RED MOON DEMON

ACKNOWLEDGMENTS

To those who helped along the way: Sally Ann Barnes, Denny Grayson, Caroline Williams, Dave Murray, Chris Crowe, Steve and Judy Prey, Jim Czajkowski, Leo Little, Chris Smith, Betty Johnson, and Raquela Perez Mejia.

ONE

"Hi, read my book or I'll hunt you down and kill you. I'm not joking."

—Caine Deathwalker

My eyes slitted open as weight on the mattress tipped me sideways off my back. Claws eased the black silk sheet off my face. An oversized black leopard stared with hungry, yellow eyes. I felt no fear. I didn't know why the spirit beast had moved in years ago—other than she liked my liquor—but we'd become family. Everyone *else* was potentially an *unhappy* meal.

I growled, "Let me sleep, jackass; it's not even dark out. Besides, this bed's reserved for sexual conquests—and I don't do cats. Now if you were able to turn into a human female…"

"In your dreams…" Her gruff voice echoed off the flat oak headboard and the bare, black walls of my bedroom. "Really, Caine, you need to get ready for work."

"Work's highly overrated."

"Don't make me drool on you."

"You're pissing me off, Leona."

"Yeah, but you don't really mind 'cause I'm so adorable." The sleek leopard lashed her tail and flashed clenched fangs at me.

I sighed. *Always freakin' great to see a feral grin first thing in the evening.*

Rolling off the bed, I padded naked to the kitchen with her slinking at my heels. My glance went to the gray granite counter where a metal tree held assorted cups ready for use. Next to this sat the coffee maker, its timer activated. A few minutes separated me from bliss. I went to the smoke-tinted glass table by the kitchen's bay window. The micro-blinds were gun-metal gray and shut tight. I opened them and looked out at the blue Pacific. Its streaked center was a fire-red dazzle, glazed by the setting sun.

I settled into a padded chair, waiting for the brewing to end. Leona bitch-slapped the second chair out of her way, squatting on her haunches where it had been. Her head level with mine, she expected to be served a cup, too. Though she couldn't drink anything but fresh blood, she liked the smell of steaming coffee. It reminded her of the Amazon jungle.

I said nothing about my poor abused chair, appreciating an attack cat willing to eat anyone breaking into my house. A thought occurred to me. "Hey, Leona, how'd you know about my job today?"

"Well, you know that ass-wipe demon you call 'Old Man,' who desperately needs a hooker, or some kind of life?"

The coffee maker spluttered in indignation, offended on behalf of my adopted father. I went to get some brew. "Yeah."

"He's been in your *office* for an hour, bending my ears over your many failures, as if I care," Leona said

I grunted at the news, filling two cups, taking them back to the table.

The leopard spirit took a whiff and closed her eyes in aromatic ecstasy.

Old Man—better known as *Lauphram* in the ancient texts—was one of the few pure-blooded Atlantean demons left. Seven foot, built like Mr. Universe, with winding scars and nautical-themed tats decorating his powder-blue body, he followed a somewhat twisted code of chivalry and honor, chaotically good instead of evil most of the time anyway. A legend among his peers, Old Man was the closest thing to a father I'd ever had. He'd raised me when my parents abandoned me on some long forgotten pagan altar. I understand they'd been dropping acid at the time.

I took a bracing sip of coffee, smooth, rich. Carefully, I put my cup down and pushed to my feet. I strode from the kitchen, through the living room, using voice commands and a little magic to open windows and turn on lights along the way. The next room I entered had once been a family room until I improved it with massive quantities of alcohol. My house was a plus size, five bedrooms, six bathrooms, two living rooms separated by a dining room. The whole place was a *gift* from a client.

When I was fifteen, I'd saved a Hollywood lawyer's whole family from a Sumerian fertility demon that had been summoned without a proper offering. The lawyer had been grateful, until I'd asked for his house in payment. I got the house with only a little fuss. People see you kill a demon, while wearing an unwavering smile, they don't say no. Of course, being a minor at the time, Lauphram's name had gone onto the deed.

I was almost thirty, but passing for twenty-one, don't ask me how, but Old Man still hadn't signed over the property to me. When I asked about it, he only said I shouldn't have what I can't take proper care of. I think truthfully he was just a tight-fisted bastard. Not that I called him that to his face. I wasn't a spirit beast; I could still die.

In the bar, I stared past the fireplace and the furniture huddled there, past the book shelves, the desk, the long wall of windows, and the twelve foot bar complete with bar stools.

No one's here.

A hand—I knew to be made of shadow—*whacked* the back of my head, shoving it six inches forward. I pulled back to a vertical posture. "You're fucking early, Old Man."

"Don't cuss, and put some pants on," Old Man spoke with soft regality, but his eyes were red coals of smoldering rage. He thought my cursing a sign of poor upbringing, and took it personally being the up-bringer.

I went behind the bar, lined up six glasses, bottles of vodka and Blue Curacao, and added lemonade and lime juice from the miniature refrigerator under the bar. They were all for me. I may be an alcoholic, but I'm totally functional. Blending the alcohol, and lime juice, shaking well and pouring through a strainer into a glass with ice gave me three Blue Kamikazes.

Swapping lemonade for lime juice gave me three Blue Lagoons. I'd have gone for a Blue Orchid instead, but I was out of cranberry juice. In another age I'd have been a hell of an alchemist.

I looked up to see Old Man watching me work. I glowered at him. "Hey, why'd you tell Leona my business?"

"You'll need her help on this one. I found out more on the assassin; she's a kind of demon you've never faced." Old Man waved and a scroll materialized in a flash of blue flame that matched my drinks. The scroll hung midair, the yellow parchment looking older than Old Man himself. He snagged the scroll and pried it open.

I scowled. "Every time you pull something out of your ass that looks *that* old, I get a new scar."

I carried two kamikazes around the bar. Contaminated by an impulse of generosity, I handed over a drink.

As if in payment, Old Man gave me the scroll. I opened it and studied a demon contract written in Japanese—in blood. "I had no idea our clan collected contracts in Japan."

Old Man took a gulp and put the empty glass on the counter. He helped himself to a Blue Lagoon. "Thanks," he said.

I thought it weird such a powerful demon bothered with manners. Matter of fact, Old Man was the only demon I'd ever heard saying please, thank you, or anything nice at all. No, now that I thought about it, there's one time *every* demon mellows out, getting polite—when begging for their life at the tip of my sword.

Old Man said, "Demons are demons; we go everywhere. There are plenty of Japanese demons—*oni, yokai, call 'em what you will*—that make contracts outside of Japan."

"Speaking of foreign demons, next time you send me after a *yuki-onna*, make sure I don't *know* her in the biblical sense. And make sure the client's not total tool." Old Man lifted his shadow hand in a threatening manner.

I held up a finger. "Hey, *tool's* not a cuss word. Put that hand away."

Old Man lowered his hand. His face writhed into a grin. "How was I supposed to know you were friends with benefits and that the client was a stalker with a demon fetish?"

"Don't apologize to me," I said. "Go next door and tell *her*. She still spits ice, every time your name comes up."

Instead of following my good advice, he drained the second glass and set it on the bar as well.

Motion drew my attention to Leona entering the room. I smiled, waiting to hear her take on things. She used a grunting cough to get Old Man's attention. "Lauphram, you of all demons should know better than to judge a gal by her reputation. Pull your thumb out of your sphincter and do a little thinking next time."

Old Man's face went *shadow* like his killing hand, but flickered back to its usual pasty blue, as the impulse to kill left him. Though they argued frequently, I knew Old Man was actually quite fond of Leona, and versa-visa.

I handed him my untouched drink and went to get a few for me. I threw them down quickly, savoring the taste. I set the blood contract on the bar, studied the writing, and tapped the parchment lightly. "Okay, I see here we get paid every time the client calls on our clan for protection, but I have no idea how much."

Old Man used a too casual voice, "Fifty kilos of gold."

My eyes widened. I tried to figure out how many high-class hookers that would buy; *about ... uh ... well, a lot*. I picked up a drink, slammed it back, draining it all, and set the glass down. I picked up the scroll with a great deal of reverence. "Fifty kilos, that's over a hundred pounds. So what's my cut?"

Old Man met my greedy stare. "Forty percent and—if you do a good job and don't let any of the client's family die—there might be a bonus."

I slapped the bar with my free hand. "Okay, Old Man, I'm in. Where are we going?"

"The job's here in Los Angeles. The Kirishima family has a skyscraper downtown, and has agreed to stay there until this is blows over. It's better for us to deal with this in our own territory." A hint of worry appeared in Old Man eyes as he handed over a business card with an address on it. "By the way, the main target is the next heir of the family, Haruka Kirishima. Her father, Hiro Kirishima, will meet you at this address."

I reached across the bar to take the card.

Old Man said, "Please be nice, and not your normal self."

I grinned. "Come on, I'm a perfect gentleman, the very soul of sensitivity."

Old Man looked at Leona then back at me. "All you've done today is mix drinks—"

"Like you didn't guzzle two of them," I pointed out.

"—and strut around naked as dragon's lust."

My face displayed mock confusion. I shrugged. "So, what's your point?"

He shook his head sadly. "I should have beaten you more often."

With a tiny bit of sympathy, Leona looked at Old Man. "Don't blame yourself. He was fucked sideways from the start."

TWO

"I make death look good."

—Caine Deathwalker

I got dressed in one of my all-black Italian suits; you have to look good while kicking ass, and hey, if I should one day get killed, I'd leave behind a spiffy corpse. As always, I had my toys: twin PPKs semiautomatic 9mm. with hollow and mercury tipped rounds in various clips. I had other ammo for regular humans. I even carried a clip with silver rounds for werewolves, though they'd been banned from L.A. years ago. When wearing my complete combat harness, I had another set of PPKs, flash bombs, smoke bombs, and twin short swords that hung upside on my back. And I had my *baby*, a demon sword that came across any distance to fill my hand when called. It was a folded-steel katana made by Old Man, with the help of a dragon in human form who'd used his own fire in the forging.

The same dragon, Red Fang, ran a tattoo shop. He'd covered my body with enchanted tattoos. Years of horrific pain had been involved. The very memory brought a shiver of ecstasy. This type of tat can only be done by old dragons that have mastered their magic, using their own blood in the ink to stabilize and seal demon curses in living flesh. With such dormant power waiting to be awakened, I could never be unarmed by an opponent, but I always felt better having cold steel on me as well."

I made my way to the three-car garage. Only one car was inside, a black '96 mustang with solid rubber tires. There was more than a hundred thousand dollars invested under the hood, and sixty thousand in the rest: fingerprint door lock and ignition, armor, and more luxury than you'd ever want. A 50 cal. machine gun unloaded on the windows would do nothing.

Techno-magic; how great it is.

I slid behind the wheel and started her up. The deep grumble of the engine was all it took to get Leona out in the garage and into the car. As a spirit leopard, she ghosted into the vehicle without opening her door, and sat in the seat next to me.

I said, "Hey make sure this time I'm the only one can see you. Last time you made that poor little girl piss her pants"

The leopard *humphed*. "Yeah, that was freakin' funny. Hey, turn on the seat warmer."

"You're wearing a fur coat," I pointed out.

She glared at me like I was putrid zombie slime about to get her fur dirty.

I sighed. "Fine, I'll turn it on."

I used a remote to open the sliding door to the driveway. We backed out of the garage with its concrete floor, work benches, and tool racks. Neon signs—advertising various brands of liquor—shed blue and red light in our wake, making it seem like we were escaping some nameless hell dimension. The vehicle backed and turned into the street then went forward.

Wearing skin-tight jeans and a loose, white blouse, my next door neighbor watered her flowers. I had to slow and stare.

Izumi had perfect pale skin with long straight black hair. Her eyes were large black mirrors. Five-foot nothing, maybe a hundred and five pounds, but she could freeze your blood in ten seconds flat. I'd always loved "lethal" in a woman. Her heart-shaped face had high cheek bones with the palest of blush that made her look like a perfect doll. With a smile that could melt a man and drive him insane, she carried herself with dignity and had a mouth you longed to kiss. Smart and witty, she never cursed, except at Old Man. She was so good natured—for a demon—I liked messing with her. A couple times, I'd provoked her into casting a miniature blizzard, nothing my protective spells couldn't handle.

Seeing me, she waved.

I stopped. I didn't want to be late, de-icing my tires. Again.

"Good evening, Caine, Leona."

Leona never hid her presence from Izumi. They were good friends.

The ice demon bent forward to talk and I had quite an interesting view inside her blouse. She didn't seem to mind so I kept my attention focused there. She used that special smile of hers, and I grew another *stick-shift* in the car. She said, "The neighbor on the other side of your house moved out abruptly. I was wondering if you knew why."

Actually, she was checking to see what I knew about those she'd moved into my territory. "Last I heard, he got mad and hissy-fitted across town because a Yeti moved into his basement. A friend of yours?" I asked.

She shrugged off my question. "You know how vampires are; they have to bitch about everything."

"Come fuckin' clean, Izumi." I knew F-bombs irritate her, but hell, that's how people talk. How Izumi and Leona got along I couldn't understand. Compared to the leopard, my language was mild and minty fresh.

Izumi sighed. "You've heard about it all, haven't you?"

Leona growled. "Your wolves moved in. I don't like wolves. They're loud, and those wild all-weekend party's…"

Izumi's eyes widened as she protested. "They're not like other werewolves. Their Alpha is a business man, not too old, only seventy though he looks twenty. Most of his pack are the same, even the bitches are very nice, a bit territorial, but nice."

I pretended to be shocked. "Bitches? You used a bad word!"

"But that is the right word for female wolves. You know I wasn't talking about humans. That would be wrong."

I shot her a hard glower. "Go ahead and cuss. You're a friggin' demon, remember?"

My foot hit the pedal. Acceleration shoved me back against the seat. I left Izumi thoroughly scandalized by my suggestion, but not so scandalized that a barrage of snow balls didn't whack my rear windshield.

She and I needed to have a serious discussion, but I was pressed for time; it would have to wait. Suburbs gave away to the highway which dropped me into downtown L.A among the skyscrapers. They were much alike; tall with too much glass and little of nature. Trees were in short supply. Everything should have a little green. A park here or there wouldn't hurt. Not that Leona needed a tree to piss against when there were panhandlers around. The city's so beautiful at night when the predators came out to play.

I threaded traffic, tearing past high-rises until I got to a dwarf building that was only six stories—a restaurant hotel combination that had only endured to modern times because it was a historic landmark. Almost a miracle, I wanted, and found, a parking space.

I turned to the leopard. "Okay, Leona, stay hidden and don't eat any one … if you can help it."

"Yeah, I know; but you should remember that there's a whole lot I can't help."

"Just don't get blood on my car."

I left the car and went over to the double glass doors. Inside, were white marble floors, art deco chandeliers, and walls painted a soft shade of sage. An oversized redwood receptionist desk blocked my way. I'd have to move right or left to reach the elevators, or the wide staircase that circled up to a second floor restaurant.

Looking like linebackers, two men in dark suits were lined up on each side of the desk, and one stood behind. Two more were at the elevators, making seven. Bulging coats showed they were packing large weapons.

While I got the lay of the land, Leona padded up to my side. None of the men saw her or reacted to her voice, "They're carrying demon slaying weapons, protective charms. Nice." She didn't say the word like she meant it.

The man standing directly behind the desk nodded. "Mr. Deathwalker … is it? You're expected. Come this way."

The linebackers let me pass, and their boss walked me to the elevator. The call button was lit. The elevator was coming. The cage opened and I went in with Leona. We were allowed to ride up alone, but they had a camera on us. Barely moving my mouth I said, "I thought you were going to wait in the car."

"Not enough people around to keep me entertained. Besides, I don't want to be the one to tell Old Man why you have seven new demon slaying weapons."

"And you figure there will be more bloodshed wherever I'm going."

"Yeah, that too. Waste not, want not."

At least the music in the elevator was Japanese classic and not some shitty, overplayed advertising jingle. The doors opened on a penthouse foyer. Four more guards with demon slaying weapons greeted us. This time, the weapons were out in plain sight. The guards parted to give access. I went through the penthouse door, Leona pressing against my leg. One of the men followed me into a sprawling living room with cathedral ceilings. On a couch in front of the fire place, Old Man sat with a tiny cup of steaming sake, talking to a Japanese man with a high forehead and white hair on the back and sides. His face was lined, and grown lax with age.

Seeing me with the guard, the Japanese man beckoned. The guard turned and left me instead of trying to throw me out—which would have been really fun. It was hard to remember that I was here to protect these people from what the guards couldn't handle.

I strolled through a light crowd, drawing curious glances from everyone. I paid more attention to the layout, looking for weak spots.

The carpet was soft red which was good if I needed to do something messy like a blood spell. One side wall was all glass. The room had too many openings, but solid wood tables laden with food could quickly be overturned and used for cover. There was a staircase to the left that went up to loft. That was a problem if someone took to the high ground with hostages. Double doors beyond the stairs were heavy, probably opened to an outside terrace.

I reached the fireplace and stopped in a casual slouch, hands in pockets. I nodded. “Hey, Old Man, you’re here too?”

“Yes, I wanted to make sure Hiro knew, even though you may not have been born to our clan, that you are our best.” Old Man never took his eyes off the leaping flames. I wondered at his fascination seeing as water was his true element.

Calling him by first name, not standing or even making eye contact while talking; these two have known each other for a long time.

I nodded to our client. “Hello, Mr. Kirishima, I am Caine Deathwalker, and I’ll be saving your family’s collective ass.”

I felt annoyance radiating off them like the heat from the fire. I grinned to show how little he cared, and took a chair next to Old Man. Caine said, “So, what are we dealing with and what have you done to get it pissed at you?”

Mr. Hiro rose from his chair and stepped away from the fire place to face both Old Man and me.

“The vile beast is what you westerners call a succubus. As for how this came to be a problem, my grandfather contracted that she would make all other rival companies fail gloriously when competing against us. In return, she could take one of his grandchildren. He thought it a great deal.” Hands shoved in the pockets of his dark blue three-piece suit, Hiro sounded angry.

“So, she wants your precious daughter and now you’re going back on your grandfather’s word.”

He unpocketed a hand to loosen the perfect knot of his tie. “I’d had no say bout the deal, only finding out when it was too late. I run the clan now. I will run it my way. I prefer to give you my gold instead of handing my only child over to that creature. She wants to make my girl into a succubus as well. That is a shame I could never bear.”

I pretended to be undecided. “You’re still breaking a contract. I don’t know if I want to be part of that.”

Old Man was getting angry, but hiding it well. He looked at me with incandescent eyes and said, “You can have seventy-five percent, and no more.

Old Man knew he’d raised me like a demon; there was no reason not to push for even more. After all, it’s greed that makes hell go round.

"Ha, Old Man you're trying to make a deal with a deal breaker? You know a succubus with a valid contract is going to be a hell of a lot of trouble."

Hiro took a step over to me. He leaned in close, as if we alone were talking. He said, "If you keep my immediate family alive, I will give you my family's sword."

"I have a sword."

Hiro locked eyes with Old Man, and then spoke to me, "It is Muramasa's last and greatest forging. All his other swords are trash before it."

In the 1600's, Japanese sword smith Muramasa created the greatest swords of his day, but he was ill-tempered and unbalanced. His insanity seeped into his blades, giving them life and a thirst for blood and war. According to legend, once drawn, a Muramasa blade has to draw blood before it can be returned to its scabbard—if not, the cursed blade causes its owner to wound or even kill himself. Such a blade could well shatter the one I owned. I felt myself getting hard at the thought of holding it.

"Okay, you got a deal. Now, show me the girl."

THREE

"Hi, I can see your panties."

—Caine Deathwalker

Hiro waved at the loft, "Haruka, Jessie, come down here, please."

I used the opportunity to grab a small bottle of hot sake from the small table beside Hiro's leather wingchair.

Old Man gave me a glare that failed to induce contrition.

Maybe next time.

I took a sip and moved away from the fireplace.

There were family members, servants, and security milling around, pretending this was a social gathering. That illusion broke as the space in front of me cleared, and two high school girls from the loft reached the bottom landing. Faces composed, dark eyes glittering, hair fanning like raven's wings; they came toward me on the way to Hiro. The girl in front would be the heir. She wore a cherry blossom print kimono, a real beauty, porcelain skin, high cheeky bones, pale pink lipstick the color of cherry blossoms. No one would ever call her cute—only amazing—I knew this much despite the damn kimono hiding her best features.

The second girl was white European, and taller, five-seven, wearing a woman's business suit. I made an automatic calculation; five-seven, twenty-two waist, thirty-two hips, and thirty-four C tits. Her ass-long hair had been dyed a soft brown and streaked with vibrant red tones. It looked like she wore colored contact lenses. Her eyes were gem-like, cobalt blue. Her bright red lipstick made me want to lick her lips for her. Her beauty was more earthly; cute with a side of come-fuck-me.

I downed the bottle while they passed me, and I noticed every man in the room targeting the girls, facing them like sunflowers moving with the sun.

I heard the distinctive slither of steel blades, leaving their sheathes in the foyer. The main doors opened and the guards staggered in, weapons in hand. Their eyes were empty, their faces slack. Facing their demon-slaying weapons, I felt my own magic stir in resonation, as if cascading feathers were lightly brushing my skin, leaving a warm tingle. I cross-pulled my twin PPK nines.

They were already cocked, so I only needed to thumb off the safeties. I called out to all those *not* under the mind-bending influence, "If you don't want to die, get your collective asses outta here." I shot twice, hitting two of the advancing guards between the eyes. "Old Man, get the girls and Hiro out on the balcony."

Female screams sliced the air. The women scattered, ducking behind furniture, hurrying toward the stairs to the loft, and breaking for the balcony where we were heading. Old Man put his arm around Hiro, making him look like a confused child, and hurried him around the free-standing fireplace to the French doors. Haruka followed, her friend stayed a step behind.

I targeted the leading edge of attackers, squeezing off carefully accurate shots. Red dots appeared between their eyes. The exit wounds in back of their heads were quite a bit messier. With scrambled brains, the puppet strings were cut. The bodies collapsed and did not rise again.

Male relatives that were inside the room when the attack began were now lurching at me, taking the place of those down. And they had less distance to cover. There were even bodies launching themselves from the upper loft, with no thought of the damage they were acquiring.

"Leona, a little help," I suggested.

She hit the closest group of men, ripping them apart with slashing claws, and bites that removed entire faces, whirling from one enemy to another in a constant, smooth play of feline muscle.

Elsewhere, one of the last mind-controlled guards advanced with his demon-slayer blade raised above his head. I shot out an eye. The sword fell to the carpet beside its wielder. Another enemy snagged it, slashing. Scampering aside, Leona barely avoided damage.

"Go to Old Man," I told her. I retreated as well, dragging a loveseat along to wedge in a French door. A body dropped near me and collapsed a small wood table. On his belly, the puppet clawed at me, flailing slowly at my ankles. I pulled the couch over him and kept retreating. Seeing what I was doing, some of the women united their efforts to copy me, blocking other balcony doors as best they could.

A guard with a crossbow aimed. His bolt sped through the air, as I shifted my hips. The bolt glanced off one of my shoulder holsters, deflected into a lamp that shattered. The weapon's design allowed a second bolt to be fired before reloading. That bolt zipped over my shoulder and broke a pane in the French doors. A small scream from outside told me it had hit somebody.

I emptied my clips, taking less care where my shots went, and then I was outside, holstering my weapons. I wedged my loveseat as best I could while the guard with the crossbow reloaded.

As the puppets reached the barricades, they clawed at hem. I took the opportunity to race away; joining those huddled across the rooftop garden. There was a fire escape. Many of the guests were stomping down the steel stairs, headed for the street. Old Man yelled down at them, "Don't stop for anything."

I looked back at the barricades. They were being pulled clear. We were running out of time.

The guard with the crossbow stepped out on the expansive balcony deck. He raised his weapon for another couple shots. The human puppet behind him staggered past, accidentally loping off the man's head, one small favor to be grateful for. A wild shot went up into the air.

I changed clips in my weapons as a swarm of bodies staggered at me. For some reason, I was everybody's favorite target.

A sword came at me. My right gun spat flame and lead slugs. The men made no effort to dodge my withering fire.

"Wow, you guys suck," I told them.

Old Man called out behind me, "Come on, we're the last."

I backed to the edge of the building, firing methodically as I went. My clips emptied and I holstered my guns. "After you," I said.

Man looked at me like I was too stupid to live. "I'm an Atlantean demon, remember. Get the hell outta here so I can cut loose.

Having no wish to be part of that, I vaulted the wall and landed on an iron grate with a drop-down ladder that reached the street. The ladder was clogged with desperate women, Hiro in their midst along with Haruka and Jessie. I saw no sign of Leona—until she faded into view next to me, her yellow eyes flaming bright with excitement.

I heard chanting, shaped by a voice that was no longer human. A demon spell was being forged, word by word, burning the air's oxygen into ozone. Had anyone human tried to pronounce such words, his larynx would have shredded and his throat filled with blood. It was one of the reason I used dragon-style magic instead of demon.

I dropped down on my knees, keeping my head low. Leona nudged in next to me so that if there was any backwash from the roof, I'd take the brunt of it for her. Spirit leopards are often too cleaver for everyone else's good.

The sky above turned dark. Purple-white jags of lightning webbed the gathering storm, licking the underbellies of roiling clouds. A sulfur-scented rain fell, mostly on this one building.

Old Man hollered, "Fire in the hole!"

Balls of lightning dropped onto the building, the ultimate flash bang grenades. Damp winds screamed obscenities in a thousand demon tongues, spiraling off the roof, tearing at me as they expanded out across the alley to the next building over. At the core of the windstorm, a funnel formed, reaching down from the overhead clouds. A blue-gray funnel detached, inverting in the air so the base was wide and the upper portion a narrow tip, a water-spout looking for a place to kill. This was Old Man's trademark. Most demons used fire or ice, but not him. His demon magic had been good enough to sink Atlantis; he saw no reason to change just because a few thousand years had passed.

"We are about to get very wet," I told Leona, visualizing a flood of water scouring everything out of the penthouse not nailed down.

"Climb on," Leona said. "I'll give you a ride."

I shouted over the wind. "There's a time and place for sex you know?"

She growled. "A ride down to the street, you idiot!"

I threw a leg over her back, getting a good grip on her shoulders, as her tail wound around my waist like a seatbelt. "Why didn't you say so?"

Instead of answering, she leaped off the fire escape. Silver-blue fire swirled around her paws, giving her traction midair so we didn't fall as we crossed the alley, ping-ponging off our building and the next over while dropping to the alley pavement. We landed running, but slowed after several steps. As Leona's tail pulled away, I stepped off her.

She went invisible and intangible—a useful trick I didn't have. I could only put my arms over my head and take a deep breath as something resembling a flash flood dumped off the building, fragmenting into a hard rain as it fell. I felt one of my tattoos heat up on my flesh, a protective spell anchored to my back by ink mixed with dragon blood. A shell of shimmering red enveloped me, extending talons of energy deep into the bricks under me. The activation caused pain I wouldn't have felt if I were a dragon, instead of a human using dragon magic. My skin burned as if caressed by dragon flame. Choking on a scream, teeth gritted, I took no real damage, but had to look at my body to convince myself I wasn't charring away to ashes,

Passing by, a wall of water crashed against me. I wasn't moved. I didn't even feel it.

Down below on the street, Hiro's family and servants weren't so lucky; milling in indecision, waiting for someone higher in the clan to tell them what to do, they were swept out into the main street where fishtailing vehicles plowed into them. The rain was gone, but Hiro and the girls fell off the ladder. Fortunately, enough of their people had fallen under them to provide a half-way soft landing.

Oddly, I noticed that no meat-puppets had been swept off the rooftops. Old Man must have opened a demon vortex to get rid of the corpses. Hard to prove mass murder without bodies. He'd probably also call in a cleaning crew from the sorcerer's guild to remove blood splatter and inconvenient memories from the witnesses. There was an iron rule that all preternaturals—PNs—could do as they liked, as long as the supernatural community weren't exposed to a paparazzi feeding frenzy. *Those* guys were scary.

On a one to one basis, humans were weak, not counting me of course, if I still qualified for human that is. But there were billions of humans on the planet. United by fear, armed with modern weapons, roused to violence, mankind could break our rule from the shadows, reclaiming the top spot in the food chain.

All this flashed through my head as the red glow around me dissipated, and I was free to walk over and help the girls to their feet. Hiro was on his own; I didn't want to get in trouble by moving him if he'd accidentally broken a hip.

I walked the girls to the corner where several washed away relatives shouted in Japanese, reaching out for our assistance in untangling themselves from each other. They sounded hysterical with fear. I laughed at them, hurrying my charges on by. Something about my smile must have been the final straw. Several women fainted, slumping on the ground like drowned rats.

"Odd," I said. "I usually only have that effect on woman after I've fuc—"

I paused, watching a woman who stood in the mouth of the alley. She studied the scene of chaos, a tiny smile on her lips, intrigue playing in her eyes. She wore a scarlet, wide brimmed hat that matched her lipstick. A clunky looking antique necklace hung around her neck. Her dress was black with a red leather belt. She wore red leggings that ended in cuff style, black boot.

Nice figure.

It seemed to me that a faint wisp of magic blew toward me from her, but the air was so fouled with occult energies I couldn't be sure. My hand eased inside my jacket, as I reached for one of my PKKs. This could well be the succubus in human form, gloating over her work, coming directly for Haruka now.

"Caine!" It was Hiro, calling from the back of the alley. "What is happening, where are you going?"

"Where *are* we going?" Haruka asked.

I pushed her behind me with my free hand while the other emerged with my handgun. In the split-second I'd looked away, the stranger vanished.

I activated a tat along my spine. Briefly, red-hot needles pricked me all over, the price I paid for mystic awareness. Yeah, the hot chick really was gone; an evil, bile-green glow on the pavement indicated a transportation spell had whisked her away. I holstered my weapon as Haruka came around me.

"What was that all about?" she asked.

I hurried her around the corner, my hand at the small of her back. Jessie followed, oddly silent and composed.

"It's been twenty minutes since my last drink," I said. "Obviously, we're looking for a bar."

"There's a bar in the restaurant right here, on the second floor of the building," Jessie said.

"Great!" I steered them toward the front doors. We went in. Whoever had attacked us probably thought we'd run off to a new hole to hide. I didn't think they'd think of looking so close for us again. Then again, I may have simply been rationalizing. Booze often plays a bigger role in my decisions than even I like to admit.

Inside the building, the guards were gone. They'd probably been part of those sent against us earlier. We darted across the lobby and hurried up the grand staircase to the second floor, kicking over the red velvet rope and the brass stands that tried to bar our way. The runners on the stairs were blood red, an ill omen I chose to ignore. We reached the upper landing and entered the restaurant. A lot of buzz was generated by the patrons who'd moved over to the windows to stare out at the weird weather that had just passed.

A black-haired hostess in a hunter green dress stared from her station, clutching menus to her delightfully endowed bosom.

"We'd like a table and some towels for the ladies." They were drenched, dripping water on the red carpet.

Before the hostess could recover, the men along the windows turned to face us, ignoring their dates. Their faces had a thoughtless hostility I recognized from our previous attackers. The diners lumbered toward us, hands out-stretched, grasping. Several of them picked up stake knives off the surrounding tables. Many of their dates called after them, puzzled at being so suddenly abandoned. Their questions went unanswered.

"Not again?" I rolled my eyes, and pulled out twin

Wakizashi from the inside of my long coat. Holding the 60 cm short swords in a guarding stance, I balanced on the balls of my feet, speaking over my shoulder to Jessie, “Get Haruka out of here. Go find a closet or something to hide in until I finish here.”

“You’ll be alright?” Haruka asked.

I grinned. “Of course, killing is what I do best.”

FOUR

"Blood orgy!!!"

—Caine Deathwalker

The girls left with no further argument. By then, the first wave of attackers was on me. My swords lashed out. Men went down in pieces. Their female family members and friends shrieked in horror. It made an interesting battle anthem, as I waded into the mind-controlled meat-puppets.

I leaped, driving one sword up through the bottom of one guy's jaw. I took a step to the left, pulling his body in the way of a chair someone had thrown. I kicked the body off my sword, and made the tattoos on my legs burn with dragon rage, temporarily boosting my strength and endurance to godlike levels.

A dinner patron in a Hawaiian shirt—with olive green fronds over a black field—lunged at me with a fork. I took his head off cleanly with one swipe. His neck spurted blood, bright arterial red, my favorite color, as his head bounced away, getting kicked like a soccer ball by other attackers.

A flurry of slashes, and the immediate area around me cleared. The fallen bodies tripped up the next wave of puppets since they were a bit too befuddled to properly pick up their feet. Those behind came on, toppling over the growing ring of flailing bodies. A woman in a dress leaped the ring, and came at me from the side. I allowed her to stab me—with a pair of clutched spoons—admiring her silicon-enhanced tits.

Wait a second! A woman? It had been only men until now.

I stabbed my sword into the headless body at my feet, freeing up a hand. I grabbed a handful of hair and wrenched the woman's head to the side, exposing her throat. She had an Adam's apple. "Damn cross-dressing transvestite!" With the hilt of the sword I still held, I smashed the wanna-be-bitch's face, driving her to the floor. Pulling my other sword from the corpse's back, I dragged the tip over to the woman and slashed upward. Another home-made soccer ball went bouncing away.

The surviving meat-puppets grew still and collapsed, their invisible strings cut. The fight was over. Maybe my unseen nemesis just got tired of repeating a theme.

A swirl of blue-green cloud billowed out of nowhere. I knew that cloud so I didn't hack into it. The cloud dissipated quickly, revealing Old Man. He looked around, appraising my work. "Done already?"

"Strings were cut." I had to yell over the room full of hysterically crying women, who doubtless realized that without the men, they'd have to pay their own checks. Perhaps it was mean-spirited for me to think so, but I was demon raised. Men existed to pay for my services. Women existed to service me in bed.

"Where are the girls?" Old Man asked.

"Where's Hiro?" I countered.

"He'll be here in a moment." Old Man slapped me in the back of the head. "Answer the question."

"I sent them to find a hiding hole while I took care of all this."

Old Man grew still as a graveyard angel, eyes wide and staring into infinity. His gaze came back to me, a frown on his face. "I don't sense them. Either they left the building, or—"

Or all this was a distraction and they've been grabbed," I said

"They've been grabbed?" It was Hiro's voice, distorted by deep shock.

I turned to see him by the hostess' desk. He leaned on it for support, face an ashen gray. He looked like he was having a heart attack. I turned back to Old Man. "You take care of him. I'll get the girls back."

"How?" Old Man asked.

I have a plan."

Old Man grabbed his chest like he was having a heart attack too. He gasped out, "*Now* I'm afraid."

I growled low in my throat. "Wise ass."

He straightened. "No, all of me is intelligent. You're getting us confused again."

He went to Hiro, taking his arm, leading his gently to an empty chair.

I put my swords away and went up to Old Man, staring at him.

"Hey, what's with the sudden consideration? You've never been exactly nurturing."

"No?" Old Man said.

"You dropped me of a frickin' cliff once without blinking, teaching me to land on my feet, but you pamper him like he's your favorite whore?" I said.

He gave me a fiery blue-green stare that let me know I was on dangerous ground questioning him, but he explained. "Hiro's father was a good friend, and I watched Hiro being born."

I didn't ask anymore. Old Man had very few human friends. He didn't make them easily, and so treasured each one. That was all I needed to know.

"The guards' weapons are mine now. Have them dropped off at my house," I told Old Man. It was a demon rule: you get to keep the property of those you kill. I'd get a good price for demon-slayer swords on the preternatural black market.

Hiro bowed his head in agreement.

I headed for the entrance, grabbing a bottle of wine off a table I passed.

Hiro found enough voice to call after me. "I want my daughter safe. Kill whoever you need to."

Of course. That goes without saying.

I went out the door without a backward glance. I went downstairs to the lobby, sitting on the bottom step where I pulled out my phone. After a swig from the bottle I'd swiped, sent a text to Izumi: I NEED A FAVOR, BRING ME TO YOU.

Another demon cloud formed; this one around me. It was white with a light blue core, a haze of ice crystals more than vapor. My tats weren't activated, so I knew the demon magic was no threat. Izumi was a friend, but even so, Old Man had taught me never to assume benevolence under any circumstances.

The cloud picked me up, rotated me, and collapsed into a theoretical dimension no scientist had yet named. My stomach registered a massive increase in gravity, then I was back in the human world with the cloud thinning to nothing. I was also in Izumi's home. She lay sprawled on a red velvet couch, wearing a sheer red negligee that tinted her flesh without hiding anything. Her eyes flamed with lust. She wiggled a finger at me.

I understood. Demon magic always has a price. No free rides. She expected me to pay her for the expenditure of magic. I really didn't have the time, but… I shed my coat on the floor and tugged open my belt and fly.

* * *

Two hours later, after making sure the clips were full; I put my guns back into their shoulder holsters. I used a handkerchief to clean my swords. Izumi lay on a polar bear rug by the fireplace, where we'd finally finished up. She watched me while recovering from her latest string of multiple orgasms.

"So, Izumi, what else do you know about the wolves that have moved into my territory?" I asked, wondering if I had the time for a fourth go at that glorious ass of hers.

"Not much, they're not even done moving in … yet."

I had no idea how old Izumi was, but unlike most immortals, she's liked to stay with the times, one of the reasons why I let her move into my territory in the first place. That the wolves had come without invitation and were still ignoring me meant that blood would soon fill the streets—none of it mine. She had to know that. Why was she acting like it had nothing to do with her? They were her friends.

She rolled her feet under her and stood. Backlit by the flames of the fire, she wore shadow as she faced me, a mysterious creature I might never fully understand. Her negligee was on the floor, ripped into numerous pieces. Naked, she sashayed past me to her room. I studied her, uh, assets until she left my sight, and walked over to the window. I moved the blinds to look at the house across the street, the wolves were close; her house lay between them and me like a neutral zone.

Moving boxes from the moving truck into the house, the wolves gave every sign this wasn't temporary.

I heard Izumi approach me from behind though she was trying to be quiet. I sometimes let her believe she could actually sneak up on me since it gave her such a thrill. She said, "I know that look. It's never good when you smile like that."

I turned. She wore a pale blue dress, a sweater vest with a fringe, and white stockings. Her feet were sunk into white boots with furry cuffs. And her hair was piled, held in place with silver snowflake pins. Platinum bracelets adorned one wrist, clinking gently as she moved.

As intended, I let my stare reveal the hardness of my soul. "Can you blame me? You know how these things go. One unanswered challenge invites another. Soon, you're fighting for respect from every imp and pixie." I concentrated on my tats, letting the dragon magic quicken to a faint suggestion of life. Waves of power shimmered, radiating from me as I turned back to the window, glowering outside with menace.

The wolves froze mid-step, looking at Izumi's house. A large man—about six foot, built like a mountain, with short brown hair, wearing black slacks and a button up-shirt—left the wolves' den. He, too, stared toward Izumi and me. His legs were wide spaced, his head high, shoulders back. I wasn't a wolf to sense the reassuring vibe he'd be sending his pack, but I knew it was there.

Fight one, fight all.

I went to the front door, stepped out, and made my way toward the wolves. They put their boxes down and formed a crescent behind their Alpha, showing solidarity; four males, two females, all very dominant and aggressive, no wimps in this group, all very ready for a battle. As I reached the property line for their house, the Alpha started toward me. I could feel the pack magic like nettles against my skin. I let my tats awaken a little more. The Alpha didn't flinch, but the other wolves cast uneasy looks at each other.

The Alpha and I stopped with several feet still between us. I looked up into the man's eyes. "You must be the Alpha," I said.

My stare was a challenge. We both knew it. Whoever looked away first would lose.

He said, "I'm William Cooper. Who are you?"

"Caine Deathwalker, Master of the City."

William's eyes went from brown to wolf yellow.

"Bill, is every thing all right," a young red-haired woman called from the doorway of the house. My wide stare caught her as a blur while I kept my focus through the body of the Alpha. Most people thought you looked at your opponents in a dangerous situation. That's not true. You use peripheral vision to absorb everything, your awareness like the light of the moon, touching everything around you. Predators track motion. It's why prey stays very, very still—until discovered.

The woman was a wolf, her movements powerful, smooth, and fearless. She walked up to William, pretending to be oblivious to the fact that he and I were about to rip into each other. She stood next to the Alpha and looked at me with a smile. I smiled too. The fact that death was in the air made her lovelier than I might have otherwise have found her.

"Hi, I'm Angie," she said.

I stared through William. "The submissive isn't very sharp is she?"

"Not when it comes to things like this," William said.

"My name is Caine Deathwalker," I repeated. "If you've been here more than a day or two, you will have heard of me."

Neither of them responded, which told me they'd been warned. I put away my smile. "There's a bar I like that's neutral ground. We should have a drink there some time and straighten out a few things."

I handed William a card. "And, please, do bring your pack so every one can relax. Say in an hour or so."

"I can come?" Angie asked.

I said, "Bring her. She just saved your life."

As if I had nothing to fear from any of them, I broke eye contact, turning and walking away. Had there been the slightest sound of a step, my magic would have flared, and blood would have soaked the lawn. The only steps were mine. Sometimes, sheer bravado is worth more than a machinegun. I passed Izumi's house, curving around to my own house. Until I was out of their sight, I could feel William's eyes on me. Asking him to bring his pack guaranteed he'd show where and when I wanted. He couldn't turn me down; he'd look weak. An Alpha can't let that happen without inviting challenges to his power.

The hour delay would give me time to find out more about William Cooper. I suspected that if I handled things right, I could make use of the wolves in recovering Haruka. I entered my house and fished out my phone, auto-dialing Old Man's number.

"Yes?" he said.

"It's me. Meet me at The Velvet Door in twenty," I said.

"Really, the bar? You should be looking for the girls," Old Man said.

"This is that plan I told you about. Now get there. I need to talk to you about something."

He hung up.

I went to get cleaned up.

Once I was done, I walked over to Izumi's house again; without my car, I was going to have to ask her for another favor, one I'd be happy to pay for later. I knocked on her door.

In moments, I felt her walking toward me from inside the house. She opened the door with a smile.

"Want to get a drink?" I asked.

"Sure, I'm already dressed; I may as well go out."

"I don't have my car so you'll have to drive," I said.

"I'll pull the car out, go wait by the curb," Izumi said.

I walked to the curb and waited. The wolves were moving things in again, working hastily to finish the job fast. They kept their eyes on me, as Izumi pulled her sky blue Honda hybrid out of her garage. She cared about nature more than most things, a tree hugger at heart. I didn't mind riding in her baby, but unless they made one that could keep up with my muscle car, I'd never own one.

I got into her car before she completely stopped. We pulled out into the street and gathered speed. I felt weird not being the one driving. Izumi drove like a bat out of hell, not really looking at the road. Not a lot of things make me nervous. Her driving did.

We made it to city in one piece, some how. Izumi pulled into a back alley. We parked behind a line of cars, and walked to the entrance of The Velvet Door. It really did have a red velvet door—and a fey bouncer just inside, drinking, pretending to be a bum.

"Hey, Claude…"

He looked up at me, his face turning ashen with fear.

I held up my hand, raising fingers one at a time in warning. "One … two…"

Claude said, "Okay, man, I'm moving. Be a little nice."

The fey got up and dragged his stool out of the doorway. He bowed to Izumi, recognizing a regular.

I paused by the fey. "Oh, by the way, there's a pack of new wolves coming here to see me, let them in," I said.

"Dark gods, no!" he said. We just got the place fixed after your last attempt at inter-species diplomacy."

I looked at him in surprise. "Are you trying to say you don't want my business?"

He sighed. "I've *never* wanted to live in interesting times."

"But you want to live, right?" I asked.

He nodded.

"Then don't you think you should be showing us to a table?"

He lumbered on. "Right this way."

FIVE

**"Big girls need loving too,
but they got to pay … a lot."**

—Caine Deathwalker

The walls of the bar were the same color as the red door, except for the black clan symbols of the local tribes. They'd agreed this was neutral territory where disputes were set aside. My house sign was on the other side of the bar, above the purple lights that shone across the various liqueur bottles. I liked the contrast of the black chairs on red carpet and bright red lights over the dance floor. The hooded lights above the six pool tables in back were ordinary. That couldn't be said for the were-frogs lining up shots, or waiting their turn.

The place had fewer customers than I expected. A couple of vampires were signing up for karaoke, their human girlfriends looked very happy keeping them company despite the fact they'd been invited here as appetizers.

The bouncer led Izumi and me past a table with four fey summer girls in stiletto heels and a few leaves plastered on at strategic points. They fluffed their boobs at me as I passed; their full pursed lips. Their painted faces were an invitation to sin.

Sadly, here on business, I declined the offer. I escorted Izumi to our table and excused myself for a minute. I'd seen

Gray sitting at the bar, no one anywhere close to him. The old half-angel said fuck-it to both sides: light and dark, siding with humans exclusively. Across the bar from him was Gloria. She owned the place.

I nodded to her as I reached the bar. She was the only pure blood I'd ever met. All the others had been made, not born to that legacy. She wore a pink leather corset with matching pants, and pink streaks in her black hair that only a twenty-five hundred year old vampire would have the guts to pull off. It helped that she looked seventeen and would always have perky tits that looked tasty on her thin, short frame.

She flashed a little fang. The usual, hellfire with a brimstone chaser?"

"Sure, and a Pink Champagne for the lady," I thumbed over my shoulder at Izumi.

As Gloria started on the drinks, I turned to Gray. "Got any words of wisdom for me?"

He took a gulp of German lager, wiped his face, and turned to scowl at me. His eyes were white, like a blind man's, but he saw everything and a lot more. The guy had a gift for prophecy that had gotten him banned from every casino in Vegas. He looked deep inside my soul, shuddered, and turned away. I guess it wasn't very pretty. His creaky voice assailed, "When it comes time to take a helluva risk, zig, don't zag."

"Is zig left or right?"

"Uh-huh."

"So I go left?"

"Right."

I sighed. "Jeez, thanks for nothing."

"Seriously, leave the *red moon* alone. No good ever comes from screwing around with alternate dimensions."

"I've got no idea what you're talking about," I said.

"You will, in time." He turned away from me, losing interest.

I returned to my table and sat down. Izumi leaned over the table, offering me a peek down her dress. "Caine, what was the 'one … two…' about with Claude at the door?"

I grinned. "The last time I got to three, I pulled him out the door and kicked him off the dumpster, the one with the big dent in it."

"This gets you better service?"

"What do you think?" I winked at Izumi, and scanned the room, waiting for Gloria. She came with two drinks on a tray, infernal red for me and a pink one for Izumi.

I said, "Gloria, bring Old Man some honeyed mead. He should be here any second now."

"It's been a while," Gloria said.

I nodded. "By the way, there's a pack of wolves coming, as my guests. Don't water the drinks down."

"Why, I never!"

I looked at her.

She said, "Well, just that once, but it was prohibition…" She was joking with me, but her eyes had gone blood red, the mark of a pure blood vampire in a pissy mood. Vamps and wolves don't get along very well.

"Are you going to destroy my bar again?" Gloria smiled. Mad, happy, sad, pissed beyond sanity, her expression tended not to change. I liked that about her, even if it creeps me out at times.

"I'll let you know," I said.

Gloria rolled her eyes and walked back to the bar to make Old Man's drink. I couldn't help looking at Gloria's ass as she walked away, which eventually redirected my gaze to a stranger at the end of the bar, further down past Gray. The man sat nestled in a midnight blue long coat that hid his bar stool and any weapons he may have carried. He exuded a foul aura of magic that had gone undetected until my senses zeroed in on him. If it had not been for Gloria's ass, I'd have missed him altogether—*the man from my dream, who went for the chicken.*

He ran a fingertip around the rim of a wine glass filled with something dark red, too translucent to be blood. As if feeling my eyes on him, he stood up. Just under six feet, his spiky blond hair looked out of place on his head, as if he'd just pasted it on and hadn't gotten it quite centered. Turning his back to me, he strolled toward the restrooms. I heard only the faintest whisper of sound from his steps.

Gray watched him go.

Mixing drinks behind the bar, Gloria didn't look concerned. She welcomed anyone in her bar as long as they respected her rules, or at least asked permission before breaking them. Still, I'd seen her back tense up just a little as he passed her. I wondered what she knew that I didn't.

I drained the glass, pushed my chair back, and stood. "Have to use restroom, be right back."

Izumi nodded. "I'll have Gloria brings you a refill"

I walked pass the bar. Gray looked right at me and then toward the restroom. The way he looked at the restroom made me think something was up with the spiky blond guy. Gray doesn't bother himself with small problems and insignificant people, except in the line of duty.

I walked into the restroom. It had three urinals, two stalls, and a pair of sink; that was the usual part. The baby blue floor tiles and the Winnie-the-Pooh pictures on the walls were

Gloria's idea of a joke, as were the lavender-plum scented hand soap bottles. There were no windows. No one snuck out on Gloria without paying their tab.

I took the pisser next to the man with the midnight blue long coat.

"Never seen you around here before," I spoke looking straight ahead. It's a straight guy thing. If you actually look at a guy taking a wiz before he puts his junk away, you endanger your "real man" status.

"I'm here for a job," the man said.

"A job for someone like you? Must be big."

"One of a private nature, Caine Deathwalker."

Oh-ho! He'd done his research and knew who I was.

"Deathwalker? Is that really your name?"

I slipped Big Willie back into my pants and zipped him in. "Yep, had to pick a last name to live in the human would, and everyone told me I 'walked with death' so there you are. And you would be?"

"Kris Salem." He zipped up slowly, carefully, trying to imply his *size* was so monstrous he had to be extra careful. I made a mental note to remember that trick.

"Well, Kris, don't fuck around in my town too much. The big problems eventually get passed to me."

He nodded and moved with me to the sinks where we washed up. The baby-blue wallpaper started to melt and twist as if space were distorting. The white porcelain sinks deepened to lilac. Running water became warm, iron-smelling blood. It cut through the sink like hot water through ice cream. The picture of old Winnie widened his grin. The bear's eyes were red flame—like Gloria's. I turned to look the rest of the room over. It had become *unshaped.* A miasma of sickly yellow and mauve mists formed leering, demonic faces that were torn apart as fast as they formed.

I extended all my senses, mystical and otherwise. There was no emotional tampering attached to the scene, so I decided this wasn't a fey trick of glamour. And I sensed only us two, nothing else alive and threatening, misty faces aside. Either Kris Salem was using a helluva lot of power to shred reality, or he was a magic-user, trying to drown me in illusion. Our piss-off had become a pissing contest.

I could feel the floor under my feet but it looked like I was standing on a humongous tongue. It was pebbly rough and grooved down the middle. I couldn't help thinking that I was about to be swallowed by something very big.

Kris faced me. His eyes were empty sockets, his skin grey as a zombie. The midnight blue long coat tore in the back as demon wings thrust free, fanning behind him. The struts were ebon, the membranes baby-shit green. He sang, "In the jungle, the mighty jungle, the lion sleeps tonight…"

I answered with, "Kiss my ass."

He laughed and walked away. Reaching out into the mists, he

pulled open an invisible door. Over the threshold, I could see the outer hallway. He went through and let the door swing shut behind him. The room went back to normal. I stood there, deep in thought. His magic hadn't felt right; not earned, borrowed, or given into his care. *Stolen from others.* I decided. That told me what he was.

Damn warlock. I was going to have and keep an eye on this guy, on top of all else I had to do. Warlocks are scum. Wherever they go, bodies pile up as they feed their magic. Normally I wouldn't give a crap, but warlocks don't care about hiding their work. That brings human attention to our community, and trouble.

What worried me more than his presence was the fact that he wasn't acting on his own, but claimed to be working a job. Someone might well have hired him to kill me, a bid at opening up my territory for someone else to claim. *William?* I didn't think so. Wolves are pretty straight forward. They want you dead; they come after you personally—and eat you alive. They don't give their prey to others.

I dried my hands on a towel from the dispenser and tossed the paper in the trash. If only all problems could be handled so easily… I left the restroom and returned to the bar. Salem was back on his barstool. Gloria, as always, was smiling blithely. I smiled all the way back to my table where Izumi waited, along with my refilled drink.

"Why are you so happy?" she asked.

"I foresee a lot of bloodshed in my future. When Old Man hears about this…"

Movement at the door caught my eye. "Speak of the demon," I said.

Old Man had walked in and was looking around, unimpressed with the clientele and the décor. Only Gray and Gloria—and the soon-to-be-dead warlock—didn't look like they wanted to haul ass and run. It's always funny to see how things that go bump in the night react to *him*.

Old Man came over. I kicked the third seat over to him.

He snagged it and sat. "Why am I here, Caine?"

I said, "Why do I have wolves on my street and why didn't I hear about it from you?"

Old Man looked at me in silence until Gloria walked over and put a drink in front of him. The mead came in a horn shaped goblet that magically didn't fall over.

"I'll put it on Caine's tab," Gloria said, walking away.

Old Man downed the drink. "I've heard nothing about this till now. Tell me more."

"The Alpha is William Cooper. He has three males and three hot females," I said.

Old Man put two fingers in the air, signaling Gloria for a second drink.

Izumi was still working on her first drink, not even halfway through.

"When did they move in?" Old Man asked.

"They're not even done moving in, but the house hasn't had a for sale sign for at least three weeks. That says something." I said.

"Could they just not have noticed it was a claimed territory?" Old Man asked.

"I don't see how. I have runes all over the damned city. Hell, they're so strong even some humans can feel them. And yeah, they're working, we just came from there," I said.

"They could have bought the house before knowing it was your territory?" Izumi said.

"When was the last time you saw someone buy a five bedroom house without looking at it first?" I asked.

"You have a point," Izumi said.

"So, Old Man, can you look this up while keeping Hiro safe?" I asked.

He arched an eyebrow, grinned, and sipping mead from the horn. "Yeah, no problem, but I'll be keeping Leona with me, at least for now."

"No problem, I don't need her for my plan anyway," I said.

"I don't like it when you take a scenic route to your missions. You should be more focused on direct action," Old Man said. "Getting fancy is often a mistake."

"I'm killing two pigeons with one brick." I took a drink from my cup. "The Alpha and his pack will be here in a few, and it would be better if you're not here, Old Man. I don't want them to panic, just yet."

Old Man gulped down his mead, got up, and slid his chair back to the table. He nodded goodbye to Izumi. Looking over his shoulder to Gloria, he said, "If any of Caine's guests damage the premises, bill him double. He's good for it."

I hate it when he makes me pay for the crap I break.

"That's why you never get Father Day cards, Old Man," I said.

He patted me on the head and went his way.

SIX

"God kills a kitten every time a girl masturbates. Save a kitten—sleep with me."

—Caine Deathwalker

We still had time before the pack showed up, if they were on time. I wasn't counting on it; they'd make sure to look around for traps before coming in. The Alpha would leave some outside to watch his line of retreat, but most would come in with him. Basic tactics the old man had beaten into *my* head by the time I was ten.

Izumi and I played a game of pool. I let her win. That's my story and I'm sticking to it. I was about to rack up the balls for another round when the place went dead quiet. I shot a glance toward the door and saw the Alpha stroll in. He wore black cargo pants, a black long-sleeved tee-shirt, and steel-toes combat boots. A male wolf was one steep behind in a navy blue suit. Two more were behind him in jeans and button-up shirts, one chocolate brown, the other paisley green. That last guy was either metro-sexual or queer. All of them looked like they lifted weights with religious devotion. Their muscles stretched their clothes tightly.

This was all standard operating procedure for wolves, the most dominant in front, the weak ones in back, but only four wolves? He really didn't know who I was.

Only William made eye contact, though he didn't hurry to come over. The other wolves scanned the crowd, seeing who I might have on *my* side. That was smart. The Alpha and his wolves flanked the bar. Gloria welcomed them with a smile. William smiled back and took a seat, placing his order. The other wolves did the same, but didn't relax their vigilance. They probably wouldn't even taste their drinks without William's nod.

I was about to go over when three female wolves came in off the street. Angie was in the lead. Her long red hair was braided, nothing loose to get grabbed in a fight. She wore a teal vee-cut, skin-tight blouse that displayed a magnificent rack. Skin-tight jeans and boots with one inch heels complemented her legs and ass, making her look like a runway model.

The two she-wolves behind her were the ones I'd seen unloading the truck with the guys back at the Wolf's Den. The female wolves looked a lot better in evening wear. The short-haired brunette had on a tight, midnight blue, short sleeved shirt. I felt deep disappointment that she showed no cleavage. Her jeans were a little loose. Her robin-egg blue sneakers made her look ready for battle, or maybe high school. The other girl was ash blonde and too perky to live. She wore a silk shirt and tight leather mini-skirt. She was texting on her cell phone. I knew if William saw that crap, he'd ream out at warp speed.

William looked over his shoulder at the ladies and took a massive pull on his drink.

I couldn't help but smile; I wasn't the only one who had trouble with subordinate woman.

I set down my pool stick and waited as Izumi did her job, crossing the room to William, a smile on her face. She invited the Alpha to my table. As he followed her, I also headed for the table so we could both arrive at the same time. This showed we were on equal footing, technically. It's so much easier just to kill and be done with it, but I had to bite the bullet on this one; I needed cannon fodder on this job. Plus, if I make them my enemies right now, I'd not have a chance in hell getting into Angie's pants.

William timed his approach with mine so we pulled out chairs at the same moment, sitting down. The other customers in the room stirred, finally taking deep breaths of relief. They seemed to know they weren't about to get chewed up in the middle of a turf war.

I waved Gloria over, as Izumi and the three she-wolves took a seat at the next table over. They avoided looking at me and the Alpha. I let a little dragon magic burn on my skin to let William know that even though I looked relaxed, I was ready for anything. Gloria arrived to take our orders.

"Eighty-year-old bourbon and six glasses," I said. "The guys at the bar are on their own." I only order bourbon when I'm trying not to rip someone's head off.

She looked at the patrons of the bar, her stare commanding their attention the way only a very old vampire can manage. The bouncer turned off the jukebox. There was a mass exodus for the door. By the time Gloria returned with my order, only Gray and the male wolves remained to watch the coming show. Gray turned on his bar seat to face my table. He clutched a bowl of pretzels, munching avidly.

Gloria put a glass in front of me, William, and Izumi, and left the other three glasses at the other table. Gloria filed the glasses all around with the reddish brown bourbon.

Angie looked at her. "No ice?"

I shuddered at such sacrilege.

William only sighed.

The wolves back at the bar split their attention between my and Izumi' table, and Gray, who ignored them with an ease they ought to find irritating. I saw one of them take a few steps his way, sniffing the air delicately for Gray's scent. Gloria watched as well, showing no sign of interfering in what might happen.

William and I didn't say a word for a long while.

I was trying to picture the red-headed wolf naked with open lips wrapped around my engorged—

"She'd eat you alive," William said.

With that, I won the standoff. I looked at William, and grinned. "Yeah, but talking about biting off more than you can chew." I picked up my drink and took a sip. The scotch tasted like smoky oak, and had a hell of a kick. I set my glace down, ready to talk. "I think we should reintroduce ourselves. I am Caine Deathwalker of the Atlantean Clan, wielder of dragon magic, Lord of the Territory. You have taken a house in my domain without giving notice or offering respect." To make a point, I flared one of the small runes along my spine. I paid a price in gut wrenching nausea and temporary cramps in my left hand. Magic must always be paid for.

All mystic talismans and devices in the room revealed themselves to me alone, glowing the soft green of baby puke. Those like Izumi who directly wielded magical energies glowed as well, silver in her case, and crimson for Gloria since she used blood magic. William and his wolves glowed the same color as their eyes—sulfur yellow, the color of pack magic. Since the tattoos I wore on my skin were a mixture of ink and dragon blood, my own glow was a shifting rain, unable to make up its mind.

One of the cool side effects of this rune was that it made my pupils thin and long, like a dragon's. Across the table from me, William inhaled sharply, a sudden tension making him rigid. Everyone in the bar stilled at the feel of my magic except Gray, and the redhead.

I put my magic away, feeling my skin cool, and the muscles of my left hand relax.

The Alpha broke the silence. "I am William Copper, werewolf and Alpha of my pack."

We picked up our glasses, saluted one another, and threw back the drinks. I poured us refills. Izumi and the she-wolves had yet to take a sip.

I cradled my glass in both hands, keeping my voice soft and mild, "Tell me Alpha, couldn't you tell you were in claimed territory?"

William shrugged. "I felt the boundary magic when I got here, but knew not many would fight with a wolf pack over territory. I didn't catch the uniqueness of your magic at the time. I assumed you were fey."

"No, definitely not fey. This must be the first time you've came across dragon magic?"

"Yes, it is. I didn't even know there were dragons on this continent."

"I'm no dragon, either," I said.

Angie had turned to straddle her chair, resting her arms on its back. She studied me with intense eyes. "You don't smell exactly human either, Mr. Caine, so what are you?"

William didn't object to her intrusion in the conversation, waiting for me to answer.

It was my turn to shrug. "Your guess is as good as mine, and unlike the fey you've known I'm quite willing to fight."

William's wolf-yellow eyes burned brighter, an indication of strong emotion.

My runes tingled in response. Every muscle in my body begged to be used to kill the wolves. My demon-blessed weapons all but wept to be used.

The wolves at the bar growled, crouching aggressively, hands thickening into claw-tipped paws. They were ready to attack but waited on their Alpha's orders.

Eyes ice blue, Izumi stood at her table and pulled her chair out from behind her so she could back away from everyone.

The she-wolves bristled, wolf-yellow eyes locked on the pulse in my throat.

As William and I stayed seated, as pack magic filled the room like an invisible mist, thick and consuming.

With my tats active, I smelled something like burning roses.

Gray didn't skip a beat on his drinking, throwing back a freshly filled mug he' helped himself to. Gloria had her back to the pool tables. She watched with cool interest for the other shoe to drop.

William said, “You’re outnumbered, Mr. Caine, and matched by our own magic. Still, if I can help it, I’d rather not fight Miss Izumi. We’ve become friends, sharing hospitality.”

Hmmmm, I wondered just what she *had* shared with him. I shook off the thought, needing to focus. “William, I think you’ve got the wrong idea. She’s not here to fight for me. She’s my ride. As for the rest…”

The runes that ran from my left wrist, over my back, to the other wrist burned as if someone had poured liter fluid over me and set me on fire. I absorbed the pain, becoming one with it so it wouldn’t break the force of my will. The runes along my collar line came to life as well, markings combining my most potent spells. I kept those runes from completing their spell, but let their power flow out of me, battering back the pack magic.

The room darkened even more. A male wolf collapsed, wheezing like his ribs had been crushed, driven into his lungs. I was almost positive that hadn’t really happened. I hadn’t wanted it to. The brunette she-wolf followed him to the floor in full collapse. The other wolf soldiers dropped to their knees, trying looking anywhere but at me. Sweat dampened their shirts, dripping from their faces.

Gloria’s eyes shone blood red.

Izumi retreated a few more steps, radiating an icy cold I could feel across the room.

Gray put his drink down while a golden sword formed on his belt. I thought I saw the suggestion of wings at his back, wings made of charcoal shadows.

In my hand, the drink in my glass started to boil.

When a light curl of smoke eased up my throat and past my grin, the Alpha lunged to his feet. I wondered if he thought I was about to breath fire. I shut down the runes, letting him feel my power recede.

“I am not a poser. I can kill most of you easily without magic, using just the training I was raised with.” I held William’s gaze. “Only you might last a while, a short while.” I broke eye contact, glancing over to Gloria, raising a hand to signal her. “Hey, can I have a new glass. I hate boiled alcohol.”

Looking surprised, William stared at the steaming glass I held.

Izumi’s heels clicked on the floor as she returned to my side. She spoke to the room at large, “Don’t worry, guys, if Caine wanted blood, he’d have completed that spell and slaughtered everyone in the room.”

That news somehow failed to relax anyone.

Izumi pressed on, “So pick yourselves up off the floor and have a drink.” She glowered at me. “And Caine, stop being your normal self and just talk to William."

She didn't understand; that was only possible now that I'd demonstrated absolute dominance.

Gloria hadn't wasted time. Her eyes were their normal emerald as she arrived with a fresh, empty glass she placed in front of me. She went on to help the she-wolves back to their chairs and pushed their table to mine, and dragging a third table over to form a long line. I looked at her, wondering what she was doing.

She said, "Okay now, everyone sit and talk, and don't worry, the drink are on Caine."

I scowled. Just like a woman to turn a perfectly good psychological beat-down into a peace conference. If the bitches in my life weren't so damn hot, I'd have killed them both. I looked at Izumi, then Gloria, envisioning them naked, and put all my magic away.

SEVEN

"What!?! They had it coming."

—Caine Deathwalker

Time for a gesture of trust—as if I trusted anyone. I grabbed both my guns and put them of the table with the handles facing William, an old custom Old Man once showed me. This demonstrated I wasn't looking to kill anyone … for now.

"Fine, there," I said.

Izumi and the wolf in the navy suit revived the male wolves, guiding them to the table and to chairs. William looked at Izumi and Gloria, a little confused with what was going on. His eyes were now light brown, deceptively human. Angie took a seat to William's right, the brunette in the next seat down. The wolf in the navy suit took the first chair to William's left. Other male wolves fell in past the navy suit in order of dominance. One wolf had to come on my side of the table. Izumi sat between him and me. The wolf seemed happy as a scampering pup to sit next to her. I guess he had a thing for ice princesses—the real kind.

William said, "If we are not to fight, then what?"

"I need someone with a better nose than mine for a job I'm on," I explained, "and the way I see it, you're in my territory and still alive, so you owe me."

William's voice finally warmed with anger, "You think I'd let one of my wolves wear your collar just because we're here uninvited?"

"Think of that wolf as a liaison, while I make up my mind on what I should do about all of this," I poured a refill in my cup and drank it down at once. I wanted them to know I was better at *everything* than they were.

His wolves relaxed as the ones who'd passed out began to stir awake. Izumi was also flirting with them, a pleasant distraction. I could see they liked her company. She'd been right; these wolves were better than most.

The bourbon went fast. I called for more, "Hey, Gloria, can you bring us a bottle of Faire tears?"

"What's that?" Angie asked.

"Faire tears, it clears your mind when you get hit by too much magic, expensive as hell on a Saturday night," I said.

"There's no way you can get me so drunk," William said, "I'll give you one of my wolves."

That was true. Alphas are super protective of their packs. Every wolf is family. It would take more than just me saying I wouldn't kill the wolf in my care. It would take a binding oath.

"Fine, I'll give you my word as a member of the Atlantean demon clan, no harm will come from me or mine to any wolf that's with me."

I might be demon in heart only, but my word's as good as any accursed hell spawn's. No demon in our clan has ever broken his word. Words form contracts. Contracts bring power and gold. Breaking one's word has only one punishment—death. There is an *Accord* to the universe that constrains demons, fey, angels, and most other inhuman things from breaking their word. Those stupid enough to do so tend to die in awful ways—those that *can* die. Those that *can't* often wish they could.

William knew this. He finally looked convinced. "Okay, but before we get to this liaison business, allow me to introduce my pack, those that are here."

He pointed at the redhead, "This is Angie, our attorney. She's very good. Next to her is Kate she's an artist who's had numerous gallery shows, receiving much critical acclaim."

I pretended to look impressed without taking my eyes off Angie's breasts. I said, "Hello Angie, Kate."

"Hello," Angie said, "I'm up here by the way."

"Sure you are," I left my eyes where they wanted to be.

William was trying hard not to laugh, doing a poor job. He'd have done a better job if Angie were the female Alpha, and not a mere submissive. He continued introductions on his other side. "This is Andrew, my second in command. He has a PHD in genetics and a doctorate in internal medicine."

Andrew said, "It's a unique opportunity to meet a dragon mage, first time I have even heard of someone like you."

"No one else is like me," I said. "When God saw me, he had the mold maker drawn and quartered, shot, and stabbed three times."

William sniffed at some Faire tears, sipped, and then drained his cup. He said, "The wolf clutching his side, trying to wake up, is Jake. He's young, but handles himself well. He does construction, and occasionally works as a male dancer." William pointed at the wolf beside Izumi. "The kid trying really hard to get into Izumi's pants is Nick, our accountant and financial planner. He's insightful, and god-awful intuitive."

I nodded at him, murmuring, "We'll have to talk sometime."

This was going very well, maybe a little too well. Not ten minutes ago, we were about to kill each other. Nothing like booze for bonding.

I asked a question, "Who's the best tracker in the pack?"

He jerked a thumb at Angie. "The wolf you've most pissed off. She has the best nose of us all."

Great, this was going to be fun. I hated lawyers. The only good ones are those that have been beaten to death with a sack of dead rats, while getting Sodomised in public by a tranny. But lawyers *do* pay well. And then there were those tits…

"Okay, if she's your best," I said. "For being in my territory without asking, I'll give you guys a pass, but I need to know why you're here and why that particular house."

The wolves grew still, suddenly on edge. William said, "Sarah liked the house and fell in love with it. She wrote me about living there, how wonderful everything was. Then her letters stopped coming. We're here to find out why."

I asked the obvious question. "And Sarah is?"

"My granddaughter. I raised her from childhood, after her parents were killed in that space-zombie thing back in the sixties. She's half fey, so she wanted to be out west, where most of the fey have settled. She wanted to explore the non-wolf part of her heritage."

It made sense. Both L.A. and San Francisco have large fey communities.

"She may not be pack," Angie said, "but we helped raise her, and we love her, so if she's in trouble, we're going to fix it."

Andrew said, "Damn straight."

"Well, good luck with that," I said. "Meanwhile, do we have a deal?"

William looked at Angie. She met his gaze. Some silent message passed between them I couldn't catch. He looked back at me and nodded. "Sure."

The pack stayed for a while longer, drinking, talking. Gloria took a seat next to me and made sure they knew they could come back anytime, explaining her bar welcomed anyone willing to behave. Though few vamps care for wolves, she was quite warm to them. Her hand went under the table and the next thing I knew, someone was playing with my joystick.

Izumi joined the wolf-girls, chatting about the shops in LA, which ones were owned by fey and other kinds of creatures of the night. I lost interest when they started to talk about shoes, and Gloria began licking my ear.

William abruptly stood. "We should go before it gets too late. Mr. Caine, I'll leave Angie you with you. Don't take any liberties that might displease me."

I gave him my soul-of-discretion, misunderstood-innocence look.

For some reason he didn't buy it.

The wolves got up, said goodbye, and left. Izumi, and Angie were still talking, so I pried myself loose from Gloria, and went to bug Gray. That sword he'd materialized interested me. Besides, I had to rip him a new one. Carrying my glass and a tumbler of Faire tears, I took a seat next to the half-angel. Gray's mug had gone empty. He held it out to me. I poured in the last of what I had, setting the empty tumbler on the bar.

I hit him with a cold stare. "Next time you make use of your angel abilities to make me happy and get along with everyone, I will rip your wings off and thumbtack them to my wall." I smiled so he'd know I meant it. "So who put you up to it? Izumi? Gloria?"

Gray drained his mug dry and belched. "Nope, your Old Man asked me here, and by the way, these aren't Faire tears.

Close, but no tinker-bells."

"So what the hell have I been drinking?"

Gray smiled and leaned in close. "I'll never tell."

"Bastard."

He patted me on the back, and fell in on himself, moving without moving, flushing himself down a wrinkle in time. I stared at his empty barstool a moment, then got up and went over to the girls, who were trading phone numbers. Weird; a vampire, a werewolf, and an ice demon, telling jokes, drinking, all hot enough to melt steel. I didn't know if I ought to be scared out of my mind, or start fantasizing immediately.

I caught Izumi's eye, "Hey, can you drop me and wolf-girl off somewhere?"

"Where?"

"Where a cold trail is getting colder."

* * *

Outside the hotel, we parked behind my car. Angie and I got out and looked for signs of the former apocalypse. Nothin'. Old Man knew how to pull strings; the clean-up was perfect, reality now reflected total normalcy.

I slammed my door. "Let's get this done before I sober up."

Izumi waved and drove off.

Angie and I walked inside the hotel. A uniformed security guard sat at a central station in the lobby. A Japanese man spoke emphatically to him, asking for a limo to be brought around. Hiro's bodyguard broke off seeing me. I saw recognition in his eyes and dislike in his face, though he hurriedly masked his response. It was good he was handy. It would save me an elevator ride.

The man took a few steps to meet me. His eyes were cold and dead. I could tell he was packing a gun under his jacket. In accented English, he said, "What do you want, *gaijin*."

"Call me that again and I'll shoot you."

Angie looked at me like I was bluffing, or possibly being humorous. She didn't know me too well.

"Why our master needs a *gaijin* dog, I do no know."

I whipped out an automatic and shot the man just above the knee, making it a clean in and out wound. Guy was lucky I wasn't sporting explosive rounds. He fell, hands pressed to the wound, screaming like a girl. I pointed my weapon at his good leg.

Angie gasped and seized my arm.

I raised an eyebrow at her. "What? I told him not to call me that."

Coming off the elevator, several men in dark suits ran over. One had a gun out. I shot it out of his hand. If the Lone Ranger could do it, so could I. I pointed at the dark suit on the floor. "You, call Hiro, or do nothing ever again." In no mood to deal with flunkies tonight, I was speaking the international language, violence.

The man pulled out his phone, speed-dialed, and waited. A few seconds later, the sitting man spoke Japanese, staring at me like I was some kind of slavering beast—the dangerous kind. After a moment he said, "Your name, sir?"

"Caine Deathwalker," I said. He didn't remember my name from the last visit. I didn't think he'd forget it again.

The man repeated my name and listened some more, looking at me again with ever widening eyes. Possibly, my real nature as a demonic agent had been explained to him. He put his phone away and said something in Japanese to the dark suits surrounding us. They had their weapons out, but pointed down at the floor—ready just in case. They holstered their guns and very slowly formed a line behind the fallen man. They faced me and bowed, even the cripple on the floor.

I holstered my gun.

A few minutes later, Hiro arrived. By then, the wounded man had been dragged off and someone else was on duty in the lobby.

"You have news?" Hiro asked.

I smiled, flashing him with my false confidence as I ignored his question. "I need something Haruka may have worn recently."

He nodded understanding, made the call, and a woman in a tea green and gold kimono soon appeared with a sweater. She gave it to Hiro. He gave it to me. I gave it to Angie. Angie looked for someone to give it to, found no one, and turned back to me, confusion in her eyes.

"Are you sure you're a wolf?" I asked.

I dragged her over to the stairs. We climbed up to the restaurant where I'd last seen the girls. It was clean. No meat puppets. No screaming customers. No blood. A new hostess was on duty.

She smiled at me. "Table for two?"

"Two café mochas, to go," I said. I turned to Angie, pointed at the sweater and said, "Take a deep whiff then sniff the carpet. Find me a trail to follow."

EIGHT

Being evil is easy: you just have to perfect your craft on those who don't deserve compassion — pretty much everybody."

—Caine Deathwalker

She didn't need to get down on all fours to sniff the carpet. Her nostrils simply flared. "Good thing the clean-up crew used magic instead of bleach to get the blood out of the carpet; otherwise, we'd have no trail." She walked past the hostess station, into the kitchen.

People looked at us strangely. A male high school kid wearing a hair net and an apron over his street clothes asked, "Can I help you with something?"

"Probably not." I strolled past him, following Angie to the walk-in freezer. The door was oversized, steel, and set flush to the wall. Angie seized the handle, turned, and pulled it open effortlessly—even in human form she had a large chunk of her werewolf strength.

"Are you sure about this?" I asked. "I remember the girls heading out into the hall, not coming back here."

"My nose doesn't lie. Maybe someone clouded your mind. No wait, I've seen you drink. You cloud your own mind pretty well, all on your own." She went in.

I closed the door on her.

The door opened from the inside.

Angie stood there looking at me. "These things are designed to open from the inside so someone can't accidentally be looked in."

"I knew that," I said. "I just wanted to be sure it hadn't been tampered with."

She looked skeptically at me, but I'd told her the truth. I'd taken an oath to keep her safe. Until I had a damn good reason to break that oath, I'd keep it.

"So what do you smell now?" I asked.

"Her scent stops right here, and then … nothing." Angie walked out of the freezer. I closed the door again. She continued, "When I say nothing, I mean nothing at all, I can't smell anything in this area, not even what I should be able to smell."

I nodded. "The girls were magically removed, and the scents went along for the ride. Someone's being very thorough. Let's go."

"Where to?" Angie asked.

"A few places I know, where fey and others go to play." I grabbed our mochas and paid on the way out. "Here." I handed her the other drink and kept moving, entering the hall, heading for the stairs.

"Thanks," she said.

I nodded and took a sip. "Being a demon lord and all, the restaurant shouldn't have charged me. I provide a public service, killing gutter trash that pisses me off."

She went oddly silent, as if I'd somehow threatened her.

We passed through the lobby where everyone gave us a wide birth. Outside, my car was still in front of the building. I'm so glad it didn't get destroyed, again. I go through them quickly.

Angie looked at my vehicle in surprise as she slid into the front passenger next to me. "For an old car it looks pretty new."

"Don't call her old. She's vintage," I said, "with a few improvements."

The engine came to life when I touched the finger print scanner. I pressed a special section on the underside of the dash, and small, magical holographic screens materialized all around me. The multiple control panels were touch-sensitive, glowing ion blue in two dimensions. They were arranged so that if I ever had to throw myself from the car, they wouldn't slow me up. The hub of the steering wheel opened and a flat green beam raked my eyes, taking a retinal scan. Sure, someone could cut off my finger and pluck out my eyeball to steal the car, but if they could do that, they deserved a reward.

The green beam produced the floating symbol of my clan. I'd passed the test. I gripped the wheel, and a woman's voice came out of the speakers.

"Oh, baby, lets get it on."

Angie looked at me with wide eyes and said, "Izumi's voice?"

"Yep."

"Does she know?" Angie asked.

"Nope," I said.

"We ought to talk later about privacy laws and the misuse of someone's likeness, actual voice, and pirating of said intellectual property rights," Angie said.

This is why I hate lawyers.

"We'll do that," I said, "when I give a crap."

I hit the gas, making us both sink into our seat. I cut off a white stretch limo. Angie's nails sunk into the arm rest and seat. The sound of my engine made me happy, as I rumbled past numerous cars, weaving in and out of traffic. We stopped at a red light and I checked the GPS. We were two miles from an underground nightclub I knew of. I pointed at a blip on one of the floating blue screens. "This is a good place to start putting word out that I'm looking for the girls."

She looked at the blip on the screen. "What is this place?"

"*Aes Sídhe.*"

"Icy?"

I pronounced it slowly for her, "*Ice-shee*, a nightclub for fey and other nightwalkers. The name means 'People of the Mounds.'"

"Sounds fun, do they have stripers," Angie asked

The light turned green and I took off. "Yeah, but you never get what's offered. Ever heard of elfin glamour?"

We got there in no time. The outside looked like a normal night club with a long line of humans, fey, and others waiting to get in. A troll with a broken tusk guarded the door, weeding out the wanna-be preternaturals from the real thing. The bouncer's knuckles nearly dragged the ground. His feet were bare, and he wore faded denim coveralls held up by one strap. It was Fred. I knew him. I'd once broken a barstool over his head.

I drove past the door, looking for a place to park. It took me a few minutes. I really hated the way people parked here. Surely they could have found spaces further away so as to not inconvenience me. I got out and Angie followed. I pinned her with a cautionary stare. "This place is nice, but it's been a very long time since they've seen a wolf, so keep your head down and don't kill any one. And if anyone gives you crap, tell them you're with me."

"Okay, I'll be good," Angie said.

We cut in line right in front of Fred. He waved me through, tapping the scar on his head to show he remembered me. I handed him a hundred and went on in.

The club was on the Goth side of things, go-go girls posed suggestively, hanging from the ceiling from wide swaths of brightly colored silk. Black lights all over the bar gave many pieces of clothing an annoying glare. The dance floor lit up as people and things stepped on different colored tiles. The bartenders worked fast, putting out more alcohol then a distillery.

Overpaid and undersexed patrons prowled for partners, danced, and did assorted drugs with no idea that no matter how much *juice* they had, here, they were at the bottom of the food chain.

But this was L.A. Everywhere you looked, there were cameras and too many high profile Celebs that would be missed, so the fey had learned to feed with restraint, and to protect the frail humans from less scrupulous predators. The demons followed suit, seeing the advantage to nightclubs where humans could get so wasted and high enough they didn't remember what had happened to them, or what contracts they may have signed in blood.

Angie and I walked toward the back room were the piece-of-crap owner had his office. Fey and demon could look like anything. Not Angie. She gathered speculative stares as we went along. It had been a very long time since a wolf had been anywhere near here. A few decades ago, the fey elders shoved the wolves out of the territory and made it stick. If I didn't handle this right, there could be war on the streets again.

Two fey guards loitered down a dark hallway, outside a black door. They studied Angie and me. More Angie than me. The massive one on the right smelled of peat bog and dead things. His eyes were yellow with red vertical pupils. He wore all black and seemed to possess a few extra arms. The other guard was thin, not so much a broadsword as a rapier, light on his feet, ready to lunge. There was a jitteriness that got expressed by hands that couldn't stay still.

He said, "The wolf can't come in."

"She's mine," I said, "and where I go, my pet goes."

I smelled Angie's anger and I was hoping—if the fey sensed it—they'd assume they were the cause, not the fact I'd just called her my pet. Wolves had killed people for less. The big man opened the door and waved us past. Instead of an office, there were stairs. They led up to a second story room above the dance floor. We walked into a large space with sandalwood wood furniture, Elvis pictures on black velvet, but fortunately, no sad-faced clowns. There was an entire wall of one-way glass. The human sitting behind the white desk wore a white suit. His hair was bleached white, as were the foot long, fine lines of coke on the desk before him. The white powder told me Albino John was in a party mood, not a good thing with so many fey around. A little coke in the air could have dangerous, unforeseen effects on them—and anyone close to them.

I nodded a greeting. "John."
The man lifted his face to me, eyes pink and watery.
"Great, I suppose you're here to destroy my club again," John said.
"Tell me, John, how can you do so much coke and still be such a fat sack of rabbit pellets?" I took a seat on his desk, grabbed an erotic paperback on his desk and dropped it on his coke, creating a chalky cloud. I felt the protective ink on my back glimmer to life under my shirt. I bit down on a curse as my blood seemed to turn to lava in my veins.
Always a price for magic—my kind anyway.
John sighed. "What do you want, Deathwalker."
"I'm looking for a new succubus in town. She took two human girls from the Kirishima Building a few hours ago, and I want them back, so put out the word," I said.
"And why would I do that?"
"50K reward," I said.
John stood and waddled to the two-way mirror. I hate people who wear white suits; they think they're better then everyone, as if the purity of their look reflected their miserable little souls.
He spoke without turning, "Okay."
I started for the stairs, Angie falling in behind me.
"Deathwalker," he called, "what's with the wolf?"
I told him what he'd believe. "An illegitimate daughter that wants to bond."
He turned and leered at me. "I can imagine the type of bonding *you* have in mind. Wouldn't mind getting a piece of that bitch myself."
I smiled at him.
He blanched.
A migraine hit like a knife to the skull as I warmed another tat. It would take him awhile to notice, but his lines of coke had turned into cocoa powder. With any luck, he'd snort some before realizing what he was doing. I hoped so. I'd heard of a crack-head made to snort cocoa once. It's funny how they choke, and cry, and paw at their noses, cursing at the blinding pain.
Smile widening, I led Angie downstairs.
"Not a lot of people like you, do they?" She said.
"Surprisingly, no."
We got back to the car, and headed to the next night spot favored by Preternaturals.

NINE

"Vampires and whores are related species; neither have souls."

—Caine Deathwalker

Rhino's Bar and Grill was owned by Rhino, a former lineman in the NFL. He was big as one of the African brutes, and almost as intelligent, hence the nickname. His afro was close-clipped, and he sported a goatee and mustache. His 4X shirt was a Hawaiian monstrosity; olive green palm trees on a field of arterial red. Above his head, a large screen TV set to the sports channel displayed a soccer game re-run.

He looked up from wiping the bar as I came in. His nose had been broken several times, actually improving his face. A huge grin appeared. One of his teeth had a snap-on gold sheath.

"Gonna start trouble?" he asked. "Been a while since we had a good fight in here."

"Just might be your lucky day," I said.

"Looks like yours, fer sure." His glance slid over Angie who trailed me in.

I slid onto an empty bar stool. Angie took the one to my left.

I said, "Give me a Bacardi Hurricane, and a Cosmo Cocktail for the lady."

Down the bar from us, a couple of werecat ladies had both hands bracketing strawberry daiquiris, as if afraid someone might snatch them away. I understood their attitude. The *kitties* were often picked on by the rest of the shape-shifting community because they were perceived as weak. That was true here in L.A. but up in Sacramento, a stranger had recently blown into town, bonded with a local tabby, and had broken the back of the local wolf pack. He'd ripped out the heart of the local Alpha, as well, carving out his territory with brutal efficiency.

I'd heard he was a wereliger, half lion, half tiger, weighing in at twenty-five hundred pounds after changing. Mass usually didn't get added with shape-shifting. This guy broke a lot of rules. Sounded like someone I'd like to meet, when all this trouble was over.

The kitties sniffed the air, turning their faces toward Angie.

She smiled at them, showing a little fang while in human form.

I'd never seen a person literally go white with fear, but the kitties did. They looked to be in their late teens, and reeked of nervous inexperience. Since I might need a little good will with the cat clans one day, I intervened. "Angie, down girl."

She looked at me like I'd stolen her chew toy.

I put steel in my tone. "Be nice or go wait in the car."

Looking forward, she grumbled beneath her breath, but was glad enough to pounce on the cranberry vodka set in front of her. A tall electric blue drink with a slice of lemon on the rim appeared in front of me on a napkin.

"There you go," Rhino said, his towel thrown over a shoulder.

I nodded thanks, and jerked a thumb toward the kitties. "Their next drink is on me."

"*You're* buying a drink, Rhino said, "and there's no gun to your head?"

I glared at him. "You trying to say I'm cheap?"

My glower bounced harmlessly off of him the same way a two-by-four might have. He grinned, not when you're spending on yourself. "Hey, Caine, have you heard…?"

At the casual dropping of my name, the supernaturals in the room went deathly quiet—for some reason. Only the humans with their normal, weak hearing were oblivious. The tension around the kitties got thick enough to carve with a katana.

I met Rhino's cold, dark stare. "Heard what?" I asked.

"There's strange folk in the city, making the rounds."

Took a sip from my drink, testing the flavor. "Wolves?"

He shook his head. "No, humans, but tough bastards all the same. They're well strapped, and don't seem to like your kind."

Angie offered a comment, "Maybe some kind of government taskforce, or spooks, looking into PNs?"

Just what the preternatural community needs." *Just what I need; something else to look into.* I slid Rhino a hundred. "Thanks. You hear anymore…"

He smiled, flashing that gold-capped tooth. His meaty palm slapped over the bill. "You'll be the first to hear."

I raised my voice, wanting the kitties and other shifters in the bar to pick up on what I had to say, "By the way, you hear of a succubus working my territory, I want to know. She'll have two abducted women with her. I'm offering fifty K for information leading to their recovery."

Several PNs hurried from the room, wanting to get a running start on that reward. Word would go out. Fast. Even things that go bump in the night need cash. My work here was done, but I lingered over my drink.

The werecats finished their drinks and ordered two more. One of them got up. Circled Angie at a respectful distance, and came around to my other side. "I want to thank you for the drinks," her voice had the faintest suggestion of a purr to it.

"No, problem."

"You're Caine Deathwalker," she said.

"I know."

"I mean, dude, I thought you were just made up, an urban legend or something."

"That too."

"Look, normally I mind my own business—"

"Good idea," Angie growled.

Eyes wide, on me, she ignored her. "—But seeing as how you bought us drinks and all…"

"Get to the point," I suggested.

"Yes, Sir, I thought you outta know, these strangers in town, they're not feds. Word is they're looking for some kinda stolen artifact, and waving around some woman's picture."

"Interesting. That all you know?"

"Yes, Sir."

"You have our thanks and mayest now leave our exalted presence." I waved her away. Too bad I didn't have a ring for her to kiss. I think she'd have been thrilled. It is good to be the king.

We finished our drinks and moved on to few more bars. The one I saved for last was going to be tricky. I parked the car across the street and turned to Angie. "I don't think this is a place where you want to be. You should wait here for me."

She looked out the window at the club. Above double doors painted crimson, a black panel sported neon lettering; *Pandemonium*. The first three and last three letters were yellow. The word demon in the middle was rendered in red. The bouncer outside was dressed like an old black-and-white movie version of a vampire. He had slicked-back hair, a widow's peak, a dark Victorian suit, white gloves, and a red-lined, black cape.

"Isss that a vampire?" Angie slurred.

"Probably not. They have too much pride to do so lowly a job. That's probably a human with plastic fangs. There will be a lot of wanna-bes inside, and a few of the real thing feeding on them discretely. The place serves a great Bloody Mary."

"You think I can't handle a few Vampsss?"

"You are rather drunk," I said. "And I'd like to get you back to William in one piece."

She blinked at me. "I'm in one piece."

"So far," I said. "Look, just stay here, and if you feel like throwing up, open the car door and stick your head out. I just had this vehicle detailed."

"I wanna go in and get another drink."

"Stay here and I'll buy you some beef jerky."

"Don't want beef jerky. Wanna drink." She opened the door and slid out, tottering toward the door.

I got out and went around; closing the door she'd left open. I hurried after her. She was halfway across the street where a '62 cutlass convertible low-rider had stopped. The vehicle was full of Latinos wearing black and gold bandanas. One of them stood up in the back, making beckoning motions toward her. "Hey, *chica*, c'mon, come party with us. We'll treat you right."

Angie pointed at the club. "I'm going in there for a drink."

The man in the front passenger seat held up a twelve pack of Tecate beer. "I got your drink right here, chica."

By then, I'd caught up to her, taking her arm, pulling her back from the car's grill. "Lady's with me," I said.

"Fuck you," the driver said. "We saw her first."

I looked at him, warming up my *Dragon Voice* tat, feeling meat hooks yanking on my spine. I growled through the blinding pain and shouted, "Go drive into a street light."

My voice shattered the windshield. The driver's eyes glazed over. He floored the gas pedal and the car peeled rubber, tearing away. I steered Angie for the nightclub door, figuring I'd better keep her somewhat near me.

We'd just reached the bouncer, cutting to the front of the line, when the sound of a car crash reached us. A moment later, there was an explosion. A fireball rose in a cloud of oily smoke. Finding this hilarious, Angie had a fit of giggles.

"You can't cut the line," the bouncer told me.

I handed him a hundred.

He pointed at Angie. "Don't you think she's had enough already?"

I handed him another hundred. He started to say something else. I opened my coat and showed him one of my guns. "If you say anything else but '*come in*,' I'm going to empty a clip in your face."

He moved to the side and waved us in.

Who says you can't get good service anymore.

The décor reminded me of an old school insane asylum; cracked concrete walls, lanterns swinging on chains, chains and manacles on the walls, a bedlam of voices, and bartenders in straightjackets with the sleeves torn off. There was a girl band on stage with pink and green hair, orange coveralls, matching lipstick, heavy black and purple makeup around the eyes, and spiked dog collars. The lead singer was hot with a body made for sin. She wore combat boots and a diamond chip on the side of her nose, and razorblade earrings. Unfortunately, her voice sounded like she'd gargled with Drano. Her lyrics stabbed through the haze stage lights, the mash of screaming guitars, and thudding drums:

Broken dreams cut my feet,
Ill winds drive me into the street,
Sanity's just a mask I wear—
Take some pain— I'm glad to share—

Angie started dancing, her boobs bouncing pleasantly as she jerked and weaved about. I let her go, figuring if I made it fast, I could get back quickly and round her up. As the crowd absorbed her, I went to the bar and caught the eye of a bartender with a handlebar mustache.

"What can I get you," he asked.

"Tell Adrian I want to see him."

"And you would be?"

"Just tell him to move his ass. I'm in a hurry."

"Hurry to die," the bartender said. "You stay right there. I'm passing your message on *verbatim*."

"Reading the dictionary again?"

He flashed fangs at me that were real. "I just hope they leave a little of you for me to taste when they're through."

I smiled at him. "Can we just get this party started? It's been a long night."

Like smoke from a fire, vamp goons appeared on both sides of me, taking my arms. They squeezed so I'd feel their unnatural strength and tremble. Vamps like their prey scared. It's supposed to enrich the flavor of blood. They hustled me to a private room where a small part was in progress. Three scantily clad girls were strewn on a long table, eyes glassy, throats ripped out. At the head of the table stood Adrian, a Champaign glass filled with blood in his hand. He wore a black suit, with red shirt and pocket handkerchief.

A female vamp hung on him like a barnacle. She had black hair, too red lips, and pallor borrowed from a corpse. Her dangerous curves had been shimmied into a little black dress. She eyed my throat hungrily.

Adrian smiled without baring his fangs. He understated what he was, having a distaste for the usual posing that's so much a part of vamp culture. "Caine, didn't I tell you that the next time I saw you I'd put stakes through both your eyes?" The passion in his voice told me he meant every word.

TEN

"There's a razor thin line between dancing and dying if you do it right."

—Caine Deathwalker

"Yeah, I missed you too," I said.

He waved his goons off me.

They went about their business.

Adrian said, "Are you here to get yourself killed, or are you finally going to admit this is *my* city?"

I grabbed a chair and took a seat, putting my feet on the table. "You couldn't handle running the city if I gave it to you on a bed of roses. The older vamps would continue ignoring you, and without the Old Ones approval, no master of the city can do his job."

I wasn't pure demon, not a demon at all, but the demons followed me. They feared me. That had been enough to bring the Old Ones over to my side as well, that and Gloria's support.

I continued, "Not only that, but all the *big bads* I keep out would swarm in for a piece of the pie. Take this new succubus that I'm planning to kill…"

His eyes brightened with interest. Vampires love gossip on other vamps, even those of a different species. "There's a succubus in town? I hadn't heard."

"No contacts in the street. Another reason you can't do my job. Face it; you're good for all-nighters, but being the master of a city means being available *all* the time. Trust me, it's a headache."

Adrian twitched a finger toward the door. Most of the vampires left in a blur of movement, but not the hot number draping herself all over him, and not the whores spread out over blood puddles on the table top. "You still have a gift for annoying me." Adrian's eyebrow shot up. A small amount of red glazed his pale blue eyes. His eyes-of-flame trick was nothing compared to Gloria's. "What do you want, Caine?"

"The succubus. She has taken two humans who were under my protection. To save face, I must be the one who gets them back. The succubus is my prey. I want to be sure you know this. Don't side with her, don't get in my way. I know all you vamps like to stick together."

"Do not compare that creature to our kind," the lady vamp attached to his hip glared at me.

I think she felt threatened by those of us sexually superior to herself, namely the succubus and me. I hate being immodest, but I am an urban legend for many reasons. I met her vamp stare easily. My protective magic prevented her from rolling my mind like a drunken sailor.

I shrugged. "Well, you suck blood and she sucks life force. You both use sex as a weapon of male destruction, and … oh yeah, you're both bottom feeders going after the weak. Did I get any of that wrong?"

The vampire girl blurred. She had a lot of speed on me, but my tats were faster. My shield turned itself on, and she was thrown back, her lovely vamp nose broken. I got up and activated the tats on my legs that let me match vamp speed temporarily, a gift I'd pay for in an hour. As she surged back to her feet, I caught her by the throat and lifted her off the carpet. She grabbed my arm, straining to snap it.

"You want this in one piece?" I asked Adrian.

He shrugged. "Getting a little tired of her actually."

I snapped her neck and dropped her body. She'd wake up when her neck healed, hopefully with a great deal more restraint.

I strolled for the door. I was almost there when Adrian spoke up, "How's *she* doing?"

"The bitch on the floor?"

"No. Gloria."

"Your mom's just fine, but you should call her. I'm sure she worries about her stupid son."

I stepped out of the room. The two vamp goons that had escorted me in were at the edge of the dance floor, telling Angie she couldn't take her drink onto the dance floor. They were having difficulty getting this across because she was so drunk. They didn't seem to mind explaining this to her slowly, while staring at her boobs. Finally she got it, throwing back her drink and handing them an empty glass.

By this time, Angie was swaying on her feet.

"You don't look so good," Goon One said. "Why don't we show you a place where you can lie down for awhile?"

Goon Two took her arm, smiling, oozing vamp seduction. "Come this way."

I reached them as they turned my way. "It's late, Angie. Let's go. You can be a blood donor some other time."

"Night's young," Goon One said.

"Party's just getting started." Goon Two gave me a look meant to back me down. They had a drunken wolf and knew it. Shape-shifter blood has a kick human blood lacks. They wanted a pint or two.

I smiled and shot them a look of world-weary innocence. "C'mon guys, don't make me kill you."

They bared fangs at me.

I pointed down at my right foot.

They stared down at my steel-toed boot.

The magic I'd used to enhance my speed was still running. I swung my foot, a hook kick across their faces. Broken teeth fell to the carpet as they reeled back and were swallowed by the dancers. I picked up the teeth to add to my collection. I pushed Angie toward the door as a fight erupted behind us. Apparently, the vamps had been overly rough trying to escape the crowd and had given offense. By the time I got to the door, a full blown brawl was underway. Somehow, I knew Adrian would blame this on me.

We got outside and crossed the street to the car. Already, Angie's werewolf metabolism was neutralizing the alcohol, taking the stagger out of her walk. I just hoped she wouldn't puke in my car.

"Hey, Caine?"

"Yeah?"

"Did the vamps agree to help you out?"

"I didn't ask them. I made it very clear they were not to get involved, that the succubus is *my* prey, a matter of honor."

She looked at me over the top of the car as I went around to the driver's door. "So, they'll do what you want them to in order to spite you, and they'll think it's *their* idea."

"Yeah. I love being me."

We got in and drove off. Half a block from the club, police had taped off a section of street where a car had wrapped itself around a streetlight. EMTs had responded, but there was no hope. The passengers were all crispy critters. Up on the side walk, the twelve pack of Mexican beer had been thrown clear and had miraculously survived. The beer was being taken into custody as material evidence, but doubted I would reach the evidence locker at the station.

Seeing the crash made me happy. I turned on the radio as we continued on. Angie did a sort of dance with her upper body in the seat next to me. It was fun watching her large breasts bounce as she clapped, and tried to sing along to the songs.

"I'll drop you off at William's place. You can explain to him how you got in this state." I said.

"No, I wanna go to your place."

"Why?"

"I'm your liaison to the wolves. You're stuck with me until this whole mess is over. And William might yell at me."

I took the ramp onto the highway. "Aren't you afraid I'll take advantage of you?"

"I'm a wolf," she said. "I can't even spell fear."

"That doesn't surprise me, but I'd rather not have you underfoot." *At my house where you can pry into my secrets.*

She stuck her head out the open window, enjoying the wind stream, smiling and waving at the traffic in the slow lane. As we went along, more of her scooted out the window, and she started lifting her shirt, flashing her boobs. One driver gave her a thumbs-up. Another honked encouragement. After a while, she just left the shirt up, and let her tongue wag in the wind. If I had a dog, this experience would have been much the same.

"Oh, hell, at least you're a happy drunk."

We reached my house as the sun began to gray the eastern sky. I pulled into my garage and parked. The garage door lowered, and multiple locks automatically activated. I led Angie to the kitchen door entrance. In the kitchen, she peered at every little thing, following me from room to room. Going through the living room, I pointed at the couch. "You can curl up there if you'd rather not share my bed." Why a hot chick *wouldn't* want to share my bed, I didn't know, but I offered her the choice, gentleman that I am, not bothering to mention I had empty bedrooms available.

She stopped to stare at the couch as if she'd never seen one before. I kept going. In my *office*, I went to the bar and hit a button on the master remote I'd left there. All the windows went dark. The curtains closed. The room lights dimmed to a soft yellow glow. A whirl of black fog condensed into a feline shape. I heard soft paws and hard nails approach as I made myself a pitcher of drinks.

"Hey Leona, Old Man's done with you?" I asked.

"For now. He's going to be with Hiro during the day," she said.

With Leona a step behind, I carried my pitcher back out to the living room. I'd intended going straight to my room, but seeing each other, Leona and Angie went rigid. There was tension in the air like a storm about to break. The scene was made ridiculous by the fact that Angie still had her shirt rolled up.

"Some kind of problem here?" I asked.

Leona's tail lashed. "You didn't tell me you'd brought a slut home with you."

"Hey," Angie's eyes were bright wolf-yellow, "I'm a bitch, not a slut."

I smiled at Leona. "We're going to have a house guest for a few days. Try not to kill her. It would touch upon my honor."

Leona sat on her haunches, studying Angie's boobs. "Are those even real?"

Angie took them in hand and gave them a little flounce. "Hell, yes. What, jealous?"

I walked to my room, set the pitcher on the nightstand, and went to the closet. My guns and swords went inside along with my long coat. My image was caught on the far side of the bed by a giant mirror on the wall. I changed into my black silk PJs. Once I was done, I lay on my bed and stared up at the plasma screen TV attached to the ceiling. Remote in hand, I began to surf channels, keeping one ear open for savage animal screams and the sound of breaking furniture.

Such sounds never came. That was far more ominous.

In the back of my mind, a clock had been running since I used my tat for vampire speed. I knew when an exact hour had passed because the bill came due with a vengeance, without any adrenaline in my system to take off the edge. Every muscle in both legs locked with severe cramps. I cursed, slid to the side, and fell out of bed trying to get weight on my legs to ease the pain. It didn't ease. It piled on, spiking to higher levels as I screamed for help.

Angie and Leona appeared in my doorway, staring down at my writhing with looks of polite interest on their faces.

"Get me up! Get me up!" I yell.

"What a perv," Leona stalked off.

Angie went after her.

Bitches. If I could have walked, I'd have gone for my gun.

ELEVEN

"My sweet dreams are your nightmares."

—Caine Deathwalker

I dreamed of hot blood drizzling from the sky, and the sweet screeching cry of dragons wheeling through the clouds, fighting. I sat on a beach chair, katana across my lap, drinking a skull full of wine. A young dragon—only three tons—romped over and sniffed at my drink. I smacked him in the snout. "Get your own, you freeloading bastard."

He swung his head toward me and a long wet tongue flailed out.

I opened my eyes to see Leona next to me, her tongue sliding back into her mouth. Sphinx-like, her head tilted in curious interest, she posed an unspoken question.

I said, "Yes, damn it, I'm awake. Keep your slobber to yourself."

She flashed a leopard's less-than-comforting smile. "One; you looked too happy, and two; your wolf's snooping around the house while you're sleep, asshole."

"Great, one more bitch to worry about. I rolled out of bed and checked the door. It was closed; the magic runes were activated, keeping our voices from leaving the room. I sometimes had "screamers" in my bed. This kept everyone in the neighborhood from getting jealous over my manly skills.

I'd added the sound barrier after someone called the cops on me, claiming I was killing a whore. Not that I have a problem with that; whores aren't really people. Since they don't have souls, they can't even make a binding contract with a demon.

As Leona jumped down, I turned to her. "Hey, can you mask your scent?"

"Oh heavens, do I offend?"

"You know why," I said.

"Yeah, her wolf senses are good, but I'm better."

My smell was already all over the house so Angie wouldn't scent me—unless I got too close. I'd use Leona for that. I opened the door and she led the way out into the hall. I tried to keep my tread light. I had to be very careful not to make noise. A wolf can hear a pin drop across a silent house.

The hallway dead ended just past the other bedrooms. I went the other way, to where it opened at a junction that offered access to either the kitchen or the living room. I could smell Angie's musky scent. Silent, Leona looked at me, and headed into the living room. I followed from several feet back, sliding a foot forward and out, planting it, then shifting my weight forward. The crescent step technique was borrowed from Phoenix style Kung-Fu.

Quiet as a Shou-lin monk, I moved along the wall to the door of my office. It was open, but Leona waited until I reached her. As I arrived, senses straining, she slunk on through. I watched her ass, having taught her a kind of sign language she could send with her tail. She made a circuit of the room, pausing by the spell-guarded patio doors that led out to the pool and the pool house. Her tail made a hook, followed by two quick flicks. Angie hadn't gone that way and she wasn't in the bar.

From the bar, the only other place she could go was into the wine cellar, if she'd found the concealed elevator. Apparently she had. Now I was nervous, and not about the wine. Everything I hold dear is in a secret vault behind one of the walls down there. She was way too close to my biggest secret. I used one hand to sign, telling Leona to go invisible, go downstairs, and wait for me.

She flashed a happy, obedient grin that was both feral and threatening.

The good news was that the wine cellar was fairly well sound-proofed. Angie wouldn't know I was onto her until she heard the elevator running. At which point, she'd either hide, or bluff it out, bottle in hand, claiming she only wanted a decent drink. Were she to go violent, well, Leona would be hovering close, ready to take on form. *Spirit beasts make life so much easier.* Of course, before I went down there, I needed to be in a hell of a lot more than black pee-jays.

I jogged back to my room, no longer concerned about noise. Before changing, I went to the huge mirror beyond the bed. Worked into the ornate frame, hidden in curlicues and other abstract patterns, were random Atlantean runes: the complete alpha-numeric orthography. I touched various symbols in a specific order. Had I needed emergency access, I could have powered up a tat, swallowing the pain, but that kind of urgency wasn't required—yet. As I touched the last rune of my personal code, the glass surface ghosted away. I stepped through the frame, into my secret vault. Sensors noted my presence, turning the lights on. A frosted white light filled a vast warehouse. All my treasures were here, safe from the I.R.S. and other demonic forces.

I extended magically amplified senses, feeling a kick in the guts as a penalty. I staggered, bent by the blow, then straightened up. Smell and hearing assured me I was alone. Angie hadn't got in. Neither her physical nor mystic resources had been up to the job. It didn't help that the vault door waiting for her to find in the winery was a fake. She could spend the next year on it with no luck. The fake door was best money could buy, made to look real with three interlocking, multi-combination dials, an unlocking wheel that would only turn if all three dials had been turned in the right order.

Reassured, I left the vault with its extra-spatial dimensions, and returned to my bedroom. A few minutes later, I wore slacks, steel-toed boots, and a dark pullover shirt. I shrugged into shoulder holsters with sheaths hanging down my back for my short swords. The harness let me use a cross-draw for my automatics, and over-the-shoulder draws for my twin short swords. I slid a knife into my boot sheath, and added infrared goggles, letting them hang around my neck until needed.

I went back to the bar and the elevator, stepping into the car. Punching the control panel started the cage moving down. The mechanism hummed until the cage jarred to a stop. The door slid open. I'd been ready with a major spell in case Angie sprang in, bringing the fight to me. This didn't happen. The lights hadn't been disabled either. I stepped out, making no effort to hide.

I made my way forward, passing a number of refrigerated coolers, the shelves lined with wine bottles. My nose told me she was at the first basement. Somehow, I didn't think she'd be hiding. I was right; I found her in the munitions corner, standing in plain sight, checking the tools I used to make my ammo. She was admiring some of my generic blades and body armor. I knew she'd barely started trying to breach the hidden vault door because she'd hadn't set off any of the protective spells, or electronics waiting for the incautious.

Off to the side, atop a stack of ration crates and jerry cans of water, a black mist whirled and solidified into Leona. I signed that she should stay put and wait on further developments.

Angie turned as if just now sensing me. She had one of my bottles of wine under her arm. "Cool place you have here," she said. "Hope you don't mind me sampling the private stock."

"The secret vault giving you trouble?" I asked.

She smiled, lacking a real poker-face. That grin told me I was right.

"I've killed people for less, you know?" I said.

Angie shifted the bottle from under her arm, taking it in both hands. I think she planned to throw it if necessary. "I'm not trying to steal anything. I'm just looking for something."

"In my vault?" I asked.

"I just need to look, so can you could please open it…?" Angie was on edge, looking at me like the enemy. Whatever she sought was important, but I'd not put anything in my vault for a while.

"Why don't you tell me what you're after and I'll tell you if it's in there," I said.

Angie looked to be thinking very hard. I looked at her ears for signs of smoke. I didn't think that thinking was something she did too well, outside a courtroom.

Leona sat on her haunches, swishing her tail.

Angie said, "Sarah is missing. We have no idea where she is. We can't find a trace of her. Her house barely has her scent. Nothing seems out of place or broken, but the place feels wrong somehow."

"And what does that have to do with me?"

"You live on the same block, and you are demon scum."

"Powerful demon scum," I reminded her.

"Exactly," she said. "We're thinking you probably took her."

"And why would I do that," I asked.

"Sarah is half fey and very pretty. She has a lot of power, but no idea how to use it. That makes her as easy target," Angie said. "So, can I look at what's behind the door?"

I walked away laughing heading for the elevator and the bar.

"Hey," she ran after me, "I'm serious. It would be a sign of good faith."

I stepped onto the elevator and turned my smile toward her. "Tell you what, you keep the bottle, and I don't kill you. There's your good faith."

"But I trusted you. I told you everything."

"I know." I looked at her with sad pity as the door closed. The elevator started running with a happy hum. I wasn't concerned anymore about Angie being in the wine cellar. Leona would keep her out of trouble. Meanwhile, I had some thinking to do.

If I help the wolves find Sarah, they'll owe me. I can have the whole pack looking for Haruka and Jessie—free labor.

The door opened and I stepped out behind the bar. I didn't stop to get a drink. I just wanted to go back to bed and sleep. I made it back to my closet and shed my weaponry. By then, Angie burst into my room.

She said, "If you don't have Sarah, let me see inside your safe."

Naked, I turned to her, "Angie, I don't have Sarah. I'll help look for her, but I'm the only one going inside my vault. Now get in my bed or go away."

I closed the closet door and strolled over to the nightstand where I picked up my phone. I sent a text to Izumi and the old man, telling them what was happening, and to put the word out that we were now looking for Sarah as well. I asked Izumi to get a picture of Sarah from William and to text it to me and the Old Man. Setting the phone down, I slid into silk sheets.

Angie stood there, glowering at me, fuming in silence.

I clapped my hands. The lights went out.

She clapped her hands, turning the lights back on, and stormed out of my room.

Yeah, that will show me.

I clapped the lights off again, and waited. A few moments later, a heavy weight dropped onto the bed. Leona stretched out beside me, rumbling softly, waiting for me to say something.

"What?" I asked.

"Don't fuck around too much," Leona said. "Wolves aren't known for their humor."

I waved her away.

I was glad to be alone. I'd used a lot of magic and needed more sleep. I sighed from the depth of my soul. Angie didn't know what she was missing, sleeping on the living room couch.

* * *

I woke up a bit early. The sun was still up, but it was happy hour. That was good. I used my private shower, put on my black suit, but left the tie undone. My usual weapons were hidden under a long coat. I heard Leona and Angie in the kitchen, and smelled bacon, eggs, potatoes and steak.

The Old Man must have put food in my fringe again.

I went to the kitchen. Leona had half a plate of food in front of her. Izumi sat across from her, while Angie cooked on the center-island stove.

Grab a chair." Leona had a piece of steak hanging out of mouth. "That bitch can cook"

I put on the Brazilian coffee and took a seat.

"You really like strong coffee, don't you" Izumi said.

"Oh God, is that stuff nuclear grade?" Angie asked, "The smell alone is giving me a rush."

"Just what I need to jumpstart my day," I said.

We all sat at the table and dug in, except for Izumi who just had tea. I put some Irish cream in my coffee. Just for taste.

My phone played *Tears of the Dragon.* I touched the screen to pick up. "I've received word on a girl matching Sarah's picture. I'm texting you the address. Now go find the two you should have been looking for all this time, you drunken, horny bastard." Old Man hung up.

I wasn't sure, but he seemed a little pissed at me. Fortunately, it didn't spoil the taste of my food.

TWELVE

"There are worse things than death, but nothing quite so fun."

—Caine Deathwalker

The address was Mission Catholic Church, currently providing a food service for the homeless. The church felt weird, like the energy here was uncommitted, neither black or white. Just … pure energy, waiting on tap. *Interesting.*

I'd parked in the church's parking lot on the side. The stairs going up the outside of the building led to the second floor, and were very well crafted. The place was mostly handmade before machines were used in construction. The stone blocks had seen a lot of time go by.

Angie and I walked to the front, noticing the six bells were clearly handmade. They'd been hanging there longer then I'd been alive. The double wooden doors were hand carved. I may hate all religions, but I had to hand it to the Catholics; they know how to make beautiful places.

I sent Angie in by herself and waited at the doorway. I could see the priest at the end of the line giving a wafer to homeless people too embarrassed to come to regular services to get their fix of God. Lay people made up most of those helping. The homeless hanging out were of all ages and ethnic groups. Standing there, I took sips from my flask; nothing like rum to help you endure being where you don't want to be.

A little girl in pink leggings with a black, frilly layered skirt and pink tee walked up and looked me over. Her short hair was black as my own. I stared into her innocent eyes, and did not shield her from the darkness inside me.

She smiled.

I let the door close between us and went back around the corner to the stairs. Most likely, Angie would ask around and make me wait, and wait… I sat down.

The little girl appeared, having followed me. Her clothes were worn and faded with age, obvious hand me downs from somebody. Her hair needed to be washed along with her face, and she was downright starved looking. Still, she smiled, offering me a wafer.

I took it and absently thumbed its edge. It would be pretty hard to kill someone with this. Probably wouldn't even fly straight. I liked shurikens better.

She sat next to me.

I said, "Little girl, you should not be so trusting to people you don't know." I looked around to make sure no one was looking and smiled back. "Where are your parents?"

She nodded at the church, and stopped smiling. "Mom tries hard, but we're not like others."

Now that she spoke, I heard something special in her voice, the inflections of Old Tongue. She was ninth or tenth generation dragon. I been around Red Fang, my tattoo guy, long enough to know what dragon tongue sounds like.

I used the Old Tongue myself, "Is that so?"

She looked surprised that I knew what she was.

A lady hurried around the corner looking panicky till she saw the little girl. The woman ran up to us and went to grab the girl, but froze in fear as our eyes locked.

"You're her mother?" I asked.

The woman nodded yes, barely daring to breathe. Her glance slid to her daughter.

"She's not afraid of me," I said.

"I'm sorry, Sir, if you've been bothered," the lady said.

"Don't be. She has guts. That's a good thing. Tell me what you're doing here?" Using my *Dragon's Roar* tat, I put just a little power in my words, feeling a burn between my shoulder blades as if a hot poker were pressing in.

"We just came to get some food, Sir."

"No, why are you *on the street* when your daughter has dragon blood in her?"

"Her father's dead. He owed a lot of money to the wrong people. I have no family, and didn't know his." She used simple words, making sure I got the point without taking to long. This woman had been around people with power and had paid for it. That was clear. She smelled human. I think she feared the dragons might take her child away if she went to them for help. Such things had happened.

I looked around to make sure no one was watching, and that Angie was still inside the church since I didn't want any whiteness for this. "Here." I pulling out all the money I had on me, a little over two thousand dollars, and I grabbed a card from an inner pocket of my long coat. "Go to this place. Ask to be taken to Red Fang. Tell him your story and make sure your daughter speaks to him, but first get both of you some new clothes."

Her teary eyes on the crisp bills I offered, the woman took my gift in trembling hands. The little girl stood up and took hold of her mother's ratty coat. The child leaned down and gave me a kiss on the cheek. Her eyes changed to those of a dragon; elongated black-diamonds pupils on oversized swamp-green irises, leaving no visible whites. A second lid slid out from under her outer eyelid, coving her eyes with a transparent film normally reserved for swimming under water. She gave me a fearless stare, embedding my face in her memory.

"Don't think I care for either of you," I said.

The mom drew away, smiling, pulling her child along. "Oh no, of course not, that would be absurd." She put the money away, and read the card, twice, pausing in her departure. "Would you happen to be a—"

"If you ever abandon the kid, or tell anyone about this, well—it won't be pretty."

The little girl's smile returned. "Come see us one day. You can wave from a across the street."

They left, turning a corner in many ways. G*ood deed of the day; did not kill someone who was not afraid of me. Future bad deed of the day; piss in the holy water. Have to keep the balance.*

I was idly tracing my left arm's tattoos with a finger when Angie came out. I stood up and walked over to her. "Any luck" I asked.

"She was here, I can still smell her scent, but with so many unwashed people it's hard to pinpoint her," Angie said.

A piercing scream sounded from the near distance. The shrillness and pitch indicated someone very young. *The little dragon-half girl…*

I shoved past Angie, running flat out, and whipped around the corner to the front of the building. The scream came again, from a knot of fifteen or so vagrants on the next corner of the church. Bouncing and rebounding, they appeared to be slam dancing without a mosh pit. Faces slack, emotionless—this looked the succubus at work once more.

The girl was alone, sitting on the ground, holding a skinned arm. I think she'd gotten a little too close to the action. Hearing my steps, she turned to me with an infinity of pain pooling in eyes that were human. The rest of her face had shifted, acquiring scales and a faint greenish tinge. Her lower face had lengthened. With her mouth open in horror, I saw multiple rows of sharp dragon teeth. Her voice broke with a sob as she turned back to face the stomping mob of meat puppets. She pointed. “Momma’s in there.”

A twist of molten agony shot through my head as I warmed the tat on my collarbone, invoking *Dragon Roar*. “Stop!”

The word rolled like thunder, hammering at the crowd, but lost force way too quickly as the crowd ignored the command, really pissing me off. The succubus was strong. I’d have gone to Dragon Flame next but I sensed a dulling in the air; something was draining magic, feeding on it. This wasn’t a normal succubus trick.

“No choice then.”

I drew my PPKs and started snapping off head shots down the middle of the crowd. I took time to also shoot right and left as I went in. I didn’t want my line of retreat compromised. I emptied my clips and replaced them, shoving a last couple derelicts out of my way. They fell like puppets with cut strings, no longer needed, their work done. I holstered my weapon, looking down at what was left of the girl’s mother. Broken splinters of bone protruded from skin. Her face was swollen, mangled. Her hair was matted from where her blood had pooled on the ground.

She’d been stomped to death.

Careful of my expensive shoes, I didn’t get too close.

The little girl streaked past me and threw herself on the body. “Momma, momma, wake up!” I think she knew death when she saw it, but hope dies hard in the young. The girl fell silent except for the sound of sobbing.

This attack made no sense. The mother was human, no body important. A warning to me? Maybe. The succubus could have somehow seen me with them earlier and assumed they were important to me. I had given them two thousand dollars.

What they say is true. No good deed ever goes unpunished.

Angie appeared.

“What took you so long?” I asked.

“I was searching the area, trying to find the one controlling the men.”

“Any luck?”

“No. Some kind of stupid magic was killing scents again.”

The sun was setting. Darkness was creeping in incrementally. The few people in the area, not inside the church getting a free dinner, made a point of looking away and scurrying off. Dead bodies will do that.

"There's two thousand dollars of mine on the body. Grab it, get the girl, and let's go." Another thought occurred to me. "There's a blanket in the truck that will keep the blood on her from staining my upholstery."

The girl moved like someone in a dream as Angie shepherded her along.

An old bag lady came out of the church and stumbled past me.

One of my protective tats warmed on its own. I felt my heart clench in pain to pay the cost. The sensation staggered me a second while my body tensed, getting ready to take a punch. I stepped left, dodging the old lady's knife trust at my heart, and grabbed her arm. I was about to break it, and stab her with her own knife, but Angie shoved the old lady out of reach, letting her keep her weapon.

The bag lady dropped her glamour, showing me a teenage girl that looked oddly familiar. If only I paid more attention to women's faces… The plain, steel blade in her hand changed to a rippled dagger—a stylized sunbeam—with a dark purple-green liquid dripping off the edge. The liquid smelled bitter. Sarah shot around Angie and tried to stab me again. Angie could have stopped her but was busy wringing her hands.

I stepped to the right, and lifted Sarah off her feet with a knee to the gut, letting her drop like a brick. I danced away, glaring at Angie. "Last chance, get the little bitch under control, or I will."

Sarah scrambled up to attack me again.

Angie pleaded, "Sarah, please, let's talk about this, huh?"

I saw a gold necklace around Sarah's throat. It was ancient, reeking of dark magic. I'd seen something like I recently. The woman in the red hat back at the hotel, the one I'd thought might be the succubus. It was her! The small red jewels in the center of her necklace spun against each other like gears. The evolving design changed the texture of her magic, its very scent. *Demon magic? Fey?* I wasn't sure. I needed to take a closer look.

She lunged at me, one slash, two…

I gestured with an extended palm. My whole body shuddered, lightning felt like it was roasting my liver as the necklace tattoo along the top of my collarbone came to life. This was the *Dragon's Roar*; I was done playing.

Angie stepped between us, offering me a growl, like I was the one needing to behave. I shouldn't have been surprised. Sarah was William's blood. William ruled the pack. Angie was pack. She had no choice, but to side with Sarah.

Unfortunately for Angie, I'd already paid for my magic and couldn't call it off. A series of concussive waves materialized in the air and engulfed Angie. She was picked up off her feet and slammed backward by a boom of thunder.

I winced, pretending sympathy.

Both girls went down in a tangled sprawl, landing at the dragon girl's feet. She stared down at them, expressionless, numb, waiting for someone to tell her to do something.

Angie had taken the brunt in human form, not as a werewolf, but was still tough enough to survive. Sarah struggled to her feet, half dazed. I was glad. I needed her alive.

Her necklace clicked into a new combination, changing into a ziggurat shape. A shimmer of light danced around her, and the damage she'd taken sloughed off. She looked fresh enough for a beauty pageant, and still determined to kill me.

I waited until the last second to dodge a knife trust and ran afoul of Angie who scrambled low to the ground, wrapping her arms around my leg, locking on with her blunt human teeth. In the split-second of distraction, Sarah cut across the tats on my forearm. All my limbs felt leaden. My balance went off keel, as my vision blurred. Angie let me go, staring up at me, her face a pale blob.

What ... the hell ... is going on? My protective spell... didn't ... do a thing.

"She cut you," Angie said.

"Tell me about it." I dropped to one knee, feeling blood warming my skin. I tried to focus on Sarah, but her necklace continued changing, clawing at my mystic senses. My arm hurt, sending tremors of agony up my arm, to my chest and eyes. They burned.

I blinked.

Sarah was gone. That damn teleporting spell of hers.

Angie climbed to her feet. "Where did she go?"

I gritted my teeth, and got up despite the feeling that my joints were melting like candle wax. I strained for any sign of Sarah's curious dark magic. Nothing. The necklace blocked me. Still, if I got out into the street fast enough to spot her... No good. I couldn't stay on my feet. I sagged back to my knees.

Looking at my forearm, I tried to activate a healing tat. Whatever had been on Sarah's blade was in my wound, breaking my focus, sapping my force of will. My tats stayed dormant. The poison wasn't letting me heal.

Angie's voice sounded distant, as if shouted down a long tunnel. Her tone was fuzzy with urgency. "Caine, Caine? Can hear me?"

I don't remember moving, but sky suddenly stretched over me. I lay on my back with Angie kneeling next to me. The girl came over as well. The same shocked, expression haunted her face as when she clung to her mom. Her voice came out in a whisper. "Don't you leave me too."

My arm felt like it a piece of meat on a spit. Beads of sweet trickled down my face. My chest ached as if I'd spent a lifetime screaming.

Angie said, "Caine, your arm looks bluish-black. It's swelling and starting to smell like spoiled meat. You need a hospital."

"No, take me home," I said.

"But Caine—"

Darkness was swamping my mind. I was loosing consciousness. I knew I only had time for a single threat. I made it a good one. "Fail me in this, and Lauphram will destroy your entire pack."

I opened my eyes. Angie had put me in the passenger seat of my car. She was trying to start my car and failing. This had her yelling at my baby. I reached out and hit the voice input. "Voice command," I said. "Override sensors, engine start, GPS function, home."

The engine started. The inside of the windshield displayed a GPS map showing the way home. The image blurred. My eyes were getting worse. I felt ice and fire as my magic level fluctuated wildly.

Angie sent my vehicle surging out into the street. "I love this car!"

The street lights we're overly bright, making it hard to keep my eyes open. I swam in and out of consciousness. I roused at one point to her the little girl muttering a sort of mantra, "Don't die, don't die, don't…" Reaching around the seat, her small hand tightly gripped my coat. Dragon girl seemed to think I'd live as long as her hand was there. I didn't move it off my expensive coat in case she was right.

My phone rang, sharpening my focus at one point. I tried to pull it out, but my arms were useless. Angie reached over and pried my phone from my pants, tearing the pocket in her haste.

She said something, but I couldn't hear what. I watched her anxious face, as I passed out. Again.

When I reawakened, my eyes wouldn't open. I felt my magic, like the coils of a python winding around me. My skin felt flayed where my tats had been inked.

I heard Angie talking. The car was still moving so she must have been on the phone. "Caine got cut by Sarah. No, he's not healing.

His arm looks terrible. One of his tattoos is cut in half, but it's not deep. The wound smells like poison. GPS says ten minutes. Okay…" Angie sounded scared. It must have been her Alpha or Old Man on the phone. I really hoped it was not Old Man. He'd be pissed at me for really screwing things up.

We stopped and I was pulled out of the seat. Her face intense and grave, the little girl climbed out of the back, and watched Angie swing me toward the house. Being a werewolf, she was strong enough not to break a sweat carrying me down the walk and up onto the porch. She kicked in the door.

A jar went through me, kicking up the ache in my skull by several magnitudes. That woke me up even more. “Hey,” I said, “what did my house do to you?” No one came running to see what had happened, so I guessed Leona out was with Old Man. I didn’t have time to wait for them. “To my bedroom.”

“You just don’t give up, do you?” Angie said.

She carried me there and was about to put me on the bed.

“Wait, take me to the mirror,” I said.

“Trust me; you don’t want to see how you look”

“Just do it”

“Last request?” She said, “Sure.”

She was right; I didn’t like seeing myself. My arm was oozing pus, swollen with poison. My magic shimmered red and violet, sizzling over my skin, coming out of every part of me. One of my eyes was that of a dragon, my nails were black and long. This was bad; the dragon magic of the tats was straight out-of-control. I’d never felt this happen before. What the hell was that poison?

Never mind. Focus.

I put my hand on the mirror’s frame, having her move me left and right. The mirror gate opened. “Just step in,” I said.

“Yeah, I don’t think so. That smells like demon,” Angie said.

“I got cut because you got in the way.” I looked at Angie and pointed at the mirror.

She growled. “Fine.”

The code I inputted wasn’t to another mirror, but to a point in space I frequently visited. Angie and I came out in front of Red Fang’s Tattoo Shop in the demon *Underground.* The little girl came along, having a death grip on the tail of my coat. The gray stone storefronts had neon signs over the doors. The red, green, and violet-black lights made sigils of the shop names in twenty languages that were far older that anything human.

I used the last of my strength pointing. “That door … there!”

THIRTEEN

"Hey, Red Fang, look what the wolf dragged in."

—Caine Deathwalker

We walked in. Red Fang looked at me with widening eyes that were clear topaz, lacking irises or pupils. He stopped cleaning his tattoo gun, and ran over, grabbing my arm, sniffing it. He pried my eyes wide open with his other hand. His face stretched into a mask of amazement. "How did you get *dispel* poison in you, and over a rune at that? Did you go retarded or something?"

Tall, thin, and full of magic, his long white hair aged him. His stony skin was hard as scales even in human form. The frequent use of dragon magic had turned his skin, front and back, a vibrant crimson and his sides blue-green. He could have probably spelled the weird pigmentation away, but I just think he was too lazy, or simply didn't care.

"Good to see your perverted self too," I whispered, my voice rough and frail.

"Lady Wolf, take him to the back room. I'll call Lauphram," Red Fang said. "He'll be pissed as Hell."

Angie hauled me away; pausing in the open door as the overpowering sweet-iron stench of old blood hit our senses.

The room was large and dragon runes scurried down the walls, writhed across the floor and clung to the ceiling. The stone altar in the center was where I usually bled, taking on tats. My blood stained every part of the slab; we were old friends.

"Put me there," I told Angie.

"What? That looks like a sacrificial altar."

I smiled. "It kind of is."

"Damn!" she said.

Angie carried me over and put me down. She looked back for Red Fang. We could hear him outside, yelling on the phone. I heard my name a few times, as well as "moron", "idiot", and the phrase "too stupid to live". The stone was cold and hard under me. Angie's hands withdrew. I missed them at once. Above me, my gaze traced the dragon runes, laboriously deciphering the grimoire until it dimmed out, and my thoughts sank into velvet darkness.

* * *

The gray cliff was high with a steep slope, loose shale, and few handholds. It had almost killed me getting up here. Old Man sat at the edge, feet dangling over the drop. Blood discolored his front teeth as he tore at fresh—raw—venison from a deer I'd killed. Hauling the butchered meat on my back hadn't made the climb any easier.

He said, "You've done well this time out."

I was ten and he'd left me in a forest for three months with only the most basic supplies so this was a compliment. I took a seat next to him

He handed me a well-gnawed bone. I was surprised he hadn't cracked it and sucked out the marrow.

"I've decided to let you get inked...," he said.

My first rune tattoo, a proud moment. Red Fang had been ready for years, I'd just needed to get Old Man's nod.

He stood; feet planted midair, and brushed himself off, as if he'd climbed up here instead of using demon magic. Abruptly, he pointed to something down below.

My heart glowing with anticipation, I leaned out to look.

He jerked me off the edge. Gravity did the rest. I skidded down, heels digging into the surface, rocks gouging my ass and legs.

"...If you live," he added.

Darkness washed in, smothering the scene, swallowing me for a time, then another dream formed...

Gray hovered next to me. The half angel looked like he needed a shave. His blind white eyes had a bit of a glow to them. He wore jeans, a polo shirt, and his usual Raider's jacket.

"What's going on?" I asked.

"Prophetic dream," he said.

"So I ought to pay attention."

"I would, if I weren't blind."

I looked down from the enveloping darkness, my words bounced around my head. Like being in a cave...

There were additional murmurs, sibilant, heated words expanding and echoing back from unseen walls. Dreaming, I floated in darkness, a disembodied spirit. Below me, a meeting
was in progress. A table stretched like a runway. The dark wood shone; glossy, catching highlights from two antiques Tiffany lamps, one at either end. There was no paperwork, no files, such as might be expected in a corporate boardroom. Water pitchers and a coffee mess waited on a trolley off to the side. I counted a dozen chairs, all occupied, mostly by men, but a few women were present as well. From this angle, I had an excellent view.

Ah, cleavage! Gotta love it.

The woman with the largest breasts made them jiggle by slapping the table with both palms. Her nails were bright red. "This is ridiculous! Obviously, I should go first."

A man in a midnight blue long coat, with spiky yellow hair, leaned forward against the table, staring straight across at her. "There's nothing obvious about it to me. This family has long retained my services for matters just like this. You wouldn't even be at this meeting if you weren't sleeping with—"

The gray haired man at the head of the table roared, "Enough! Such bickering has no beauty to it. All of us need to test the upstart so we will know if he is worthy of the blood he carries, and we will do it in an orderly fashion as always."

"Rock, paper, and succors?" the woman asked.

"No," the boss stabbed the table in front of him with a jeweled dagger. "We will gut a chicken and read the haruspicy."

The spiky-haired man stood, pushing his chair away from the table. "I'll go get the chicken."

* * *

My eyelids felt too heavy to lift. I heard the tattoo gun humming. It hurt worse than normal. My right arm felt like it was melting in magma. Someone screamed. The voice was familiar.

Oh, me.

I stopped and forced my eyes open a crack. Red-Fang held my arm, trying to fix the tattoo to stop the feedback loop of magic gone bad. The swelling and discoloration was gone. The poison had been drained from my arm. From the marks, I think he'd used leeches; talk about Old School. Of course the leeches hadn't gotten all the poison out of my system. The crushing weakness I felt testified to that.

Red-Fang's focus made my arm his entire universe. I don't think he realized I was even awake. The fresh ink he infused me with had a dark red hue. It changed into various colors as it hit my skin. He'd finished half the repair. Magic trickled into my veins and arteries.

Red-Fang paused and looked into my eyes. He forced my right eye to open wide, and then checked the pulse in my neck. I felt the warm slither of magical residue tingle across my face. He'd used a *helluva* lot of magic to *still* have that much lingering on his hand. He didn't say a word, just went back to work.

I heard the creak of a chair on my left. A wet cloth appeared to wipe away my sweat. As the cloth withdrew, I rolled my head to see who else was here.

It was Angie, looking half as sick as I felt. Her face was tight, pale, her eyes were werewolf yellow. Her red hair was a mess, and her shirt had my blood on it. A small table crowded her. Several folded washcloths lay there beside a basin of cool water. I saw an empty, murky purple bottle with a black and gold label. The label had the picture of a unicorn beetle on it, antlers raised in defiance.

That's when a vile taste finally registered in my mouth.

What the hell have they been pouring into me?

Angie put the wet cloth back in the basin. Her hand shook. Looking tired, she laced both hands together. "How long have you been here?" I asked.

She looked at me and then down at her own shirt, brushing at various stains. "A while."

I grunted at her non-answer. "Do I want to know what you guys made me drink?"

Red-Fang said, "A potion to counter the poison. It will take a while to do its job, but you won't die."

I rolled my face toward him, "Not ever?"

"Not from this latest disaster anyway," he said. "By the way, what's with the dragon child? You adopted?"

"No family," I said, "murdered. I was hoping you'd take her in."

He nodded. "What's another mouth to feed? I'll have my mate come down and pick her up."

"Thanks," I said.

Red Fang looked at me with an expression I couldn't decipher. "We dragons take care of our own."

I tried to stay awake, but was too weak. Slowly passing out, my mind reviewed what had happened. I'd never had a poison hit me like this. How could I have let a little girl cut me? How had she—and that freakish amulet of hers—pulled this off? I had the feeling that when we met again, she'd be dying to tell me.

* * *

I fell out of perfect darkness into shadowy gloom. Huge, yellow piles of gold caught my attention. Assorted pieces of armor and numerous swords cluttered the aisles between them. Among the gold, faceted jewels flashed—rubies, sapphires, and emeralds. Pearls, black and white, formed necklaces. There were even tiaras and crowns as if someone had raided a royal treasury

Precious. Shiny. Bright. I wanted it all

I looked toward the sources of light. Skeleton arms were embedded in smoke-blackened rock walls. The attached hands gripped the base of pitch torches. Where the rest of the bones were, I had no idea. The torches orange flames danced, wagging in a gentle breeze that suggested an opening to the cave system wasn't far off.

I looked down at myself, and through myself. I was translucent like a ghost with a blob of hazy golden light where my heart ought to be. I wore black-crystal armor worked to suggest a reptilian theme with scales and spikes. My armored boots had claw-tips at the toes. And I stood midair.

Yep, definitely a dream.

A guardian hunched near the piles, a great scaled beast, eyes bright, tail rippling. A real dragon. His long neck swung so he faced me. The same as Red Fang's, his eyes were topaz, pulling me into a crystal sea. Words like black smoke hissed through my mind. A greeting? A warning? I didn't know. At least the beast wasn't attacking. There was no hint of dragon magic searing the air.

I looked to see who else might be here, and spotted Old Man standing next to a young couple. My adopted father held a white cloth bundle in his arms. The bundle was small, pressed against his chest. A small fist rose up from the cloth. A baby explored the textures of his face.

The strange male had the biggest sword I'd ever seen strapped to his back. A yellow tanzanite adorned its pommel. His short, black hair had smudges of gray that didn't match his energetic, youthfulness. His craggy face caught shadows easily, wearing them like a mask. He wore strategically placed piecemeal armor—plain and matte black—over vital points; a true warrior's armor that had passed through many battlefields. The choice of pieces over a whole suit of armor told me his fighting was built around speed and skill, more than power. He was a hit-and-run fighter, not an impregnable fortress in his mentality.

The woman stood a few feet back from him. Her long, black hair had highlights of red and silver. She held her hands to her face, shielding it as she cried. Her liquid silver dress reflected the gold piles everywhere. Drawn by her sobs, the dragon waddled over and dropped his huge paw on top of her head, clumsily comforting her.

The man stepped closer to Old Man, reaching to the bundle that held the baby. The warrior brushed the baby's hair, his obsidian gauntlets glinting with white-gold runes on the cuffs, the same kind of runes I used.

He backed to the woman's side. They couldn't have been more mismatched. She was inches taller, thin, and delicate. He was short and extra-wide. Under the armor pieces, you could tell he was all rock-hard muscle, the type always ready for battle. But when he reached out to claim her hand, he was gentle.

He said, "We'll be back one day, Old Man. Keep him alive 'til then."

A silent specter to the meeting, indignation flooded me. Old Man had always told me my parents were drugged out hippies that had abandoned me on a Wiccan altar in some nameless forest. The bastard had lied!

* * *

I woke up on my back, under soft sheets. There seemed to be something particularly important I needed to remember from the depths of a dream, but as I tried to hang onto it, the dream faded, leaving a faint taste of rage in my mouth. *What the hell had I been doing in my sleep?*

The pillows under my back and head propped me up so I could see. I was back in my own room. The curtains were pulled back, the window open. Sunlight brightened things unpleasantly. Black and red décor was meant for night viewing. My guns and blades occupied a kitchen chair that had been placed in front of the window. The clothes I'd worn lay under them, washed, dried, and folded.

I pulled my aching arm from under the sheet and saw bandages. Well, at least I still had the arm.

I eased off the bed. Someone had put me in gray sweatpants. I hated sweatpants. I didn't even own any. I stripped them off and left them on the floor. Whoever wanted them could pick them up.

Leona and Izumi were talking outside my room in the hall. Normally, I'd have paused to listen in, but I felt too weak for casual loitering. With aching slowness, I made my way toward the master bathroom. The room was large with a four-person Jacuzzi. In addition to the usual amenities, a condom dispenser was attached near a gold-plated sink that matched the showerheads, and toilet handle.

I went to the frosted shower door and opened it. The inside space could also hold four people, if they were very friendly. I turned on the water, feeling the spray with my good hand. I balanced the temperatures until the stream reached the warmth of fresh spilt blood—just what I needed to feel better.

I left the shower door open so steam could warm the room, and went to face the mirror. My hair was spiky and tangled. The bags under my reddened eyes were dark. I hadn't looked this bad since my first hangover. The only color on my chalky skin was from my tattoos.

Carefully, my arm over the sink, I took off the bandage. Underneath, the tattoos looked great. There was a new, white scar four inches long—sensitive as hell—in which fresh ink had set. My tat had been restored, completing the once broken circuit. First time I ever needed this kind of a patch job; I was glad it came out good. Normally, my tattoos healed as slowly as anyone else's. Red-Fang must have felt sorry for me, throwing in a booster spell. I wondered if he'd bill me for that.

I returned to the shower, closing the frosted door behind me. The water burned my healed arm a little as I applied body wash everywhere, enjoying getting clean.

I heard soft, padded footsteps as someone walked into the bathroom. Touching the glass near the latch, my finger traced a small rune. My side of the door cleared, giving me a perfect view of Leona. The leopard didn't say anything, waiting, her bright yellow eyes fixed on what would still be a frosted glass door to her.

I finished up, killed the water, and stepped out.

I grabbed a towel off a shelf, dried, and dropped it in a hamper. By then, Izumi appeared in the doorway, her gaze molesting me in a good way. Ignoring the ladies, I pulled a drawer open under the sink and extracted the box that had my straight razor inside. The boar's hair shaving brush floated out. A can hissed and provided it with lather. Leona did such things for me when I was hurt. I used the brush to prep my face and I pulled out the razor.

"You sure you should be doing that?" Izumi said.

"I have to shave," I said.

"But your hand's shaking." She said.

I looked at her in the mirror as she came in and stood behind my shoulder. "Izumi, unless you're going to help, shut up and bail. I can use some privacy for what will probably be a dangerous little ritual."

They both went.

I threatened my hand with a soul-withering glare. It stopped shaking, and I got the job done. I put everything away and returned to my bedroom. The girls were sitting beside each other on the foot of my unmade bed. The sweatpants I'd left in the floor had been picked up, folded, and placed on my pillow like a gift from a cat. *Leona?*

Still naked, I walked to a chair by the window. I stood there looking out at crows hopping on my lawn; had to be an omen though I didn't know *of what*.

The small hairs at the base of my neck tingled. Shifting my hips, I checked over my shoulder. Leona was looking past me, out the window toward the crows, as if she knew they were there. Izumi was looking at my ass. Women are hornier then man, they just hide it better, most of the time.

"Take a picture it will last longer," I said.

"I already have, the camera is in my safe" Izumi said.

"What! When?" I asked.

"Who do you think changed you?" Izumi said.

"Leona, you let a demon near me when I was vulnerable?"

"Hard to turn down a grand for every picture, and can you put some pants on already. I've seen more of your junk lately then I have all year."

I put the laundered clothing back on and secured my weapons where they could easily be drawn. Weighed down with them, I felt human again.

So what now?

I needed to find out quite a few things. I was going to have to do some research, one of the many reasons why I hate jobs like this. Good thing my office was a bar. I was going to need a very large drink. The only kind of research I'm normally good at involves undressing nineteen year old supermodels and putting them to bed.

I grabbed a few books from my shelves and took them out into the hall. There was no sign of Old Man. I went slowly, not quite a new man, and felt tired again by the time I reached the office. Walking in, I saw Leona sitting on the bar. Izumi sat on a bar stool. They watched me with piercing stares as I settled in a well-padded recliner by an unlit fireplace.

I opened a book, holding it up in front of my face. "Hey, can someone get me a drink?"

Izumi's icy tones lowered the temperature in the room. "You're hurt, you look like hell, and you want to drink?"

"I deserve a drink precisely because I am hurt and look like hell," I said.

Leona jumped off the bar and headed for the door, her tail a stiff club swaying in her wake. She said, "We'll be back in a few. Izumi, let's get him his drink."

Izumi rolled her eyes, and followed Leona out.

I rolled my eyes as well. I hate it when people *watch over me* when I'm hurt. Hell, I'd be happy left alone, without an ice princess or spirit leopard to help lick my wounds.

On the coffee table was a new stack of books. Old Man had been here, doing research of his own. Curious, I looked at what he'd gathered. They contained folklore on succubae. Bookmarkers were set in numerous locations. I put aside my books on ancient talismans and thumbed through what he'd left for me to find.

There were three bookmarks on one page in the middle book. *Ah-hah! A clue.* The marked passage highlighted a very special succubae clan. They didn't give birth to children, but recruited from humans, turning them through some kind of dark ritual involving a kiss beneath a dark moon—usually followed up with an orgy. He'd hoped for details, and pictures, but there weren't any.

There was plenty else on the demons, one of the oldest succubae clans around. Few in number, they'd been around a long time, steeping themselves in the oldest magic. Most other demons feared them. The succubae were known to enthrall large numbers of humans just being near them. The thing that got me was that they'd wait as long as it took to get a special human they liked. By turning a human female, they didn't run the risk of giving birth to a domineering incubus, or to a weak succubus. They made sure every generation was stronger—and female.

I set the books aside, sliding deep into thought. A ritual that turned a human female into a demon would take a lot of power, and a spell caster that knew the ritual. The succubus would require a place of power. It had been no coincidence that he'd found Sarah at the Mission. She was working with the succubus. I'd seen high-level spells in action before. There was little chance a spell-caster could control and focus that amount of power, and do the spell at the same time.

Unless...the amulet. It could run any spell—no matter how advanced—all by itself. That explained why a lone succubus needed Sarah's help to transform Haruka. The succubus was probably the source of the dispel poison that worked even on me. The deeper mystery was where Sarah had laid her mitts on a relic that was almost alive.

Could it contain trapped souls? They have a lot of power. I remembered back to the battle at the mission. The amulet hadn't seemed to possess life force, only magic. *That thing's going to give me a headache yet, I can tell. There's no way I can go after Haruka until I come up with a counter to what Sarah's using.*

Izumi came back with my drink, but without Leona. Instead, Angie strolled behind. They swept toward me, their faces betraying nothing. *Mental note; never play poker with these two. And here I'd thought Angie didn't have a poker face.*

Izumi offered me the glass. I smelled rum.

I took the glass that was frosty cold due to her hands. "That's more like it."

Izumi stepped back and faded magically in a swirl of snowflakes, her voice lagging a little behind, "Later, love."

Angie dropped into the other recliner, sitting cross legged in the chair. The bouncing of her large breasts told me she wasn't wearing a bra. That's what I like about lady werewolves; they seldom do. Something about cleavage diminished the rage I should have been feeling.

"What do you want?" I asked.

"Sorry I got in the way before."

"You didn't just happen to get in the way. You turned on me in a fight. I've killed people for less."

"I'm ... sorry."

"You should be. Fortunately, I know how you can make it up to me."

"How's that?"

"We could start with a lap dance. I'm sure other things will occur to me. Later, I'll even let you get on top."

"*Let* me? I'm a *wolf.* I take what I want." Angie looked to the open door, then back at me, her eyes burning amber. She bit her bottom lip in indecision, staying in the big yellow chair that dwarfed her. "I can't give you what you want. You're hurt and weak. I'd break you."

"You can try." I downed half the drink, feeling it burn down my throat. "I may be hurt and weakened, but part of me definitely isn't dead." I pointed at the pup tent in my trousers.

Through the cloth, she eyed the humongous size of my engorged package, and unconsciously licked her lips. "Well..."

The door creaked open a little wider as William walked in.

Come on! Can't a man get laid after a close call on his life?

William sniffed. As a wolf, his nose would easily pick up on the sexual tension in the room. He looked at Angie. "Give us a moment."

She nodded, unfolding her legs, sliding them to the floor while leaning forward. I had a wonderful if frustrating view down inside her shirt. Standing, she hurried off, closing the office door behind her.

William turned to me, staring down. I really didn't like that, or the look of blood in his eyes. Here was a wolf thinking of killing something.

FOURTEEN

"Vodka? No, just water. Ignore the empties in the trash."

—Caine Deathwalker

"Angie told me what happened at the Mission," William said.

"Yeah, your granddaughter's a hand full."

"She can be, but family is family." He paused, searching for the right words. "I need to know you're not going after her for what she did. I don't know why she did it, but I'm sure she had a good reason."

"I can't promise anything when she's liable to try and kill me again. And I'm pretty sure she's involved with a succubus I need to kill. I don't see how we're *not* going to clash."

"Then there not much left to talk about." William lunged.

Drawing a silver dagger, I sliced at him to force him back while rolling sideways, over an armrest. I hit the floor and a grunt of pain escaped me. Sparks danced before my eyes as the world tried to go gray. Dragging my feet under me, I braced for whatever he'd do next. *Damn so weak. I felt like a girl scout could knock me over with a cookie.*

The chair was snatched up and flung across the room, crashing into a barstool and the side of the bar.

Crap, Old Man will make me pay for that even though it's my own house.

I stood crouching, watching his face crinkle in fury, the bones melting, flowing into a more bestial shape. His nails lengthened into claws. He didn't completely change since it was daylight, but an extra twenty pounds of solid muscle ghosted onto him from nowhere, and his eyes *were* full wolf

I tossed my knife, hoping to bury it in his heart.

He blurred to the side, letting it safely pass through the spot he'd vacated, hitting the far door. *Damn!* He had full wolf speed. I didn't dare try a spell with my arm not quite healed. All my tats were interlinked, tapping my life force. Something could go deadly wrong if they weren't back in balance yet. It would be an irony I'd never live down if I killed myself trying to save my life.

I cross-drew my twin PPK's, trying to remember if either of them had a silver clip ready to go.

Kicked, the door exploded inward.

William paused, glowering over his shoulder at the intruder.

"It was unlocked," I yelled, "thanks for costing me money."

Angie ran into the room. Forgetting William was her Alpha, with power of life and death over her, she screamed at him, "What in hell do you think you're doing?"

He growled.

Realizing she was challenging him, she lowered her eyes meekly, stopping, dropping to her knees in submission.

William swung back to me, utter disdain in his eyes over my choice of weapons, until a swirl of black mist appeared between us, solidifying into a hundred and forty pounds of Spirit Leopard. Leona crouched, muscles bunched, white fangs bared, as she hissed in white-hot fury.

"Hiding behind a kitty cat?" William asked.

"Yeah," I said, "you know all about courage, attacking an invalid and all."

Angie was up off her knees, but still low to the floor, edging around William, giving him lots of room. Leona caught the movement, switching her baleful stare to the she wolf, sending a growl that way.

"Everyone, stand down," I said. "This is over."

Leona gave no sign she'd heard me, but William made a show of relaxing, shaking the tension from his body, offering me a wolf's friendly grin.

I didn't buy it. I kept my guns extended, covering William *and* Angie. She'd turned on me in a fight once before. I don't forget things like that.

William's hand, the one closest to Angie, twitched.

Reading the signal, she lunged, scooping up Leona, carrying her off to the side. Leona squalled, squirming, her claws slicing and dicing. I heard Angie cussing passionately as blood was drawn. At the same time, William leaped for me, into the rapid-fire thunder of my automatics. I guess one of the clips did have silver, cause he flinched aside, crashing to the ground, twitching like a junkie, claws gouging the floor,

Angie tried to break away from Leona, only to find that next to impossible. Leona had every claw hooked into Angie while straining to reach the wolf's throat. Angie's face had coarsened, shadowed with fuzz, turning bestial with a partial change. Her wolf yellow eyes were losing all trace of human control as I watched. Their struggle would soon be one only death could end.

"Leona," I called, "let her go."

She continued to ignore me. I couldn't really blame her. It had probably been a long time since she'd been able to pull out all the stops. Still, I didn't want two dead wolves on my hands.

William started writhing. I wondered, *How the hell isn't he dead yet?*

The windows crashed in, and more of William's pack arrived, I knew the answer. Pack magic. As Alpha, he had the power—the magic and the life force—of all his wolves to draw upon. His wounds spat out the crumpled silver slugs, closing up. Silver wounds normally are difficult for wolves to heal. This was the difference being an Alpha made.

William's eyes were open, centered on me, promising me an orgy of pain.

His wolves were coming on fast. I knew I couldn't outrun them. Fortunately, Old Man and I had contingency plans for just such events.

The chimney was right behind me. I crawled inside, and grabbed the lever built into the fireplace grate. A steel door dropped, sealing me. I didn't worry about Leona out there with all those wolves; she could fade out whenever things got too rough. I pushed the lever back in place. This activated the dumbwaiter I was in. The small platform I was on dropped smoothly. In moments, I'd be in the wine cellar.

Above me, the steel barrier dented, booming as William battered it with preternatural strength.

I grinned. "Good luck with that, buddy, it's charmed."

The battering continued.

The dumbwaiter reached the basement where a wall panel hinged out of my way. I crawled out, stepping down to the floor. I walked over to the desk in the armory section. I had emergency guns, ammo, and swords from all over from those I'd killed. I grabbed extra handguns, paying little attention to what type, and looked for silver ammo. I was glad I had the backup armory in here, but could have also used some armor.

Note to self: put some in here ... if you live.

One sword wasn't a trophy, the one Old Man and Red-Fang had

made for me. Displayed above its black lacquered sheath, the katana was all black, four and a half feet long instead of the usual three and a half. The round hand guard was a circling dragon wreathed in flames.

It begged to be used, wanting to spill blood in my name.

I lifted my hand, reaching toward the sword on the wall. "C'mon, baby, let's go killin'" The repaired rune on my right arm burned like acid, but the pain was welcome, a sign that magic was awakening to my call. I needed to be sure of that before going back upstairs to take on a whole pack of wolves.

The sword disappeared in a pale gray cloud of smoke, creating a soft *whump* of imploding air, and reappeared in my closing hand. *Excellent.*

Carrying the blade to the cooler, I took a bottle of wine out and opened it. Four hundred years old, just right for a possible last drink. I guzzled with abandon, corked the bottle, and put it back.

Now, to get back upstairs. Angie knew about the elevator. Activating the dumbwaiter had deactivated its controls, but it would be watched along with the chimney. That left only one way to go—the treasure vault. Despite what I'd led Angie to believe, the chamber couldn't be physically accessed from here. The only portal there was magical; the mirror in my room. I went to a jumble of old furniture, each piece an antique covered with a sheet. Throwing a sheet aside, I uncovered what looked to be second mirror. There was a third inside my vault, but not really. They were all the same mirror, occupying three different points due to a set of magical wrinkles in the time-space continuum. Stepping through any one could take you out of either of the others.

My fingers traced the runes carved into the frame. No pain came as the portal opened. The magic of enchanted objects is paid for by the one who fashions such things. The glass rippled like water as I stepped through the full-length mirror, entering my vault.

A living room set surrounded me, an office desk and laptop off to the side. At the far end were two Mayan-style pyramids, one made of silver, the other gold. Between them lay heaps of gold coins and precious jewels. Another pile contained ancient relic and enchanted artifacts. A large cooler held my rarest wines. Wafting overhead, several will-o-the–wisps hung like silver-blue stars, throwing soft light everywhere.

One of them came over, shifting to a yellowish green in agitation. It wined at me, "We want to go home. The iron here hurts us."

I shrugged. "You should have thought bout that before leaving the land of Faire to cause trouble in *my* territory. Killing people draws too much attention."

"They were old and sickly. They couldn't swim worth poop."

"They were senior citizens, someone's grandparents. Only I'm allowed to put them out of their misery."

"We won't do it again. We promise."

"I know you won't. I need the free power."

I was just about to turn around and use the mirror to go to my bedroom when I felt demonic energy coming in. I scanned the room. A blue-green haze shimmered in the air. Old Man stepped out of it, turning to face me.

"How did you get in here?" I demanded.

"I taught you everything you know, not everything I know."

"Yeah, well just don't take anything."

"As if. This is trash compared to my vault."

"Really?" I said, "Where did you say you kept your stuff?"

"Isn't it too soon to be going back on the job?" Old Man said.

"Like I got a choice. Have you seen what's going on upstairs?"

"No, I came straight to you."

I explained what had happened, until Old Man put a hand up for me to stop, and pulled out his phone. He dialed, waited, and said, "Achill, I have a problem with one of your Alphas. Yeah, I'm still in LA. His name? William Cooper. He and a large number of wolves have broken into my home. Yes, that is unfortunate. Well, I could tell him to stand down, but he might not. Then I'd be forced to…"

He listened quietly, nodding his head now and then, and said, "Sure, I'll let you handle it. We are friends after all. What? Oh, sure, I'll bring the wine and the old chess set. I look forward to another game. Goodbye, old friend."

What the hell…!

I knew each country had its *Fenrisulfr* or "Wolf of Hell" to rule over its Alphas, the original being the son of the Norse god Loki. On trips out of the country, I'd partied with Brazil's master wolf a few times, but I didn't know the Fenris for the United States. He kept a low profile, often talked about only in mythic terms and tones of awe.

And here Old Man had him on speed dial.

I looked him in the eye with my best don't-bull-shit-me stare. "When did *you* meet the US Fenris?" I asked.

"Civil War, back when Sherman was burning Atlanta. Those were the days. We did quite a lot of hell-raising back then. Achill's a good man, good wolf. We stayed in touch."

"We're going to talk about this later," I said.

I used the portal to transfer to my bedroom. Old Man followed along. We headed for the office. There was no sign of wolves overrunning the house. Things were strangely quiet. Guns in hand, I burst into the office. William's wolves wee squatting around him in postures of dejection. Several of them looked like they'd been mauled by a leopard. Leona was on the bar, licking blood off her paws.

Sitting on what remained of a broken loveseat, William sweated bullets, holding his phone to a fuzzy, pointy ear. He didn't even make eye contact, cringing at whatever Achill was saying. Angie was doing the same; with her wolf hearing she didn't need to be close to the phone.

Calmly, Old Man strolled past me. I fell in behind him, ready to back him up in case the trouble wasn't over. Oddly, I should have felt tired as hell, but the adrenaline rush seemed to agree with me.

William put his phone away, stood, and gathered his people, leaving by way of one of the broken windows. Angie shot a look of regret over her shoulder, and mouthed the words "I'm sorry."

I gave her my stone-cold stare until she was gone. Izumi had let these guys into my territory. The smoldering anger in me was for her more than anyone else. She might look *hella* great, naked, legs spread for me, but there were limits to this kind of stupidity.

I went back behind the bar and poured some white wine, for everyone. Old Man sipped his, absently, obviously distracted. Leona lapped at what I set before her.

As if reading my mind, Old Man said, "Bill Izumi for the damages."

"Suits me." I threw back my drink and headed for the same broken window the wolves had used, knowing it faced Izumi's house.

"Where are you going," Leona called.

"I gotta see a bitch about getting the hell outta town."

FIFTEEN

"One should never cut off one's penis to spite one's face. It hurts."

—Caine Deathwalker

Still convalescing, every step barely seemed to move me ahead. The weapons I carried gave comfort, but they also weighed me down. Or maybe I just didn't want to do this. Izumi had lived next door for years, a first class demon, both in and out of bed. The dragon magic in my tats could deal with her—if I could pay the price in pain. The bitch had destabilized my territory. She had to go.

Didn't she?

Unbidden, memories came: Izumi in my arms, in tangled sheets, lathered up in the shower, on her knees before me her warm mouth sheathing my—

I shook off the vision and growled at the scent of opium smoke in the air, laced with demon herbs. The smoke came from her house, an aromatic spell designed to waken my intensions. *Subtle.* It wasn't the attacks I'd see coming I had to worry about, but the ones I'd never see.

Mentally, I traced the pattern of one my tats and felt it burn to life, a sensation similar to a bullet kicking a hole in my head. I staggered, stumbled, but didn't go down. After a moment, my vision cleared and I could breathe again. With the defensive shield now around me, it would take a high level spell to do more than irritate me. Already, the narcotic smoke in the air transformed to purifying sage.

Point to me.

I reached her fence. Usually I stepped over. This time, I kicked it in. Boards cracked and flew like a bomb blast had gone off. My foot was hurting—it bitched me out.

Shut-up.

I limped up the walkway to her porch, climbed the stairs, and stopped in front of the door. Every mystic alarm she had was probably clamoring for attention. She'd be expecting me to kick the door in. I would have, but knew I needed to conserve all the strength I could, no matter how pissed I was.

I kept my voice low and gravelly, "Open up."

I counted heartbeats. One … two … three… The door swung open silently. No one was there to greet me. *How rude.*

I stepped inside and noticed that the house temperature had to be somewhere around twenty below. The air I breathed sandpapered my lungs. Exhaling, my breath hung as a cloud in my face. I went down the hall, into a deserted living room, and brushed a frosted bamboo tree in a small pot on a long narrow table behind a white leather couch. The main bamboo stem and the two that spiraled around it snapped off and fell to the table. The dead growth lay before a silver frame. Inside the frame was a picture of me at a party, pounding a piñata into submission. The blindfold I wore only covered one eye. It was easier that way.

Another picture showed me laving ice cream off her pale torso. We'd been out of waffle cones, but not ice wine, wine frozen by her touch to remove water and make the final product extra potent. Izumi had her uses, I had to give that to her.

"It's not going to work," I called out. "I don't get sentimental when I'm about to kick ass."

"Worth a try." Her voice drew my gaze to the bedroom door. She stood in the doorway, without a stitch of clothing, looking utterly relaxed. She pirouetted, giving me a 360° view. "Isn't there something else you'd rather do to my ass than kick it?" she asked, peering over a creamy shoulder at me.

Well, I knew she wasn't about to fight fair.

I let cold indifference glint in my eyes as I lied to her, "I've seen better. Pack your crap and get out of my territory. I'm putting word out that my protection over you is rescinded. By dawn tomorrow, you'll be gone or dead. And don't think the wolves will stand for you. Their Fenris has called them in for an accounting."

I turned to go.

"Caine…"

I stopped. "What?"

"We've been friends a long time. Doesn't that count for

something?"

I laughed, a wounded sound, thin and sharp as a katana. "Sure, I haven't killed you myself, have I?"

The blizzard hit then, a wall of snow coming out of some nameless frozen hell. Slashing winds wound around me like barbwire. The temperature dropped another twenty degrees. My blood felt like *it* was turning to ice wine in my veins and arteries. My defensive shield buckled under the onslaught, but stronger, automatic wards activated.

She vanished in the white-out, merging with her storm, as snow flurries whirled and drifts formed on the carpet and furniture.

Heat built at my core. Electric current crackled in my blood, the price I paid for the *Dragon Aura* spell that warmed my muscles, keeping organs functioning, and my flesh fever-hot to the touch. The magic would last for six hundred and sixty-six seconds, but required six days, six hours, and six minutes to be renewed.

The snow touching me evaporated, refreezing once the vapor reached Izumi's blizzard. Winds howled, hiding the sound of her movements.

I was sure she'd hit me from some unexpected direction. I kept my face down, which changed my range of vision, letting me see further behind me. Not that I was focusing. That's the common mistake that half-assed martial artists make. To focus is to limit your perception. To anticipate is to limit your responses. By being ready to respond in all directions to everything, I wasn't going to be blindsided.

Except for the killer snow men that formed from the snow all around me, leaping in with icicle teeth bared in old, savage aggression. They had indentions for eyes—not even lumps of coal, poor bastards—and they actually thought they had a chance.

A spinning heel kick took their heads off, splattering them against a distant wall I could no longer see. Somewhere in the storm, I heard a lamp crash over and a picture fall. Headless, they still grappled with me, becoming slush as my furnace level metabolism melted them. As ineffective as this attack against me was, it had to be a simple diversion. Izumi had to be close to making her real attack.

I almost missed it when it started.

The wet slush around my feet became a block of ice, anchoring me in place. For her ice to stand up to my magic-fuelled heat, she had to be expending a huge amount of energy. Still, ice could be dealt with in an old-school manner. I drew my guns and fired around my feet, freeing myself...

...As she slid down a stalactite-sized icicle grown from the ceiling, landed on my shoulders. Her bare legs wrapped around my neck, but before I could act, she arched backwards, her dead weight flipping me along with her. Fortunately, my ankles were free; otherwise, this little maneuver of hers would have broken them. As it was, I sailed over her, out the front door, and rolled off the porch, onto the walk way.

Rising from the sidewalk, I noticed she'd followed me outside. Dressed in armor made of blue-white ice, she stalked toward me with twin swords made of ice. They had serrated edges, and were curved like sabers. Another of her threats, the blizzard following her out of the house like an eager puppy.

She flew from the porch, lifted by the screaming winds of her storm. They added to her power as she slashed.

I threw myself to the side, squeezing off two shots that fractured the ice over her heart, presuming she had one. With a snow demon, you couldn't always be sure.

Her sword blurred past, missing me by a mile.

But then I wasn't he target. My left gun was sheared in half, made super brittle by the focus of her magic. That still left the gun in my right hand. I spun to keep the muzzle centered on her. The sidewalk iced over as her feet touched down. She wheeled toward me, the swords continuously swirling around her upper torso. In another moment, she'd lunge back and I'd be a twig in a wood chipper.

Extended, locked onto her head, I pulled the trigger, ready to empty the full clip into her. The gun exploded in my hand, made too fragile to fire bullets by Izumi's winter stare. The icy air made the explosion sharp and clear, only muted by the screaming and cursing I was doing as my trigger finger separated from my hand and spun through the sir, trailing smoke. It fell in the grass as I bit off the flow of my own profanity, ripping my shirt to staunch the blood. My thumb was shredded but still attached.

If not for an impossibly high tolerance of pain, I might have passed out, or given in to shock. As it was, my thoughts were fuzzing up, running in circles. Get out your sword … get your finger a good surgeon can reattach it… Wait! What's Izumi doing?

One of her swords slashed low as she tried to separate me from my knees.

I leaped onto her sword, my weight taking it down, shattering it.

Her other blade came straight at my face, point first.

I ducked under it, ramming my head into her armor. The pain of impact cleared my head a little. She directed the sword I'd ducked into the air, bringing the spike on its pommel down into my left shoulder blade. On my knees, I grabbed her legs, driving my head between them, lifting her into the air, flipping her over my back.

She crashed down hard. Pieces of her ice armor broke off. As she slowly rolled over, orienting on me once more, I used the strip of cloth

I'd torn free to bandage my hand, tightening it with my good hand and teeth, all the while glaring at her. Like a wounded wolf, I was done with playing around.

But her blizzard hit me like an eighteen wheeler, slamming me across her lawn, though a section of fence, into a car parked at the curb. The whiteout of dancing snow blinded me. Sleet pelted me, rattling off the car behind me. I activated the tribal-style *Demon Wings* tattooed to the back of my shoulders and my upper back, above the shoulder blades. Paying for the magic felt like taking a spiked mace to the head, but at least it distracted me from my hand, what was left of it.

The blizzard lost focus. Its attacks faltered, spreading randomly over the area. I walked through the storm, back the way I'd come, until the air cleared. Izumi stared through me, at her pet blizzard. The cloaking magic I used didn't allow her to notice the footsteps I was leaving in the snowy ground. I walked right up to her—and punched her in the throat.

Her sword fell as she did. I stepped on the ice blade as she scrambled to pick it up. Coughing, choking, wheezing, she made the sweetest music as her larynx swelled, cutting off her air flow. On hands and knees, she shuddered with the knowledge that death was very close. I kicked her in the face, shattering the helmet she'd made from ice. She dropped back, sprawling on her back. I stomped her chest, right over her heart where the ice armor was crackled. The body armor fractured off her.

She flopped around, managing a sort of mewling sound.

Her pet blizzard came running, but its magic was thinning. The ice and snow dropped on the lawn and quivered like amputated limbs. The air cleared as Izumi lost consciousness, growing still.

I staggered over to her. My heat spell had left me. I was shivering. The demon wings spell was burning through the last of my strength. Izumi had put up a hell of a fight. For what? It had been a pointless battle. Was she so afraid of whatever had chased her here that she preferred having me kill her?

Now there was an interesting thought.

I sat on her stomach, my knees pinning her arms to the snow covered ground. Using my good hand, I pulled out my tanto, putting the point between her breasts, right over her heart. That's when I noticed Old Man standing beside me, watching with great interest. "Take a picture," I said. "It will last longer than this bitch is about to."

"I'd hurry," he said. "Her breathing is getting easier. The swelling in her throat is going down. She appears to be healing herself even in an unconscious state. I'll have to try that some time."

I looked at her pale, sleeping face. Tears had jeweled her eyelashes with chips of ice. Her mouth hung open, inviting.

The tip of the knife cut into her flesh as I shook my head, refusing to indulge in any of the memories we'd made together. I leaned forward, a second away from plunging the knife into her.

Her eyes fluttered open. "Do it," she begged. "Please."

I drew the knife back. "Like I'd do you any favors."

"Stay there," Old Man said. "I'll go get your missing finger. I just might know a zombie spell for restoring damaged flesh.

I put the edge of the knife against Izumi's throat. "There are worse things than dying, you know. You better hope he can fix my hand."

"Let me stay," she said. "Wasn't this the best fight you've ever had? And imagine what the makeup-sex will be like."

"I can get sex a lot of places. You'll have to do better than that."

"You need something to nullify the grimoire necklace Sarah is using. I know of a relic that can do that."

"All right. You've got my attention."

SIXTEEN

"Why does everyone want me to kill them?"

—Caine Deathwalker

Izumi and I popped out of the human world and fell through a heavy, green-tinged darkness. There was a brief moment of slamming pressure, like taking a corner in a too-fast sports car, as we broke into the fey world. A spectacular view awaited us. The setting sun—an icy ball of light—seeped through veils of cloud on the far horizon where forested mountains gnawed the sky. Overhead, the low-hanging clouds were thicker, darker, spitting snow down upon us.

The Ridge Road we stood on was pitted and rutted by passing horses and wagons. There were other tracks, reptilian, maybe some kind of giant, flightless bird. Along the winding road, some of the shrubbery still had green leaves showing through their ice glazes. Clinging to webbed branches, thin icicle's provided a festive look.

Looking down the steep embankment from the road, I spotted azure balls of light dancing in the air. The will-of-the-wisps played tag in small orchards, but avoiding well-lit farm houses painted riotous colors. From the distance, the buildings looked like miniature models, toys abandoned to Fate.

A chilling wind bore the scent of mistletoe and winter berries. The freshness of the breeze spoke of a place that had never known industrialization. This place was an environmentalist's wet-dream; a land with more life than back on earth. Here, if you hugged a tree, it just might hug you back, if it didn't drink your soul. Nature isn't as warm and fuzzy as some would have us believe.

We pushed on, traveling past a bed of lavender that should have been long dead. I saw stick-figure humans the size of my small finger, ice fairies floating about on hummingbird wings. They were tending the plants, brushing off the frost, strengthening the growths with their Faire light. The glow indicated that the creatures didn't do magic—they were magic.

Ahead of us, the road stretched up a bank to an ice bridge that spanned a frozen river. The road continued into a city labyrinth shadowed with soft blues. The icy spires, blocks, and domes were carved from glacier ice.

I grew aware of a new silence; it had been a while since I'd heard the clack of high heel boots. I turned to see Izumi standing motionless a dozen feet back. The look on her face was one of painful longing.

"Is this it, Izumi?"

My words snapped her out of brooding abstraction. She started toward me, scuffing along like a convict toward her execution. A very hot convict. She wore a glittery body sheath of midnight blue. Blue diamond earrings studded her earlobes. An ermine half-cloak was her only concession to the weather and its hood was thrown back to expose the artful pile of her hair. Black diamond chips glinted from the butterfly pins keeping her hair in place.

"Yeah," she said, "Winter Court, they run this corner of Underhill. Once we reach the bridge, they'll know we're here. I'll be all right, but I can't guarantee you'll even get across. The ice trolls are always hungry."

She'd brought us to this road just outside the fey city limits, dropping us into a domain off-limits to anything non fey. This pseudo-space counted as an entity itself, one that kept demons out. Always. Without her, I could have materialized in a web of illusion, never knowing I was anywhere close to anything fey. That she could bring me past all defenses contradicted what I knew of her.

I stopped her with a hand on her arm as she made to pass me on the road. "Izumi, you're not a demon, are you?"

She sighed softly. "No, I'm fey. My glamour disguises my magic's feel, and lets me pass for demon, or Japanese snow woman. I can even do Santa Claus."

"Please don't."

"Old Man knew."

Of course he did. And he couldn't bother telling me. He probably wanted me to discover her nature the hard way; on my own.

The dirt road acquired thicker coats of frost the closer we got to the bridge until we were treading ice. We paused, one step from the moon bridge. The posts lining the sides were square pillars extending into the frozen river below. The posts were capped by round spheres. Whatever wood they'd used was a mystery, covered by ice. Or perhaps the whole thing was ice.

I stared through the arch of the bridge, as if I could see what lurked in its shadow. "There really are ice trolls under there?" I asked.

"Two of them."

"You're going to help me with them, right?"

She looked at me. A slow smile appeared. "It will cost you."

"How much?"

"I need a promise."

"What kind?"

"You have to promise to kill anyone who I'm ever forced to marry—preferably before the honeymoon."

I grinned at her. "Sounds like fun."

She nodded and started up the bridge.

We reached the middle before the brutes climbed over the sides to block our way. The frost trolls were twelve feet from curl-toed boots to horned helmets. Their clothing was a patchwork of animal skins—fox, rabbit, wolf, and elk. PETA would be pissed. The trolls had ice-white beards and pale flesh. Leather straps held their kilts in place as well as assorted knives that would have counted as swords in the hands of small men. They'd made the climb over the railing one-handed, moving with speed and grace. Their free hands clutched the hafts of war-hammers, the heads flat on one side, spiked on the other.

They crowded each other while road-blocking the bridge, grunting in wild-eyed menace, grinning balefully. The one on the right had sapphire eyes, the one on the left, hazel.

Blue sniffed the air. "Demon stink."

Hazel said, "The stench of a *dead* demon, you mean."

Blue looked surprised. "He's not dead."

Hazel laughed; a hard bark of joy that boomed loud enough to crack ice. "He's dead, he just don't know it yet."

I stepped forward, demon sword fading into my hand.

Blue lunged to meet me, giving no advance warning of his attack. I approved. My sword flashed as I swayed out of his path. He came to a sudden stop, staring at the stick in his hand.

The head of the hammer lay on the ice bridge. I'd cut its handle in passing. Still moving, I closed with Hazel. His hammer fell toward the top of my head. I jumped into the air and caught hold of it, letting my weight add to the power of its fall. The hammer hit the bridge with a bone-jarring WHAM! The underlying bridge cracked.

I knelt and placed a palm to the cracked surface. I felt a dull, metaphysical knife gouge my spleen—the price I paid for activating one of my tats. A shockwave edged with infernal heat shattered the middle of the bridge. The trolls and I dropped to the frozen river, a hard white ribbon of ice. Pieces of broken bridge bounced around us, skidding every which way.

The trolls landed on their feet.

I landed on all fours, then stood, careful of my balance while I watched for the next attack.

Izumi looked over a stub of bridge, doing nothing else. Her glamour faded. Her eyes went western, no longer Asian, blazing like sun fire on ice. And her glossy black hair turned snowy white. If I wasn't in the middle of a fight, I would have stopped to admire the change.

I called up to her. "I thought you were going to help me with these guys,"

"I am," she said. "I'm absorbing their bitter cold so you don't shatter like a rotted twig. Why do you think your protective ward hasn't activated, draining your energy?"

Leaving the grunt work to me.

Blue stared up at Izumi. "I know you."

The other troll nodded. "The little girl with a human heart."

Izumi scowled at them. "Damn it, I'm fey to the core. You want a piece of me?"

Hazel laughed. "If I get to pick the piece... You've filled out nicely since running away, little snowflake."

Izumi raised a fist in the air. A javelin of ice formed in her hand. She thrust it down with a relaxed, smooth throw so it pierced Blue's collarbone and heart. He clutched the protruding ice shaft as his legs collapsed under him. *Thu-thudda.* The troll's knees indented the river ice without breaking through. He fell backwards onto bent legs with a *whump* and lay spread eagle on the ice. His blue eyes went flat and dull, fading to silver. His big chest lost air and no longer filled with breath. As if conquered by cold, layers of ice seeped out of his skin, making an ice sculpture of him.

"Shouldn't have pissed me off," Izumi said.

"Sonuffabitch!" Hazel looked at his fallen comrade. Tears welled in his eyes. The drops fell, turning into beads of ice that rattled and bounced on the ice. He tore his gaze away, facing Izumi.

Without regret or remorse, she stared down from above, now wearing armor made of ice over her clothes, a blue-ice sword in her hands. This reminded me that no matter how warm and soft I'd her heart, it had a frozen core, like all the winter fey.

Hazel set his hammer on the river, kneeling toward her. His head bent in submission, his huge fist pressed in a sort of salute over his heart. "Your pardon, Princess. May I have the honor of escorting you to your mother's throne?"

Princess? I glowered at Izumi. If she was fey royalty, than the Japanese snow demon persona had been her cover, down to the Japanese features of her face. I wondered what her true appearance was like without her magical glamour.

I muttered, "Keeping secrets much?"

She shrugged at my accusing stare, and nodded to the surviving troll. "I will await you on the other side of the bridge." Her sword tip bit into the broken edge of the bridge.

In moments, the shattered ice grew into its previous shape, letting her walk across.

I, of course, climbed up the bank the hard way, refusing to let the troll *help* by tossing me up like a bag of ice. We rejoined Izumi, escorting her past buildings carved from ice, with thinner sheets of it serving as windows, letting light through. To those inside, we were probably smeary shadows.

We hit a market area where heavy pillars supported an overhanging roof. Dividers of ice separated displays. Tables were littered with clothes, arts and crafts, preserves, metal work, ceramics, wood carvings, and local produce—probably magic-assisted—grown out of season. There were some fur cloaks, boots, and jeweled daggers that I wouldn't have minded getting a closer look at, but I was expecting the local guards to intercept us soon and channel us to the local palace.

It was a little odd seeing all this going on so late in the day, but this was Faire after all. The fey always marched to a different drum. It's what made them so unpredictable. *So dangerous.*

"The merchants privileged to supply the Court," Izumi said, "Have private shops that are quite better than this. I wouldn't be surprised if a lot of this was glamoured to look more appealing and hide defects."

"Something to keep in mind," I said.

I drew a lot of attention but Izumi even more so. Fey of all kinds stepped out of the way, heads bowing after an initial flash of startlement. The smell in the air wasn't fear. Many of the fey smiled, happy to see her.

"You're important to them," I said.

Izumi's face tightened, flushing a delicate pale rose. Her eyes shied from the crowd.

"Feeling shame?" I said.

"It's that easy to read my emotion?" she said.

"I know you," I said.

She looked at me and smiled. "Yes, you do. But you've barely touched my secrets. You might want to remember that."

Like a misplaced Buddhist monk—a bald, fey in bright orange robes with a gold jacket—manned a table piled with fruit. He used a hand-cranked device to churn out crushed ice that went into cups hollowed out of fist-sized hunks of ice. There were also pitchers with various flavors of fruit juice. The guy was selling the local equivalent of smoothies. The man called out to us, "Strangers, come and refresh yourself. First drink is on the house."

I thought of how drug dealers work. "Of course the first taste is free. It will probably be magically irresistible. I'll wind up emptying my wallet and selling myself into servitude to end the cravings. Thanks…"

Izumi shot me a warning glance.

The vendor's eyes flared with triumph. I knew why. You weren't supposed to say thank you to them, ever. It implied that you were indebted to them, giving them power over you.

I finished my sentence "…that's what I might have said if you were actually doing me a favor."

The merchant widened his eyes in mock outrage, turning blustery, "Why I never…! Of all the lunatic accusations…! I am offended, I tell you, offended and insulted … and…!"

I nodded wisely. "And speaking in sentence fragments. You haven't denied what I said."

He scowled, crossed his arms over his chest, and turned his back, waiting for us to go away so he could try his line on the next passerby.

But the area was suddenly full of soldiers in ice-blue uniforms. They bristled with swords, pikes, and axes as they surrounded us. Their Captain ignored us for the moment,

Stalking up to the merchant who'd turned to take in the disturbance. The Captain of the guard snatched the man by the hair and forced his own beverages down his throat. The merchant sputtered and gagged, spilling much of the fruity slush down his front. A second cup and a third followed.

As the captain of the guard approached Izumi and me, the merchant continued swilling his drinks, victim of his own magic.

I had to smile.

SEVENTEEN

"Is it my fault if they just left it lying around, under heavy guard?"

—Caine Deathwalker

The guards stood in a relaxed manner, haughty, proud…

Confident? They had reason to be, all of them skilled warriors who smelled strongly of fey magic, a scent not unlike lightning above a pine forest. Stimulating. Their Captain occupied an entirely new level. His feral magic was rich and potent as a moonlit jungle. His eyes were pale gray coins with vertical pupils that suggested he might be a shape-shifter. There was a spring in his step, a liquid flow to his muscles, no wasted motion.

Dangerous.

His gaze flicked my way, absorbed me, and passing on to Izumi. His fist went over his heart as he gave her a shallow bow. This indicated he was high in the aristocracy. His words emerged glacier cold, "Nieve, it is good to see you again." Something in his voice convinced me not to believe him. In addition to the tone, he'd not used any honorifics. If he wanted to see her, it wasn't for a good reason. And what was this *Nieve* stuff, a nick name?

She nodded once. "Frall, my mother's faithful hound. Are you still doing her killing for her?"

Hmmm. Izumi's tipping me off that he's as much assassin as soldier. Good to know.

I moved closer to *Nieve* and offered the captain a dead black stare. This was the look I usually wore just before blowing someone's brains out.

He stared back like I was dung clinging to the heel of his boot. "And what are *you*."

I smiled, my voice a loud whisper, "Your death, if you push me. Do your job and lead us to Winter Court."

"Sure." He matched my smile. "I look forward to seeing your arrogance crumble before our queen." He turned to the ice troll, his voice sharp with command, "Don't you have a bridge to hide under?"

The troll grinned in a friendly fashion—the way a shark might before taking a bite—and turning, lumbered off, as the guards quickly cleared out of his path.

"This way." The captain stomped off. His men pressed in, urging us to follow. We did.

Soon, the city lay behind us and we were climbing up a hill past terraces where ice sculptures glinted in ranks like giant chess pieces. White wolves were pawns. Wishful thinking I decided. There were knights, warriors on horses, swords lifted in challenge. The rooks weren't castles, but black ice crows, fanning wings, eyes rubies. Bishops were druids in dark cloaks with roughhewn staffs in bony hands, but there was something vaguely reptilian about the faces.

Other terraces contained menageries of animals, many twisted and strange. A sly-eyed pooka, a river-dwelling pony, stood next to a proud unicorn. A griffin and hippogriff faced each other in poses of combat. A python with six legs—carved from soft-green ice—reared up to snatch fruit from an apple tree. The carved detail surpassed anything I'd ever seen, making me wonder if these thing had once been real, before falling afoul of Winter Court magic.

The road we were on passed a high ice-brick wall. The gate itself was a frozen mass of thorns and white roses, all encased in ice so its beauty might last forever. Beyond, I saw a sprawling castle with spear-point turrets rising like diamond shafts against the charcoal clouds. The towers were lit green and blue by will-o-the-wisp swarming the structure. Like a painting, so perfect I didn't want to look away.

We pushed on toward the castle's main entrance. Two ice doors, each fifty feet tall and twenty feet wide, turned on central pivots, balanced on the threshold. Additional guards waited, coming to attention, snapping swords in salute to *Nieve*. Their ice-blue armor shimmered as their protective magic reacted to my aura.

The palace doors rotated open with a soft grating sound. We went in, onto an ice floor chiseled to resemble fancy tiles. They bore a pattern of berries and holly. More of the Will-o-the–wisps danced inside, fracturing their light against seven-tier chandeliers. On the lower walls, silver rimmed mirrors threw our images back at us. Blue-velvet cushions on thin limbed benches and chairs allowed unimportant guests to cool their heels until someone in power wanted to see them. Ivory tables were graced with weapon racks where jeweled knives and swords rested, as well as occasional spears and morning-stars. All were made of silver or bronze. No iron allowed. That was understandable; iron had a tendency to disrupt fey magic.

"You will need to leave your weapons here," Frall said.

"Not in your lifetime," I muttered.

The surrounding guards edged closer, threatening without brandishing their weapons.

The runes tattooed on my neck burned like I was being branded as I let some of my magic seep out. The fey respect power, but not much else; I'd have problems if they were to see me as prey. What they hold in contempt, they slowly torture and kill. As it was, every guard looked ready to pounce, taking by force what I wouldn't give.

"Try it and I'll eat you alive." I used my *Dragons Voice* spell so my words echoed in their heads, their hearts, and throughout the great hall, shaking the chandeliers so that ice crystals fell and shattered on the tiles.

The guards jerked back.

Frall didn't move, but his eyes were fixed on me, intent and measuring.

Izumi yawned, doing her best to simulate boredom. "Caine, this way."

I broke off the *Dragon's Voice* and followed her across the hall, ice crunching underfoot. As we got further from the outside walls, the translucent blues became deeper, darker.

Before we got more than halfway across the hall, Izumi stopped, crouching like a beast scenting danger, deciding whether to fight or run. I felt the air around us deepen with cold. My breath emerged as a white banner. Her breath stayed clear as if she was the same temperature inside as out. Her lips were parted, her eyes wide with fear. This made her even more beautiful to me.

Ahead of us, a broad staircase stretched up to the next floor. The steps were extra high and thirty feet wide, made for the boots of heroes, not common men. The scale of everything was meant to intimidate. Not that I let it.

Feet thumped loudly on the staircase as massive creatures came into view. Frost Giants, three of them. I'd thought the ice trolls, a related species, were big. These guys made trolls look sickly and anemic. Though only a couple feet taller, they were easily twice as wide, with three times the muscle mass. The giants wore animal pelts held in place by wide leather strips winding around arms, legs, and waists.

Hammered bronze wristlets and necklaces adorned them. They wore horned helmets and sported outrageous beards encrusted with ice.

Two had ice-white eyes—staring eagerly at Izumi. The one in the middle glowered at me for being near her. He had yellow-red eyes, as if they'd been set on fire and the flames suspended in time. I think I'd heard that the frost giant's royal family had eyes like that.

I looked at Izumi. "Why are there frost giants in Winter Court?"

She ignored my question, saying, "Caine, please don't do anything stupid, I beg of you."

I tried on a look of injured innocence, one eyebrow cocked. "I don't mess with things like that without collecting a lot of money up-front. You want to give me some context here? They've been at war with the Winter Court for generations. What the hell's goin' on?"

The giants reached the ground floor and stomped our way. They got bigger the closer they got. I'd thought their skin was white, but close up, detected a faint blue tinting.

A five-foot vortex of snow flurries condensed in front of Izumi. The frost giants lurched to a sudden stop, attentive and careful. That worried me. A barely legal girl jumped out of the whirling snow which collapsed. A foot shorter than Izumi, the girl's lavender-blue hair and cobalt eyes shone with the light of industrial strength magic. I wondered how much of what I was seeing was real and how much of her was glamour. You couldn't take the fey at face value—ever.

The new-comer radiated excitement, peering into Izumi's face. "Sweetie, I'm so glad you're back. I've been so worried."

Tears glistened in Izumi's eyes as she melted into the girl's embrace. Pulling back, she kept hold of Izumi's hands. They smiled at each other.

Side doors in the hall exploded open and fresh guards rushed to converge on us. These were hard fey, scarred, mauled by past conflicts, with death in their eyes. Their weapon harnesses were worn and oiled, not the type put on to impress visiting dignitaries. I warmed with the joyous desire to kill them all. Such a challenge! My hands stayed pressed to my thighs, ready to draw the automatic pistols holstered in that part of my gun harness.

The girl turned the full force of those icy, electric eyes on me, deadening my muscles like a killing frost. "And what have you here?" She smiled; it wasn't fake. That was really bad. Having the attention of a fey with this much random power wasn't good.

I looked into her eyes and smiled. "I am Caine Deathwalker." I forced my body to move, making it look easy. I seized the girl's hand, kissing it. "And who would you be?"

Before I could even make an obscene suggestion involving a feather bed and a trapeze, I had four blades at my neck, coming from behind and both sides. I kept looking into the girl's eyes. Projecting enough confidence for a legion of demons, I waited for an answer.

She said, "I am Kellyn, the Heart of Winter, ruler of the Northern Court, Queen of the Ice Fey."

"My mom," Izumi added.

The queen waved the guards back.

The blades at my neck withdrew as the guards retreated.

Kellyn stepped closer to me. Her hand settled against my chest. She studied me. I'd had powerful fey do this before; they had a hard time getting a *feel* for what I was.

Kellyn didn't look away, but spoke to Izumi, "Is this yours, my daughter?"

The hand on my chest became warmer. She pulled it away and stared into her palm.

Before Izumi answered, the middle frost giant's voice thundered in the hall. "Enough of this. I demand my prize now, fey queen."

Kellyn turned to face him.

Izumi looked angry as all hell.

The queen's guards didn't move, but the faces I saw were masks of frozen rage.

Kellyn's face aged ten years as she spoke with imperial ice edging her words. All sign of the barely legal vixen fading away. "In due time, Aybran, we will discuss the matter."

Aybran, the frost realm's heir apparent? What the hell have I walked into?

"Izumi," I caught her eyes, "what's going on?"

Izumi looked at the floor as if she were avoiding me, but whispered, "I was named the prize to stop a war; it was decided that we should marry. Not that I was ever asked."

"That's why you were hiding in my territory?"

Kellyn turned her attention back to me. "You are something that has a territory?"

"I really nice territory," I said. "I rule L.A. in the human world."

"El-lay?" Kellyn's face was blank. Apparently, the human city didn't mean much to her. She gestured to the surrounding guards. "Take them to Nieve's old room and see to it she doesn't wonder off again."

Izumi grabbed my hand as a heavy escort led us away.

Aybran didn't look happy, but was smart enough to swallow his protests.

I looked at the frost giant prince, and smiled in contempt. "You will die before you ever touch her."

I shot Kellyn a glance as well, one that traveled down her hot fey body and back up again. I gave her a little goodbye wave.

The queen looked surprised, but gave up a little smile of her own.

We were hustled across the hall, out a side door, and down a passage with blue crystal orbs set halfway in the ice walls every few feet. Ice, ice, and more ice… I was starting to see a theme here. A few minutes later we came to stairs made out of ivory. Izumi still held my hand. I didn't think it was for my benefit. She smelled of fear, powerless in the face of palace machinations. Despair darkened her eyes, robbing her face of animation.

It was a look I really enjoyed seeing on my enemy's faces, but not on Izumi. Maybe she was more to me than an accomplished fuck. Maybe.

The guards stopped us in front of a white door with small handprints melted into it. Each print was bigger then the next, each a deeper blue as the prints got bigger. I wondered if she'd marked her territory with each birthday. Me, I preferred drunken orgies myself.

Izumi opened the door with a wave.

The guards followed us in and stood in a cluster like bowling pins, watching us like their lives depended on it. Maybe they did.

I looked Izumi in the eyes, and kept laughter out of my voice, "Well, should we just kill them all now and run for it, or would you prefer ripping my clothes off and having your way with me?

EIGHTEEN

"You should tell me what you know. I don't know how much longer I can keep my gun from killing you."

—Caine Deathwalker

"Don't tease the guards," Izumi released my hand. "They might think you really mean it."

As she drifted away, I shrugged and took the opportunity to look around. The bedroom was a potential treasure trove of information on the person Izumi had once been, and who she still might be deep inside. Bright colors dominated the hand-woven tapestries that hide the ice walls. The Victorian style bed was rich mahogany with sea foam green sheets, pillowcases, and an overhead canopy of leaf green trimmed in gold. The hope chest at the foot of the bed was red cedar, every surface carved with a forest scenes of running stags, wolves, flying geese, and river swan.

Izumi passed a mahogany armoire with black quartz handles, and settled on a loveseat framed in cherry wood, its upholstery blood-red velvet, trimmed with golden tacks. She watched me intently as my gaze scanned each piece of opulent indulgence. I turned until I faced grape-colored curtains, a room within a room. An alcove held a miniature antique stove, something Ben Franklin might have cobbled together. An orange glower of burning coals could be seen through an ornate brass grillwork. A chimney conducted smoke up through the ceiling with no any indication the ice took notice. Fey magic at work.

Oak shelves wrapped around three walls, well within reach of anyone sprawling on the alcove's padded ledge with its numerous tasseled cushions. The pillows were enormous and apple colored; red, gold, green. A small, child's harp lay among them. Carved from rosewood, inlaid with gold vines, the strings looked like they'd been frozen and shattered by fey magic gone awry. The space felt like the heart of Izumi's domain. It suggested a solitary spirit hungry for beauty, music, poetry, and flights of imagination that were the only escape from the ever encroaching ice of the Winter Court.

Izumi's voice overtook me from behind, "I cried for three days after destroying my harp, and I wouldn't let them take it away. Not everything sent for repairs was returned to me; not all of my interests were considered *appropriate* for a princess of the realm."

I shot a glance at the loitering guards, as if it had been their personal fault. "Bastards! Picking on a little girl."

A few of the guards looked away, faces red with embarrassment. An older fey met my stare with icy dignity. His milk-white mustache bristled with indignation, like an ice-glazed caterpillar. He said, "The queen's will is absolute."

I considered whipping out a gun and placing a slug dead-between his eyes—but didn't. I was here on a mission. Work first. Fun and games later. I had to come up with a plan that didn't involve starting a war. With both frost giants and fey, it would be a very short war … for me. The queen alone was the greatest threat. Bonded to her kingdom so the very land obeyed her, drawing power from the fealty of her people, and already having a massive amount of power by birth, she could easily shrug off most of my dragon magic and crush me like an ice sculpture.

I had only one spell that could deal with her. The *kiss-my-ass-goodbye* spell tattooed on my right ass cheek. Looking like the three blades and hub of a fan, the tri-foil—the international symbol for radiation—represented my own version of Armageddon. Problem was, it was a one time only spell. Depleting all of my life-force, swallowing the life force of all living things within the kill-zone, it assured that anything able to put me down for good would also die. In fact, anything within fifteen miles would be vaporized toast.

If I had a religion outside of sex and booze, it would probably be vengeance. What can I say; though raised demon, I was still human at heart.

Breaking me from my mental abstraction, Izumi rose and stalked toward me as if drawn by an irresistible force—*damn this animal magnetism of mine.* She seemed a new person; icy eyes alive with dancing passions, her white eyebrows arching delicately, her pointy ears longer than I remembered. She took my hand and dragged me to the alcove, shoving me toward the padded ledge and its mob of pillows. She pulled the purple curtains closed to give us privacy.

I heard one of the guards mutter, “Damn lucky round-ear.”

Yes, I am.

She rushed up to me, placing a hand over my mouth before I could say a word. She gestured down at the floor and a ring of golden light rippled outward, followed by several more. They faded at the edge of the curtain and the surround walls. I felt the carpet lurch under me as if turned to quicksand. Her hand muffled the “what-the-fuck!” that came automatically to my lips.

“Just a conveyance spell.” She wrapped both arms around me and held on as we sank to our knees, hips, chests, and then heads. If Izumi hadn’t been coming along, I might have suspected betrayal. What can I say? Just because I sleep with someone doesn’t mean I trust them.

We fell through a hunter green mist, sliding down a tunnel made of shimmering white-gold rings. As a carnival ride, it was pretty cool. I didn’t think this ability of Izumi’s was common among the fey. It was no wonder they’d not been able to hold onto her once her powers kicked in.

The conduit spit us out on a balcony clinging to a tower. A four foot ice wall separated the balcony from a sheer drop that would have landed someone’s mangled body outside the palace walls. A large, full moon glazed the ice with silver light, making it glow, giving us both blue shadows. Roses and thorny vines had been etched into the tiles underfoot. All we needed was an orchestra playing a waltz in the distance. Maybe in there… The adjoining hall of the tower was a dark blue ice cave behind sheer white curtains that rippled in the wind like ghosts hung up to dry.

I went to the balcony’s edge and peered out at a carpet of dark-shadowed forest laid over rugged mountains. There were lights from a few scattered farms, but not much else.

Izumi spoke as if reading my thoughts. “This part of the castle faces away from town. During one of the many remodels my ancestors made to the castle, access to this section of the tower was blocked, and later forgotten about. I played here as a child, and when it came time to escape without a trace, this was how I did it.” She paced like a caged animal until she ran out of space and stopped, hiding her face from me. Her back was tight with tension. “If you want to go, and leave me to my fate, I can send you home from here. I’d do that for you.”

I followed the wall up to her, took her shoulders, and turned her around. There were no tears in her eyes. They were dull white stones. She had the drained, emotionless look that comes to a person shortly before they give up their most cherished desire.

I sighed. "So, your people sell their own quite easily. Blood kin is nothing more than a bargaining chip.

If I liked it," Izumi said, "I wouldn't have run away all those years ago, but it's not that simple. We'd been at war with the frost giants for generations, on and off. The struggle was doing no one any good, but no one could afford to look weak by calling the whole thing off. Peace through marriage seemed the only way. If my intended husband had been anyone but Aybron, I could have endured it for the sake of my people."

"He's especially bad as frost giants go?" I asked.

"He wanted me as his bride, desperately."

Sure, Izumi is hot. "I don't see the problem."

"Among the fey, thirteen is legal. I wasn't even that old at the time. I've been kinda hoping he might not want me, now I've grown up. No such luck. I'm fey; I have glamour. I can be whatever he desires."

I nodded in sympathy. "Yeah, sucks being you."

"So, I'm sending you back?"

"I need to know two things: where is the treasure room and where is Aybran staying?"

"Caine, what are you going to do?"

"Once you ice me up, I'm going for a walk. You stay here."

"Ice you up?"

I began stripping off my non-fey clothes and weapons, making a pile at Izumi's feet. "I've seen some of your people walking around with pieces of armor made from ice. Give me chest and back plates, a helmet with an ice visor across the eyes, frost everything else over lightly, and give me an ice sword and shield. I'll blend right in."

"Wait, if any one finds you skulking about they'll…"

"Make me more dead than they already intend to?"

"You have a point." She smiled a little, her hand freely roaming over my body in rampant admiration. The moisture in the air became a white mist settling on me. I was already cold. It got colder as her hand caressed, leaving a trail of ice. She made a point not to ice up my joints, immobilizing me, and added little creative touches to the armor like the six-pack on the piece over my abs, a map of the palace areas where I'd be going on the inside of my shield. The extra weight and cold was a liability.

She saved the helmet for last, leaning in to kiss me as her hands spread ice over my hair. "You will be careful, right?"

"Sure, but where's the fun in that?" I hoped I didn't have to break off the armor to kick ass. Naked combat wasn't really my thing.

All that was left for her was to make the thin ice visor across the eyes. "Use your *Dragon's Voice* spell if you need me," she said. "I will hear you and come at once—with your weapons and clothing." She waved a hand past my eyes and translucent ice formed, adding a slight distortion to everything I saw.

"Okay, pop me as close to the treasure room as you can without setting off magical alarms."

"If I haven't heard from you in an hour, I'm coming after you," she said.

I smiled. "Always great to have a backup plan."

The hunter green fog returned with its white-gold tunnel of shimmering rings. A moment later, I stood in an empty hall lined with closed doors. I looked at the map inside my shield. A tiny flickering mote of azure light showed me my current position. Two other locations were color coded. The gold light seemed likely to be the treasure room. Knowing what Izumi thought of Aybran, I figured the black dot would be him.

I turned and took several steps, trying to move naturally like I wore ice armor all the time. I watched the blue mote. It moved on the map, showing the progress I was making. Great, I had my guide.

I followed the hallway, seeing only servants scurrying about. None of them paid me much mind, probably grateful I didn't add to their duties. Once I left the back of the castle and approached the central core, I saw guards on patrol, or posted to protect places where frost giants were not allowed. Or people like me for that matter. Thanks to my armor, I didn't look out of place. After the first dozen or so guards, I relaxed and pretty much ignored them.

When I reached the treasure room, there were no guards. This told me high level magic was being used, so guards would have been a waste. Still, I couldn't loiter long in the hall. If I were seen here, all hell would break loose. Someone was bound to sound the alarm. The doors were double-wide, painted bright arterial red; probably a warning to the stupid. Red veins branched out off the doors, into the surrounding walls, both décor and fey magic, though the power there was dormant.

Needing more insight, I concentrated on the Dragon Sight tattoo on my back, near the spine. It came to life with a flare of heat as if a fireball were charring my left lung from the inside. The sensation was blinding agony, but very short lived. In exchange for the pain, I saw through my ice visor as if it weren't there. In addition, a smoky amber glaze covered the world. In that haze, spells and magical items revealed themselves to me with a color coding and a numerical rating that indicated their power level like I was walking through some kind of an online RPG, only this role-playing game could get me killed if I was careless.

The magic of the doors was low-key, a simple magical alarm activated by any movement of the doors. But beyond the door, a blurry blob of light, like a violet x-ray, showed a high level threat. This was dormant too, for now. The numbers attached to it made me cringe. Old Man had numbers like that.

Okay, I had a spell that just might work here. My upper back and shoulders flared awake as my *Demon Wings* activated. This spell was supposed to make all supernatural creatures refuse to register my reality. It had worked back home in the fight with Izumi and the living blizzard. It ought to suppress the alarm, and let me steal past whatever it was gently slumbering inside the vault.

Drawing a deep breath, I pushed one of the doors open a crack and looked inside.

Daaaaammmmnnnn!

NINETEEN

"Cry me a river … so I can drown your ass."

—Caine Deathwalker

The first five feet into the treasure room was a narrow passage. I could reach out and touch left and right walls at the same time. They matched the ceiling and floor—blood red ice, dimming to purple where drifting will-of-the-wisps happened to cast shadows of blue light. The ceiling was cathedral-high. I came out of the passage and the chamber belled out, doing a good job of matching the distance above. My sense of smell was blunted by the cold, but I knew what the chamber was made of; blood, fey blood. You don't get *this* rich shade from food coloring.

Directly ahead of me, a twelve foot statue of an ice dragon occupied a three foot dais. The beast looked far from lifelike, covered as it was in scales of white jade, with gold claws and teeth, and star-sapphires the size of my fist for eyes. Its silver wings were mechanical, probably dwarf made, and just a bit too cute for my taste. I didn't think they'd even lift the dragon off the pedestal if activated. All the joints were hinged so the device could move when brought to life. That made sense since this was the source of all that freakin' huge energy I'd detected outside the door.

Mental note: do nothing to wake up the mechanical dragon. I think it holds the soul of a real dragon inside.

Treading lightly, I circled around the sculpture and studied the many treasure laden shelves, tables, and pedestals that formed a labyrinth.

One section of the maze had a pocket where three vanity mirrors in obsidian frames guarded a rack of jeweled gowns. The dresses were woven from pure silver thread and beaded with blue pearls. There were matching handbags and feathery masks with goblin faces. Should there be a surprise costume ball, the queen would be ready.

There were chests full of gold and crown jewels.

Izumi had said the relic might be hidden under a glamour, but that didn't bother me. I let my magic enhanced vision scan everything in sight. I was looking for an item with even more power than the dragon guardian near the door. Half the things in here had minor spells attached, some for protection, and some for seduction. Screwing and getting screwed seemed to be a major fey pastime.

I wound through the labyrinth taking multiple paths, crisscrossing my own trail, and eventually returned to where I'd started. *Nothing.* So what did that leave? If I wanted to hide a magical item that gave off a powerful aura, I could either cloaking the whole thing—which would take a helluva lot of power—or, better yet, I could simply mask the aura with another. I returned to the dragon to give him another look.

I circled the mechanical beast, studying it carefully. The object I wanted could be in plain sight, or even built into the sculpture, maybe a hidden compartment. I reached out, my ice-gloved hand hovering inches from the white jade scales. The dragon's tail twitched with a soft hum of power.

I froze in place, holding my breath.

Mecha-dragon's long neck swung my way. His whiskered snout stopped a foot away. Star-sapphire eyes wobbled in his face as he stared through me. Panning constantly, his gaze never stopped. At last, he returned to his resting pose, shutting down with a whispered sigh of dropping power.

Too friggin' close.

Breathing shallowly once more, I withdrew my hand and circled the dais. Facing the somnolent dragon, I knelt with my back to the entrance and examined the pedestal more closely.

Ah, hah! A hairline crack along some decorative gilding indicated a secret compartment. The door had a series of mother-of-pearl moon shapes set in the black lacquer. They detailed the phases of the moon, left to right, from a thin ring of inlay that represented a new moon, to a crescent moon, half moon, gibbous moon, full moon, and back eventually to a dark moon. The shapes had a faint glow of ice-blue magic, a very low key spell.

A magical combination lock. I smiled. This had to be what I was looking for. I'd probably only get one try. An incorrect sequence would set off an alarm, and the big guy looming over me. I looked up at his gaping maw, at those gold teeth, the jewel eyes fixed on the door behind me. There had to be some way to keep him shut down while going into the drawer, unless he was attuned to the queen and only she could safely open the drawer.

My gaze dropped to the top of the dais. Just under mecha-dragon's head lay a crystal lotus that could fit in my palms. Normally, you'd expect a giant pearl. The lotus was unusual and its placement screamed that it was important. *Ah, yes. The moon shapes are decoys. The lotus is the true catch.*

Putting my theory to the test, I reached out and gave it a quarter turn counterclockwise.

There was a soft click. I looked down and saw that the drawer had popped open. The dragon hadn't moved. I'd guessed right.

I reached inside the drawer…

And mecha-dragon lunged off the dais, picking me up with the power of his charge, slamming me back into the narrow passage and the door at its end. I hit the door with a loud *thoom!* The ice shield and the armor back plate shattered, hailing to the floor around me as I dropped to hands and knees. Separate from me, the broken ice was no longer shielded by my *Dragon Wings* magic. Of course, the sound of me crashing into the double doors had already betrayed me.

There was no time to figure out what I'd done wrong. Mecha-dragon was at the opening of the narrow passage, peering in. His star-sapphire eyes spilled a radiant silver-blue. This was like being hit by halogen headlights on high beam. His jaws cracked open even wider, like he was planning on swallowing me whole. This shifted his eyes' glare upward and let me see the inside of his throat frosting up. I had a second or two before being engulfed in the liquid hydrogen mist-breath of an ice dragon.

I could have backed out the doors into the hallway, or switched my power from *Dragon Wings* to my defensive barrier, but some nameless instinct had me use my *Dragon's Voice*. I didn't call for Izumi, I called out to the dragon soul lodged inside the mechanical dragon. I wasn't even sure what I said, except that it was in the oldest language of dragon kind, a phrase I'd heard Red Fang use once in drunken rage. Some kind of oath involving fire, ice, blood, and wind…

With a clack, the dragon's mouth clamped shut on the impending deluge. A little swirl of white mist escaped the nostrils, but that was all. Between me and the white jade dragon, a ghostly image formed of a true ice dragon. Mecha-dragon's dragon soul was now awake … and curious. His phantom stare raked my body, lingering on the tats drawn with ink made from dragon blood.

His thoughts touched mine. *And what are you supposed to be?*

"Everyone keeps asking me that," I said.

Answer the question. Your life depends on it.

There was only one way to have him respect me. I concentrated on all my tattoos, warming them up with a trickle of life force. The exposed ink on my torso and arms brightened from black to a dull red, then warmed to the color of fresh blood. This had the effect of wrapping me in a miasma of dragon magic; identification and threat all rolled into one.

The ghost dragon sniffed. *The earth magic of the Red Dragon Clan, but there's something underneath. Show me your true power, not what you've borrowed.*

I stared. All my magic was borrowed, dragon blood blended into the ink of my tats. I had nothing else to show him.

The dragon soul collapsed back into the mechanical dragon. Its mouth hinged open. I knew what was coming; ice breath. That left one option; kicking over the game table. I let all my tats go dormant, except for one: *Dragon Flame.* Saving nothing back, I let it all go out in one explosive blast, shoving fire down mecha-dragon's throat, washing his scale, claws, and wings with the equivalent of a solar flare peeled off the sun.

I couldn't see the dragon very well in the flame I hurled. There was a blue-white billow between us as his breath vented my way, but it was absorbed in the fire stream, flung away from me. After a moment, it seemed as if his gold fangs were melting like ice. The jade scales blackened, scorching, and the silver wings lost shape evaporating. The mechanism retreated, as if sensing its death. My fire pursued. I had to stay close, keeping the hottest part of my flame on target.

In the vault, my fire mushroomed, swirling out to wash the far walls, whipping itself up in a rush to the high ceiling. I poured even more fire into the attack, knowing if it became diluted, what was left of mecha-dragon might be enough to kill me in my exhausted, weaponless state. I looked down to see that I'd blazed away the rest of the ice armor. I stood naked against a threat stronger than any other I'd ever faced.

Mental note: don't do this again.

My fire was falling in on me, the outer edges thinning to nothing. Furthermore, warm blood was climbing up my legs to my knees; melt off from the blood ice in here.

I got a good look at the mechanical dragon. Its wings were stumpy, twisted strands of silver slag. The jade had blackened, fusing in places, cracking and pitted elsewhere. Its eyes were unchanged, but the gold claws and teeth were gone. Still, the machine was at least a couple tons of enraged killing fury. It waded into the dwindling spray of my fire.

I all but felt death breathing down my neck, his bony hand on my shoulder, whispering of the delights of eternity.

Hell, no, I'm not ready to go.

Some unknown door deep in my spirit swung open a crack, and new magic filled me like nothing I'd ever known. My flame still condensed, but it grew hotter than ever. The red of blood-flame turned an eye-searing gold. The blood under it bubbled and steamed.

Mecha-dragon was slammed back onto his dais, his body superheating from solid directly to a gaseous state. Sweat poured down me in slick sheets. A feeble flicker, my protective barrier tried to come on to save me from my own power. The dragon sculpture melted into the blood. The top of the dais burst into flame, releasing an oily black smoke that made me choke.

And suddenly, the dragon soul was back, free with no body to anchor it. He cried out; *Enough, I yield!*

Good thing too, my solar flare snapped out, leaving me an aching tiredness that went deep inside my bones. My vision blurred and a roar filled my head. I sank to my knees, doubting I'd be getting up any time soon.

The spirit hung near me, reproach in its eyes but gratitude as well since I'd broken the ice queen's hold over it. He said; *You should have just told me who you were, Halfling. Had I known, not even the queen's geas could have prevented me from aiding you. Now you've wasted both our strength.*

His words were a riddle I couldn't fathom. *Who I am? And what the hell was with that fire spell going gold on me?* Thinking hurt my head, so I shelved the mystery for another time.

He began to fade, shifting out of this reality, leaving me with a final thought: *I am Wyrmmfrey of the Ice Clan. Call on me seven times, and this debt will be paid.*

I grinned. "Good to know."

But he didn't hear me, having returned to Earth. I wished I was there too, in a bar somewhere, a large frosty mug of beer in my hands.

The chamber had to be well warded. Our ruckus hadn't drawn any attention. Not even the massive out pouring of magical energy. My luck wasn't totally bad. I half crawled, half swam over to the flaming dais. The open drawer in its side had filled with blood. I plunged my hand inside and felt around. I no longer had the strength to power my *Dragon Sight*, but I had to believe there was something in the drawer to justify all this effort.

My hand thrashed inside, making the warm blood frothy. The iron scent was thick and cloying. The drawer was empty except for my hand. I drew it out and cursed softly under my breath for several long minutes.

My baleful stare raked the crystal lotus. It had undergone a transformation, stripped of its glamour. The thing was no longer clear crystal but as red as the blood I was squatting in. I reached out to touch it.

And the world went away in a crimson burst of cold light that stole all my senses. The red wash dimmed and I dropped into a lightless abyss.

TWENTY

"Never stop your enemies
from screwing themselves over."

—Caine Deathwalker

A kick to the ribs woke me up. Someone stood over me, getting ready for another kick. Forcing my eyes to work, I recognized Izumi. "You can stop now," I said.

The high cathedral ceiling and the surrounding walls were winter blue now, no longer red. For that matter, falling down, I should have drowned in the melted blood. There wasn't a bit of it on my clothes. And didn't the space seem a little bigger?

I got on hands and knees, ready to force myself to my feet.

Izumi kicked me in the stomach.

Seeing it on the way in, I hardened my abs, but it still hurt. "Here you are, having fun without me, almost getting yourself killed, destroying the vault and one of our greatest treasures, with no thought to how I'm tearing my heart out with worry over you."

"It's been an hour already?" I asked.

She pulled back for another kick, but stopped herself from following through. "What happened? Did you find the relic?"

"Oh, yeah, the crystal lotus…" I looked around for it. Nothing. I frowned. "That's funny; it ought to be right here."

"It is." Izumi pointed at the inside of my right forearm.

I stared at a new tattoo: a crystal-blue lotus combined with a purple dragon. The whole thing was four by five inches. It hadn't come the usual way. There was no pain, no reddened skin I'd need to keep lotion on, and a bandage, while it healed. It might have been simple skin art except for the throb of dormant power in the ink. I think it had absorbed all the dragon blood in the room—waste not, want not.

"What the hell…" I said.

"Looks good on you," Izumi said, "but mother will be pissed."

"Then let's not tell her." I climbed to my feet, shivering from the cold. I activated my *Dragon Flame*, barely waking the tat up. A brief burst of pain went through me, like my spine had snapped like a whip. The pain went away, replaced by the magic I had bought; a warm haze that flushed through my muscles, blood and organs, loosening the stiffness that had come from sleeping on ice.

"A warning about the lotus," Izumi said. "Using it requires a special price. Until I've explained it properly, keep it dormant."

"Why, what does it do?"

"It gives you access to a pocket dimension where *She* has retired from the worlds of men and fey."

"*She*?"

"King Arthur called her the Lady of the Lake. The Japanese know her as Kagomi, Princess of the moon. One of her children was the first of all vampires. We fey talk of being Under-the-Hill. She *is* Under-the-Hill, the Red Lady who defies even the *Wilde Hunt*.

I stared at her. "And your mom stole a relic from her, binding it to a murdered dragon's soul in a chamber shielded by dragon blood? How many wars does she want to start? Is she crazy?"

Izumi looked at me like I was crazy. "All fey are insane. It's a matter of degree. You don't get to rule a Court of Faire without being an extreme personality. Speaking of which, we need to get out of here. She's bound to call for our presence soon."

"All right then," I sighed, "Ice me up again, then go back to your room and wait."

"We got what you needed. Why not just go?"

"And have your people come after me for taking the relic? No," I pointed at the melted sculpture on the burned dais, "we need someone to pin this on. And there's the matter of your prospective husband to deal with. Just a minute." I returned to the labyrinth of treasure and found a particular trinket, a rare, old necklace with a blue stone that reeked of fey magic. Just holding it in my hand caused a drop in my own energy, causing my invisible magic shield to flicker on and caress my skin.

I returned to Izumi and let her do her thing. Mostly encased in ice, I left her and went back into the outer hall. Several twists and turns and a staircase later, I reached the main floor, looking for my next target.

Various guards milled in the great chamber. They were agitated, falling back to line the walls. I didn't have to seek out Aybran. He and the queen were strolling towards me. I moved out of their way. Along with the rest of the guards, I bowed in respect as the queen passed. For a second, Kellyn's gaze scraped across my visor. I felt the cold stab of her power and an unaccustomed flutter of fear in my stomach. I wondered if she knew me beneath the ice. The edgy dread went away as she climbed the stairs I'd just come down. Aybran lagged a couple paces behind her, veering now and then to jostle guards, hoping to provoke a fight for entertainment value. Frost Giants were like that.

As Aybran passed me, I dropped the stolen necklace in his pocket. Proud and intimidating, he put out so much magic he didn't notice the extra bit he'd acquired.

Idiot, everyone knows never to let your own power mask what's around you. You're king's heir by name and fear only. A squirrel has more brains.

After a moment, I followed them back up. Aybran started talking, his voice booming but slurred as if he'd drunk too much wine. I couldn't make out what he was saying; probably not anything important, not any more.

As soon as I could, I broke off and used a variation of my *Dragon Voice,* a carrying whisper, to call Izumi. The price for the magic felt like someone was bathing me in hydrochloric acid—and drying me off with sandpaper.

Izumi pulled me to her, to the curtained alcove with its shelf bed and abundance of pillows. She was naked, eyes like diamonds, coldly ablaze with desire. The lust I felt diverted me from the fading pain. At her touch, the ice armor I wore softly shattered. She tugged me closer. I fell, pinning her down, flattening her ample breasts between us.

I whispered, "Your mom's on the way here with Aybran."

She smiled with deep joy. "Perfect. This is just how I want them to find us."

I shrugged.

She shifted to settle me more comfortably between her legs. Her hands cupped my ass, squeezing as she gnawed my neck hungrily.

I felt myself getting excited, and whispered, "Any chance your mom might want to join in?"

She bit my neck harder and pulled her head back to stare into my eyes. "Ass!"

"Yeah, I am."

She shook her head. "No, I mean; get it moving. How long are you going to keep a lady waiting?"

"We don't have time to do this right, so let it wait. We just have to make it look good for your mom."

She looked at me. "Seriously?"

"Don't worry," I said. "I'll make it up to you later."

She tangled her legs with mine, and rested her head against my chest as if listening for my heart. "Okay," she said. "Later."

Lying on my side, I held her, brushing her hair back from her face. Her fingers scraped down my torso, tracing a line across my hip that left a small slick of frost. Her hand stopped on my thigh. Her face lifted and her eyes opened, staring into mine. "You're very good at making love, Caine, but can you love? Really. After being raised as a demon, how much human is left in you?"

"Old Man would say 'too much.' Me, I don't look for answers that I don't really want to know."

Her face sank and returned to my chest. "You know, whenever I feel like wallowing in self-pity, I think of your situation, and start counting my blessings."

"Hey! I like my life."

She laughed, but the sound had an empty ache to it. "I know. And that's … so sad."

The curtains parted and we suddenly had an audience. I rolled over and looked straight at Izumi's mom. "It's not what you think. Okay, so *it is* what you think. How about a little privacy? I still have one more orifice to go."

There was a thunderous growl from behind the queen as the frost giant scrunched down to peer over her shoulder. She spun on him, pointed a royal finger in command. "Stay, I'll deal with this." She drew the curtains shut, and approached the bed. Kellyn's face went from livid to shocked as she saw the size of my equipment. "Winter's Heart! What are you, part centaur? Never mind. Put it away and get dressed. There are matters of state to attend to."

"Are you sure you couldn't give me another twenty minutes?" I asked.

She held out her hand, closing it on thin air. A sword of ice formed. She swung the tip. It caught me under the jaw, lifting my face, more than implying a threat. "I am not one you ever want to keep waiting."

"Fine," I said.

She withdrew the sword, willing it to shatter and fall, adding to the ice on the floor. I slid off the shelf and moved to where my clothes and weapons were piled. Keeping my new tattoo turned from her view, I dressed.

As Izumi roused herself, sitting up, Kellyn turned to her. "Are you trying to break my plans by outraging your betrothed husband?"

Izumi swung her feet off the shelf, leaning toward her mom, diamond eyes hard and cold. "You're trying to get rid of me through marriage to a piece of frozen crap. Why should I care about you?"

I liked the way her boobs bounced as she said that.

Kellyn slapped her daughter across the mouth. The queen's voice lost all trace of warmth, cutting like a blizzard. "I have never spared myself from the demands of duty. You shame our family, asking me to spare you. Get dressed, and pray I need not kill your well-endowed friend to appease Aybran." She shot my cock another look as I slowly zippered up.

Dressed, we filed out of the alcove. Aybran waited, a killing rage dominating his face. His whale blubber stench in close quarters was less than enjoyable. Kellyn waved the guards from the room. They seemed especially glad to escape from the drama about to unfold. Kellyn pushed the giant toward a seat. "Sit, and try not to break the chair." Planting fists on hips, she glanced at all of us. "We need to come to an understanding here. Aybran, after all this, do you still want my daughter?"

He looked at her, hunger and viciousness mingled in his expression. "Oh, yes."

The queen nodded. "Then the wedding will continue as planned."

"What of him?" The frost giant pointed a massive, square-shaped finger at my face.

"He's my maid of honor," Izumi said. "You can't have him."

"He has tarnished my honor!" the giant roared.

"You have to *have* honor to get it tarnished," I said. "Besides, you've no claim against me; you're not married *yet*."

Kellyn quelled us with a glance. "The stranger is my daughter's guest. Guest rights apply. Touch him and you touch my honor. Whatever grievance you imagine you have, settle it outside my court."

The frost giant glowered, eyes ablaze. "Oh, that I will."

There were thudding feet in the outside hall followed by banging on the door.

"Now what?" Kellyn raised her voice, "Enter!"

A guard rushed in, hastily bowing. "My Queen, the treasury has been despoiled by thieves."

She looked calmly at the guard. He froze over and shattered in little pieces, many of them the color of blood. She spoke mildly, "You should not have let that happen."

"I doubt he will repeat the mistake," I said.

The giant was back to pointing his finger at me again. "There's your thief. It must be him."

"I've been here under guard," I said, "but you can certainly look through my things. Of course, if you really want to find your thief, I have a spell for that."

Kellyn gave me a nod to continue.

My mid-back tat burned like hell on a Saturday night. The crawling, peeling sensation almost convinced me my skin was blackening from internal heat. Using *Dragon Vision*, I saw the flow of magic within the room. Kellyn was a pyre of silver-blue magic. Izumi looked like her, but not nearly as bright. The frost giant was a muddy indigo, his fierce aura tainted by the necklace I'd palmed off on him.

I put a look of surprise on my face and did some pointing of my own. "There! He's got something on him. Check his pocket." I powered down my magic, saving my strength in case this didn't work and I had to fight for my life.

Leaping to his feet, Aybran yelled, "Lying cur!" The fury in his voice caused several guards to enter the room, faces set in grim masks.

Kellyn looked at me. "You had best be right. Such an accusation, proved false, will strip you of my protection."

"Turn out his pockets," I said. "You'll see."

"I will not suffer this indignity," Aybran said.

"You will," Kellyn said. "Or the Wilde Hunt will drive you from this land, or to your death, depending on how fast you run."

He paled, swallowing any further protests. Apparently, the greatest terror of the fey legend was not unknown to him.

Aybran dug in his pockets and turned them out. The necklace I'd stolen fell to the floor. The necklace's stone shone like a small blue moon. The giant's face showed shock and surprise. He stared at the necklace, stuttering his indignation, not actually forming any words.

Queen Kellyn cut him off mid-bluster. She did this with a sword like the one she'd earlier threatened me with. Its point pierced the giant's chest and his heart. "I hate a thief," she said.

I wisely failed to mention that most of the things in her treasure room, like mine back home, were stolen from other people.

A thick silence settled as the giant slumped and sprawled on the floor, covering the necklace with his corpse.

Izumi cleared her throat. "So, does that mean the wedding is off?"

TWENTY-ONE

"Blood, death, and chaos ...
my work here is done."

—Caine Deathwalker

Kellyn had the frost giant rolled on his side so she could retrieve the necklace. The guards then dragged him away. They closed the door behind them, leaving me and Izumi alone with her mom.

Kellyn said, "I didn't see you plant the necklace downstairs. You have good hands, human, but poor sense, releasing the dragon ghost. Who knows where he will have taken the Red Moon relic by now. It may take me centuries to track him down again. You were a bad boy."

Yeah, keep looking for that ghost. Don't even suspect I've got your treasure tattooed to my arm.

Kellyn wandered over to me, stopping inches away. "In one thing, you've done me a favor. With this, the frost giant elders will be inclined to grant concessions; their honor is at stake. Of course, their king could restart the war anyway, sharing the pain of his grief with us all."

Izumi looked stormy, eyeing the small distance between her mom and me. "I don't care. I want what I want, and that sack of shit was in my way."

Kellyn graced her daughter with an approving look. "Spoken like a pure-blood fey." The queen returned her attention to me. "I, too, take what I lust after."

"He's mine," Izumi said.

"Here, a rental fee." Kellyn tossed the necklace to her.

Izumi caught it in cupped hands. She left the bauble on the bed, standing, coming over to join us. "As I said, he's mine, and we have urgent business elsewhere."

Kellyn shook her head. "No, Nieve, you will stay here. Izumi is no more. No more running away. You must learn the duties of a future queen."

I might be heartless and self-serving, but I stand by my friends, when convenient. Still, I had no rights in Winter Court. I was out powered and outnumbered, which was why I'd been relying on stealth. I had no right to object, but when had I ever let such things bother me?

Besides I need Izumi's muscle backing me, and I'd hate to lose a hell of a lay.

An idea hit me. I just needed Izumi to be quick on the uptake and play along.

I stepped in front of her, cutting off her view of her mom and gave her a quick wink. "Your mom is totally right." I took her hands in mine. "Duty is very important. We must always sacrifice to meet our obligations. It is the path of honor." The expression of surprise on her face was so fleeting, I could have imagined it. She knew I didn't believe in personal sacrifice. Let others die for their causes, I'd kill for mine. "I'll say goodbye now, if you want to open up a gateway back to L.A. for me."

She stared into my eyes. "If you think it's for the best."

She gestured. An oval plane of dark green, edged with white-gold energy, swirled open. We were only a few feet away from escape, but I had to make sure no one would be sent to drag Izumi back here once we were gone.

I nodded solemnly. "I will miss you terribly. Sure it was a burden, taking you into my own home, feeding you, clothing you, cleaning up after your messes. The incredible sex barely made up for the inconvenience, but still, a certain *price* must be *paid* to befriend a committed party girl."

I saw the light of understanding blaze in her eyes. She threw herself into my arms with a theatrical sob, clutching me desperately. "Oh, Caine, I can never thank you enough. I owe you so much!"

"Nieve, be silent!" Kellyn's shocked voice lashed out, but it was too late.

I smiled. "Yes, you do, a debt that will take years to repay."

Turning, I faced Kellyn. I saw defeat in her face. She knew as well as I did that fey law required even royalty to pay an acknowledged debt. Izumi had no choice now except to come with me.

"Relinquish your debt-right," Kellyn said. "I will ransom her with a gift of magic or treasure. I will even pleasure you enthusiastically amid silken sheets until you lose desire for anyone else."

"Yeah, you'll throw a glamour on me so I'll think I'm having the best sex ever, and *I'll* wind up the one enslaved. Sorry. I've got other plans." I walked toward the open dimensional gate. "Come on, Izumi."

I didn't have to look back to know she was following.

Kellyn sighed. "I can afford to wait a few years. Fey are long lived. Eventually, I will have my way."

At the edge of the gate, I turned back to see Izumi hugging her mother. They broke apart and both approached me. I pulled out one of my cards and handed it to Kellyn. *Often what I lust after makes its way to me.*

"We will always have room in our bed for you." *My bed is spell-proof and glamour proof.*

She smiled. "Be careful what you ask for. You just might get it."

Izumi smacked me in the arm. "Really, stop hitting on my mom; it's weird."

"Hey, I'd be doing her a favor. An ice queen needs defrosting now and then, like everybody else."

"Ass," Izumi said.

I smiled. "My favorite feature, or so I've been told."

As we plunged into the silken depths of the gate, the chill of the palace peeled away. Currents of chaos pried at the shimmering rings that formed our path, jostling them out of perfect alignment. Magic whisked us through the hunter green space, but it seemed as if we hung in stillness while the rings zipped past *us*.

This kind of travel wasn't anything new, but Izumi reached out from behind me and her arms wrapped around me. It was a little late for post sexual cuddling, but I didn't mind, until we emerged in her front yard and her leg tangled mine. She rode me down to the ground, laughing. My face sank into the grass as I absorbed the impact with my arms.

Sitting on me, Izumi lowered her boobs to my back, taking me by the shoulders as she whispered in my ear. "That's for hitting on my mom." She shoved off my back, getting to her feet.

I noticed the gate hadn't closed. "Are you just going to leave that thing running?"

"For a while. Now that I know mom can't keep me against my will, I'd like to go back and catch up on all the time we missed—for a while at least. I need to pack a few bags." She headed for her house, and the way she swung her hips told me she knew I was watching, with great enjoyment. She called over her shoulder, "See you in a few weeks."

"Wait a second," I stood and brushed myself off. "You were going to tell me something about my new tattoo?"

"Oh, yeah, never go into its altered space alone. A sacrificed soul is required, or it's a one way trip."

"Good to know," I said.

She continued on. I wasn't going to ask her to stay and help me out. She'd charge me by the hour. I went to my own yard and made my way to the front porch. Leona sat on its edge, watching me. She bared clenched teeth in that Gawd-awful grin of hers as I passed.

"Enjoy the show?" I asked.

"Always a pleasure to watch you eat dirt."

Go catch a mouse."

I went inside. The TV blared. Someone's talk show was in full swing. Apparently, someone had slept with her sister's husband and had gotten pregnant, but a jealous ex-boyfriend was insisting that he was the real daddy and a DNA test was pending—"Right after a word from our sponsors!" A woman appeared on-screen holding a tube of gel. "Ever wanted product that would both whiten your teeth and bring soothing relief from vaginal itching? Well, Toof-Fer-One is for you!"

"Sometimes, I think I'm already in hell." I headed toward the office-bar for a well-deserved drink, and to look for Old Man. I knew he was going to bust my chops about all the time I was spending *not* searching for Haruka, even though we'd needed an answer to Sarah's weird-ass transforming necklace first.

As I pushed through the door, I pulled my phone and checked the calendar and weather. *New Moon tonight and clear skies. Good night for unleashing old magic.* I had a feeling a rescue in the nick of time lurked in the wings. *I'll hit the Mission again after sunset. Meanwhile...*

Going into battle sober didn't seem a good idea. I proceeded to make my own version of a top-shelf AMF (Adios Mother-Fucker!). This involved Captain Morgan rum from a one-use barrel for maximum flavor, a shot of French vodka, a shot of Karma tequila, a shot of aged gin, a shot of Crown whisky, two shots of Blue Curacao, two shots of sour mix, two shots of 7up, and a 151 Bacardi top layer. Instead of attacking this the usual way with a straw, I poured it all in a blender and gave it a whirl.

The challenge of the drink is to try not to die before finishing the first cup. I didn't die. Barely. Nursing my second cup, I drifted off to my room to check my guns and ammo clips, adding them to the special combat harness I intended to wear over my night suit, an all-black second skin that simplified going over fences and hiding in shadows. I laid everything out on the bed, adding the long coat I'd been wearing. Later, it would keep my weaponry concealed until I reached the battlefield.

I finished my second drink, shed the rest of my clothes to the floor, and staggered off to the bathroom for a shower. The world slid sideways. Next thing I knew, the floor rushed up to greet me.

I don't know how much time passed, but the darkness eventually released me. My head rocked to the side. Old Man bent over me, slapping my face.

Stretched out on the tiled floor, I squinted against the glare of the bathroom lights. *He must have turned me over.* My head hurt. I needed another drink.

He hit me again.

"You can stop that now," I said. "I'm awake."

"But it's so much fun." He walked away and started the shower. I listened to the hiss of water as I struggled to sit, and climb to my feet.

"Clean yourself up," he said, "then join Hiro and me in the office. There's news. Bad news." He walked away.

I made it to the shower and added more hot water. Standing under the spray, I wondered what had hit the fan now. Torn by curiosity, I hurried things along and soon emerged a little more awake. I shaved, gelled my hair, and returned to my bedroom. The light coming in the window was dimming. Sunset wasn't far off. I needed to dress for battle, but my stuff was no longer on the bed.

Off to the side, a martial arts head and torso on a stand had been brought in. The limbless rubber dude was usually used to practice pressure point attacks where clearly marked. This guy had been turned into a clotheshorse of sorts. My night suit, weapons harness, and long coat were settled over it. The gear looked better on me, but I was glad to have the dummy. It spruced up the place nicely and gave me someone to talk to for intelligent conversation.

Speaking of which, I was running late. Dressed, I ran across the house, seeing no sign of Leona. I entered the bar and swerved toward the fireplace and the furniture there. The chair William had destroyed had been replaced by a wingback chair with crimson leather and brass tacks. Hiro sat there. Old Man stood at the fireplace, his back to me.

I walked over and dropped on the couch.

Hiro look tired and years older.

"What is it this time?" I asked.

"They've found Haruka's friend Jessie. Her body's in Japan."

TWENTY-TWO

It hurts to kill; it never lasts long enough."

—Caine Deathwalker

I frowned. "The succubus took the girls to Japan and killed one of them?"

Old Man turned from the fireplace. He smoldered with rage. There were actual blue flames leaping out, obscuring his eyeballs. "Jessie's been dead for at least three weeks."

"Damn, I *really* need a drink." I felt like I'd been sucker punched. "Hey, why didn't we see it, Old Man, why didn't we sense that the Jessie we met was a demon?"

He locked his hands behind his back. The flames of his eyes settled down, becoming sapphire coals as he went introspective. "Probably a doppelganger spell; lets you look and feel like someone else, but it's tricky to keep it going and harder to mask it from people like us. It's why the succubus needs Sarah."

I said, "Okay, this sucks, but at least now I only have one person to get back." I turned toward Hiro. "Did you speak about us in front of Jessie?"

He nodded sharply, eyes widening. Claw like hands gripped the armrests of his chair. "Yes, every time I spoke about the situation, she was there with Haruka."

"How much did you tell her?"

"I told Haruka she would be safe"

"Did you tell her our clan name?"

A name like a smear of shadow in the mists of legend, a name respected far and wide in the preternatural communities.

He said, "Yes."

"No wonder we were attacked as soon as we hit the scene." I thought of the Catholic Mission where Sarah had been mucking about. The place offered power to anyone able to corrupt the holy site. "Well, at least we know where the ritual will be taking place. I need to head out."

"I'm coming along," Old Man said.

"Me too," Leona added.

I jolted in place, half drawing one of my PPKs. "Where the hell did you come from?"

She snorted in amusement. "I'm a spirit beast, remember. Fading in and out is what I do."

I scowled at her and holstered my gun.

"I'm coming too," Hiro said.

I glared at him. "I'll kill you myself before I let you breach our contract by getting yourself killed."

Hiro cast a glance at Old Man, a silent appeal.

Old Man shook his head. "Sorry, my friend. The pup is right. Your battles are fought in boardrooms. If we have to divide our attention to keep you safe during a rescue, it puts Haruka in greater danger."

Hiro sighed and nodded. "I understand. I will wait here."

The rest of us headed out to my car. Old Man could have opened a demon gate, but the magic might set off alarms where we were going. As I started the engine, Izumi's computer simulated voice came out of the speakers, greeting me warmly.

Old Man raised an eyebrow at me.

"What?" I said.

He looked forward again, saying nothing.

We didn't talk much while I drove to the Mission. Once in the neighborhood, the air grew heavy, dead with foreboding. Old Man studied the church as we parked across the street. Leona did the same. The church looked closed, but I could feel an aura of old magic peeling off it in cold, clammy waves.

Old Man's eyes blazed for a moment. The blue-green glow caught my attention. He pointed at the shadows around the church and the elm trees near it.

I watched the shadows stir. "That's not the wind." I counted seven of them and put up fingers, telling the Old Man how many I saw.

He raised an eyebrow and put up ten fingers, then four. I'd guessed wrong. A moment later, he put his hand on his face and shook his head in blatant disappointment.

I gave him the bird.

"Can you tell who or what they are?" Old Man asked.

Always testing. "Yeah, I can. Can you open the glove box?"

He did. "When did you put a mini bar in here?"

"A few weeks ago when I got charged five hundred bucks for a single drink at a trendy new night club."

Sometimes L.A. really sucks.

"And humans call *us* demons." Old man handed me a shot of Jack Daniels and poured one for himself.

Leona butted in, "This is what you guys talk about when you're on a stakeout?"

We looked at each other, turned in the seat to stare back at Leona, then faced the church. I said, "Sometimes, Old Man gives me coloring books and crayons, but I'm not very good about staying inside the lines."

We climbed out and got half way across the street before pack magic hit us, like a wall of ice. Ignoring it, Leona disappeared like the spirit beast she was. The air smelled sour as stale fear. Gibbering laughter crackled like goblin song, scraping the pavement like fallen leaves. Four-legged shadows with hell-fire eyes scampered around us.

"Illusion," Old Man said, "an attempt to stampede us so we can be run to ground."

We staggered, but managed another few steps. Undaunted, Old Man rumbled low in his throat, a sound of gleeful anticipation. My protective shield warmed to life and I winced, a splinter of ice driving like a nail between my eyes. Touched by my expanding shield, the red-eyed shadows dissolved. The wild laughter thinned and died with a last ghostly moan, and the air went back to smelling as polluted as ever. The wolves had just tried to take me out with pack magic.

We looked back toward the trees where the shadows had come from. There were more of them now, these ones real. Half of William's pack came out into the open, spreading out between us and the church. Angie hung back, staying close to the building's front double doors. William himself approached us, mostly in human form, but with hands turned to claws, his jaw distended, bristling with large pointy teeth—the better to eat you with.

William locked eyes with Old Man.

Big mistake.

The wolf was used to staring down his own kind. Someone should have told him meeting demon eyes was uniquely dangerous, depending on the demon in question. Old Man didn't need pack magic to induce the chill of death, the paralysis of fear. He just had to bring his deeper self out of hiding. Tens of thousands had died to wash his honor clean.

He was the Power that had shattered an island continent at the dawn of time. The towers of Atlantis had crumbled before his rage. The seas had answered his call. Savage storms had howled with madness, writing his name in runes of lightening on winding sheets of rain. With everything dear to him, Old Man had consigned his own demon race to a watery grave. It was why he *was* the last Atlantean.

William's inner beast wouldn't understand these things, but he'd feel nightmare squeezing his heart, melting his courage to the bone. He broke eye contact, his feet rooting to the pavement.

Old Man smiled. Darkness shadowed his face and his killing hand. Dark clouds piled up overhead. Thunder grumbled. Writhing snakes of lightning spun from thunderhead to thunderhead. The earth shuddered like a cowering behemoth.

I called to Old Man, "Don't damage my city."

"Not likely," he said. "I am not as powerful as I once was."

"Okay, I'll take William and Angie. You take the rest."

"No," he said, "I've got William. You take the rest."

Fading in, in mid-leap Leona shrieked, "Mine!" She dropped like a buzz saw onto William. They hit the ground in a whirling, snarled mass of fur, teeth, and claws. Blood streamed from gaping wounds. Blindly, William tried to pry the jungle cat off him. She had his head in her jaws, trying to crack it like an oversized egg. William went to pounding on her sides, trying to drive her ribs into heart and lungs. Making herself solid enough to attack, she was solid enough to take damage.

Old Man went to help her.

I spun to face the street behind me. Three new, oversized wolves were almost on me. I opened fire, glad a lot of my clips tonight were silver hollow-points. The wolves shook as I stitched with fire, round after round. Shredding silver carved up their internal organs, creating wounds that could not be healed by a werewolf. Their roars collapsed into hacking barks and yelps as they fell twitching at my feet, eyes glazing in death, blood pooling on the pavement.

I spun back to the Mission, resuming fire on the rest of the wolves.

I expected them to charge, but they held their ground, lifting muzzles to the sky, howling. Their song pierced the night, ringing out, stirring the short hairs at the nape of my neck. This wasn't pack magic. Something worse. From the surrounding blocks, the call was echoed by new voices. There were even howls from inside the church.

The wolves had been recruiting. That meant the priests, the homeless, wandering thieves, pimps, and hookers tending their corners had been blooded, infected on a massive scale.

William had seen how things might go, and had sent out the missing members of his pack to build an army. The new converts wouldn't be experienced wolves able to control themselves, able to take human form at will. They'd be driven by blood lust alone.

William was past caring about that, into a win-at-all-costs mentality. Worse, he was exposing us all to the human world. This kind of thing was why wolves had been banned from L.A. years ago.

As all that went through my head, I emptied my clips, reloaded, and resumed fire. The wolf voices at the Mission fell silent. My gaze slid to the doors of the church where Angie glared at me with utter hatred. Eyes blazing amber, she backed into the church.

The young wolf voices in the near distance fell silent. They'd come in now, looking for those that were pack, those that had called. When they found the wolves dead, the new ones would start killing everything in sight. Those they'd wound would rise as new wolves too, spreading the contagion in a feeding frenzy. From the screaming police sirens, I knew that the carnage was spreading.

Only their Alpha could stop this.

I yelled over to Old Man, "Hey, we're going to need him. Don't—"

C-Crack.

Damn. I know the sound of snapping vertebrae when I hear it.

I looked over. Leona was gone, probably ghosting away to heal and reconstitute herself. Old Man held Williams so his feet swung, toes scraping the sidewalk. The Alpha's neck looked broken. His head swung loosely. His eyes were closed, his muscles lax. Old Man thrust a silver dagger into the wolf's heart for good measure and tossed the carcass away, turning to stare into the surrounding darkness.

Lightning flashed, bleaching the world white for several heartbeats. Darkness crashed back in, and Old Man said. "They're coming."

"The new wolves? Yeah, I already figured that out."

"No, something else." His head lifted as if scenting the wind. "I feel a presence in the storm, riding in my sky."

Leona reformed next to him, looking her usual self. Even William's blood was gone from her black fur.

There was a shimmer of dark energy. Sarah appeared in a black robe, wearing that god-awful necklace of hers. She snatched the knife from William's torso, pinning his face to her breasts. Tears dampened her face. She looked at me with human eyes filled with hate.

I bolted toward her.

Leona and Old Man swiveled to see what was happening.

Before any of us could reach them, William and Sarah vanished into thin air. I had the feeling I'd find them inside the mission. I started for the doors where Angie had retreated. "You guys got this?" I asked.

"Sure," Leona said. "Go have fun."

I pulled my straight katana out of thin air, still sheathed. The demon blade begged me to let it out to feed.

Soon, I promised. Soon.

TWENTY-THREE

"If you don't want me to piss in the holy water, don't invite me to church."

—Caine Deathwalker

In the mission's front vestibule, a suspenseful silence held sway. The outside street lamps backlit the stained glass windows, spilling primary colors across midnight-red carpeting and up a wall. In the glow, I saw a wooden stand and a basin of holy water. Out of the light fall, both sets of double doors into the nave were open.

There were no smoldering red eyes in the inner shadows, but I knew an ambush had been set, so, of course, I had to go in.

Against my usual habit, I went in on the right, scanning empty pews that smelled of lemon Pledge. It wasn't perfectly dark; the left wall had more stained glass. Shafts of red, blue, and gold knifed across the gloom. Sheathed katana in hand, I glided past the closed doors of confessionals. Alabaster saints on pedestals stared down at me from lofty heights, their expressions troubled.

I had the feeling they didn't want me here.

As I passed the last confessional, its door splintered, ripping off the hinges with a loud crack echoing in the vaulted space. A wolf in human form leaped at me. Everything slowed in my mind as I dipped and wheeled out from under his fangs and claws. My sheathed katana trailed me, staying in his path. It struck him midair, glancing off his shoulder, breaking his collarbone as he went by. He landed on the carpet, tumbling into the end piece of a pew. Rebounding, the wolf spun, looking for where I'd gone. Pain and injury weren't slowing him down. Werewolves heal too quickly for that. I swung the sheath a second time and broke his jaw.

Enough playing around.

As he staggered, I unsheathed my blade. Its voice strengthened, as did the hunger it shared with me. The blade was as much an opponent as the wolves. It would do its best to drain my will, to make me an extension of it, so it could kill forever, creating oceans of blood. This was the price I paid for so powerful a weapon. It was why I'd hesitated to draw it—until I heard the soft padding of wolves rushing me in the shadows.

There were plenty of red-eyed shadows now the trap was sprung, and Angie was in the lead, her face fuzzy, distorting as her change began. Without looking at the wolf I'd been fighting, I stabbed him through the heart. The meteoric iron of my straight katana couldn't stop the wolf without taking off his head, but the demon blade possessed a soul of its own—a vampiric soul. The blade burned with a crimson aura, and I heard the howl of a wolf spirit as it was ripped from the wolf, into the blade.

More, the sword demanded. *More.*

Larger than regular wolves, possessing the full mass of the humans they'd been, four of the werewolves sprang, only Angie digging in and drawing back. She retained enough of her human side to understand the damnation my weapon offered.

In the heat of battle, things continued to pass with aching slowness. Not that I was slow. My sheath in one hand became a flail. The blade in the other cut the air, weaving a rune of death. Hitting solidly would have stopped my energy, immobilizing the weapon. I used it to scratch. Being a demon blade, a scratch was enough for it to slurp out the life force of two wolves in a moment. My sheath brained a wolf, making it shake its head in annoyance, shooting past me, missing. My sword took out another wolf with a cut on its spine.

The phantom voices of captured spirits thickened the air, wrapping around my sword, sinking into the metal.

I crouched with my blade next to my left hip, waiting for the return of the wolf that had lunged by. I didn't look at it directly, but gazed across the pews so peripheral vision could catch both the turning wolf and anything Angie might do at the same time.

She turned tail—literally, fully wolf now—and ran for the front of the church. The last wolf charged. Claws scraped the air, barely missing me as I danced away, slicing my blade across Achilles tendons. The wolf's spirit howled in despair, drawn into the sword as its body collapsed, in death.

I stared as the katana grew silent, temporarily sated. That wouldn't last. The blood on the steel sank into the steel, an after dinner drink. I sheathed the blade once more. Dropping it from my hand sent it back to the armory in my vault.

With any luck, Angie was now leading me to Sarah and the Succubus. And Haruka of course. It had nearly escaped my mind that I was supposed to be rescuing her. Perhaps I get distracted too easily by my passions.

My automatics in hand, I stalked toward a door someone had opened for Angie. In her wolf form, she didn't have hands to work the knob; she'd have busted through. And if the door had been ajar, I'd have spotted light bleeding into the sanctuary from the well-lit hallway. Halfway there, I heard the sound of shattering glass. I stopped to crouch and swing my guns toward the high, stained glass windows. Several of them had caved in, spraying razor-edged shards and broken lead fretting into the air. Amid the debris, Old Man and Leona hung a moment, then dropped as gravity caught up to them.

As a spirit beast, Leona hadn't needed to break her window. I think she'd just thought it a fun thing to do.

I relaxed, straightening, focusing my senses on the door to the hall once more. Crunching glass underfoot, Old Man ambled up to me, Leona a step or two behind.

"This is as far as you've got?" Old Man said.

With the muzzle of the gun in my right hand, I pointed over my shoulder. "I stopped to play with some wolves back there." I pointed the gun ahead at the open door. "Angie went that way. I was just about to go after her when you crashed the party. Why aren't you guys outside, dealing with the new wolves?"

"That new force I sensed in the clouds?"

"Yeah?" I said.

"Slayers with glider packs, swords, and automatic weapons."

"Quite a lot of them," Leona said.

"We left the wolves to them," Old Man said.

I couldn't believe my ears. *Slayers? In my town?* Slayers were humans with a hard on for killing whatever goes bump in the night. They're a secret society all about purifying the planet of preternatural threats. "We shut down their L.A. operation years ago."

Old Man nodded once. "Guess they're back in business."

As if things weren't complicated enough.

Leona said, "Maybe we'll get lucky. They and the wolves could wipe each other out."

Old Man and I looked at her silently.

"It could happen," she said.

I started for the door. "I don't have that kind of luck. Come on, let's go."

Low to the ground, quite a bit faster on four feet, Leona rushed ahead. "I'll take point."

"Okay," I said, "but be careful. They know we're coming, and Angie has a good nose."

"Bitch will find out I've got good claws," Leona said. "I never liked her."

The hall took us to a kitchen where dishes filled a sink, trash waited to be emptied, and a few bodies cluttered the floor. A woman lay at my feet, black hair in a bun, eyes glazed by death, vacantly staring, her mouth opened in a silent scream. Her dress was tattered and soaked in blood as was the underlying flesh. A teenage volunteer,and a priest in black suit with white collar, were missing essential organs. They'd been attacked by wolves, and had not survived the transition into new wolves.

So much blood, a pretty contrast to the bloodless flesh, the frozen expressions of horror—*beautiful! Wolves do good work. If only they were tidier about cleaning up…*

I went into a dining hall with tables and benches. Cold food aged on paper plates. Paper cups were overturned, spilling Kool-Aid to mix with blood. There were more bodies. From the smell, quite a few of the homeless had unloaded in their underwear as death came for them with claw and fang. There were kids here too. Many of hem had simply been batted across the room into walls, leaving red smears as they slid to the floor and fell over.

For some reason, my gaze snagged on an infant near a crumpled blanket on the floor. A rather large bite had removed half her torso. Tiny ribs were exposed. From the angle of her head, her neck looked broken. She had curly blond hair and small hands clenched in fists that had done her no good. Her life wasn't any more valuable than anyone else's had been. I couldn't understand why my heart felt so dense inside my chest. You'd almost think I cared.

"No wolves here." Leona paused to lap up some of the pooling blood.

I felt a cut across my pectoral muscles and jumped back, looking for the source of the attack. It hadn't felt like a blade or claw tip. *Magic?* My protective tat had let it happen. I knew who this had to be. *Sarah.* Another cut opened, a rip across my side. *Bitch!* The wounds were shallow, teasing. The one that cut across the dragon tattoo on my chest had already healed since poison wasn't involved this time. Was she hitting from a distance, or in the room, invisible to our senses? With that necklace of hers, either was possible.

"Old Man," I yelled. "I need some fog. Fast!"

Not bothering to ask me why, he muttered beneath his breath, throwing out an arcane gesture or two. The air went from dry to damp at warp speed. Clouds formed around him. Billows expanded to choke the room, making us shadows to one another. Holding my PPKs out in at a forty-five degree angle, I scanned the fog for a human-shaped gap in the mists. If Sarah was here I'd know it. If she was attacking by some kind of remote viewing, I thought this would mess up her targeting.

Listening, I heard no footsteps trying to avoid me. Sweeping through the cloud, I found no gaps. "I think Sarah is homing in on us with a magic attack," I said. "Can you keep the cloud cover with us as we move on?"

He snorted. "Please, ask me for something difficult."

Old Man and Leona were near me, blurry but identifiable from their silhouettes. "Stay close," I said. "We want to avoid friendly fire if we can."

Leona padded past me, sniffing the air. He tail lashed with excitement. "I've got Angie's scent. This way." She moved on, but not so swiftly that we lost her. Stepping over bodies, we reached another open door. Our fog went ahead, billowing down a flight of stairs into darkness.

"Obvious isn't it?" I said.

"As soon as someone creaks on a stair," Old Man said, "all hell's going to break loose. They'll have us in a bottle neck, all bunched together."

"Good strategy," I said.

"Not good enough," Leona said. "Give me a minute."

She went ghost, not just invisible but intangible too. Dissipated, there was no target to hit, no weight on the stairs, no warning at all for the poor sons of bitches down there waiting on us.

A few heartbeats later, harsh, bestial screams erupted from inhuman throats. There was gunfire, a sound of struggle, of things breaking including bones—then an ill-omened silence. Leona's voice reached us, "Haul ass, the coast is clear."

Old Man and I hurried down. He kept the mist thick around us as we reached the bottom so there was very little to see, except for the wolf bodies we stepped over as we entered a hallway that was lit at the end by a single bare bulb in the ceiling.

I said, "Sarah's got to be running out of wolves down here."

"Doesn't mean her necklace isn't an army all by itself," Old Man said. "Are you sure you can counter it now?"

"I sure hope so." I thought of the new dragon and lotus tattoo on my arm. As a last resort, I'd use it, but I'd try everything else first.

Playing around with altered spaces when you weren't really demon or fey was highly dangerous. Messing with a micro-universe belonging to a Goddess—even worse.

Leona was halfway down the hall, in plain sight. The clouds were thinning to nothing. We were exposed to anyone who might leap out of a doorway. "What's the idea, Old Man?" He muttered a curse, shocking me. I'd never heard him curse before. "Sorry," he said. "It seems like Sarah has found an answer to my weather magic."

"She *so* needs to die!" I said.

A voice behind me made me spin, taking aim.

"Maybe I can help you with that." It was Kris Salem, the warlock from Gloria's bar. His off-kilter hair was still a spiky blond embarrassment. He had an Uzi hanging on a strap at his side. Developed for urban combat, the machine pistol was good for bouncing bullets off of pavement, spraying under cars, that sort of thing, but not a precision weapon. It jammed easily and tended to break when dropped. He'd traded in his midnight blue long coat for black Kevlar body armor and a harness that held a sword on one hip and a western handgun on the other, a desert eagle with pearl handles.

Old Man looked him over. "The slayers are recruiting warlocks now?"

Salem shrugged. "Murder brings odd people together. You want my help or not?"

TWENTY-FOUR

"Best rule I ever learned: shoot first, shoot some more, change clips, ask questions, shoot again."

—Caine Deathwalker

"Okay," I shot a glance down the hall, making sure hostiles weren't popping out to gun me down, "truce, for now, but later we're going to have words about you and your slayer friends being in my territory without observing protocols."

"Yeah, whatever." Salem swung his dangling machine pistol up, holding it braced in both hands. "If there is a later."

"Can we get a move on," Leona called back to us. "The new moon will be in position soon for fueling dark magic. Do we really want Sarah getting stronger?"

I nodded and moved ahead, slipping one of my PPKs into the right shoulder holster, replacing the gun with the one from my right thigh. The substitute weapon had explosive tips and had hollow cores filled with mercury. Regular ammo just leaves big holes. These rounds were better, guaranteed to tear apart torsos and amputate limbs. They wouldn't stop the charge of a two ton golem, or a millennial dragon, but just about anything else would go down and stay down.

We waited in the hall, crouching, balanced on the balls of our feet for quick evasion, while Leona pulled ghost recon on each door we passed. Only after she faded back into view, nodding the all-clear, did we go on. At the last door, we heard chanting, Sarah up to no good.

"Recognize the spell?" I asked Old Man.

He shook his head. “No but I think I caught a reference to elder gods in there.”

The warlock listened intently. He turned dark eyes my way. “A necromantic invocation used to raise the dead.”

“That means zombies.” I growled. “I hate zombies.”

“Me too,” Leona said. “I like my kills fresh, not gamy.”

“Never mind that,” Old Man said. “Leona, ghost inside and create a distraction while we hit the door.”

She faded out while walking through the wall.

The drone of Sarah’s chant seemed to do something to the air, making it glacial heavy. There came a female yelp. The sound of growls and scrambling bodies reached us. I think our leopard might have bitten Angie on the ass. There was a slight pause in the chanting, then it resumed with a brisker pace.

Salem pitched himself through the door, fanning the flaming muzzle of his Uzi around with no attempt to aim at specific targets. I went through right after him, Old Man on my heels. The space was tight for fighting, especially with assorted boxes piled here and there, boxes now stitched with fire from the Uzi. Leona and Angie were tearing into each other, blood and fur flying. The warlock went for the succubus who was still wearing Jessie’s form. Old Man and I charged Sarah who was hemmed in with smoldering braziers to either side. They were filled with red-hot charcoal briquettes, putting tendrils of smoke—like pale dragons—in the air. She clasped her necklace in two hands, standing behind a wooden table where Haruka was tied down, eyes closed, chest rising gently as she stared vacantly in a light trance.

On the floor, stretched parallel to Haruka, lay William’s corpse.

My senses magically enhanced, I was able to keep track of Salem as well as Leona. The warlock dropped an empty clip, reloaded, but then switched over to his desert eagle. I noticed he wore a wristband on his gun hand. The band was platinum, framing a sapphire that pulsed with blue light like a second heart. I wondered if the stone magically increased the accuracy of his shots, or if he just thought it made him look cool. My magic also informed me that all the bad guys were accounted for, with Angie being the last of the wolves.

As I cut toward the right end of the table, Old Man slammed Sarah with a violet-white bolt of lightning. It thinned out as it reached her, briefly making visible the thin, blue shell of a protective barrier. I cut toward the left side of the table, but didn’t quite make it. William’s eyes were open. He’d reached out at werewolf speed, and held my ankles like iron shackles.

Ah, the necromantic spell! Sarah’s brought her Grandfather back from the dead. Doesn’t she know this type of thing always backfires?

I had the gun with explosive rounds lined up on William's right wrist. The gun with silver ammo locked onto his head. I snapped off two shots. The wrist disintegrated in a froth of blood. The silver round made a neat hole in his forehead, a larger hole in the back of his skull. That should have stopped him. It didn't. He flipped over and surged to his feet. Resurrected, he possessed his usual werewolf speed, but none of the silver allergy common to those with lycanthropy.

I fell backwards, my left ankle gripped tightly, held up in the air. The wolf shifted forward, jaws cranking open, bearing white fangs. He used the stub of his right wrist, trying to scrape away the legging of my night suit to expose the underlying flesh.

I tried to warm the tat that controlled my *Dragon Flame*, but pain didn't come, the magic didn't answer. Sarah was chanting again, the texture of her words indicated a different class of magic being used. She was damping out Old Man's magic, and mine too.

I placed an exploding round in William's left wrist, amputating his other hand, while using my free leg to drive a heel into his groin. He bent at the waist, a savage growl vibrating his throat as he drooled. I drove a second kick in, but he twisted his hips, and my kick slid off his thigh. Splattered with his blood, my left leg dropped free. I rolled heel-over-head, gaining distance.

Belatedly, it occurred to me that the zombie had felt pain. Zombies aren't supposed to feel pain. That meant he was something else. If only my magic-enhanced senses weren't back to human levels...

The sound of splintering wood pulled my attention to Old Man. Holding a ripped off table leg, he clubbed at Sarah as she retreated. My attention snapped back to William as his head caught another stray round and became a crimson cloud, bone fragments flying everywhere. That had to have been Salem's Desert Eagle, using large-bore .50 rounds. Packing in twice as much gunpowder makes a bullet fly faster, doing more damage, but sometimes the gun can blow up in your hand, and the stronger recoil can break your wrist if you're not careful. Another drawback is that you're slowed down by having to re-aim after every shot.

The reanimation spell Sarah had used lost its grip on William now he was headless. He went limp, dropping to his knees, then to his chest.

"You owe me one," Salem yelled from across the room.

"In your dreams," I said. "You know that was just an accident."

I heard police sirens wailing closer to the mission. Time was running out. I hoped the slayers and new wolves outside would keep the cops off my back until I was done down here. I also hoped my car was all right. Parking it at the edge of a battle zone might have been less than clever. My insurance doesn't cover werewolves.

The table, missing a leg, still stood between Sarah and me, but not for long. Old Man swung the wooden leg in a blur, a killer storm driving Sarah before him. In a moment, she'd be rounding the head of the table, coming into the open. Not that I was going to wait for that.

I pointed both guns at her.

And went down as Angic and Leona, still locked in furious combat, barreled into the back of my legs. I fell on them and bounced off onto the floor as they rolled on and smashed through a remaining table leg. The table came down on them. They scrambled out from under it and reengaged. Sprawled on the floor, I turned over to get my feet under me. My gaze slid to Haruka, still tied to the table. Her kimono was loose, one nicely formed breast exposed to view. Her head lolled to the side, eyes opened wide.

"Help me!" she cried.

"Working on it," I said.

Old Man no longer swung his club. He'd stopped moving, peering down at his feet in puzzlement. I saw the problem. The wooden floor had been stimulated with earth magic by Sarah. The boards sprouted roots that writhed up Old Man's legs, coiling like pythons, pushing out twigs that bristled with tiny oak leaves.

Old Man sighed. "Always something." He dropped the table leg, using both hands to bend the roots, ripping chunks of them away with demonic strength.

Sarah turned her back on him, running to help the succubus who exuded an air of rampant sexuality that raced my pulse from across the room, but had no effect on the warlock. One-handed, with great relish, he slowly choked the succubus. Her arms hung uselessly at her side. Both looked broken. One had splinters of protruding bone.

She looked ready to sweat blood.

"Sorry," Salem said, "I'm not into women. Too bad you're not an incubus."

She managed to gasp, "Please…"

He said, "You were supposed to wait your turn, and not get in my way. All of us agreed..."

I took a look at her boobs, trying to imagine them from a high, downward angle. Yeah, they were familiar. *The succubus is the woman from the dream Gray showed me.* That meant that there were more enemies waiting in the wings. Nothing was going to end here. I needed to tell Old Man about this. But for now…

On my feet again, I snapped off a shot, sending an explosive round for Sarah's head. My shot hit her protective shield, deflected as easily as Old Man's lightning had been. I figured the short swords strapped to my back would be equally useless. I needed a weapon she couldn't neutralize, one able to carve through her barrier. I holstered my guns and ran at her, calling my demon blade once more. In its sheath, the katana materialized in my right hand.

Salem took a second to help me out, sending several .50 rounds sizzling in to grind against her shield. The rounds didn't get through, but Sarah flinched from them.

This let me close the distance, drawing the blade, slashing at the back of her neck. Her shield struggled with my blade. It was like hacking into over-cooked calamari … with a butter knife. I poured my strength into the effort.

The howling of the sword filled my mind as it strained with me, thirsting for blood and another soul. An aura of dark red mist wreathed the demon blade. Obsidian flames danced along the steel, gripping it in places like dragon claws. Once more, the thin shell of Sarah's barrier shifted into visible light, a haze of electric blue that tinted the sword's red aura into violet. The barrier began to indent under the sword, deforming as the blade progressed by inches. Its hurricane shriek in my thoughts gave me a headache.

"Is that really necessary?" I asked. The howl didn't abate. Long used to pain, I focused through it, my teeth clenched, a growl on my lips.

Sarah faced me now, her necklace in hand, click-clacking into a rounded diamond shape. A haze of red surrounded her. The necklace sprouted black flame as it copied my sword's aura, fighting hellfire with hellfire.

Old Man appeared at my side, Haruka hanging on his arm. His gaze locked onto the necklace. "Break off! It's a soul-sink. Your sword's about to—"

The shield went down and Sarah caught my descending blade with the mechanism on her necklace, risking her fingers. Necklace and katana touched. A blinding flash and deafening boom of thunder erupted. A concussive wave picked me off my feet and threw me backwards. I hit the floor skidding.

And the piercing howl in my head dwindled into an eerie silence passed. Only after she faded back into view, nodding the all-clear, did we go on. At the last door, we heard chanting, Sarah up to no good.

"Recognize the spell?" I asked Old Man.

He shook his head. "No but I think I caught a reference to elder gods in there."

The warlock listened intently. He turned dark eyes my way. "A necromantic invocation used to raise the dead."

"That means zombies." I growled. "I hate zombies."

"Me too," Leona said. "I like my kills fresh, not gamy."

"Never mind that," Old Man said. "Leona, ghost inside and create a distraction while we hit the door."

She faded out while walking through the wall.

The drone of Sarah's chant seemed to do something to the air, making it glacial heavy. There came a female yelp. The sound of growls and scrambling bodies reached us. I think our leopard might have bitten Angie on the ass. There was a slight pause in the chanting, then it resumed with a brisker pace.

Salem pitched himself through the door, fanning the flaming muzzle of his Uzi around with no attempt to aim at specific targets. I went through right after him, Old Man on my heels. The space was tight for fighting, especially with assorted boxes piled here and there, boxes now stitched with fire from the Uzi. Leona and Angie were tearing into each other, blood and fur flying. The warlock went for the succubus who was still wearing Jessie's form. Old Man and I charged Sarah who was hemmed in with smoldering braziers to either side. They were filled with red-hot charcoal briquettes, putting tendrils of smoke—like pale dragons—in the air. She clasped her necklace in two hands, standing behind a wooden table where Haruka was tied down, eyes closed, chest rising gently as she stared vacantly in a light trance.

On the floor, stretched parallel to Haruka, lay William's corpse.

My senses magically enhanced, I was able to keep track of Salem as well as Leona. The warlock dropped an empty clip, reloaded, but then switched over to his desert eagle. I noticed he wore a wristband on his gun hand. The band was platinum, framing a sapphire that pulsed with blue light like a second heart. I wondered if the stone magically increased the accuracy of his shots, or if he just thought it made him look cool. My magic also informed me that all the bad guys were accounted for, with Angie being the last of the wolves.

As I cut toward the right end of the table, Old Man slammed Sarah with a violet-white bolt of lightning. It thinned out as it reached her, briefly making visible the thin, blue shell of a protective barrier. I cut toward the left side of the table, but didn't quite make it. William's eyes were open. He'd reached out at werewolf speed, and held my ankles like iron shackles.

Ah, the necromantic spell! Sarah's brought her Grandfather back from the dead. Doesn't she know this type of thing always backfires?

I had the gun with explosive rounds lined up on William's right wrist. The gun with silver ammo locked onto his head. I snapped off two shots. The wrist disintegrated in a froth of blood. The silver round made a neat hole in his forehead, a larger hole in the back of his skull. That should have stopped him. It didn't. He flipped over and surged to his feet. Resurrected, he possessed his usual werewolf speed, but none of the silver allergy common to those with lycanthropy.

I fell backwards, my left ankle gripped tightly, held up in the air. The wolf shifted forward, jaws cranking open, bearing white fangs. He used the stub of his right wrist, trying to scrape away the legging of my night suit to expose the underlying flesh.

I tried to warm the tat that controlled my *Dragon Flame*, but pain didn't come, the magic didn't answer. Sarah was chanting again, the texture of her words indicated a different class of magic being used. She was damping out Old Man's magic, and mine too.

I placed an exploding round in William's left wrist, amputating his other hand, while using my free leg to drive a heel into his groin. He bent at the waist, a savage growl vibrating his throat as he drooled. I drove a second kick in, but he twisted his hips, and my kick slid off his thigh. Splattered with his blood, my left leg dropped free. I rolled heel-over-head, gaining distance.

Belatedly, it occurred to me that the zombie had felt pain. Zombies aren't supposed to feel pain. That meant he was something else. If only my magic-enhanced senses weren't back to human levels...

The sound of splintering wood pulled my attention to Old Man. Holding a ripped off table leg, he clubbed at Sarah as she retreated. My attention snapped back to William as his head caught another stray round and became a crimson cloud, bone fragments flying everywhere. That had to have been Salem's Desert Eagle, using large-bore .50 rounds. Packing in twice as much gunpowder makes a bullet fly faster, doing more damage, but sometimes the gun can blow up in your hand, and the stronger recoil can break your wrist if you're not careful. Another drawback is that you're slowed down by having to re-aim after every shot.

The reanimation spell Sarah had used lost its grip on William now he was headless. He went limp, dropping to his knees, then to his chest.

"You owe me one," Salem yelled from across the room.

"In your dreams," I said. "You know that was just an accident."

I heard police sirens wailing closer to the mission. Time was running out. I hoped the slayers and new wolves outside would keep the cops off my back until I was done down here. I also hoped my car was all right. Parking it at the edge of a battle zone might have been less than clever. My insurance doesn't cover werewolves.

The table, missing a leg, still stood between Sarah and me, but not for long. Old Man swung the wooden leg in a blur, a killer storm driving Sarah before him. In a moment, she'd be rounding the head of the table, coming into the open. Not that I was going to wait for that.

I pointed both guns at her.

And went down as Angie and Leona, still locked in furious combat, barreled into the back of my legs. I fell on them and bounced off onto the floor as they rolled on and smashed through a remaining table leg. The table came down on them. They scrambled out from under it and reengaged. Sprawled on the floor, I turned over to get my feet under me. My gaze slid to Haruka, still tied to the table. Her kimono was loose, one nicely formed breast exposed to view. Her head lolled to the side, eyes opened wide.

"Help me!" she cried.

"Working on it," I said.

Old Man no longer swung his club. He'd stopped moving, peering down at his feet in puzzlement. I saw the problem. The wooden floor had been stimulated with earth magic by Sarah. The boards sprouted roots that writhed up Old Man's legs, coiling like pythons, pushing out twigs that bristled with tiny oak leaves.

Old Man sighed. "Always something." He dropped the table leg, using both hands to bend the roots, ripping chunks of them away with demonic strength.

Sarah turned her back on him, running to help the succubus who exuded an air of rampant sexuality that raced my pulse from across the room, but had no effect on the warlock. One-handed, with great relish, he slowly choked the succubus. Her arms hung uselessly at her side. Both looked broken. One had splinters of protruding bone.

She looked ready to sweat blood.

"Sorry," Salem said, "I'm not into women. Too bad you're not an incubus."

She managed to gasp, "Please…"

He said, "You were supposed to wait your turn, and not get in my way. All of us agreed..."

I took a look at her boobs, trying to imagine them from a high, downward angle. Yeah, they were familiar. *The succubus is the woman from the dream Gray showed me.* That meant that there were more enemies waiting in the wings. Nothing was going to end here. I needed to tell Old Man about this. But for now…

On my feet again, I snapped off a shot, sending an explosive round for Sarah's head. My shot hit her protective shield, deflected as easily as Old Man's lightning had been. I figured the short swords strapped to my back would be equally useless. I needed a weapon she couldn't neutralize, one able to carve through her barrier. I holstered my guns and ran at her, calling my demon blade once more. In its sheath, the katana materialized in my right hand.

Salem took a second to help me out, sending several .50 rounds sizzling in to grind against her shield. The rounds didn't get through, but Sarah flinched from them.

This let me close the distance, drawing the blade, slashing at the back of her neck. Her shield struggled with my blade. It was like hacking into over-cooked calamari … with a butter knife. I poured my strength into the effort.

The howling of the sword filled my mind as it strained with me, thirsting for blood and another soul. An aura of dark red mist wreathed the demon blade. Obsidian flames danced along the steel, gripping it in places like dragon claws. Once more, the thin shell of Sarah's barrier shifted into visible light, a haze of electric blue that tinted the sword's red aura into violet. The barrier began to indent under the sword, deforming as the blade progressed by inches. Its hurricane shriek in my thoughts gave me a headache.

"Is that really necessary?" I asked. The howl didn't abate. Long used to pain, I focused through it, my teeth clenched, a growl on my lips.

Sarah faced me now, her necklace in hand, click-clacking into a rounded diamond shape. A haze of red surrounded her. The necklace sprouted black flame as it copied my sword's aura, fighting hellfire with hellfire.

Old Man appeared at my side, Haruka hanging on his arm. His gaze locked onto the necklace. "Break off! It's a soul-sink. Your sword's about to—"

The shield went down and Sarah caught my descending blade with the mechanism on her necklace, risking her fingers. Necklace and katana touched. A blinding flash and deafening boom of thunder erupted. A concussive wave picked me off my feet and threw me backwards. I hit the floor skidding.

And the piercing howl in my head dwindled into an eerie silence.

TWENTY-FIVE

"I understand what you want, it's just that I am prepared not to care."

—Caine Deathwalker

I held my katana in both hands. The steel was as strong as ever, but the sword had been broken, no, that wasn't quite right. The sword had been eaten alive. The souls it had feasted on and its own demonic soul had drained into Sarah's necklace. I tried to will it back to my armory, but the blade remained. Empty. Powerless. Just another sword. My eyes misted, but manfully, I refused to cry.

Old Man rumbled. "What matters is stopping her." He held out his palm, purple lightning haloing his fingers as ragged jags of fire spun away, falling against Sarah's shield. The energy burnt the air, making her shield visible around the contact point. As streamers of lightning curved around the barrier, all of it came into view. The fire play became blinding as Old Man poured more strength into the attack. Inside her shield, Sarah could no longer be seen.

Haruka's gaze was forced away from the struggle. She noticed Salem gripping her friend "Jessie" by the throat, in the act of murdering her.

Pleading in her eyes, the succubus locked stares with Haruka.

Haruka broke away from Old Man, running to help her friend.

I was on my feet, the soulless katana abandoned on the floor as I ran flat out to intercept Haruka.

Salem backhanded her as she arrived. Her head rocked viciously. She went down hard, not even trying to break her fall.

Ignored by the warlock for the moment, the mask of defeat on the succubus' face slipped. Her lips curled into a tight smile of victory. Her eyes went hot-coal red as a silver shimmer seeped from her skin, followed by a concussive blast of light that slammed Salem away.

"Jessie" burned away as her true form emerged. Her broken arms mended in a moment as she shifted, sporting cute little devil horns—one inch protrusions of white bone—on her forehead. Her hair became a cloud of midnight black, her eyes red-violet stars. Dainty, black, bat wings sprouted from her back. Her hands became long-nailed claws tinted with crimson polish, and her figure acquired even more dangerous curves. Her breasts swelled, bouncing on her chest with no regard for gravity at all as her pointy tail lashed the air.

Her amped up aura of rampant sexuality stopped me mid-step, pouring molten desire into my veins. I wanted her. I needed her. I needed her naked under me. *Now!*

My protective shield snapped on, and I could suddenly do more than stand there like an idiot and drool—I had my guns in hand, locking muzzles onto her face.

But Salem hadn't been idle; from the floor, he reached back toward the battle between Old Man and Sarah. Great ribbons of lightning leapt from Sarah's shield to Salem's hand, deflecting up from there, burning a path through the spot the succubus had occupied. Scooping to gather up Haruka, the succubus had inadvertently saved herself.

I held my fire, having to be careful with my shots so I wouldn't hit the client I was supposed to protect.

Salem redirected the stolen lash of lighting at the two women.

I swung a gun toward his head. "Cut it out." I ordered.

Instead of obeying, he sent ribbons of fire sizzling my way, splashing against my shield.

This let the succubus spring into the air, skimming just under the ceiling, heading for the door.

Salem's lash caught them, coiling around their flesh. They screamed and crashed to the floor, smoking. The lightning thinned away. Old Man had broken off the attack on Sarah, so there was no loose energy for Salem to steal.

Old Man ran for Haruka.

Sarah relaxed for a split second as she found herself neglected on the battlefield. Big mistake; one of William's severed hands scurried under her shield and grabbed her ankle. Startled, she hopped around, shaking one leg in the air. She fell and her necklace pitched away from her, rattling across the concrete floor. The chain settled over the second severed hand which jerked up on fingertips in surprise, scuttling off, dragging the necklace with it. From the rapid collapse of its shape, and the various combinations it sequenced through, the amulet acted like it was in a state of shock.

I ran for the necklace.

Salem did the same.

We exchanged shots, fanning each other's faces with the vapor trails of our slugs. The stupid hand lurched toward

Salem, letting him claim the prize as I stopped to empty both clips at him with greater accuracy. Unfortunately, a protective shield surrounded him as he gripped the necklace. My shots were deflected. He grinned at me like the cat that swallowed the proverbial canary.

I grew aware of an odd silence in the background. The squalling and growling from Leona and Angie had ended. Exactly when, I didn't know. I sent a quick, appraising glance across the room and saw the ladies side by side, sitting against some boxes. They were covered in blood, drooping with exhaustion, having declared a ceasefire.

Hmmm. Angie's tougher than I'd thought.

I returned my stare to Salem, expecting renewed aggression. What I didn't expect was Sarah, back on her feet, slinging herself at him, and bouncing off his barrier with a grimace of pain.

Hah! That will teach you.

In Salem's hand, the necklace shuddered through another change, becoming three pronged. The space inside his shield became a muddy blue swirl of light, hazing his body into a two dimensional silhouette. The blue brightened to a neon hue, casting off a coronal wash that burnt the air, producing ozone.

The barrier collapsed like a dying star, dwindling to a pin-prick in the air before winking out.

We all stared at empty space. Salem had taken his prize and escaped.

I put my guns away as Old Man came over. "We've got to go," he said. "There's nothing left here to be gained."

I nodded and walked to my soulless katana, picking it up. Blade in hand, I turned toward Sarah, remembering a little dragon girl and her murdered mother. "Still one piece of business to take care of," I said.

"No!" Angie was on her feet, running awkwardly to intercept me.

Old Man said, "No one's paying us to kill Sarah."

I paused. "Every now and then, I balance the books with a little righteous judgment."

Old Man slapped the back of my head. "Are you a middle schooler, or the heir to a demon clan?"

I glared at him. "You know she's got this coming, and a lot more besides."

Angie skidded to a stop between me and Sarah.

"She's all that's left of my pack," Angie said. "I owe it to William to protect her."

"Protecting her is what got William and the others dead," I said.

She flinched from my words, but didn't move out of the way.

"Killing two isn't much harder than killing one," I said.

A solidifying black mist, Leona faded into view. The leopard stood between me and Angie, giving me one more person to go through.

I rolled my eyes. "Fine, another day then." I slid the katana through a harness strap to free up my hands.

Angie stayed between me and Sarah, moving her toward the door. Leona saw them off, and waited at the doorway for Old Man and me. He crossed to her. I followed, pausing to gather up Haruka's body, beautiful even in death. Cradling her against me, I left the room with a last glance behind. William's headless body was sitting up. His severed head lay on one ear, facing me, eyes open and ablaze with hate, lips mouthing curses. The amputated hands were still scuttling around the room, bumping into things, blindly searching for William's body in hope of reattachment.

This whole fucked-sideways mission is going to haunt me for years.

Out in the hall, Old Man took Haruka from me, gently draping her over a shoulder like a garment bag.

"Better get the cleaners in here to sanitize," I said.

He nodded. "I'll call them from the car."

We hurried down the hall to the steps. Leona led us up to the kitchen. We stepped out and stopped, taking in a fresh scene of horror. The corpses that had been at peace, were now straddling the border between life and death. Not fully reanimated, muscles twitched and spasmed. Nerves fired incoherent impulses. Dead eyes were empty of emotion. Teeth gnashed. Arms and legs flailed without coordination, like fish out of water.

"What the hell!" Leona said.

"Sarah's spell, when she brought William back," I said. "I think her range was wider than she knew."

"She overpowered the spell," Old Man said, "no finesse. Must have learned spell-crafting from *Necromancy for Dummies*."

"Always wanted to read that book." I kicked away a homeless-dude corpse that flopped too close.

We heard the sounds of large trucks pulling into the side parking lot. The *whump-whump* of a helicopter came seconds later. Sirens were screaming closer.

"We don't want to get caught around all this carnage," I said.

"Your problem, not mine." Leona faded from sight, going ghost on us.

Old Man and I used mincing steps, and a few jumps to clear the half-assed zombies writhing on the floor. We reached an exit and stepped out into the night. Nothing unnatural was stirring anymore. The grounds were littered with new wolves. Many had been hacked to pieces. Many were beheaded. A lot were human once more with bullets riddling them. The wounds were edged in black, a sign of silver poisoning. The Slayers were gone too, taking their fallen with them.

Neat. I like that.

I studied two parked eighteen wheelers disgorging federal marshals and soldiers with automatic weapons. There were tech guys in white lab coats toting laptops, and equipment I didn't recognize. A man-in-black wore leather gloves and an infrared visor, snapping out orders. A police helicopter buzzed them, a spotlight stabbing down on the red vehicles. A radio message was sent from the ground troops and the chopper withdrew. I didn't need to see the plates on the trucks to know they were government.

I said, "PRT, Old Man."

He nodded. "Preternatural Response Team. They must have known something like this was going to break out. They're here way too fast. Guess I won't have to call the cleaners after all."

"They might have followed the Slayers into town," I said. "Hey, stay close. I'm going to use my *Demon Wings* to keep everyone's attention off us so we can get the car."

"Worth a try," Old Man said. "Just remember that the PRT employs magic-users, and some of them are top-grade seers."

"I know. I've run into these guys before." I thought of Cassie back in east Texas, and smiled. *There's a girl that can nail me any time—but not with live ammo.*

The tats on my upper back and shoulders warmed. The ink felt like it had turned to acid and was eating into the muscle. The pain grew in intensity as I extended the magic to cover more than my own skin. Old Man helped reduce the strain on me by going all shadow, loosing distinction and color. His camouflage extended to Haruka, still draped over his shoulder. Shadow blanketed her, stealing color and definition.

Half the soldiers were setting up a perimeter, turning away the cops that were hitting the scene. The feds would make sure all this went quietly away, our tax dollars at work. The rest of the soldiers and a few geeks in white coats nosed across the battlefield, piecing together what had happened.

Old Man followed me as I moved away from the church. Keeping a leisurely pace, we skirted the PRT personnel. I wasn't worried about the normal humans, but running steps might have drawn attention from anyone with heightened senses or unnatural gifts.

Several of the fallen wolves were hauled off to the trucks for quick field autopsies. I heard the black suit order a cleanup of the spent rounds. A guy with a laptop paused to pull a knife out of a fallen wolf. The hilt had the black rose and sword crest of the slayers. The tech dude carried his find to the black suit, as a woman with green hair walked up. I had the feeling the green was her natural color, not a dye job.

As Old Man and I passed the three, she looked up, straight at me.

I put a finger to my lips—the international symbol for shut-the-hell-up-and-stay-that-way.

A smile turned up one corner of her lips. She turned her attention away. Clearly, her loyalty was divided, but that was to be expected; she smelled fey. A fey really only has *one* side—their own.

We got out into the street, and passed some cops bitching about the feds having pulled jurisdiction on them. Wouldn't be long before the news crews arrived and the meat wagons. They'd need several for this mess. The whole thing would probably go down officially as a gang war. This was L.A., after all.

Old Man put Haruka's scorched body in the trunk, then we piled into my car. Leona was in the backseat, waiting. Her window was down, her face sticking out. "Great way to keep a low profile," I groused. "What if someone had seen you?"

"I'd have killed them, what do you think?"

"Oh, well," I said, "as long as you had a plan."

Old Man shot me an evaluating look. "Caine?"

"Yeah?" Going through the usual routine to disable the security system, I started the engine.

"Can you hold the whole vehicle in your spell? We really don't want to draw notice leaving here."

"For a short time, yeah, but even I have limits."

"You're admitting that?" Leona said.

"Yeah, I learned a long time ago; lie to anyone, but not yourself. That can get you killed."

I sent the car cruising slowly past various vehicles. We soon reached the highway, and headed for home.

TWENTY-SIX

"I hate dead clients. You don't get paid for those."

—Caine Deathwalker

We pulled into the garage. The opener closed the door, sealing us in from the night. The automatic locks engaged. We bailed from the mustang. Leona ghosted away, going about her business. I opened the trunk and pulled out Haruka's body, hefting it over my shoulder. Rigor mortis had yet to set in. The eyes weren't clouded. She might have been deeply asleep, awaiting a prince charming.

There was a thin chance I could still make that happen. A very thin chance. The grimoire necklace had resurrected William to the degree that even now, his body parts struggled to live after his second death. If I could get the necklace from Salem and use it on Haruka, then maybe I could still collect my fee. I certainly needed a new demon sword. I handed my old one to the Old Man.

"Here, do something with this."

He took the soulless blade, back in its sheath, and headed for the kitchen door. "I'll hang it over the fire place. What a night. I think I'll see how many drinks it will take to drop me on my posterior region."

"Hell of a good idea," I said.

Old Man paused in the kitchen doorway, looking back at me as I went to the big double wide freezer in the corner of the garage. *Too bad Izumi's not here. Haruka would be better off flash frozen.* I opened the lid and settled Haruka inside. This wasn't the first time I'd used it to store a body for later disposal. I closed the lid and caught up to Old Man.

"Hiro's still here," I said. "You're going to explain things to him?"
"He's my friend, so yes, I'll do it. What's your next plan, after getting drunk of course?"
"Don't give him the body. I need it."
"I know you have aberrant sexual needs, Caine, but…"
"I hardly ever do that anymore. Anyway, that's not why I need her. I think I can bring her back, better than a zombie." I passed through the kitchen, heading for the living room.
Old Man stayed a step behind. "Full resurrection? The necklace?"
"Yeah. No matter what he says, keep Haruka here on ice. I'm her only chance."
"Sadly, I agree. Very well. I'll try to make Hiro understand that all is not lost."
From the living room, he headed for the office. I took the hall to my room. Once there, I stripped off my gear and hung everything on the martial arts manikin. His rubber face was blank. No recrimination there. I knew when I showed up in the bar, Hiro's face wouldn't be so restrained. I went to the other side of my bed and activated the stored magic of the full-length mirror. Naked, I stepped through, emerging in my armory under the bar.
Regular gear hadn't been enough. With Salem powered up, I needed a hell of a lot more before taking him on. I went to the work area where I had some new gear I'd been working on: a light Kevlar battle suit with woven tungsten fibers and small pieces of plaiting over vital areas. The thing was matte black with a harness over it that contained PPKs, various grenades, a combat knife, and short swords in back where they could be easily reached. I'd been soaking the new armor in eldritch energy for months now. I hoped the suit could withstand the worse of Salem's magic and let me use mine—at least long enough to take the warlock out. This was my zombie apocalypse suit. I'd been saving it for the end of the world.
This next battle was close enough.
I put the suit on and grabbed a bag with equipment for fine-tuning my guns. The elevator returned me to the first floor. I stepped out behind the bar and started to make myself a few drinks. I watched Old Man over by the fireplace, trying to calm Hiro down, and doing a poor job at it. Understandable considering his only daughter was chillin' in my garage freezer. Finishing the manufacture of Margaritas, I lined them up on the bar next to my bag, and opened the drawstring mouth. I drew out several clip-on laser sights. Two PPKs went on the bar as well. I clipped the sights to the undersides of the barrels.
Panning the guns at the empty end of the room, I checked out the sights. They threw out thin red beams across the windows. I changed a

few things inside the PPKs to make them full-auto. The clips would empty in a single burst unless I lightly tapped the trigger for single shots. I also changed out the regular clips for 24 round banana clips. *Perfect. Now for the other two guns.* As I worked, I listened to the Old Man.

"Yes, she's dead, for now, but Caine has a plan."

"Did he not have a plan the last time?" Hiro asked.

Everyone's so picky.

"Well, yes, but he does get the job done when pushed this far toward vengeance. It's his only redeeming trait," Old Man said.

Wow, a complement and a backhanded at the same time.

"Lauphram, she's dead. My daughter is dead. I just want to take her and give her the honorable burial she deserves."

My fingers worked automatically as I sneered. *What she deserved was freedom to learn how to protect herself. And giving her a .38 special wouldn't have hurt*

Old Man laid a hand on Hiro's shoulder. "Please calm down. We will bring her back to you, alive. I give you my word of honor."

Old Man was putting a lot on the line; the head of the clan saying something like that meant failure would come with a heavy price. He rose from his chair, walked over to me, and stole two of the drinks I'd made. Without a word, he returned to Hiro and gave him one.

Hiro took the glass, and looked up at Old Man with the eyes of a child doubting consolation, the tooth fairy, and Santa Claus all at once.

Old Man smiled and patted Hiro on the head, like that small gesture fixed everything wrong in the world.

I remember Old Man doing that to me when I was hurt, or going nuts, killing everything around me. That head pat had done more for me than any spell could have.

Old Man said, "The warlock has an amulet that can bring Haruka back with no problem. We are keeping her body safe—and cold—to prevent further damage."

"If you bring life back to her, will she be the same as before?" Hiro asked. "I have heard stories that things like this never go well."

Old Man shrugged. "Well, since we're not depending on the Necronomicom, it should all work out, somehow."

I was suddenly aware that Leona had faded in, taking one of the stools at the end of the bar, watching Hiro and Old Man like I was.

Old Man said, "Caine is my son. I trust him to get this done, Hiro. He may be a lot of things, but a pushover isn't one of them. If that were true, my training would have killed him long ago."

True.

Hiro drained his glass in a gulp.

I put my fine-tuned weapons onto my harness and went about throwing back a drink of my own.

I was already making more when Old Man came over to grab refills. He waited as I mixed them, eyes boring into my skull. I saw how much this meant to him, giving his word of honor, comforting Hiro, even giving me a half-assed complement. If I was a better person, I'd have cared about Hiro's pain, but being me, I just wanted payback from the warlock bastard—that, a new sword, and having a fine hottie like Haruka grateful to me was all that mattered.

"I need you to do me a couple favors," Old Man said.

"Depends on the favors," I said.

"Bring the long mirror from the armory up here and put it by the fireplace."

"Why."

"Just do it. And one more thing…" He extended a finger across the bar and touched the Kevlar I wore. Over my heart, a storm-blue shimmer of dancing motes appeared. The mystic light died a moment later, leaving an addition to my armor. I looked down at a self-adhering disk against my chest. It was a three-and-a-half inch mirror framed by polished, white jade.

I looked back up into Old Man's eyes. "What's this, some kind of protective talisman?"

"Better," he said. "You'll see."

Leona snorted. "That old mirror trick of yours? I haven't seen it in years. Are you sure it will work?"

"One can always hope." Old Man took the new drinks I made and went back to Hiro.

I was getting damn tired of people treating me like their personal bartender. I threw back another drink and went to fetch him the mirror he'd asked for. I hauled it back upstairs, out from behind the bar, and set it up across the room.

Hiro eyed the glass with quiet calculation.

Old Man nodded approval and brought his hands together in front of him. His fingers curled as if he were holding an invisible sword. Electric blue light shot up five feet into the air. The light took on the shape of a broadsword, then the light snapped out, leaving a real sword in its place. The thing had a blue pearl the size of a golf ball on the pommel. The hand guard was a stylized squid with a ruby for an eye. The iron tentacles curved around the grip to create a protective basket for the fingers. The blade was wide, possessed a blood groove, and was made of white coral etched with ancient Atlantean runes.

The relic was Old Man's personal sword. When I took over the clan, it would become mine. My hand itched to hold the coral weapon and learn its many secrets.

Old Man told Hiro, "We, too, will have a part to play, but we must wait for the right time."

Hiro crossed his arms protectively across his chest, staring at his image in the looking glass. "How will we know when it is time?"

Old Man smiled. "That is what the mirror is for. Watch."

He touched the frame of the mirror, caressing certain runes in a pattern I'd not used before. I memorized the sequence. My own gaze was pulled to the glass. Instead of reflecting what was before it, the glass became rimmed with an aqua light. Both Old Man and Hiro appeared in the glass as seen from my perspective. Their images rippled as if caught by a pond, not a mirror. I waved my fingers across the little mirror on my chest. Magnified tremendously, my fingers blurred across the larger mirror. The mirror I wore had become a vid camera and the larger mirror was displaying what I saw.

Hiro's eyes widened in surprise.

Old Man told him, "You will see the coming battle with your own eyes. You will see the efforts Caine makes on your behalf."

"It's not enough," Hiro said. "When your son goes into battle, I want him to take a force of my own men with him. They, too, failed to keep my daughter safe, and burn with the need to atone."

"They'll just get themselves killed." I said. "And get in my way."

Uncrossing his arms, Hiro faced Old Man, "Is it too much to ask, old friend?"

Thrilled by my irritation, Old Man shot me an amused glance. "Not at all. Your security force is welcome to tag along."

I shrugged. It *would* give Salem more red shirts to kill and give me time to cut through his defenses once we found him. "Fine," I said. "I'll take your cannon fodder along."

"You obey me with so little grace." Old Man sighed, and returned his attention to Hiro. "See what I have to deal with? Be glad you have a good kid."

Hiro said, "The moment I get her back, I will let her know how proud I've always been."

I returned to the bar and threw back the last of the drinks. Grabbing the bag, I took out the last items I needed, extra thin leather gloves. They'd leave no prints and not interfere with my dexterity. I checked my suit's forearm guards, pressing the releases one at a time to make sure the spring powered bayonets were working. They *snicked*, and seven inch blades popped out. Pressing the tips against the side of the bar, I pushed them back in until they locked in place again. I had to be careful. The suit wasn't field tested. It would be embarrassing if the mechanism lost its grip on the extending blade and I wound up stabbing myself in the foot … again.

“That’s nifty,” Leona said from her barstool. “Fake claws.” She raised a paw and showed me hers. “I like mine better though.”

Old Man’s cell phone went off, playing the Black-eyed Peas’ *My Humps*.

I looked at him.

Hiro looked at him.

Leona choked, laughing too hard.

“What?” Old Man said. “I like the song.” He answered the call, listened, and said “I’ll tell him.”

“Who’s that?” I asked.

“Albino John at the *Aes Sídhe*. He says he has information you’ll want to pay him for.”

“A little too late,” I said. “The warlock’s the problem now, not the succubus.”

“Old Man listened some more, nodded, and hung up. “Go talk to him. He says there are slayers at the club, ones he’s seen with a certain warlock we want to find.”

I smiled. “I’m on my way.” I looked at Hiro. “Have your men meet me there. I want to see how they handle themselves.”

“Going to destroy another nightclub?” Leona asked.

“Hey,” I said, “it’s what I do.”

TWENTY-SEVEN

***"Don't believe what they say;
violence solves everything."***

—Caine Deathwalker

The line outside of *Aes Sidhe* was shorter, conspicuously lacking preternaturals. The usual bouncer had been replaced by two slayers with black Kevlar armor under their long coats. Each chest plate bore a fancy crest; a bleeding, black rose with a sword superimposed over it. The aura of fey magic around the nightclub had been replaced with one of earth magic.

As I walked past the line people hoping to get in, the slayers gave me a once over, studying what they could of the zombie apocalypse suit under my own long coat. If I'd had a crest on my chest instead of what looked like a compact mirror, they'd have assumed I was one of them.

"I need to see Albino John about a warlock," I said.

The bouncer on the left blocked me with a palm. "Wait in line, freak."

The bouncer on the right waved on a couple at the head of the line.

I took half a step back and kicked the first man in the jewels. He gasped, wheezed, and bent at the waist. His cheeks flushed, puffing out.

His partner lunged at me.

I used the heel of my hand to shunt his elbow as he threw a punch. This made his fist miss my head. As his fist hung over my left shoulder, I used a *leopard paw* strike against his throat, cutting off his air. He dropped to his knees, choking. Mercifully, I slammed their heads together and they collapsed to the pavement, unconscious.

Mesmerized by the sudden violence, those at the head of the line stared at me.

I stared back. "I really hate waiting in line."

I stepped over the slayers and stopped on the threshold. It was new. In the center was an ancient Hebrew symbol, the circles of Solomon. Had I been a true demon, I would have been stopped here. As it was, I crossed over with a smile in place. *Screw you, Solomon.*

Inside the club, the festivities were going more full-throttle than usual. Scantily clad women hung from the ceiling on wide bands of silk, doing routines more common to Las Vegas. The slayers were everywhere, in battle gear, many of them baring wounds they'd taken from the wolves at the Mission. The fey bartenders and waitresses were gone, replaced by biker chicks that looked like they could handle a lot more than drinks. Anything fey had been stripped from the walls. The slayers had moved in and the placed had become *human only.*

Either Albino John had been pressed into service during the on-going transition, or he'd traded masters. Either way, he'd probably not called me on his own. Chances were good I was walking into a trap, despite the attitude I'd been met with at the front door.

I pushed through the human crowd to reach the back hallway. The black door past the restrooms drew my eyes. Two slayers guarded it. They wore headsets, muttering into them as I approached. I stopped in front of them. "Do I have to go through you guys too?" I asked.

The one on the left spoke, "We've been told to let you through."

"Someone around here has some common sense," I said.

They moved aside, opening the black door. I went through, up a flight of steps, and kicked in the upstairs door to the office. When no gunfire sprayed out the door, I cautiously took a fast peek. No goons were waiting to unload. There were several slayers seated inside near the wall of one-way glass. Behind the office desk, Albino John had his feet up, his hands laced behind his neck as he leaned back in his leather chair. A lit cigar occupied one corner of his mouth, a curl of blue smoke spiraling up from the end.

I strolled into the office, my guns holstered.

Albino John's eyes stabbed like a stiletto of hate, the effect somewhat diminished by being red and teary. His nose looked inflamed. This time, there were no lines of coke on the desk, waiting to be inhaled. John flashed a vicious smile. "About time you got here. These gentlemen want to have a discussion with you."

I stopped where I could see everyone in the room.

There was a click. I tensed but didn't go for my gun since no one else was in motion. Slowly, John brought his hands into view. One of them held a remote control. I heard a hum. Directing my attention, John pointed the remote at the ceiling where the hum came from. I glanced up. *A black light lamp?*

I looked down at the carpet. Ultraviolet paint now glowed neon green around all around me—the seal of Solomon; four concentric rings surrounding the Star of David, scribbling all over it.

I laughed, and shook my head sadly.

Near the one-way glass that overlooked the dance floor, one of the slayers stood, kicking over his chair. "What's your problem?"

I pointed at the phosphorescence on the carpet. "You guys actually expect that to work?"

Another slayer made a restraining motion toward him. That second man had steel gray hair, a clean shaven face, and green-slate eyes that peered at me, one brow lifting. He was the oldest. An aura of strength seeped from him, a feeling of earth magic. I smelled freshly turned earth, and dew-dampened foliage from him, the residue of the plant's life force. It had touched him many times. Of the slayers, he was openly unarmed, as if mundane weapons couldn't threaten him. This was no one to take lightly.

Next to him, also seated, was a female slayer in black leather. Her hair was midnight black, her eyes dead black. Her skin was bleached white, her nails crimson and long. A sawed-off shotgun lay on a loveseat next to her. She smiled at me, flashing a bit of fang. I noticed her gaze dropping to the little mirror on my chest, her brow furrowing in puzzlement.

Vampire? Keeping company with slayers?

The leader of the slayers asked, "Are you not a demon, son of Lauphram?"

I said, "Actually, no. He's my adopted father."

The leader nodded. "I see." His gaze slashed across the room to Albino John. "We were misinformed."

John slid his feet off the desk, sitting up. "I didn't know, Carson, honest."

"You should have." Carson switched his attention back to me. It didn't seem to bother him I had a psychological advantage, peering down at him. "Caine, we've come looking for Sarah Cooper. She was one of us, for a while, a slayer in training. She took a relic from our vaults, something dangerous."

"Very dangerous," the woman said.

"I know," I said. "I've faced the power of the necklace several times now."

"And you're still alive?" the standing slayer said.

"Apparently," I stared at the woman, "though looks can be deceiving."

I was fishing for an explanation and she knew it. She said, "I look vampire but I'm not."

But not human either. I nodded in sudden understanding. "A dhampyr; your mother was human, your father a vampire."

"Right," she said. Her gaze flicked to the mirror again. She couldn't figure out why the thing was featured so prominently on a battle suit. She had no way to know that Hiro and Old Man were keeping tabs on me.

Carson spoke up, "My granddaughter is human enough to be a slayer, and vampire enough to be one of our best."

She stared through me. "What about you? Are you anything other than a traitor to your race?"

Briefly, I indulged a fantasy where I killed every male in the room, stripped the girl, and spanked her into submission. I shook off the vision, reminding myself I had business to conduct here.

"We want Sarah," Carson said, "and the necklace."

"Don't you already have the necklace?" I asked. "Salem was working for you guys, right?"

"He has it?" the woman said.

I said, "Yeah, until I find him and rip his spleen out, along with a few other internal organs."

The slayers looked at each other, an uneasy tension gripping them.

"Betrayed again?" I said. "Hard to get good help."

The woman scooped up her shotgun and stood. "That black-hearted bastard. I'll kill him!"

"You know where to find him?" I asked.

"I have a good idea," she said.

"Can I come," I asked. "After all, you're engaged in operations within my territory."

"Hell, no," Vivian said.

The unnamed male slayer glared my way. "This is slayer business."

I shrugged. "Well I could just kill you all and be done with it, after I make you talk of course."

My protective tattoo burned, activating against a sudden attack. Motion at the edge of sight drew my attention to the source of the threat. Albino John stood with a nasty grin on his face and a shotgun in his hand. Gilded runes were inset on the barrel. I didn't need to take a chance, and it was time to leave anyway, so I activated the tatts on my legs—knowing I'd pay the cost for vampire speed an hour from now.

I ran straight at Vivian.

Afraid he'd hit her, John held his shot.

With dhampyr speed, Vivian swung the butt of her shotgun at my head as I closed with her. She underestimated my speed.

I ducked under her swing, speared a shoulder into her midsection, and lifted her off her feet. Together, we sailed through the one-way glass. It shattered around us and the noise of the bar hit us like a wall. We dropped in a rain of razor shards, and I made sure the dhampyr hit first, cushioning my fall for me. The impact knocked her out. I checked for vital signs. Her breathing was strong. Takes almost as much to stop a dhampyr as a full vampire. That was good. As a hostage, she'd get me out of here, and after I interrogated her, I'd know where Salem was. Overall, things were looking up for a change.

The crowd, sprinkled with broken glass, screamed and roared in confusion. A general stampede from my location began, which made it easy to spot the four slayers running flat out for me, against the press of the crowd.

I pulled Vivian up and over my shoulder, her head hanging in front of me, not behind as was usually done. I had a PPK with laser sight in my hand, the muzzle against Vivian's head.

The slayers broke free of the retreating crowd, but stopped dead. They knew if they got their leader's granddaughter killed, they'd soon be dead as well, or worse. One of the slayers whipped out a Glock 23, the official service pistol of many FBI agents and other law enforcement agencies. He barked a command, "Put her down, now!"

Yeah, I'm going to make myself a target so you can blow me away. I don't think so.

"I'm leaving," I said. "Try anything and she dies."

"Wait," another slayer holstered his colt .45 and pushed down the Glock that was aimed at my head. "Take me instead. I'm on my feet. She's not. Make it easier on yourself."

"I'm heading for the door," I said. "If I take any heat, she takes a bullet to the skull. Understand?"

Another slayers said, "We understand. There will be no trouble. Just leave her outside on the curb, and we won't follow."

Like I believe that.

I smiled. "Sure, I'll do that," I lied.

The slayers in the room provided crowd control, holding the civilians back so I had an open corridor to the front door. I faced the room, moving sideways for the door, my back to the bar and the bartenders. I figured one of them would try something, but I counted on my protective shield to handle it. I was halfway to the door when something shattered against my shield, from the sound, a bottle. I spun and tapped the trigger for a single round. My slug hit the bar-bitches' shoulder. I spun back around to see all the slayers in the room pointing their weapons my way. However, having seen my protective shield in action, they didn't waste their ammo.

Things were going too good to last. I sensed disaster breathing down my neck. Hiro's men burst into the bar, blocking my escape route. They bristled with guns, every last one of them in black suit and tie, with sunglasses in place. It looked like a men-in-black convention. They ducked for cover, as the slayers opened up on them, screaming, "It's the Yakuza!"

TWENTY-EIGHT

"The purpose of a human shield is to keep one's armor from getting dirty. This doesn't always work."

—Caine Deathwalker

The band played a metal cover of *Barroom Blitz* as the crowd screamed and ran for the back exits. The Slayers held their fire through the exodus, turning over tables to use as shields. I started to move with the human herd, taking advantage of their cover, but several of Hiro's men raced up and surrounded me in an attempt to provide protection.

I shoved out from between two of my protectors, carefully balancing Vivian on my shoulder. As I ran, more of Hiro's men followed, firing wildly to keep slayers ducking so they couldn't shoot back. I felt my shield flicker, as if undecided about turning on, and was driven to my knees as someone landed on me. I rolled. Vivian slid off my shoulder and sprawled, groaning, her eyelids fluttering. Next to her was a scantily-clad young blonde with way too much makeup, one of the acrobat-dancers from off a dangling silk ribbon. She'd picked a hell of a time to lose her grip, probably panicked by the gunfire.

I understood why my shield hadn't activated; nearly naked woman throwing themselves at me was a common fantasy, not what I'd consider a danger.

I pushed to my feet and reached for Vivian once more. As I touched her, bringing her inside my shield's usual activation range, she lunged up, wrapping around my leg like a dog in heat.

"Come on," I said, "we really don't have time for this."

She sank her fangs into my thigh and held on for dear life. The suit

I wore would have stopped a slug, but her vampire fangs pierced the material, sliding between the tungsten fibers.

I cursed, "Son of a … bat!"

One of my protectors fell with a slug in his shoulder. Most of the others were reloading, crouching so I was totally exposed. *Damn! Don't they know how to do anything right? Where did Hiro get these people? Idiots Я Us?* I pulled a couple flash bang grenades off my belt and slung them across the floor toward the slayers. I threw out a couple impact smoke bombs for extra measure.

The slayers were now out from behind their tables, in full charge against us. Ignoring the bitch gnawing my leg, I warmed a dragon blood tat—and felt every nerve scream as if someone was skinning me with a potato peeler—but my voice transformed to thunder. "Everyone stop!"

The band froze. The slayers seized up mid-stride. My own guys became statues. The rest of the women on the silk ribbons fell *thudding* to the floor. The last of the fleeing crowd lost impetus, becoming even more mindless. The only one that didn't stop was Vivian. She had enough vamp in her to be immune to my power of suggestion, having that same power herself.

I didn't want to pistol whip her, her head was already damaged, bleeding heavily. Another head blow might kill her, and she was too hot to die unless really, really necessary. The smell of her own blood had probably been what had brought her around, triggering this feeding hunger. When fully back in her senses, this would probably embarrass her. She was supposed to be one of the good guys.

I pulled the mirror off my chest, turned it in my hand and said, "Old Man, we need a demon gate, now!"

Hiro's men and the slayers were now mixed in a violent dance. The danger of each side hitting their own guys was too great, so street fighting replaced gunplay. Now I saw what Hiro's men were good at. Hand to hand. The slayers went down en mass.

The way to the front door was suddenly clear.

I looked into my mirror again and said, "Never mind."

I dropped my full weight onto the knee Vivian clung to. This drove her back to the floor, my knee sinking into her abdomen. Even with the muzzle of my PPK to her head, she still didn't let go, though more sense seemed to be returning, wiping the haze of hunger from her face. I pulled the gun away and taunted her. "Like father, like daughter. He'd be so proud to see you now."

She released my leg, shoving me off her with vampire strength.

I hit the floor, skidded toward the door, and rolled to my feet while slapping the little mirror back on my chest again.

I called out to Hiro's men. "C'mon, let's go!"

Bristling with guns once more, they covered my retreat. We ran through the smoke from the bombs I'd released, and were out the door as sirens shrieked closer. We were keeping the cops busy tonight. They'd probably had to call in all off duty cops to deal with all the hot spots I was leaving.

Hiro's guys had two black vans waiting at the curb. As they loaded up, two of the Japanese paused to high-five each other.

I groaned in the depths of my soul. They slammed doors and drove off.

I headed for my own vehicle. I was rounding the hood when Albino John popped up from hiding, that rune etched shotgun still gripped in his grubby little hands. He smiled with delight, pointing the muzzle at my face. Cold fear settled in my guts as I realized that my shield was still dormant. The runes on his weapon were making my tat blind to his threat.

"Gottcha, now!" he said. "Twitch, and you die."

I saw the bloodlust in his eyes. He was going to shoot anyway, but he'd take a moment to gloat first. All bad guys were the same.

I warmed my *Dragon Flame* tat, preparing to use it.

Albino John said, "Who's the little punk ass bitch now, huh? Who's the damned—?"

Old Man's hand emerged from the mirror on my chest along with several inches of wrist.

Albino John stared in shock.

I stared in shock. Then I realized that the white jade frame had expanded magically to allow Old Man's oversized hand through. The hand flexed its fingers. A ball of violet-white lightning filled the palm, reeling off an electric storm of jags that made a blackened, crispy critter out of Not–So-Albino John. He died on his feet, blasted backwards out of his shoes. The shot gun went flying high into the air.

I caught it with one hand. *Hmmm, something new for my collection.*

Old Man's hand withdrew back into the mirror.

I got into my mustang and drove off. I was several blocks away—heading for Gloria's place—when my phone played *Tears of the Dragon*. I knew that was Old Man, asking me what the hell I was doing. For once, I had a very good answer

I flipped my phone open and said, "Yeah?"

"What the hell are you doing? We need the female slayer to find the warlock, and you drive off and leave her behind?"

I smiled. "Old Man, shut the fuck up." Startled, he fell silent. I went on. "Things are going according to plan."

There was a long silence. His voice returned, vibrating with curiosity. "Okay, what did I miss?"

"We don't need to *have* the dhampyr, just to *follow* her. She's going after Salem."

"You're not at the club anymore. How are you going to follow her?"

"That's where Gloria comes in."

* * *

I stopped my mustang behind Gloria's bar, and got out. Hiro's men parked the black vans behind me. *Old Man had to have sent them after me. I probably ought to ditch this stupid mirror—Hiro's men too. There's just so much helpfulness I can take.*

I walked to the driver's door of the van.

He rolled down his window.

I said, "Wait here. I need to speak to someone inside to find out where we go next."

Sharply, the drive nodded his head once. "*Hai*, Deathwalker-san."

The bar was closed, but Gloria's home lay on the upper floor, and she'd still be awake. Vampires don't crash until dawn. I didn't have to knock hard; with her vampire hearing, she'd know someone was here. She might even recognize my heartbeat—through the door. I called out, "Gloria, Adrian sends his love."

I waited a few seconds and heard the locks rattling open. She cracked the door and looked out. "Caine, you're here late. Everything's okay? Is Adrian…?"

"Fine," I said, "though he could use an enema."

Though concerned, her perfect smile was in place, as always. *Creepy.* Against the darkness of her hair, the pink streaks were nearly three-dimensional. She wore a diaphanous nightgown, a pale peach color that floated around her like a wet dream waiting to happen. My gaze naturally dropped to her thinly-veiled breasts. I said, "I need your help with something. Can I come in?"

Gloria opened the door and stepped to the side to let me pass. She closed the door, relocking it. Without a word, she led me up the stairs to her apartment. Her silk nightgown hugged her curves, draping her legs, whispering sexily as she moved. Her assets right in my face, I was reminded of just how beautiful she was.

Without looking back, she said, "Your pulse is a little fast. See something you like?"

"You could say that."

The magic locks on her upstairs door were strong. Not even I could break the blood magic. She opened the way and stood aside so I could enter first. The living room was like a tribute to Victorian sensibilities, but didn't lack modern conveniences. The hard wood floors were cork wood. The walls had riotous flowers painted on them, species from all over the world. The white antique couch lacked one arm and had only half a back that started high and sloped into extinction. An iPod lay on the cushions, music leaking from earphones. There were chairs that might have come from a European court. And a treadmill for running that faced a small TV on a stand. A crystal chandelier hung from the middle of the ceiling. Pink blackout curtains on her windows were heavy enough to block the sun during the day.

Yeah, this is a place where a vampire would live.

Gloria pointed at the couch, for me to sit, and headed for the mini bar in the corner. She made me a gin and pineapple drink as I took my seat, relaxing. She smiled that sweet smile of hers. "What do you need help with, sweetie?"

"I need you to use your blood magic to track a dhampyr," said.

"Why are you wasting your time with one of *those*."

"Business. The bitch will lead me to someone that needs killing."

"Well, I'll need some of her blood to do that."

"How about some of mine instead? She bit me, so my blood is in her."

"Yes, that will work." Gloria brought me my drink, and set it down on a coffee table.

By then, I'd unzipped the apocalypse suit down to my waist and slipped my left arm out of its sleeve. I pulled out a pocketknife and put the edge on my forearm. "How much do you need?" Gloria's hand enveloped mine, straightening out my left arm. "Put away the knife. I'll extract the sample, *my way*."

She smiled, flashing fangs. Her eyes turned blood red. She ran soft fingers along the radial artery in my left arm. Her smile lacked threat, friendly, not even sexual. That was a line neither of us seriously wanted to cross. The friendship would have suffered, and she was too good a resource, one I depended on.

She lifted my hand, bringing the wrist to her lips.

My phone went off. I said, "Yeah?"

Old Man yelled, "Put her on, now!"

I handed her my phone.

She paused and took the phone with a question in the lift of her eyebrows. She put the phone to her ear.

I couldn't hear what Old Man was saying, but he was talking—fast. After a moment, Gloria's eyes widened. She shot me a look of disbelief, as if Old Man were telling her I loved mankind and abhorred violence. She looked away and continued to listen, nodding now and again. She said, "And you never told him?"

What the hell?

She nodded absently. "Sure, I can see that. Okay, mum's the word." She turned off the phone and handed it back to me.

I took the phone with my free hand, and put it away. "What's that all about?"

She smiled with true regret. "I'm sorry, I can't tell you. You'll have to talk to Lauphram. Meanwhile…"

She bit into my arm with relish, her eyes rolling to the back of her head like my blood was the finest vintage ever discovered. Her breathing stopped as she lost focus on passing for human. After a while, I actually had to put a foot against her stomach to push her away. "Gloria! What the hell!"

Drifting back to me, she licked her lips, as the red fog cleared from her stare. She reached down and caressed my face in apology. "Sorry, that was … rude." Her fingertips glided past the bite mark on my arm and the punctures closed—by magic.

"Never mind that," I said, "did you get what we need?"

"I think so. Just a minute." She whirled away, her sheer nightgown belling around her legs as she crossed the room to an antique roll top desk. Lifting the cover, Gloria reached in and gathered several items that she brought back with her.

I picked my drink off the coffee table and guzzled. By the time I finished the sweetly sharp pineapple gin, she had a city map spread on the coffee table and was kneeling by it, her ankles daintily crossed behind her. She lit a small red candle. From the cloying iron scent, I'd say there was blood mixed into the wax. A pendant dangled from her right hand, a silver chain with a claw gripping a long narrow sliver of clear crystal. She rubbed the crystal across her mouth, tinting it with my blood.

The stone was now a pale shimmer of red. She moved the pendant until it cast a spangle of pink light on the map. After that, she held her hand perfectly still. Without the waver of fatigue a human would have felt, her arm might as well have been chiseled from marble.

As she looked up at me, her smile turned predatory; she'd started the hunt.

Her lips shaped words that twisted unexpectedly. Her tone was sultry and dark, almost sibilant at times. Her hand never shifted position, but the pink tangle of light slid across the map and stopped.

I bent forward and made a mental note of the street corner. That would do. My *Dragon Sight* tat would fine-tune the location once I got there. I stood and slipped my arm back into its sleeve, zipping up the suit.

Gloria blew out the candle and licked the bloody crystal clean. She dropped it on the map and almost seemed to levitate back to her feet. She came around the table to stare into my eyes. My shield stayed dormant. She wasn't trying to roll my mind. She brushed her hand down the line of my zipper, nearly to my crotch, stopping just short. She murmured, "You will be careful, right?"

"Sure, you know me."

Her eyes were dilated. There was a slight drunken slur to her woods, "Yes, that's why I worry." She was buzzed on my blood. Old Man and I were going to have a serious talk when this mess was over. He was keeping secrets from me, and some of them were mine.

I smiled and kissed her cheek. "Gotta go kill someone. Catch you later."

Her hand withdrew. She went ahead to open the locks for me. Me and my hard-on somehow made it through the doors to where the night waited like a beast, ready to pounce.

TWENTY-NINE

"War is nature's way of preventing the stupid from breeding."

—Caine Deathwalker

I hurried from the bar, flicking a glance at the black vans. A twinge in my right leg warned me that an hour had passed and that I was about to pay for the last time I used *Vampire Speed.* I hurried. I didn't want to lose it here, and display my weakness.

Makes it harder to be a bad ass in people's eyes.

I made it inside the mustang and slammed my door the same moment pain slammed the breath from my lungs. Cramps knotted all along my legs. I clenched my teeth and bit off a curse, coming off the seat to straighten my legs. I smashed my fist into the roof a half dozen times. As the pain edged down to barely tolerable, I sat and white knuckled the steering wheel, an unvoiced growl in my throat. I managed to deactivate the security system with sweat running into my eyes.

I had no time for this so I tried a martial arts visualization, imagining myself as a glass figurine. The pain was light ghosting harmlessly through me. I did my best to believe.

Remember to ride the pain, to be the pain, pain doesn't hurt itself.

Someone tapped at my car window.

My meditation dissolved. Fresh agony knifed through me. I drew a deep, staggered breath, and pried a hand off the steering wheel to power the electric window down.

One of the Japanese leaned down and peered at me. "Do we not have some place to go?" he wondered.

"We'll go when I'm ready." He flinched back from the death in my eyes, and ran back to his van. By then, the pain was slacking. I sent the mustang hurtling out into the streets. The vans stayed well back as if the vehicles were uncertain of my temper. The streets passed in a blur of light and darkness. Skyscrapers looming on every side, as cars weaved ahead and behind, and in the other lane. As late as it was, there were a lot of people that didn't want to go home yet.

I remembered Haruka—dead, frozen, waiting for me—I couldn't go home yet either, even though I was dragging, fighting the echoes of pain, and the squeezing fist of fatigue. Old Man's hand emerged from the mirror on my chest. He held a shot of something bubbly and crystal pink. I took the glass and drank. Fire pulsed in my veins. Tiredness retreated to a safe distance. My thoughts sharpened.

I gave the empty glass back to the hand. Both withdrew.

"Thanks," I said, "for whatever that was."

Eventually, we reached the right address and piled out of our vehicles. I looked up. We were in the downtown area where eight of the tallest buildings in California were located. The building we wanted didn't quite measure up to four hundred feet, but its sleek, new millennium design was impressive. Edison Tower was a behemoth of blue glass, steel, and white concrete at the base. Due to city codes, the top would be flat, and have a helicopter pad.

The windows in the face were dark, as if the building was drowsing. I knew this wasn't true. I felt magic alive in the structure, like the pulsing of blood. A scent of malice sizzled the air. *A death trap. No two ways about it. He knows we're coming.*

I could have had Old Man open a demon gate for us all to pop inside, but the warlock would be shielding himself from detection, and if we did hit his location by blind chance, he'd see us coming through the glowing gate and blast us—*Like shooting fireflies in a mason jar.* Going in on foot would be slower, but not more dangerous. At least, I hoped not.

Hiro's men stood a few feet from me. A few were missing, those the slayers had wounded, and there were some reinforcements as well, twenty of us now, including the two scouts I'd sent around the structure to reconnoiter. They returned, slinking along like cat-shadows in their black body-stockings, gloves and masks. A bit theatrical, but who was I to talk? I wore a zombie apocalypse combat suit with a fully stocked weapons harness.

The returning men bowed shallowly. One of them said, "No break in. Motorcycle in alley."

The other broke in with very good English, "It has a vanity plate; SLAYRIDE. And there's a shadow climbing the side of the building."

"Yeah, sounds like Vivian's here alright." She was heading for the roof, probably thinking it would be easier to break in from there. I liked a more direct approach. I walked up to one of the glass doors and braced myself to kick.

One of the Japanese held up a hand. "Wait, the alarm!"

"There will be no alarm," I said. "Salem wants us all to himself."

I kicked the door in. Shards sprayed inward across green and white checkerboard tiles. I kicked a few times to clear the jagged glass still in the door's frame, and waved the guys through. They ran past me, ducking under a horizontal crossbar on the door frame to get inside the lobby. They each kept a gun in hand. I headed to a hall, about to turn left in search of the stairwell entrance at the far side of the building. Most of the men were with me, but four lingered at the elevator.

I called back. "If I were you, I wouldn't do that."

The four men ignored me as the elevators dinged open. They stepped inside. The door closed and we heard the sound of metal tearing, crumpling itself up like a paper wad. The screams were cut off sharply. One of the men next to me started to say something. I held up a hand to silence him. "Wait for it," I said.

The doors opened and the elevator car, considerably smaller now, was spit out with a hell of a racket, its broken cables dragging along like dead snakes.

"Told you so," I said. *Just started, and down to fifteen already.*

The rest of the men stared in horror. A few were shaking.
One sobbed. Another screamed and ran for the front door. An older gentleman at my side shot the deserter in the back. Several men—that looked like they'd had the same idea—swallowed and got a hold of themselves.

I looked at the shooter. "What's your name?"

He bowed reflexively. "Maki, Osamu, Deathwalker-san."

Maki was his family name. His given name was Osamu. He'd impressed me. I actually wouldn't mind if this guy survived. "Can I call you Osamu?"

He blinked and bowed deeper. "*Hai!*"

"Call me Caine," I said. "You've earned the right."

He straightened, pride shining in his eyes.

"Let's go." I led us down the hall, keeping an eye out for another trap. We reached the stairwell door and went through. The thing ought to have been locked, but the warlock wanted us coming after him, especially me. This was round three in the pissing contest we'd started back at Gloria's bar.

Most of the men crowdied into the stairwell, and stared about suspiciously. The rest called in from the hall, demanding to know what was going on.

The stairwell distorted as if seen through a warped lens. The rising stairs bent into bizarre tangents that shifted as we watched. The brick walls swelled and contracted as if breathing. I put my palm against the closest wall. It felt warm, tingly with magic. I warmed the tat for my *Dragon Sight*, and felt as if a drill were ventilating my skull. After a moment, the pain dropped. I studied the area once more. The stairwell lingered like a superimposed image. We were also inside the gaping maw of a monstrous serpent, looking down its throat. Space was bending in such a way as to turn us into snake food.

I whispered. “Back up, fast.”

They didn’t have my sight, but they saw the gun I swung their way. Those around me spun and shoved back into the lobby. I didn’t have time to wait, and I doubted my usual weapons or tats were up to *this*. If I knew for sure I was about to die, I’d use my Kiss-My-Ass-Goodbye spell which would basically nuke half the city.

Yeah, I’m a vindictive son of a bitch.

The boys were wedged in the lobby door, and the roof of the snake’s mouth was descending. I could make out fangs coming together to either side of the door. The *floor* under my feet shifted, rippling, becoming a red tongue. The dimensional reality of the monster snake had yet to completely gel. There was still a chance to force the realities back apart.

I remembered the ghost dragon I’d met in Kellyn’s treasure room, back in Faerie. What had he said to me? Oh, yeah!

I am Wyrmmfrey of the Ice Clan. Call on me seven times, and this debt will be paid.

I warmed the tat for my *Dragon Voice*, barely tolerating the sensation of someone sawing me in half. My words boomed, “Wyrmmfrey of the Ice Clan, I call you to answer your debt.”

A blue-white swirl of mist formed before me, a serpentine shape that was as translucent as the stairwell. He fixed the silvery blaze of his eyes on me. His whiskered snout opened. “I answer, as I am pledged. What do you wish?”

“Tired of being a ghost? I’ve got a new body for you.” I gestured at the surrounding dimensional overlap.

His head swiveled. “Hmmm. Not bad. Not a dragon, but not bad. But I’m not going to owe you for this.”

“Oh, no,” I said. “Think of it as an act of friendship.”

The dragon spirit snorted, glaring suspiciously at me. “No strings attached?”

"None," I said. "Enjoy."

"Don't mind if I do." The ghost expanded as billows of white, soaking into the altered space around me. The tongue under me froze in place. The brick walls were startled into motionlessness as well. The fangs were no longer moving, locking against each other. Then the monster snake retreated, its body possessed, hijacked by the dragon ghost. The stairwell became its usual self, running upward as originally laid out.

I called to the milling bodies still jamming the hallway door. "Danger's over. Stop screwing around, and let's go."

I started up the stairs, staying close to the wall. The men behind me followed my example. A few floors up, one of the men opened a door only to be sucked in by screaming winds. Winds clawed us. I threw myself to the railing, hanging on with all my strength. The heavy fire door slammed shut. The wind died. I looked at the men with me.

Down to fourteen now.

I said, "Are you guys done being stupid?"

Osamu glared at his partners, then faced me, bowing deeply. "Apologies, Deathwalker-san."

"It's Caine, remember?"

"Hai, Deathwalker-san."

I sighed. *Japanese, go figure…*

A few floors higher, the air wavered. I held up a hand in warning, pausing to take in the new threat. Like a 3-D projection, a piss-yellow image of the warlock appeared. His boots were a few inches off the floor, and he held the necklace in his hand. He grinned. "Caine, I'm not going to make it easy for you, but you do need to hurry."

"Any special reason?" I asked.

His yellow glow expanded, giving me a better view of his surroundings. He was on the roof, on the helipad. *Really, a rooftop fight, can you get any more cliché.*

Off to the side, behind him, I saw Vivian. She'd made good time getting to the roof, not that it had done her much good. She was on her knees, hands behind her back, her chest heaving as she strained against … nothing. Either invisible restraints were being used, or an illusion spell—if her mind was convinced she was bound, her body would act as if this were true.

Furious, Vivian's eyes blazed a watery red that lacked the rich, blood-hue of a pure-blood vampire like Gloria. The dhampyr snarled at me, "Don't you dare help. I don't need anything from a worm like you."

I shrugged. "Okay, if you're sure."

Salem's smile died. "You need to fight on, Caine. If I get tired of waiting, I'll amuse myself with her. It won't be pretty. She can take a lot of damage, a lot more than a human." He laughed. The sound stretched and thinned as the projection faded.

I growled at the warlock. "Damned bastard gets all the fun."

THIRTY

"The only way out of an early grave is past the shovel and flying dirt."

—Caine Deathwalker

"He's on the roof," I said. "And he's right about one thing; we better do this quick. He's infused his magic in the building. It's fighting us, leaving him free to do other things. By giving up direct control, he's left us with a powerful but unimaginative enemy that can be easily confused."

Most of the men looked confused. Sweat dripped off their faces. They smelled of fear. That was good. Fear sharpens the senses, releases adrenaline. Adrenaline tweaks the muscles, helps you to survive.

I said, "Think of the building as a golem that we're inside of."

"Ah…!" That sound went around the group as the concept sank in at different speeds.

Their collective presence will continue to attract the dark magic. There are too many to protect with my cloaking magic. If I spread myself too thin, I'll only endanger myself, and I've go to survive to get paid, or all this is meaningless.

My skin felt warm for a second, the flicker of warning that I get when my shield wants me to move. I stepped back, dodging a blunt-tipped spike of brick, designed to bludgeon more than stab. The guy behind me wasn't so lucky. His spike hit at eye level. Half his skull was gone before he even had time to scream. The man behind him looked at the door to the floor we were on, and leaped to open it. There was a massive surge of fleeing men that left me in the stairwell with Osamu and three others.

Five of us now…

I pointed at the dead guy. “Take his guns and ammo, and let’s hustle. The only way out is up,” I said. This was good actually; the building would probably focus on the larger group and not come for us until they were all dead. Sad, really, but that’s the fate of red shirts; to die in battle so the intrepid hero can press on to glory.

We ran up the stairs. The activity drained me more than it should have because I was steadily feeding energy to my personal shield. Next best thing to a *spider sense*, but expensive.

We made several more flights. I didn’t expect to hear the screams of the men that had left us, and I didn’t, but I knew they were being made. In the rest of the building, there was more to attack you; cleaning closets with caustic chemicals, furniture that might take an instant dislike to you, drapery to entangle and choke. The possibilities were endless. Here, we only had to worry about…

The stairs above us started to jerk away from the wall like a living thing. I ran as fast as I could to get past the affected area. Osamu and the rest sprinted along. The last two didn’t make it, falling down the stairwell as the steps under their feet collapsed. Their screams echoed for a long time, as if each flight of stairs under them were collapsing in turn, expediting their plunge to the ground floor.

This isn’t good. I’m running out of human shields.

I flogged myself to keep the grueling pace. Osamu stayed close. He understood that following my lead was better than not doing so. He didn’t want to be a *red shirt.* I didn’t want that either. If he survived, I was considering hiring him away from Hiro. My house could use a live-in butler who wasn’t easily rattled. Of course, Leona and Old Man would have to approve.

We made good time, as nothing happened for a long time after that.

Then I noticed a vibration in the air. I felt the wall. It was there too. The stairs were developing a webbing of fine cracks. I had a feeling the rest of the staircase would soon be coming down, so I stopped at the next landing and pried at the fire door. It was locked. I shot the lock and pried again. It didn’t budge. I looked down. The cracks had reached our landing, and were widening.

Old Man’s hand emerged from my chest. His fingers were splayed. His palm pointed at the door. He was going to open it so I could save energy for the battle against Salem. I warned the guys still with me. “Get down low. I’m blasting the door, and there might be some blowback.”

They went a few steps down, pressing against the wall. Osamu stared at the hand protruding from my chest. His face was white with fear, tense with strain, but he was holding himself together. The other guy had a crazy look in his eyes that I didn't trust.

I backed from the door as light pooled in Old Man's vertical palm. I looked away as the light intensified, shooting out writhing streamers of mystic purple lightning. The burning air boomed as the fire door blew off its hinges, crashing into the hallway beyond. The heat of the concussive backwash washed around my shield as it cranked up to high. The cost of the additional protection was a kick in the gut that sank me to my knees. I gasped for breath, catching myself on the trembling landing.

The concrete gave way.

I managed to grab the crumbling lip of what remained, and dangled a few feet from the open door. The stairs were falling out from under Osamu and the other man. They scurried up onto the ledge of the shattered landing. Osamu stopped by the door, reaching down to grab my left wrist and give me a hand.

The other man never paused, bolting through the doorway. He made one step as the top of the door frame fell, acquiring a sword's razor edge that cut into the top of his skull, slicing down to both ears. His body flopped face first on the hall carpet which drank his blood.

Down to the two of us now.

Osamu had me up on the ledge by that time, but we couldn't linger; the landing overhead was fracturing and pieces were raining on us. With Osamu inside my shield, we were both protected. But the ledge supporting us would go next in this vicious game being played. I leaped through, dragging Osamu along as we trampled the fallen body, and then stomped over the blown off door. It was half melted and scorched with a hole completely through its center.

Continuing on, nothing threatened us. That in itself was suspicious.

The building's probably working up a few special surprises.

We went on carefully, especially where there were open doors to rooms from which assorted things might pounce. The floor rippled, a slight distortion setting in. The walls wavered. The only lighting we'd seen was the red emergency lights over the exit behind us, and window light from the open doors. That changed as the overhead lights came on in the distance, the effect racing toward us, a sweep of lighting that killed all shadows, clearly showing us the next threat.

Nimble chairs and more sluggish desks turned a far corner. The animate furniture paused until the lights finished coming on. Then, like a panicked herd, the furniture stampeded down the hall toward us. Osamu opened fire winging two chairs and clipping off the leg of a desk that continued to amble toward, though with a more awkward gait.

I activated a fire spell, feeling as though my brain were expanding under enormous pressure, breaking my inner skull like the shell of an over-boiled egg. The sensation passed. I focused the fire I'd summoned on the carpet and the onrushing office furniture. A few floor lamps joined the herd, slithering along the wall, and I saw a coat rack, its upper branches transformed into meat hooks.

The burning carpet smoked heavily. The flames failed to deter the attacking herd. *Odd, no fire alarm. The sprinklers aren't going on.* I chose a door at random, pulled Osamu in with me, and slammed the office door. I used a chair that showed no signs of life, wedging it up against the knob.

"Keep an eye on the furniture. Let me know if anything starts to act up."

Osamu nodded. "Hai." He slid a secretary's desk over to help barricade the door, adding a filing cabinet and a trash can. The outside of the door shuddered as the herd beat against it, trying to get in.

I went to an inner door, kicked it open and peered in. It was an executive office with a wet bar, red leather couch, client chairs, a massive desk, and bookcases on one wall. The books were thick, leather-bound, and covered various subjects on the law. *A lawyer's office, one who's very successful. Too bad I don't have time to search his files for useful dirt.* A wall of windows showed the cityscape beyond. Another door was open, probably a private wash room.

I went in, careful of the door frame. It stayed attached. This looked like a dead end. We were cornered.

I looked up at the ceiling. *Maybe not.*

"Osamu, get in here."

We dragged the red couch and put its back agaist the bookcase so it wouldn't fall when we climbed up. Osamu helped me toss books off the shelves, creating a ladder to the false ceiling. I sat on top of the bookshelf and explained my plan. After popping a ceiling panel loose, I stuck my head into the crawlspace. This let me see that the false ceiling was mostly held up by wire. However, metal posts anchored one line of tiles, making a path we could use, if we were careful.

I pulled myself fully into the space, distributing my weight evenly on the metal frame held by the posts. I headed forward towards the adjoining office. "Osamu, distribute your weight on the frame like I'm doing, or you'll fall through the tiles."

"Hai!"

We crawled on until we were well past the wall, over the next office, then the next. Then I took a chance and punched a tile under me. Ah, perfect. A conference room table. This made the drop shorter and safer. Quieter too. I slipped through, keeping my feet under me, and landed with little noise. *Not the first time I've done this.*

Standing, I reached up and tried to ease Osamu down. This didn't work very well, but the old guy was spry, landing light as a sparrow. I raised my eyebrows at him in surprise.

He grinned in silence.

We squatted and swung down off the table, onto charcoal gray carpeting. I glanced at the door to the hall. It was wide open. I whispered, "On the other side of the building, there's another stairwell to the roof. I think we're close enough that Salem will actually call off the building's attack. He'll want us on hand to flaunt his power, now that he's cut down our numbers."

Osamu nodded. We padded over to the door. I whispered, "On three, run like hell." I held up three fingers, and folded them one at a time. When all were tucked in a fist, we leaped out and hauled ass, not bothering to look and see what the furniture was doing.

There was smoke in the air, burning my throat, but the sprinklers had finally decided to come on. We ran through the spray, listening to its hiss, and the wooden clatter of pursuing chairs and desks.

We hooked the corner, entering a hallway where the sprinklers were still off. Using a PPK, I shot a vacuum cleaner that was lying in wait, kicking it over as we passed. Osamu gave it an extra stomp in passing. We raced on to the next stairwell. I threw open the door and froze.

Salem stood there, or rather, another muddy yellow image of him. He wore the necklace and held a knife. The blade dripped blood. "About time you guys got here."

"You've been having fun," I said.

He grinned and winked. "I don't think the little lady would call it that."

I was aware of Osamu, standing angled so he could keep an eye on the corridor behind us. Otherwise, he let me handle things.

"Get out of the way," I said. "We'll come up and entertain you."

"I'm sure you will," Salem said. "But you've got a final hurdle to leap before you get to me."

"What now?" I asked.

He laughed, the sound sharp as a fang, beating at us like bat wings. And then he was gone, and we saw what hid behind his mirage—all eighteen of the men we'd lost, many of them mangled to the point where they barely looked human. Blood soaked their black suits, giving them a rusty sheen. Their guns were lost. Their wounds gaped. The four from the elevator were crushed lumps humping across the threshold, more tumble weed than anything else. They got trampled by the men behind them that lurched our way in search of prey.

Osamu and I brought our guns to bear. My PPKs were on full

automatic, spraying a withering fire of explosive rounds. Anything other than zombies would have gone down and stayed down. These didn't, though I was chipping away at them, blowing out chunks left and right.

I growled in frustration. "I hate zombies."

THIRTY-ONE

"Finally, all my experience in bar room brawls will come in handy."

—Caine Deathwalker

I concentrated my fire on their ankles, slowing the zombies down to a creep. Normal zombies you can take out by splattering their brains. I'd tried this. Didn't work. These guys were driven by a potent form of necromancy that kept pulling them back together regardless of the damage. I was only buying time.

I called to Osamu, "The best we can do is to lure them past a room with two doors and use our greater speed to get behind them."

"I'll find such a room." He ran off and left me.

Still retreating backwards down the hall, I changed clips and sprayed another rapid burst of exploding rounds. This time, I concentrated on knees.

My shield flickered, warning me a massive attack was coming that required agility to escape. I jumped diagonally backwards, ducking low for extra measure. A chunk of concrete ceiling fell where I'd been, *whumping* into the carpet. My shield continued to flicker. I danced to the side. A concrete spike burst up through the carpet in my wake.

Damn, going for the family jewels!

I heard Osamu's battle cries mixed with breaking wood, and knew the savage pack of furniture was back for blood—and that Osamu was doing something about it. Karate exhibitions routinely had students breaking boards and bricks. I didn't have to turn from the zombies to know what was happening. If the building thought attacking us separately was going to be effective, it had miscalculated.

I could have used my stealth magic to become invisible to the zombies, but that would have meant abandoning Osamu, and that didn't sit right.

He took a moment between breaking up chairs to yell at me, "Deathwalker-san, the next two doors…" *Crac-crack!*

"My right side or left?" I asked. *Gotta know if I zig or zag.*

"Either," he sounded winded.

My mind flashed to Gloria's bar, back to the conversation I'd had with the half-angel Gray. He'd said, *"When it comes time to take a helluva risk, zig, don't zag."* He'd also said, *"Leave the red moon alone. No good ever comes from screwing around with alternate dimensions."*

Back then, I hadn't known about the lotus-dragon tattoo. I had the feeling that *this* was the battle he'd been advising me about, not that it did me a lot of good. I could only take the best shot open to me and hope for the best.

Still ... his warning implies something other than my usual response is needed.

By habit, I enter unknown spaces to the left, not the right. This time, I'd go against custom.

My guns ran empty. I holstered them in my shoulder rig. I drew the ones from my thigh holsters and started splattering zombie eyeballs.

"Right," I called out. "I'm going to my right."

"Hai-iiiiya!" *Ccrack!*

I took that as an acknowledgement. I passed a set of doors and continued retreating until I reached the next set. By then, I was stepping over shards of broken furniture. Unlike the zombies, when the furniture got smashed to kindling, it stayed down.

Osamu returned to my side, listing with fatigue. "The last few chairs…" he wheezed, "ran back around the corner. We've taught them fear at last."

"More likely they're trying to suck us into another ambush." He looked slightly depressed by the news. I whispered, "Fake left, spin, and go right."

We lunged left, but didn't cross the threshold. The floor inside the room shattered and dropped, piling on the next floor down which also shattered. From the crashing sounds, I could tell a chain reaction had been started. We flung ourselves across the hall, through the opposite door, and raced past the zombies, separated from them by a wall. We came out another door and wound up behind the zombie horde. They didn't seem to realize this.

Guns useless, empty of ammo, I holstered them, and ran to the stairwell, Osamu staying close as my shadow.

When my shield didn't react to danger, I led the way inside. Several flights later, we reached the roof access. By then, Osamu was laboring for breath, blinded by sweat. His gun hand shook. I was half afraid he might accidentally shoot me. The old geezer was done in. I pushed him against the wall, beside the roof door.

"You stay here," I said. "You've done enough for your honor. Leave the rest to me."

He shook his head to the side and back. "No, Death-walker-sama, we are in this to the end."

The fire in his voice and eyes told me he meant it. Because I admired his loyalty, I punched him on the point of his chin, rocking his head at an upward angle, knocking him out. The angle was important. I didn't want to break his jaw and have to hit him again, fun as that might be. He sighed and collapsed. I caught and lowered him so he sat against the wall.

Fighting the building had been bad. Fighting Salem was going to be worse. I couldn't do that if I had to divide my attention, also keeping Osamu alive. Besides, what would I do for a combat butler if he died?

I drew both swords from the back of my harness, filled my lungs, and let the breath escape slowly. I stepped out onto the roof. Air-conditioning units edged one side of the roof, hugging a wall. I barely registered them, my gaze drawn to the well-lit helipad where Salem waited, wide-legged, baring the weight of the sky on his shoulders, fists on his hips in jaunty defiance. Behind him, Vivian knelt as I'd last seen her, except her head hung, hiding her face, and the black leather had been
peeled down to her waist, hanging in clean-cut strips. Herbreasts and stomach were drenched in red.

Friggin' warlock has been busy.

A tingle raced across my skin, followed by a feeling as if something heavy and wet had wrapped around me. I tried to awaken my *Dragon Vision* but the tat stayed cold. Salem was doing something that cut me off from my magic. He seemed to have better control over the necklace he'd stolen than Sarah ever had, or maybe he simply knew better spells.

Only the lotus and dragon tat on my arm felt alive—with anticipation. The thing had too much power to be suppressed. That scared me into saving it as a last resort, so I only had my short swords and Old Man's training left to draw upon.

Have to be enough.

In the absence of cover, I walked straight toward him. Nothing came; no gunshots, mystic bolts of bedevilment, he didn't even throw a rock—I'd never have wasted such an opportunity.

His voice came, thin and sharp as the knife he held. "Caine, she's not so pretty now, but if you want her, you can have her. All you've got to do is go through me. Do you really think you can do that?" He gestured with his empty hand. A spectral green light lit up the helipad, and in that glow, he became weightless, floating into the air. His midnight-blue long coat whipped in the cool night breeze as he looked down on me.

So theatrical...

About twenty feet still separated us.

Using my wrists, I spun both swords in lazy circles, weaving a web of death in front of me. "You're above us all, aren't you?" I said.

"Well, above *you*, certainly. I told them you'd be no challenge."

"Told who? Who set you and the succubus on me?"

He shook his head. "Ah, that would be telling."

"Think of it as a condemned man's last wish." I kept the swords in motion. "Who's trying to start a war in my territory?"

"It's not about your precious city. It's about the crime committed by your parents in giving birth to a half-breed like you. It's about the reward I've been offered for taking you down."

Ten feet left to go.

I stepped onto the helipad, into the watery zone of light. I felt nothing new. Gravity did me no favors. I stayed earthbound.

Half breed. He was saying one of my parents hadn't been human. The idea didn't distress me. In fact, it might actually explain a few things I knew about myself.

I stopped, with him hovering just above my head. I stilled the swinging swords, and offered him the one in my left hand, hilt first. "You said you wanted to play. What's wrong? Scared?"

"Of you? No. I attended a military academy in Europe. Fencing was part of my daily regimen. I'm quite good, actually." He sank until his feet were only a few inches above the concrete. He reached for the sword I offered. "I hope you're fond of scars, not that you'll live long enough to enjoy them."

His hand closed on the hilt.

I went from utterly relaxed, to an explosive movement of my entire body. My right hand shot straight out, driving my sword forward. Though he wheeled sideways—never moving his legs—my edge managed to slice across his chest, through the left lapel of his long coat.

Like an action figure moved by an unseen hand, he orbited me, extending the sword I'd given him. He kept its point centered on my torso. "Nice," he said. "You just might last long enough to amuse me."

I turned with him, not giving him access to my back. "One can only hope."

He stopped in front of me, angling his body the way European fencers do. Western swordplay is all about what's in front of you.

I slid diagonally back. I wasn't about to let him pull me in into his kind of fight. Now I was the one circling, forcing him to continually adjust *his* stance. I thrust at his hip, testing him. His blade clattered against mine. I rode the energy of the blow, and spun, slapping the flat of my blade against my ribs so that as I came around, I could shove my point straight out in a blinding flash of speed.

The tight turn and strike forced him back a step. Blood dripped from his badly slashed hand. He stopped smiling. Even the little blond spikes of his over-styled hair seemed to quiver in rage. He looked at his hand while putting distance between us. The wound took a second to heal. Apparently, I was going to have to cut his heart out, or lop his evil head clean off. *No problem.*

"Interesting," the warlock said.

"Oh," I said, "there's a lot more hell to come."

The warlock flew forward, his sword aimed at my heart.

I dipped my sword tip and turned my body at the last second, stepping inside his guard. I slammed my right elbow at his neck. He caught the blow with his left hand, redirecting it to the side. I went with the motion, riding his energy while conserving mine. Slashing, I tried to take his head. The amulet sparked red-violet and he shot high into the air faster than humanly possible. His shirt was slashed, the material wet and red with a growing stain of blood. His face took on a grim cast.

"You have a nasty fighting style there, Caine."

I smiled, "What can I say? Sometimes I even scare myself."

He floated back down, drifting backwards toward Vivian. I don't think he realized that, or that she was awake now, head lifted, eyes ablaze with unconquerable fury. If looks could kill, she'd have finished Salem off in that second. But maybe I could help her out.

I ran at him headfirst, my sword held in a relaxed grip, dragging on the concrete, trailing sparks. I leaped, my sword sweeping up before me to clear my way. Aloft, I reversed the blade and brought it down full force. He blocked, but I drove him down. His feet skidded on the helipad. This brought him crowding against Vivian.

Fangs yawning, she struck at his neck.

He screamed like a drop-kicked poodle.

I laughed.

At least he seemed to know he'd tear out his own throat before he pried her jaws apart; his strength *was* only human. He stabbed at me with his sword to keep me off while his free hand clutched the necklace. Its edges whirled as it clattered through rapid-fire changes like a Rubik's cube with rabies.

Salem's whole body went spectral green like the weird light generated by the helipad underfoot. Like glass he could be seen through, actually filtering the light. Every artery, vein, bone, ligament, tendon, organ, muscle, and webbing of nerve fiber were on display in way too much detail for clarity, especially as he thrashed, keeping only his neck still where

Vivian had attached herself.

The necklace clattered a little more, fine-tuning its form, then grew silent and still.

Vivian's teeth gnashed.

The sword Salem had been wagging didn't slip from his fingers—it fell through them. He'd shifted his molecular structure slightly out of phase, becoming a living ghost.

He straightened and moved effortlessly away from Vivian, as if picked up by the wind. Since this wasn't possible, I figured there was a ghost wind in whatever side pocket of reality he'd shoved his density.

Vivian thrashed in rage as her prey escaped, coming loose from the effect that had bound her limbs, making her a prisoner. Apparently, his necklace was less effective reaching us from an altered space.

I staggered as my tats warmed, reconnecting their magic to me in a violent rush, as if I'd been drinking cleaning fluid. Again. I went to one knee, and kept my eyes on Salem.

The green glow of the helipad thinned and died, allowing shadows to rush in. The main light now came from the lights mounted over the stairwell entrance, and the city surrounding us.

With a smirk in place, he waved goodbye. Drifting off the darkened helipad, he rose a little higher, sliding sideways against the black face of the moon.

Bastard's running. No way am I losing him after all this.

There was only one way I might still reach him.

I focused my life force on the lotus-dragon tat on my right forearm. The new tattoo began a slow burn, taking its sweet time waking up. I ran toward the edge of the building, trying to stay close to the warlock. I growled at the lotus. "Come on, how much time are you going to take?"

My stare slid past Salem to the moon, and I stopped running. The moon was changing. A wet layer of blood dripped from its top, soaking the whole thing as it spread downward. The dark orb became an infernal crimson, bleeding red light into the night sky.

What the friggin' hell! Did I do that?

THIRTY-TWO

"It never fails; put on an apocalypse suit, and an apocalypse happens."

—Caine Deathwalker

Something about my expression compelled Salem to cancel his drifting and turn. He went rigid with shock. A heartbeat later, a spinning ring of red plasma enclosed us both, ghosting up from the roof, reaching my knees. The writhing fire was colder than the night. Salem's head tilted downward. He turned my way once more, gaze following the ring, then sliding to me. There was a look on his face as if I'd profoundly surprised him.

Hand touching the amulet, Salem darted away, but only made it as far as the ring. An unseen wall in the air stopped him, bouncing him back. He returned to my reality, losing the green glow, and was tinted red by the moon, and the blood ring around us.

"So, what now?" he asked.

"Now the fun starts, Salem."

"How did you do this? This is not your kind of magic."

I moved the sword, rolling my arm in a what-can-I-say gesture.

His eyes followed thc motion. They widened, as if he could see the new tat under my sleeve. "What is that…?"

The concrete inside the ring turned blood red, spilling crimson radiance into the air. It was like a piece of the blood moon had materialized under us. Why now? I think I knew. Salem had just shed his altered state. The ring could now sense two souls. That was the key. My mind flashed to Mad Max at Thunder Dome.: *Two men enter.*

One leaves.

The blood light hardened. We were bugs in red amber, but the wind-blown grit had no trouble reaching us. Soon, the glow was so thick we were only shadows to each other, haunting a private hell. He screamed something I couldn't understand as gravity flickered. Finally, I was seized and thrown by a monstrous force.

Blinded by dust, whirled madly by hurricane winds, I lost the sword. Wrapping my arms over my face, I protected my eyes, and filtered the clogged air so I could breathe.

Something that felt like a sand dune caught me, whacking my breath out of me. I rolled up the bank and then back down, as the wind slacked from *killing force* to just *pissed off.* Squinting, I shook myself and put my back to the wind, feeling for the mirror on my chest.

Good, still there.

Something else felt wrong. My right forearm felt cold. I unzipped the suit enough to pull my arm out and take a look. The tattoo was gone. I stuffed the arm back into the suit, and looked round. I found the lotus I'd stolen from the fey treasure room, it was restored, a hunk of crystal half buried in the dust. Coming to this dimension had broken the bonding.

It will probably happen every time I come here. The crystal needs to be functional to catch a soul and fuel my return. I picked up the crystal lotus and stuffed it inside my suit. With the relic there, I wasn't able to zip back up, and would gather dust in my clothes, but I needed to keep my hands free, the downside of survival.

I noticed I wasn't staying put. My knees were digging shallow furrows in the dust; a weird kind of sideways gravity pulled me. I rolled to my feet, and the soles of my feet cut the furrows then. My weight felt low as I moved with no effort on my part, like a passenger in an invisible car.

I'd lost Salem in the murk of grit. He might be miles away or on the other side of any of these dunes. His feet could be sliding nearby like mine and I'd never know, with the sibilance playing games with my senses.

I heated a tat, striving to activate my heightened senses, and a spike of pleasure went through me better than any sex I'd ever had. My feet became heavy, digging grooves in the crimson dust, dirtying the air even more. My whole body expanded, lifting my upper torso out of the billows. My magic worked in this pocket dimension, but not as expected. I needed to be careful about any spell I used.

Above the dust, I found a bloody bowl of sky with a few bright red stars gleaming through. In the middle of the sky, as seen in NASA photos taken by astronauts on the moon, I saw the bright blaze of the

Earth, a blue white swirl of cloud and ocean, and brown-green continents, hanging out of reach. Only the moon I was on was not the same Luna. This was the moon of a parallel universe, or maybe the sub-space dream of a god. This moon had atmosphere and—ruins.

Saving my magic, I released the heightened senses I'd invoked, and sank into the billows, my normal size once more.

Lumbering along in a jet stream, without effort, I drifted past half shattered buildings made of octagonal, obsidian bricks. The wind swelled, moaning as it grated across the dark surfaces. I passed a tower resembling a pig-pong ball on a skewer. Then a divided pyramid occupied two sides of a courtyard where the dust clouds flattened the appearance of gargantuan statues into amorphous shadows. These frozen warriors awaited the thaw of battles that would never come. I went on to where slanting obelisks stabbed the sky like accusing fingers.

Curious, I tried an experiment, angling myself, pushing against the dust to add a bit of resistance to the relentless drag of the horizontal gravity. I was still pulled with the billows across the ruins, but I was able to tell there was a local source to the attraction.

I'm being taken somewhere on purpose.

I wanted to resist on general principle, but I figured Salem would eventually show up where I was going, and if I wanted to get there first—to get the lay of the land and prepare an ambush—I needed to run. I started moving my legs. The dust made footing treacherous, but running into the drag made it easier to breath.

I crossed an expanse of dunes and reached the hard red face of a bluff. I jumped against it and ran up what my eyes insisted was now ground, not wall. At the top, it felt like falling when I reoriented. The filter of hissing grit almost hid the sound of grating stone as a slab swung up in front of me. What poked its head in my path was more mantis than trapdoor spider, with its long, green chitin, oversized eyes, and meat-hook claws. The size of a German shepherd, it tilted its head to study me as if humans were a fabulous, mythical thing it had never expected to meet.

I wondered what its usual prey was.

Making the best of things, it leaped to meet me, pushing off the upright door, against the sideways gravity. I had an impression of a grasshopper's oversized hind legs, as I fell flat to the ground, I hit the releases that popped the bayonets from my forearm sheathes. I slid feet first into the drag until I stood on the raised trap door. The bug's claws missed, but my bayonets didn't. I grooved the entire length of it, head to pelvis, but I don't think the injuries were fatal.

It screamed, thrashing in shock. Before the weird gravity could bring it back on top of me, I threw myself to the side and rolled into the drag. Bumping up a dune, I went a little airborne and managed to get my feet under me so I no longer felt like I was dropping. I knew I was still falling, if sideways, but the *normal* orientation was a psychological comfort.

Keeping an eye out for more opening trapdoors, I continued. The pull increased, as if whatever caused it was getting impatient to see me. The thickening gruel of air acquired a diagonal motion that tugged me out of line with the drag. I activated my magical senses once more and nearly came in my pants as the pleasure center of my brain was tickled. It was a hell of a cost I was paying for magic. This reality—to use the term loosely—could become addictive.

Expanding, I almost didn't fit the giant gate that appeared before me, set between two fanglike pillars. Resisting winds that now moved in from the side, I realized that I'd reached the edge of a vortex that would only get harder, more impenetrable with every step. However, if I could punch through to the eye of the storm, I should find tranquility and maybe normal gravity once more.

I charged all out, feeling a delicious thrill as I activated the tat on my leg that amplified my speed. I got ahead of the jet stream, but my course went diagonal. Still, progress was progress. The air was a red smear now. I ran blind, until bursting through a curtain, I found crystal clarity and a return of gravity from the ground.

The suddenness of it tripped me up. I sprawled face down, my heightened senses peeling away like layers off an onion. Spitting, I lifted my face from the dust and looked a few yards ahead at delicate bare feet with petite ankles. I raised my head and followed the view up milky legs to a diaphanous wrap hugging a woman's full, sweet curves. My gaze slid past thinly veiled breasts to a heart-shaped face framed by blood red hair. Her lips were stained the same color, and her eyes continued the motif, deep crystal red pools where shadows swam like sharks, ever in motion.

She stared down at me much the way the trapdoor bug had done.

"Am I on the menu?" My words seemed loud to me in this quiet pocket where the dust no longer scraped and hissed.

Her full lips parted, daubed a moment by the tip of her tongue. She said, "Do you want to be?"

English, great! But wait a second. Did she already know it, or did she just pull the knowledge straight out of my head?

"Straight out of your head," she said.

"That's fine," I said, "but you don't want to rummage around in there too much. You might get scared."

"Scared?" Her voice verged on laughter. "I am a goddess."

"Don't say I didn't warn you." I slowly pushed myself off the ground, rechambering my bayonets. I scanned our surroundings, hoping I'd beaten Salem here. The lady and I stood near the edge of an obsidian jungle. Broad palms, dangling orchids and vines, cross-hatched boles of trees; they all looked like they'd been carved from volcanic glass by a master craftsman. I heard the murmur of a small waterfall not too far away.

Her gaze caressed my holstered weapons. "Are you afraid of me?"

"Hell, yes! I'm not stupid."

Her well-formed body—only a tiny hint of her true essence—was a severe temptation I needed to fight. This lady had formed this dimension with a stray thought. Such powers hadn't walked the earth since the dawn of civilization. Her awareness of me posed a worse threat than the warlock I hunted. Speaking of which…

"There's another guy on the way here. I intend to cut his heart out by any means possible. I hope you don't have a problem with that."

She began circling me, studying every inch. "And if I did?"

"I'd do it anyway," I said.

"Even though you're afraid of me." She came around in front again.

"I need to sacrifice a soul to get out of here and go home. I had that explained to me. As for you, well, you may be a goddess but I figure I've got a fighting chance at fucking you into submission."

Holding still in front of me once more, she considered my words, arching an eyebrow. "Really?"

I looked around in an obvious manner. "I don't see a long line of suitors anywhere. Sure, you could *dream up* some guy, but he'll only be as good as your imagination and experience. In this one area, I surpass you." I gave her my best dead, flat stare to let her know I wasn't joking.

She stared through my head, her focus a light-year away. A small smile appeared. "You really believe you're *that* good? I'm tempted to prove you right or wrong. Too bad you're out of time."

"I am?"

Her hand lifted. She pointed at the sweeping, red-mist curtain behind me.

I turned.

And Salem was there, stepping into the eye of the storm with grace that made me hate him even more. His spiky blond hair was full of red dust, making him a redhead. *Artificial intelligence*, I thought. He had a shirt sleeve in tatters. The exposed arm bore shallow claw marks. His torso was splattered with yellow-green ichor. He glowered at me, face tight with rage. Gripping the necklace mechanism in his right fist, his knuckles whites, he stomped toward me, barely glancing at the scantily-clad woman beside me.

The guy really is gay.

I looked her in the face, noticing a bit of irritation there. Goddesses don't usually like being ignored.

He stuck a finger in my face. "The only reason I'm not shoving lightning up your ass, Caine, is that the necklace can't seem to get me back to Earth from here. You're going to open the way back for me, and in exchange, I'll make sure you don't suffer—too much—as you die."

I looked at the Red Lady, and pointed at my crotch. "Letting me die would be a terrible waste, don't you think? He's not going to want to do you."

Salem gave her a hard stare, then looked back at me. "You seem to have a gift for finding whores, Caine. You're right, she's not my type."

I smiled. This was not going to work out well for Salem.

"She's a lady," I said. "Be respectful."

"Respect this." He raised the necklace toward the Red Lady. Hazy blue fire spurted between his fingers. Mystic energy shimmered back along his arm.

Her eyes opened wide. "You wouldn't dare!"

"I dare all," he said

The energy wove into a shaft of smoke-blue light. The fire struck the Red Lady, lifting her off her feet, slamming her back.

I winced in sympathy.

Her clothed flesh dissolved where the light had hit, releasing a swirl of fiery red-gold motes to trail in the air. She hit the ground and raised a plume of dust sliding to the edge of the obsidian jungle. Black shards showered her as a hollow tree trunk shattered against her head and shoulders. The bole toppled and crashed to the ground, where it finished bursting.

Salem turned the amulet my way.

Hitting the releases on my arms brought out the bayonets. I stabbed at him.

His own version of a personal shield snapped on, saving him from a punctured lung. Though my attack fell short, I kept the pressure on. *I don't think he can fire a blast without dropping his shield.* I figured I only needed to tie Salem up for a few seconds.

I was proven right when the Red Lady materialized between us, unmarked by the violence she'd just absorbed. Her raised hand froze my bayonets midair. I relaxed and didn't resist her, as if I could. She faced Salem and shoved her hand through his protective barrier as if it were a haze of cigarette smoke. She gripped his throat and lifted him off his feet, standard tough guy pose. His body swung against hers. He choked and pried at her gripping hand. When that did nothing, he pointed the necklace at her a second time.

Yeah, because that went so well last time.

THIRTY-THREE

"It's usually a bad idea to piss in your own Corn Flakes."

—Caine Deathwalker

The stone in Salem's hand clattered through a change, taking on a Y shape, one prong pointing at the Red Lady's face. It spat green phosphorescence that settled over her. Her skin blackened, bubbling, steaming, and peeled away from the raw red muscle underneath. She grimaced with agony, baring her teeth in an animal reaction, but never loosened the death-grip she had on his throat.

Her face shimmered red and the radiance burned away the acid fog around her. The same ruddy glow melted away the damage to her flesh, restoring her beauty. Through gritted teeth, she said, "Keep that up and I will never let you die—no matter how loudly you beg."

A real bitch. Just my kind of woman.

With an effort, as if fighting against part of herself, she loosened her grip so Salem could breathe once more. But at the same time, a creamy green vine sprang from her touch, winding around his upper torso, working its way down his body, spiraling around his limbs. Along with waxy white leaves, the vine sprouted inch-long nettles that spiked into his body and made a leafy green porcupine out of him.

Pierced and constricted, he gasped, biting off a curse. His eyes rolled into the back of his head, and his fingers lost their hold on the necklace. It dropped from a flailing, claw-like hand as he shuddered.

I tore my gaze from the necklace as if it were of no importance to me. Keeping still, I willed myself to fade into the background. *I'm not here. I'm not here. Just ignore me, and the necklace. Take Salem, and go have fun with him.*

As if responding to my thoughts, she let go of his throat and turned away. Salem dropped to his feet but didn't topple over. The vines formed a kind of exoskeleton with a mind of its own. They held him upright and moved his legs for him so he wobbled after the Red Lady. The shards from the broken tree melted as she reached the edge of the jungle.

The waterfall sound died. The crystal growths dissolved into roiling smoke that took on mauve and orange streaks. The entire jungle wavered like a heat mirage and reformed into a red rock canyon with its stark planes softened by dusty-mauve creepers. The canyon bent away from her in the middle, a bright blue pond at its base. A new boulder to my left sported a three-foot lizard with blue-green jeweled skin. An incredibly long tongue swung out past needle teeth as it liked the moisture from its own eyeball.

I lifted my head. An ornate palace crowned the cliff. The sky was now a dusky purple, but the earth was still there in the sky. Many more stars burned through. Green stars. Green stars weren't supposed to be possible, something about the colors of different temperatures. I shrugged. Her universe. She could make the stars any color she wanted.

I bent, snatched up the necklace, and stashed it in the gaping front of my zombie apocalypse suit, on the opposite side from the crystal lotus. *Mental note: add backpack to suit.*

The Red Lady stepped out onto the water. It lovingly cradled her feet, refusing to let her sink. Petite ripples ringed each step as she moved toward the canyon face. Salem, a marionette now, marched in her wake.

I turned to go the opposite direction—thinking I'd come back for Salem later—when…

She called out, "Uh-uhh, you come too. I don't get guests so often I can afford to let one slip away."

"Sure," I said. "I've got nothing better to do anyway."

By the time I'd sauntered to the water's edge, she'd reached the far end, and Salem was halfway across. The water supported him, so I stepped out. I went carefully, the surface like squishy sponges that jiggled underfoot. *Weird.*

Moon pale, dark green haired, a mermaid skimmed past me just under the water, flashing piranha teeth. Her tail flicked, breaking the surface. With a burst of speed, she angled down, fading into the cloudy blue depths. On the surface, the water was the size of a pond, but I suspected it was also impossibly deep.

I wondered if the bug creatures and merfolk were pieces of the Red Lady's dreams, or what she'd made of previous visitors once she tired of them.

A staircase rose from the rock at the lady's feet. There were no side walls or rails. Heights didn't seem to bother her as she ascended. The stairs zigzagged up into the canyon wall where a dark tunnel opened like a monster mouth. She went through, and Salem started up the stairs after her. Dripping blood, he no longer fought his restraints. I think he was afraid of pitching off the stairs and breaking things he'd need to depend upon later. I imagined that, even with broken arms and legs, the vines would march him wherever the Red Lady wanted him to go.

I let him get nearly to the top before I started up behind him. I considered turning tail and running, but knew it was useless. She was absolute in her private little universe. Once she missed me, the entire world would respond to her will, driving me back into her arms. So far, I was spared her malicious attention. I wanted to keep it that way.

Salem vanished into the tunnel. I reached its huge, non-slavering maw, and discovered that what I'd thought were teeth was actually a portcullis. I passed under it and the medieval grating dropped to seal me in with a loud *chung* that reverberated loudly. The Red Lady had made her point; I'd go when *she* was ready, not before.

I promised myself that if I ever got out of here, I'd never come back.

The tunnel wound lazily around several murky blue pools. Several foot-long toads squatted at the edge of the water. They were bright green with mustard yellow eyes. They called out as I passed, "Guh-riip guh-riip!"

"Same to you," I said.

The walls started out as red rock, but quickly blended into a red quartz surface. A smooth path appeared under my feet, milky glass with a hint of blue. Vents in the ceiling allowed shafts of Earthlight to filter in and lessen the gloom, and gray-green lichen on the stalactites excreted a fragile radiance, tinting the shadow a hunter green.

As I went, there were side pockets where giant boulders had been split open to reveal the gemmed hearts of geodes. These lay at the base of spiky, red quartz blooms. Earth blue moths fluttered around one such inorganic flower.

I saw an opening ahead, spilling in a pinkish froth of light. Just two pools of water remained. I came between them when a sea dragon arched from one pool and vanished into the other. About forty feet of rippling aqua blue and sea-foam green with translucent gold fins and flippers, it gave no notice of me. This wasn't a reaction I'd gotten from dragons in the past, especially with the dragon blood tats I wore on my skin. This might not be a real dragon at all. Possibly only a figment of the Red Lady's imagination given life.

Like a woman putting on her most pleasing face for a male, the Red Lady was trying to dazzle me with her power and the beauty of its expression. That implied vanity, a weakness I could exploit. I smiled to myself, continuing on.

I left the tunnel for a courtyard the size of a football stadium. Underfoot, red octagonal bricks surrounding square ones, sweeping on to a massive hall with towers and flying buttresses. Narrow, red paned windows were everywhere. Black gargoyles were ranked on the edge of the hall's roof, staring down at me with interest. Their eyes were vermillion stars. One of them fanned great, ribbed wings as if he wanted to swoop down and crush me with his glossy jet limbs. The adjoining gargoyles stared at him and he settled down, folding wings, becoming just another statue.

The Red Lady and Salem had drawn closer together, and both were way ahead of me. They took a flight of stairs from the courtyard, and passed through open double doors that had to be fifty feet high. They were black oak, banded with black iron, adorned with the same type of hinges. The circular knockers were spiraled like rope. There were no guards at the entrance, another sign of her power; only the weak required protectors.

I was impressed even though I was trying very hard not to be.

I crossed the courtyard and climbed the stairs.

My magical barrier self-activated, my tat burning to life like a sonofabitch. Damn, the pain for magic was back. Me magic seemed to have acclimated to this strange dimension.

Something wet and gold sprinkled against my shield and slid down its bell to the stonework. The stone steamed and foamed a little. *Acid rain?* I looked up and saw a gargoyle standing, shaking his manhood. *Gargoyle piss.* I saluted him cheerily. *Better luck next time.*

Inside the Great Hall, I was reminded of a soaring cathedral, but there were no pews. The red-stained window let thin shafts of crimson slice the gloom. Iron braziers lining the walls held red coals. A red carpet lay underfoot. I felt like I was walking on blood as I headed for the distant dais were a jet throne waited with matching plump, red-tasseled pillows. The Red Lady stood on the dais, waiting. Forced to kneel—and bleed—Salem was several steps down from her.

The lady held out her hand to me, and a rich red-velvet gown misted onto her. Like a bloody cataracts, her hair now fell to her heels. Her sleeves were short and puffy, and a red copper armlet wound down to her wrist like a serpent. As I got closer, I could see engraved scales. Its wedge-shaped head was lifted from her skin, its mouth closed, garnets glinting for eyes. Her palm was turned up, fingers pointing down, an invitation—to what exactly, I wasn't sure.

I stopped several feet back from Salem. He was panting and groaning, his face and hair damp with sweat. He tried to turn his head my way, and failing as the vines caged it too. "Get us out of here," he growled. "I'll pay you, anything."

My hand pressed the outside of my suit. I felt the lump of the necklace under the material. "I have everything I need," I said, "except for your death."

He cursed me, until the vines choked him into silence.

I moved past him to the dais, looking up. "Hell of a show, I must say." I pointed at the throne. "Is that for me?"

She stared. Throwing back her head, she laughed, a sound like a great shivering bell heard across a distance. "Oh, your arrogance surpasses even my own, and I have reason for it."

"It's just that I'm a little tired. I was hoping I could sit down."

She turned toward her throne and waved. The floor buckled up beside her throne, forming another, one slightly smaller and less grand than her own. Well, it was better than a footstool. I took the steps, walked past her to the new throne, and sat down. I stared at her. "I swear, if a talking lion pops up and calls me a Son of Adam, I'm going to borrow a sword and hack his head off."

She murmured, "My, you are ferocious, aren't you?"

"Lady, when I was born and the doctor slapped my ass, I bit his thumb. I didn't have a tooth in my head, but they needed two orderlies and a crowbar to pry me off him. You got anything around here to drink?"

"What would you like?"

"Rum and coke."

Looking puzzled, she stared into my head. I felt fingers plucking at my thoughts. Her confusion cleared. "Ah, yes, here you are, my pet."

I've got something you can pet.

A goblet ghosted into view in front of me. Carved from brown jade, it hovered, waiting to be snagged outta thin air. I reached out, pulled it in, and set the cup against my lips, but didn't drink, remembering all the stories about the dangers of eating fairy food and such. I wet my lips, and set the cup down on the arm of my chair. After getting drunk on dwarf beer, Rip van Winkle had slept for twenty years. I wasn't taking chances.

Staring across the hall, I noticed we had a standing audience of deep-red, translucent shadows, make-believe people with rose zircon eyes shading into deeper reds. Their clothes were shadow as well, a style out of the renaissance. Armored shadows guarded the entrance now, armed with halberds.

I studied at Salem but spoke to the Red Lady. "What's going on, a public execution?"

"Why, yes. To be followed by a wedding." She sat on the throne beside me, a bright smile in place. A jeweled tiara appeared on her head, holding a gauzy veil in place over her eyes. "I haven't had one in five-hundred years. And then comes the wedding night." Her voice dipped to a chaste whisper. "You will have a chance to live up to your boasts. I am expecting a lot out of you." Her smile turned hard and threatening, yet teasing as well. "You had best hope I am not disappointed."

I loosened the collar of my battle suit, swallowing. "Man, talk about working under pressure."

An executioner appeared, a big fellow with leather pants, boots, no shirt, a hairy paunch, and a black hood over his head with eye holes so he could see. He hefted a massive battle ax with one brawny arm, using the weapon to sketch a salute to the Red Queen next to me.

She gestured imperiously at Salem. "Off with his head!"

THIRTY-FOUR

"When confronted with a dire situation it's best to 'drink' it over!"

—Caine Deathwalker

"No way!" I said. "He's my arch-nemesis. If anyone's going to kill him, it will be me."

Salem glared from the foot of the dais where the vines forced him to kneel. He said, "You can kill me, but you didn't beat me. You'll never have that."

I pushed myself off of the throne, and studied him thoughtfully as I walked forward, stepping down to his level.

The executioner glowered at me for interfering with his work.

I held out my hand.

He visibly restrained himself from biting my fingers. Instead, he handed over the ax, and stormed off. I set the head of the battle ax on the floor, leaning on the shaft as I bent forward to look him in the eye. "You have a point, but I hope you don't intend to appeal to my sense of fair play for a chance at life."

"Wouldn't think of it," he said.

"As long as we're talking, I'd like to know something."

"What?"

"You were throwing around all kinds of power, back in L.A. You were even managing multiple spells simultaneously, and not paying any kind of a cost to do it that I could see. Were you powering the necklace with the men you killed?"

I didn't know if he'd tell me anything. Spite sometimes wins out against the arrogant desire to boast. In the end, he couldn't resist rubbing my nose in his brilliance. He smiled. "I'm not surprised you couldn't figure it out. The necklace attunes itself to whoever uses it, obeying whatever commands they know enough to give. I widened that attunement to overlap with entropy itself."

"Ah, that is smart." *Stupid, I mean.* He'd powered the necklace through necromancy, feeding it from the slow death of the universe we'd left behind.

The Red Lady called from her throne, "Getting bored here. Can we move things along?"

Salem surreptitiously strained against the vines, seeking a weak spot, even though this drove the thorns deeper into his flesh. I knew if he could break free he'd try at once to snatch the necklace; going intangible as he had back on at the skyscraper was the only chance he had to escape the Red Lady.

Maybe my only chance also.

Problem was, I wasn't a magic-user in the traditional sense. My dragon-blood tats were a shortcut, a way of handling power without having to thoroughly understand it, leaping years of training. The drawback was it might take me years to bend the relic to my will. Haruka couldn't wait that long. As skilled as Salem was, I knew he could answer questions I hadn't even thought of yet. This caused me to reconsider killing him—for now.

I had an idea.

I said, "I am willing to spare your life, on one condition."

The Red Lady said, "Is anyone listening to me? I want him dead. No one is allowed to survive who is indifferent to my beauty."

"What's your condition?" Salem asked.

"You must swear a binding oath of fealty to me."

"Is that all? Sure," he said, "now let me go."

The Red Lady's voice took on an edge of threat, "Caine..."

I ignored her. "A binding oath," I said. "Here, where such an oath cannot be broken, swear it in the name of the Red
Lady,"

Salem stared over my shoulder. I somehow knew that she was right behind me, her eyes radiant with murderous intent.

"Give me the ax," she said. "I'll do it myself."

Yeah, thought so. I straightened and turned, meeting her gaze. "You're making a mistake here."

"I'm a goddess. I don't make mistakes, at least none I have to live with." She held out her hand for the weapon.

She was a goddess. That meant she could have materialized another ax for herself instantly. What was going on here wasn't about Salem, but her and me. She was staking her claim as the dominant partner in a very new relationship—that existed only in her head. Problem was, what's in the head of a goddess can wind up becoming painfully real. I needed to win this contest of wills. I also desperately need a drink.

"Listen," I said, "if you want this…" I almost choked, "*marriage* to mean anything, it's got to be done right. In my reality, there can be no marriage without certain formalities. One of these is the bachelor party. Also, a best man is usually required for the wedding ceremony. Can't we do this without cheap theatrics?" I reached out and slid my hand up her arm, then suddenly yanked her closer, crushing her against my chest. I let the ax fall over, and held her, peering soulfully into her eyes. "You're going to make me think I mean nothing to you." My lips drew closer to hers.

She'd resisted my hold at first. I felt ghostly fingers stirring through my thoughts. She was checking to see if I was lying to her. Fortunately, nothing I'd said was untrue. I'd never claimed to want to marry her, I'd just told her the customs of my people.

Her body softened, melting against mine as a new kind of fire kindled in her eyes. Her hand caressed my cheek, and slid to the back of my neck as she closed the distance, kissing me roughly, a lot of energy but little finesse. For a goddess, she was terribly inexperienced. Of course, there aren't a lot of suitors at her power level. Guys like to be in control; there's little chance of that with her.

Well, there's something to be said for a challenge.

Her arms went around my neck. The kiss went on forever, until I was desperate to escape. She might not need to breathe, but I was fond of doing so. My hands slid down her body, behind her—and purely in self-defense—I squeezed her ass, startling her into releasing me so I could gasp for air.

She saw my discomfort and reddened in embarrassment. "I'm sorry, I wasn't thinking."

"It's all right," I assured her. "We'll get better with practice. Now, about the warlock…"

"Take it, if you have to have it."

I gathered in one of her hands and kissed it. "Thank you."

She smiled coyly, batting her eyes at me. "I have a lot more for you, after the wedding. I can be a virgin as many times as you'd like."

A thrill went through me. My gaze slid down her body, imagining her dress away. The thought of a woman that could change her form for me, being anyone, anything, was sorely tempting, but not even a goddess is worth enduring the trap that is marriage. I smiled wistfully and told her a truth. "There are so many things I want to do to you…"

She blushed.

I released her hand. "Do me a favor and stop reading my mind. I want to surprise you with my passion and expertise. *Let* me surprise you. Be a beautiful bride in my arms, and nothing else. You have forever to be a goddess."

She pressed her hand to her bodice, as if to gage the thunder of her heart. "Very well, it is a small enough gift to give, but I want something in exchange."

"What?"

"I've seen in your mind that your people have a custom. You give a diamond as a token of love to those you'd claim as wife."

"I don't have one," I said.

Her hand moved out from her heart a little. My shirt went lax as the crystal lotus disappeared from my suit. The lotus reappeared between her hand and breasts. "This will do."

With that, she turned and walked toward a distant, heavily gilded side door. Without her attention, the spectral audience that had silently attended us all this time melted to nothing. Almost out of the room, she paused and called back to me. "I know your heart is sincere, but I should warn you; do not try to leave the palace without me. The gargoyles on the roof are fools that once trifled with my emotions. And they were bad in bed besides. Since you are my new favorite, they hate every fiber of your being. I'd hate it if you were torn apart … before you've proven your mettle on our wedding night."

She went out the door. It closed by itself behind her, and I was left alone with Salem.

Dripping blood from dozens of wounds, he looked up at me. "And I thought I had it bad."

"You're stuck here too," I said. "Are we going to work together, or am I going to toss you outside to play with the former boy toys?"

"All right, I'll work with you."

"Swear it by the Red Lady."

"I swear by her name to serve your best interests, until we escape this reality. Then, your ass is mine."

"I'm not gay," I said.

"Figure of speech."

There was a mounting pressure; a sizzling vibration in the air that drew a sympathetic heat from my tats.

Salem's eyes widened. He felt it too. "What the hell is that," he asked.

"You made an oath in the Lady's name. This is her reality; it has witnessed your oath. Break your word and her world will crush you."

"You're joking?"

I flashed him one of my evil grins. “One way to find out.”

Maybe later,” he said. “Cut me outta this ambulating salad.”

I raised a boot high enough to reach into the top, and drew my field knife from its hidden sheath. A whisper in the back of my mind urged me to sink the blade into his black heart. I resisted the impulse and slid the steel between him and the vines. Strands of the thorny growth snapped on the knife edge, and all of it withered, falling away as dust.

“Well, that’s easy enough,” I said.

He straightened, and his hand moved a few inches toward the necklace inside my combat suit.

“Go ahead,” I said, “betray me. I dare you. I’m kind of curious as to what will happen.”

He stepped back from me.

“Smart,” I said.

“Speaking of smart, now that we’re alone, and she’s not reading your mind, why don’t you open the gate that brought us here?”

I drifted back up the dais, and crossed to the bigger throne. I threw myself into an inelegant sprawl and looked at him. I lifted my feet into the air. A moment later, an ottoman appeared under my boots. I relaxed, my feet comfortably elevated. “Just because she isn’t reading my thoughts doesn’t mean she’s not keeping an eye on me—and you too. Besides, I can’t open the gate without the crystal lotus she took from me.”

“But you have some kind of plan. You aren’t really going to marry her?”

I phrased my words carefully, figuring the Red Lady might also be listening. “I’m going to do what I must, and so are you. Namely, as best man, you’re supposed to throw me a wake, uh, I mean a bachelor party. Better get to work”

Old Man’s hand emerged from the little mirror on my chest. His fingers gripped a little folded square of paper. I plucked the note from his hand. His hand sank back into the glass, and the frame readjusted to its former size.

Salem stared, nonplussed. “You’re full of surprises. I am beginning to seriously regret interfering in your life.”

I opened the note and read Old Man’s elegant handwriting: WHILE I AM NOT OPPOSED TO HAVING GRAND KIDS; YOU NEED TO HURRY FOR HARUKA’S AND HIRO’S SAKE.

“Screw you,” I muttered.

THIRTY-FIVE

"Let the party games begin!"

—Caine Deathwalker

Playing with the now dormant necklace, lobbing it from hand to hand, I took a tour of the sprawling palace. I needed to get a handle on the Red Lady and I thought better in otion. Every now and then, one of those shadow people with red eyes would pass by, guys wearing archaic livery, women in long-sleeved gowns with their hair teased into artful piles atop their heads. The women all seemed to have a strong resemblance to the Red Lady. The guy's faces were bland and unrefined. Besides giving her reality a lived-in look, the shadows bowed or curtsied, graciously asking if they might be of service.

I ignored them, more interested in the décor. A rich cherry wood paneling lined many of the spacious chambers. The floors were parquet, intricate puzzles made of different woods cut into different shapes. The center of the rooms almost always had large medallions at the center of the design, usually starbursts or flowers. Everything shone with a high polish though I never saw anyone actually working.

Pacing like a caged tiger, I discovered a five-story, octagonal library. Every wall was lined with ivory bookshelves, every level serviced by a railed gallery with rolling ladders. The tiled floor at ground level was a red and white checkerboard. High overhead, a massive ceiling dome was made of cloudy rose quartz.

The center of the room held three kissing couches arranged to form a triangle. Within the triangle, a wrought iron tree created shade from the pink light of the dome. The sculpted branches were festive, many of them dangling lanterns, fashioned from bright paper and thin-hammered gold foil. The lanterns cast out a soft luminosity that gave me multiple, pastel shadows as I circled the stacks, my hand trailing over the titles.

The writing was obscure, nothing I recognized. It resembled a blend of petroglyphs and Middle Eastern scrawl. I paused and picked out a book bound in red velvet. An attached black ribbon acted as a built in bookmark.

I cracked the volume and scanned a page, more of the meandering writing, written in blood on yellow parchment. I flipped a page and noticed that the writing had shifted orientation. Page after page, this happened; sentences ran left and right, then up and down, and on another page the symbols seemed to spiral from the center. No illustrations were there to help. I wondered if this were a demon tongue, or some language the Red Lady had invented.

Old Man might know.

With a shrug, and quick look over my shoulder, I proceeded to feed the book into the mirror I wore. I felt someone take the book from my hand, pulling it through. While I was at it, I sent the necklace through as well. It had done little good against the Red Lady, and if I didn't make it back—I shuddered at the thought—maybe Old Man could still do something with it to help Haruka.

If I stretched the glass enough, it could get me out of here, except my hand had been stopped by the glass while the amulet and chain went through cleanly. I understood. There was no way out without the crystal lotus and a soul to feed it.

Mulling things over, I moved on and almost ran into a shadow girl servant. She held a sliver tray with far more substance than she had. The tray contained a gold cup encrusted with rubies. Beside the cup was a dark red bottle. The shadow girl spoke with a low, sultry voice, "Would My Lord care for some wine?"

"I'd rather have a white chocolate mocha."

She looked ready to cry obsidian tears. "I do not know what that is."

I snatched the bottle off the tray. "This will do, for now." I waved her away, and she scurried out. Bottle in hand, I finished my circuit of the room and left the way I'd entered, the only door as far as I could see. The over-wide hall continued past ballrooms, parlors, assorted offices, and rooms devoted to fine collectables. I reached a solarium with a green glass table and padded chairs.

A sliding glass partition took me into another glass chamber, this one a greenhouse where riotous flowers formed a miniature jungle. Some species could easily have come from Earth or Fairie, others from the methane crevices of Titan, or a madman's dreams. A few I steered well clear of, suspecting they were carnivorous.

I found a hammock supported by more of those tree sculptures. These had no lanterns. I was bone tired from a night of fighting, and from heavy magic use. Whatever restorative Old Man had giving me in that drink from the mirror had lost its edge. Only the horror of an impending marriage had galvanized me this long.

I dropped into the hammock and popped the cork from the bottle. Off my feet, I couldn't believe how comfortable the sling was. That, and the bottle I guzzled, soon had me nodding off. The bottle fell from my hand as sleep closed in. Just before I lost consciousness, I thought I saw the Red Lady standing next to me, smiling, casting a woven throw across my body. Softness touched my forehead, a kiss. It was either that or a fragment of a dream.

I awoke, feeling hands patting me down. My eyes slit open. It was Salem, looking for the necklace.

He stilled and looked at my face.

I opened my eyes wider.

He shook me urgently, as if he'd intended this all the time. He smelled of booze and his words were slurred, "Time for your party."

"Party?" I think he'd started early.

"Your bachelor party. That's what a best man does after all."

"Oh, yeah." I slid in the hammock, swinging my feet to the floor. As I sat up, I kicked the empty wine bottle. It clinked and rolled away with a grinding sound. "Just tell me you've got hard booze and strippers."

"Hard booze anyway. There aren't a lot of women around here, ones that are real."

"Booze is better than nothing." I stood. "Wait a second, how long was I asleep?" *Please don't say twenty years. I wasn't supposed to eat or drink anything here.*

"Hours and hours."

Better than days and days. Okay, I guess the food and drink are safe here after all.

A trifle off balance, he led the way back to the main part of the palace.

Sauntering along my earlier path, I noticed subtle changes in the floor plan and the décor. It reminded me that all I saw was built on a whim, and that whim could change without notice. This unseen threat hung overhead like a sword, no matter how benign the scenery might be.

Salem went into the library, around the loveseats and sculpted tree with its lanterns, and out a back door that hadn't been there last time I was here. The doors were made of aqua-blue glass with glass door knobs. Salem threw them wide open and went into a hall lined with deep blue curtains. He crossed a Prussian blue carpet to a cluster of tables and chairs.

The furniture made me uneasy. I kept thinking about those under Salem's command that had attacked me earlier. *Well, he'd had the necklace then. It should be safe enough now. He's under oath.*

Like sea foam, pale green tablecloths washed off the tables, almost spilling to the floor. Silver place settings waited. Silver cups gleamed and sparkled with fire opals and sapphires. Silver buckets containing bottles on ice. In place of the usual wine bottles, I saw vodka, gin, and Kentucky bourbon. A cart off to the side was laden with pizza boxes. Over on a stage, an ensemble group prepared to wow us with cello, violin, flute, and piano.

Oh, joy.

"The Red lady provided all this?"

"Yeah, once I made it clear this was for a pre-wedding ritual common to our world. She provided the guests too."

I eyed them with something less than pleasure. More shadow people she'd dreamed up. A lot of them were women, in theory anyway.

He said, "I tried to get across that this was supposed to be an all guy thing, but…"

"I suppose it doesn't really matter since they are all aspects of *her* anyway."

"That's what she said." Salem pulled out an empty seat dropped heavily into it. His voice went oh, so casual, "By the way, what happened to the necklace? You did want me to instruct you in its use, right?"

"You can just tell me what I need to know. I've got it stashed for safe keeping."

"Do you now?" His gaze shot to the mirror on my zombie apocalypse suit.

So did mine. The frame expanded. Old man's hand poked out again, offering me a folded paper. I took it and read the note. The hand withdrew and the mirror shrank.

"What's it say?" Salem slurred.

"Old man's yelling me about a book he read."

Dear Pain in my Ass,

The script in the book isn't demon, Faire tongue, or human language, nor does it come from any known oracle, extra-terrestrial or otherwise. The palace—and its books—seem to be an unconscious manifestation of the Red Lady. Reading the books isn't possible because the part of her mind that made them doesn't draw from her brain's language center. You might be able to override small parts of her reality when she's not actively maintaining it.

P.S. Stop screwing around, get the lotus, and come home.

—Lauphram

I wadded up the note and shoved it back inside the mirror. "Easy for you to say," I muttered.

The ensemble played something light and airy that made me remember Izumi. I dropped into a chair next to a shadow woman, and stared. Under my gaze, she seemed to grow more solid, her hair paling to star fire. Her face and figure shifted until she became a shadowy imitation of the fey princess.

Showing interest, Salem watched what I did and then peered at the shadow man next to him. That guest became a young boy with long curly locks of hair.

"Robbing the cradle?" I said.

He shrugged. "It's not like he's real, or like there's anyone around here that will arrest me. Besides, I became a bad guy so I could do what I want."

"Just don't do anything that will kill my appetite." Someone brought a pizza box over and set it in front of me. I opened it and studied a three-meat pizza with mushrooms and peppers. It even smelled real.

"Speaking of killing, you do realize that my oath prevents me from harming you, but doesn't require that I actively defend you in anyway, right."

With a slice of pizza halfway to my mouth, I answered. "Yeah, so?"

He smiled in huge anticipation. "So we have some entertainment to look forward to."

I glowered at him. "What have you done?"

He smiled; a look of innocence that was almost as good as my own. His eyes were wide as he shook his head, hands up, showing me his empty palms. "Why, I've only arranged for a little floorshow. I thought a little dancing might be nice."

I tensed. Dancing meant many things; recreational dancing, sure, but it was also a street term for fighting.

He stared straight up.

I stared straight up, at a high, vaulting ceiling set with more blood-red stained glass, each irregular pane separated by black, lead fretting. There were shadows on the glass—*winged* shadows—until the glass burst, and the gargoyles crashed the party.

THIRTY-SIX

"Marriage? Oh, the horror!"

—Caine Deathwalker

The attack was not as disquieting as the surreal responses; the ensemble played on, the shadow guests stayed seated, passed pizza boxes around, laughing, mumbling banter as they fulfilled the role they'd been created for. Salem grabbed the wrist of the pretty boy next to him. The youth became more solid, more real, at the touch, drawing life from the warlock. Salem dragged the boy under the table as shards of glass splintered into smaller pieces on top of it.

I covered my head, trusting my sturdy apocalypse suit to weather the abuse. I had no swords, my guns were empty, my bayonets and the field knife in my boot weren't going to do more than scratch a gargoyle's stony skin. That left my tats, but they were acting unpredictably in this altered space. They could save me, or get me killed.

I could always scream for the Red Lady to come and save my ass, but then I'd owe her, and besides, a man has his warrior's pride. I wondered though, how all this was going on without her doing anything. Was Salem shielding the gargoyles from her perception in some way? Or had he convinced her this was normal for a bachelor party, some kind of rite of courage for a groom to prove his worth?

Never mind. Fight now, figure out the answers later.

The shower of glass ended. I dropped my hands, one of them still clutching a slice of pizza, and looked up again. The jet black gargoyles were in the chamber, ribbed wings slicing the air as they wheeled in tight circles, slowly spiraling down. There seemed to be some question as to which of them would tear my head off and who got to eat my heart and liver.

Okay, time to improvise.

I held the pizza slice in front of me, ignoring the sounds of sexual activity coming from under the table. I focused on what I wanted to see. The pizza slice darkened to shadow, loosing its warm greasy scent. The shadow flowed. A second later, I had spare clips of ammo. I loaded my guns, put two back in thigh holsters, and kept two guns in my hands.

I used laser sights to lock onto the lowest of the gargoyles, and tapped the triggers to get single shots with the automatic weapons. Holding down the trigger would have empted the clip, and that would have wasted too much ammo, assuming of course the phantom rounds functioned as I imagined.

The guns bucked in my grip, muzzles spitting flame as red as the eyes of the shadow guests at my party. I was irritated. Here I was—bold as hell, heroic, and awesome—and not one of them bothered to even look my way.

The mercury rounds punched four-inch holes in gargoyle chests which proved to be hollow. The creatures' backs sprayed away from ten-inch exit wounds. Their wings were blown loose. Inorganic hearts shredded. Wingless, they plunged to the floor, faces displaying comical expressions of disbelief. They crashed headlong into the floor, breaking into pieces.

That got the attention of the other gargoyles. They broke off from the wheeling formation and streaked toward me from all sides.

I spun, emptying the clips. Half the gargoyles had heads or hearts that exploded to gravel, causing them to drop like—well, stones. The rest of those I'd hit managed to block shots with their arms. Though armless, waving stone stumps in fury, they were still a threat, dropping toward my head like rogue meteors.

As I holstered my empty guns and drew the fresh ones, I focused on the floor. A sheet of carpeting, and the stone beneath it, curled up to catch and deflect them. Though many were shunted aside, a few gargoyles broke through my barrier. I was clubbed off my feet, and sprawled in the rubble. The spell-reinforced suit took the brunt of the force. I'd be wearing deep dark bruises for weeks, but I hadn't broken anything.

From the floor, I tapped the trigger of a PPK, sending single rounds sizzling into the obsidian skulls of the gargoyles still trying to move. Soon, they were all inert. My left glove torn, my hand bled from the broken glass scattered about. I picked out a few shards, and carefully climbed to my feet. From the sounds under the table, Salem was finishing up a party game of his own. The party guests were still carrying on like nothing had happened.

And I was incredibly pissed.

I went to the table, arriving as Salem surfaced, adjusting his pants. He looked surprised to see me. "You're not dead yet?" he asked.

I'd saved one round for him. I put the muzzle against his forehead. He winced from the heat. "Move a muscle," I said, "and you die."

Though drunk, enough reason glimmered in his eyes for him to hold himself very still.

I said, "You set them on me."

"No, not at all."

"Explain it to me," I said.

"I told them about your up-coming wedding, and emphatically warned them not to come and cause trouble because you wouldn't like it."

"Yet they knew where to come to."

"I told them specifically to avoid the room with the red stained-glass ceiling, but they didn't listen." He giggled. "Not *my* fault."

"No, of course not. Tell me, did you have a good time there under the table?"

His eyes widened. "Oh, yes, thank you for asking."

I smiled. "Good, everyone should have a happy memory to take with them to hell." I blew the top of his head away, flinching back from brain and blood splatter. His body toppled to the floor, also ignored by the party guests.

He can't be the only magic-user out there with knowledge about the necklace. I should probably have checked with Red Fang right off anyway.

With my bloody hand, I grabbed a bottle of vodka from an ice bucket, for medicinal purposes of course, and staggered across the room to the library. Swigging from the bottle as I went, I almost passed the loveseats without noticing who lounged there in a red chiffon gown with silk slippers on her feet.

The Red Lady held up a fluted glass the color of garnets.

I stopped and poured her a drink.

"Having fun?" she asked.

I thought about it a second and nodded. "Oddly, I am."

"But you don't want to stay." It wasn't a question. She knew my answer.

I thought of Haruka, dead, folded up in my freezer, her father's heart all but ripped out by grief. "It's nothing personal, but I've got too many unresolved issues that need my attention."

"I see her in your thoughts."

"You weren't supposed to look in there, remember."

She swung her feet to the floor and patted the place next to her. "Sit a moment."

I did. Leaning back, I took another pull off my bottle, savoring a starchy burn that was right on the edge of pain.

The Red Lady swirled her glass, not yet tasting what it held. Turning toward me, she pulled a knee onto the loveseat, wedging it between us. She peered into my eyes. "If I let you go, will you promise to return to me, someday?"

I stalled. "You just met me. I know that I'm sexy as hell, a real man, and all that, but aren't you moving a little fast?"

"You don't understand. I'm the real thing, not some fantasy novel goddess. Time is omni-directional to me. I've known you in my heart since before you were born. I've known we would one day be together. And I know—much as I want to hide it from myself—that your love for me is yet to awaken. In time, I will love you for a thousand years. I wanted that to be longer. I wanted to start us now, knowing all-the-while it wasn't going to happen. A goddess can do anything, even lie to herself."

"Okay, that deserves another swig."

But I couldn't take a drink. I sensed she was telling the truth. She didn't need to lie to keep me here. She didn't need the tears in her eyes either. A teardrop fell into the glass she held. Instead of melding with the vodka, the tear became a red pearl, the symbol of her sorrow. The glass and vodka melted into the air, a cascade of red sparks that left the pearl alone in her hand.

She offered it to me.

I set the bottle of vodka down by my feet and leaned toward her, my hand sliding under hers. She tipped the creamy red pearl into my palm. My fingers closed over the gift. Such things were rare, and usually powerful. This might well become the greatest treasure in my collection.

"Think of me when you wear it," she said, "and remember I loved you enough to let you go."

"Thank you."

"You won't need the necklace now." She smiled, blinking back the rest of her tears. "Go. Go quickly, before I change my mind."

"I need the crystal—"

"—Lotus. I know." She ran her fingers along my right forearm. The sleeve vanished. The underlying skin chilled, then warmed, then throbbed with magic.

I looked down and saw the lotus-dragon tattoo back where it needed to be.

She said, "The lotus has taken the requiescat soul. You can open the gate, if this world will let you."

"Why wouldn't it?"

This reality is a reflection of me. I don't want you to go, so the very walls of space will fight your leaving."

I shrugged. "Why should anything ever go easy for me? There's one thing I want to know." I rested my hand on her thigh.

She smiled briefly, tenderly. "Just one?"

"What is it about me that you love so deeply? There are those who'd say I'm a total jerk, who ought to be flayed alive."

She said, "I wasn't always a goddess. Like most of us, I had to ascend to that level. I was once a dragon." She stopped, as if that explained it all.

"That's it?"

"Yes."

"I've never found lady dragons to swoon at my approach."

"It might just be me." With great deliberation, she stood and headed for the party room.

"You're going in there?" I said. "The party's over."

I thought I heard her sob quietly to herself. She paused in the doorway, her back to me. "I know. You've made quite a mess. Someone needs to clean it up."

I felt a heavy deadness in my chest. If I didn't know better,
I'd have called it regret. I picked up the vodka bottle and finished it off, with a silent apology to my much abused liver. I dropped the bottle on the loveseat and headed out. I wanted a little distance from the house before opening a gate. The transition back to my world might damage the room. That would be poor gratitude for the hospitality I'd received.

I'll jump for home from the outer courtyard. After all, there are no longer any gargoyles to get in my way. As I reached the library doors, they slammed in my face. The lock clicked.

What the hell? Oh yeah, she'd said her reality might resist letting me go, but I can't let it make a difference.

I pointed my gun at the door and then remembered I was out of ammo. Okay, time to go old school. I raised a knee and lashed out, kicking the lock. The door shuddered, but didn't break open. Instead, the doors fused together and turned into high quality tungsten steel.

I shrugged. *Okay, I'll leave from here instead.*

I looked at the tat on my arm, willing it to life.

The books left the shelves, flapping like birds, buzzing me, smacking my body in a desperate bid to break my concentration. A particularly heavy book *whapped* me in the back of the head. I went down in a daze with the world spinning off center.

"Sonofabitch!"

THIRTY-SEVEN

"Women have a way of disarming a man."

—Caine Deathwalker

On hands and knees, I blinked dizziness away, looking for the pearl that had fallen from my hand. I reached past a steepled book on the floor for the glossy bead. The book flipped over, becoming a manacle as the pages hardened to steel and fused to the tiled floor. I growled at the checkerboard pattern. "I'm leaving. Get over it."

The floor under me turned butter-soft. I sank a few inches and stopped, the floor gripping my circumference. Overhead, the books from the shelf continued to flap in agitation.

My open hand lay a few inches from the pearl. It might as well have been a thousand yards—but under the force of my desire, the pearl rolled to me. My hand closed around it. Then I focused on the book-cuff the same way I'd focused in my fight with the gargoyles. The cuff was paper once more, old and brittle, yellowed with the passage of uncountable ages. The stuff tore loudly under the pressure I applied. Using that one arm, I tried to lever myself up. The edge of the floor wouldn't let me go.

I considered warming up the tat for *Dragon Flame*, but I had a mental vision of turning the library into an inferno with me trapped inside, and decided I needed a safer plan. Before I could think of it, Old Man acted. Thunder shook me in its teeth, blasting me several feet into the air. Looking down, I saw Old Man's sword blade protruding from the mirror I wore. Three feet of it extended from the glass. The blade was wreathed in violet lightning, a big crater under the tip. I fell and covered the hole as the sword was pulled back through the mirror, leaving me on my own again.

So I wouldn't lose the pearl again, I put it in an empty pocket for ammo clips, and snapped it closed

Thanks Old Man. I owe you one.

Old man's hand came out of the glass. He held up four clips of ammo. I took them and reloaded my guns.

Owe you two.

The flapping books were diving again. Who needed gargoyles? I shielded my face with one arm, running to the ladder that serviced the next level up. As I put my weight on the bottom rung, it snapped like a Popsicle stick. I jumped higher. The next rung broke as well. I slid down, and ran for the door to the party room. I more than half expected the door to lock itself in my face, but it opened at my touch and I burst through.

The door slammed behind me, locking with a click. This was a room I'd never seen before. The Red Lady wasn't here. Neither was the party I'd left, or Salem's corpse. I stood in a hall that stretched on forever. The walls left and right were ten feet apart, and lined with old suits of armor. The helms were plumbed with red-dyed ostrich feathers. The suits each had unsheathed broadswords, their tips grounded between iron feet. Each warrior also had a triangular shield with the top edge scalloped. The design was simple; a full, red moon on a sable sky.

A gauntlet?

I stood still, watching carefully for any sign of motion. Nothing moved, but I knew better than to relax my guard. I also had a suspicion that the second I warmed up the lotus tattoo, I'd be in the midst of an all out melee with the armor.

I took a step.

Nothing.

I took another step and waited.

Nothing.

I took a third step, getting between the next set of armored figures. I heard steel sliding on steel. Turning, I saw the first two armored suits step off their stands, blocking my retreat, like I wanted to go back and be swarmed by books. The two suits did nothing besides block my path. I turned back to face the long gauntlet, and took a couple more steps. Once more, the suits I passed filled in the hall behind me, making no other aggressive move.

That made sense. The house didn't want to hurt me. The Red Lady claimed to love me. The house would share that feeling. It had yet to actually do significant damage. Still, if provoked into more extreme measures, the house could always hurt me by accident. *I shouldn't take my safety for granted.*

I holstered the PPK I held. There were too many suits. I needed to conserve my ammo. I stood there a moment, whistling a jaunty tune, lulling the hallway into complacency, and then sprinted at my top speed down the line of warriors. The suits to the side blurred past. The ones behind me became noisy, piling into the center of the hall, clattering into each other in their haste. From the sound of clomping metal feet, I knew they were giving chase.

What they'd do when they caught, I didn't know.

The suits beside me stirred as I reached them. A few steps later, those up ahead began to move, as a wave of animation swept the hall. The suits at the end of the hall were stepping off their stands, plugging up my escape, and I still had half the hall to go.

No choice now. I warmed the tat for *Vampire Speed* and slammed full ahead. As I hoped, the house didn't react to that spell, consumed with keeping me from using the lotus-dragon tat instead.

Four pairs of suits barred my way at the end of the hall. I was lucky; instead of thrusting swords at me, they formed a barricade, presenting shields toward me. Just before I would have collided with them, I leaped. This wasn't much different from body-surfing a crowd at a concert—except their heads came off as I plowed through, skimming over their shoulders. I flew past the last pair, out of the hallway, and found myself above a rather dark, deep pit.

Surrounded by eight empty helmets with red-dyed plumes, I began to fall, feeling something like the coyote from the roadrunner cartoon. Wind whistled past my face. I fell … and fell … and fell … into a strand of something sticky and stretchy. I dropped like a yoyo and rode back up into the darkness. The second time descending, a strand caught my left boot. On the way up again, multiple cords swirled around me, wrapping up various parts of my combat suit. I couldn't see the strands, but suffered the unpleasant sensation that I'd become a fly in a spider web.

I decided not to hang around for the spider. Pain shuddered through my body as electric current jazzed through my muscles, igniting the blood in my veins. Each nerve ending screamed —the price of the *Dragon Fire* tat I activated. My suit shimmered dull red. Flames curled around my limbs, seeking out the strands. They caught fire, burning with a sulfur color and rotten-egg stench. The flames raced along the strands, and soon gave form to a web such as I'd imagined.

Sometimes I hate being right.

The webbing burned, but wasn't consumed. The web bounced.

Dark figures scuttled closer, taking on more detail. They were shadow people, eyes red as coals, female from the waist up, with arachnid lower bodies. Their hairy, spider legs were quite secure on the strands despite the swaying and bobbing.

They ringed me, using their weight to accelerate the bouncing I was going through. I recognized the tactic; they were doing their best to disorient, to break my concentration so I couldn't do magic. I had fought more evil opponents, more powerful ones as well, but nothing so unrelenting.

The webbing was tough. I could pour more energy into my spell, but maybe there was a better way. I felt as if a linebacker had stomped on my stomach as I activated the *Demon Wings* tattoo on my upper back. I expected the tattoo to cloud the house's perception of me, making it lose interest, maybe assuming I'd already escaped. I should have remembered that this reality caused my magic tats to function erratically.

My back felt an acid burn, as if skin were blackening and splashing away. My shoulder blades flowed like wax. The sharpness of the pain was a new high, suspending my breath as strobing agony filled my synaptic gaps. And then new impulses came, trying to convince my brain I'd acquired extra limbs. I flexed them, and tore free of the webbing, onyx wings slicing me free. My demon wing tat had become true demon wings, hauling me into the yawning darkness above.

The wind stream cooled my face as I plunged past the ground level, up to a third floor level where a plaster ceiling loomed closer. The ceiling used foreshortening and painted shadows to create a three-dimensional image of a dome where there was no dome. I discovered this the hard way by ramming straight into it. Blood dripping down my face, neck nearly broken, I fell, stunned beyond thought as darkness closed in.

Red light filtered through my eyelids. I groaned as I started to move, and sharp pain jagged through my skull. It wasn't as bad as a tattoo activating, but worse than a hangover—most of my hangovers anyway.

A familiar ache in my legs told me I'd paid the price for using *Vampire Speed* while unconscious.

My eyes opened. Amber tiles slid underneath me. I lay on my side. Two shadow women—fully human, dressed in toga-like wraps—dragged me by my right arm, draining my life force for the strength they needed.

I looked ahead of them to see where we were going. An arch. A kitchen lay beyond. A damn big kitchen. This was the kind of kitchen a castle would have that might need to feed hundreds. I was pulled over the threshold, past a wall of shelves stacked with pots, pans, skillets, and kettles. There were tables where food could be prepped, sinks for dishes, where vegetables could be cleaned, and a number of ovens. I smelled assorted spices and the scent of wood smoke and grease.

They jerked me through another turn and I saw a brick oven large enough to stick a whole cow on a spit. Our destination seemed to be a big wooden block, old and stained. A butcher's block. There was a large ax embedded in the block. It looked familiar. I tried to remember where I'd seen it before, but my brains still felt scrambled. Thinking was slow, hard.

It came to me in a rush that put the copper taste of fear in my mouth. This was the ax that the court executioner had carried, the one he'd wanted to use to lop off Salem's head.

The ladies pulled me right up to the block, dragging my arm across its top. I smelled the stale iron scent of dried blood as they held my arm in place. A third shadow woman walked past me. She joined the others, reached out, and placed her hand on the handle of the ax. With a sudden backward lunge, she freed the blade. Her gaze fell on my arm as she raised the ax, preparing to bring it slicing down.

They'd found a helluva way to keep me from using my tattoo. They were removing it—and the whole arm while they were at it. The building probably figured the Red Lady could grow me another. I was not about to put her to that kind of trouble.

THIRTY-EIGHT

"When all else fails, tell the truth."

—Caine Deathwalker

I swung my right boot against the wood block and shoved. I didn't break their grip. Instead we had a tug of war going on with my arm as the rope. My protective shield activated, creating a shell of red light that stopped the ax. Undeterred, Ax Girl hauled back and swung again, her shadow-face oddly bland, untouched by any violent emotions. My barrier stood up to the blows, turning them aside.

I changed my tactics, suddenly yielding to the tugging, and skidded over the block, landing between the women who had my arm.

Ax Girl shifted her attack, chasing me with her weapon's edge. She swung, slicing through another woman, doing no damage to her shadow substance. The blade found my shield's new location, slapping off it.

I stood, as the ax came around again. Reaching past my own barrier, I grabbed the shaft of the weapon. It jarred my palm, but was now in my control.

I stared Ax Girl in the face and sneered. "What now, bitch?"

The floor shuddered underfoot. The ceiling and walls cracked. Dust drifted down into the air. Pots and pans rattled. A bottle fell off a counter and shattered, splashing wine like blood on the tiles. A wooden beam crashed down from the ceiling, booming as it crashed through a table, breaking plates, scattering chairs in fear.

An earthquake?

The floor buckled. Tiled blocks turned edge up, showing the stone underneath. The maw of a basement yawned to swallow me. I leaped from the chopping block to the sink counter which was still attached to an outside wall. In the process, I lost the ax I'd just fought over. Turning, squatting in the big sink, I slammed my left elbow through diamond-paned glass, letting the suit protect me as I cleared the window and slid out.

I fell into a rose garden, glad that the whole massive structure wasn't going to bury me alive. The wall beside me began a slow topple, forcing me to roll. The wall smacked the grass where I'd just been. The level of violence had become dangerous. I think the palace had forgotten I wasn't supposed to be hurt.

The rose bushes unfurled long thorny whips. The lashes slashed across my suit. I used a forearm to cover my face, and ran across emerald grass that tried to entwine around my feet. I escaped the roses, only to become close-lined by two plum trees locking branches together in my path. My feet flew up. I slapped the grass as my back came down, spreading out the impact of the fall.

A living carpet of grass and sod curled over me like a wave, and rolled me into tight layers, without any wiggle room. Bagged up, breath crushed from my lungs, I heard cold terror whispering in the shadows of my mind; *buried alive ... buried alive ... buried alive...* Despair chimed in, telling me that even if the attack ended here, I could well suffocate. And of course, the attack wouldn't end here. If I were to escape the house, the grounds, there remained an entire moon roused against me, ready to strike me down for shunning the love of the Red Lady.

Enough is enough.

My spine felt like it was kinking, as I fired up every tat on my upper torso. I hoped this would disguise the fact that my dragon-lotus tat was also awakening. I tried to keep my regular tats to as slow a build as the dragon-lotus tat, which wasn't fast-acting, being a more complex and powerful spell.

One of two things was going to happen: either the gate back to my world would open, and I could dampen out the other tats, or the joint effect of every tats going off would produce *Dragon Breath.* This last spell was one I seldom used. *Dragon Breath* was much more intense than my basic fire spell, and more exhausting. Its cost usually left me wrung out, weak, and too drained for further magic until hours had passed. This vulnerability was not good, not with the number of enemies I had.

So ... damn hard ... to breathe.

I coughed, my throat stung by smoke. Sweat dripped down my face. My lungs filled with lava and I screamed with what little air I had.

Oh, crap! The Dragon Breath is peaking, and the gate's not open yet.

Fire licked my body, searing the sod carpet, burning it. Pressure built until every atom felt like they were vibrating loose, as if a vast corona of sun-fire were funneling down my throat and exploding my stomach. Like a water balloon, I felt stretched to bursting. I screamed in silence, my bones igniting like phosphorous. Even the darkness of my soul lost its shadows, for a moment.

Then everything ripped loose, and my dragon wings fanned from my back as I expanded to fill the sky, riding the center of a blazing vortex up to where I could grasp the stars with agonized fingers. As a phantom, the stars slid through the pale mist of my incandescent hands. And then I was falling back to the surface of the red moon, toward a blasted crater of fused red glass. Steaming magma pooled where a palace had once loomed proudly from the cliffs.

The roiling mists of my body pulled together once more; cooling, hardening, materializing as true flesh once more.

And there under me, a circular hole widened in the fabric of space, glowing a bloody crimson. The gate to my world.

By the time I reached it, I was back to proper scale, threading a spinning ring, rising from a spinning ring on the same skyscraper I'd left from. I looked up at the stars and moon. The moon was still red, but an edge of black showed that the red was slowly fading. From the position of the moon,
I judged that only a half hour of local time had passed in my absence.

The roof top solidified under me, as the ring of fire vanished away. Beyond weariness, I collapsed to my knees, my hands catching me so my face didn't smack the concrete. I felt the onyx wings jutting from my back dissolve, spreading a fine black dust into the wind. I wanted to collapse and sleep for a week or two. I didn't need a hero's parade.

Maybe a case of scotch... Uh, why is there a small army gathered around me?

I lifted my head and recognition set in. Black leather and attitude. These were the slayers from the Aes Sídhe night club. The red moon light gave their clothes a rusty sheen as they moved. Vivian pushed through their ranks. Someone had loaned her a jacket to cover up the damage she'd taken from Salem and his knife. By now, her flesh would have knitted, but the blood would still be there, and her previous clothing would still be slashed to ribbons.

She came to me at the center of the circle, and stopped so I had a close up view of her knees. I lifted my head, but not much higher. I spoke into her crotch. "Hey, nice to see you. Come here often?"

"Caine, you look like shit, but we need to have words. First, where's Salem and our necklace?"

I leaned back, putting my arms behind me for support. "Sad news there. He caught a bullet to the brain and didn't suffer as much as I would have liked."

She squatted down, presenting me with a disappointing view of her tits. The jacket she'd borrowed was way too large on her for proper definition. Still, I made a point not to look her in the eyes. It wasn't like I was interested in her as a person, or anything.

"And the necklace?" she asked.

"I lost it," I lifted my head to gesture at the red moon, "up there." I smiled. It was true, as far as it went. I knew that Vivian's dhampyr hearing could tell from my heartbeat that I wasn't lying.

She spoke over her shoulder to Carson, the slayer leader who walked up behind her. "He's telling the truth."

I pressed on, "Of course if you want to trigger the next zombie apocalypse, I may be able to get it back for you. How'd you guys get so potent a demon charm anyway?"

Carson moved beside Vivian for a better view of me. He said, "It's supposed to be the creation of Mordred Pendragon, founder of our order, despite his half-fey blood."

"Hell, no," I said. "That thing was forged by a coven of necromancers. It has too much dark power for anything else."

Vivian nodded at Carson. "He's telling the truth."

Whispers of discontent went around the group as their historical beliefs were proven to be less trust-worthy than they'd thought.

Carson cleared his throat in a threatening manner, glaring around. In the following silence, his precise, clipped words were clearly audible, "Order in the ranks." He looked back to me, then up at the red moon. The fire was washing away. It was back to half-black already. Soon, the moon would be normal. He began to quote from the Bible, from Revelations, one of my favorite passages. "And I beheld when he had opened the sixth seal, and, lo, there was a great earthquake; and the sun became black as sackcloth, and the moon became as blood."

I said, "Do you really want to know how close we came to the end of the world?"

He shook his head. "Probably not. Caine, we're going to be setting up a permanent presence in L.A. You have a problem with that?"

"The fey certainly will. You owe them for a night club, and they never forget a slight."

"I've an answer for that." He smiled coldly. "Cold iron and genocide. You're human, and you've done the world a favor, taking out the succubus and Salem." He looked at Vivian. "And you've protected one of our own."

Vivian glared at me. "I didn't need your help, but … thanks."

That had to have hurt.

Flushing, she spun around and stomped off, pushing out of the ring of slayers.

Carson's thumb and first finger made an L, forming a make-believe gun. He pointed it at me. "We're giving you a pass, this time, but the next time you get in our way…" He let the hammer fall, jerking his hand back as if with recoil.

I got the message.

He turned and headed after Vivian, moving toward the roof's exit. The slayers closed ranks behind him, following.

I stayed where I was, watching a new shadow approach.

It was Osamu. He didn't look happy with me. *Join the club.*

He stopped pretty much where Vivian had, staring down at me. His forehead was creased. His hands were in his pockets. He pulled one out and offered it to me.

I reached up and let him pull me to my feet. I swayed slightly.

His clean accent didn't have any emotion to it. "You knocked me out."

"Yeah."

"Saved my life."

"Yeah."

"I ought to be grateful, I am, only…"

I cocked an eyebrow. "Yeah?"

"I wanted to finish, fighting at your side."

"That's what I figured."

"Every man has a right to the death of his choice."

"Yeah." I decided he had the right to a heartfelt apology. "Sorry."

"Okay. Forget it. Do you need help walking? An ambulance, perhaps?"

I thought about it for a second. "If we go slow, I probably won't fall on my face."

"We'll go slow."

"Osamu," I said.

"Yes, Deathwalker-sama,"

"I feel like getting drunk. Know where I can get my hands on some warm sake?"

He nodded. "I know a place that never closes, but you may not like it."

"A hole-in-the-wall?"

"A nice place, but in your current state, I doubt if you're up to a brawl."

I frowned. "I don't tear up every place I drink in. Those rumors are unfounded."

He looked at me without conviction.

I said, "Okay, the rumors are mostly true. But this time, I only want to drink."

"I'll take you there." He supported me as I staggered toward the roof exit.

"One more thing," I said.

"Hai?"

"What would you say if I offered you a job as live-in security and occasional backup, for an obscene amount of money? It would mean putting up with me, Old Man, and a spirit leopard."

"Full medical?" he asked.

"Sure."

He grinned, suddenly looking decades younger. "I am honored, Deathwalker-sama."

THIRTY-NINE

"Every now and then, the angel on my shoulder wakes up from its drunken stupor."

—Caine Deathwalker

There was a lot at stake. This had to work, or I wasn't getting paid. The gold was fine, but I really needed a new demon sword.

The garage light was on. The place was quiet except for the low hum of the industrial-sized freezer. Haruka's body lay stretched on top of the lid. Her legs dangled off. There was a beautiful innocence to her. Fragileness defined her sleep, like an illusion about to break.

The amulet lay heavy in one of my hands. The red pearl—light as a dream—lay in the other. Two paths of magic. Two choices of insane magic.

The amulet was a tool of death, and able to manipulate its various states. Its power was god-level now, since Salem linked it to entropy. Each moment of death the universe felt was a source of energy that could make a necromancer drunk with power.

The pearl possessed power poured from the heart of a goddess. It was a thing of miracles, and would have its costs to use.

Love and death. Fire and ice. Committing to either would change me in ways I couldn't yet see. Change my magic—change me.

My dragon magic was a literal pain in the ass sometimes, but it made sense. There is a cost to all things. The necklace steals its power. There's no true cost, no balance. That offended me to the core.

I made my choice, dropping the necklace into the large side-pocket of the cargo pants I wore.

My nerves shrieked with outrage, as if a straight razor were carving its initials in my often-abused flesh. This was the price I paid to heighten my senses so they enveloped Haruka, while I invoke a healing spell to help with the lightning damage she'd taken. That took care of my contribution.

Now for phase two. I pointed a fist at her. Inside the fist was the red pearl. I opened my heart to it and a pulse of power hit me. I was suddenly able to hear the heartbeat of the universe, or maybe the heart of a Red Lady, far away in her own private universe where abandoned suitors and half-alive fragments of her own thoughts kept her company.

I heard Haruka's heart take a double beat, then a stronger one. She took a shallow breath. Then another. I was slightly disappointed that there were no Hollywood special effects from the pearl. I felt Haruka trying to live once more. Damaged by lightning, then by being frozen, her pale, sexy flesh resisted. I understood. I was calling her back to a universe of pain. It takes courage to face that.

"C'mon, Haruka, you can do this. Your father's waiting on you."

I've heard of fashionably late but this is ridiculous.

I put my hand over her heart and, with my gut wrenching from pain, used a low-grade fire spell to warm her. Her fingers and toes were frost bit, but the damage unmade itself as dragon magic hazed her. If I didn't know better, I'd think my power alone was bringing her back.

I put the red pearl in a different pocket from the necklace. No way was I taking a chance on those two things getting together, and maybe fighting it out, and taking down half of L.A.

I picked Haruka up and a soft sigh spilled from her lips. I cradled her against me and carried her into the house. The door to the kitchen stood open. I'd almost forgotten Old Man was watching. Passing him, I was pinned by his eyes. They were hard to read.

He said, "Sometimes, I am not disappointed in you."

High praise, coming from him. I said, "Done, now where's my gold, and sword."

I didn't stop for him to answer. I knew Hiro would pay his debt. I was carrying the reason for that in my arms. Her eyes fluttered as I passed through the kitchen.

I felt a shudder of revulsion. The room reminded me of another kitchen where the subconscious of a goddess nearly took my arm off

In the living room, I walked to the couch and laid Haruka down. On the back of the couch, there was a charcoal and burgundy striped blanket that Angie had used when she'd stayed the night. I picked up the blanket and spread it over Haruka.

Old Man went to the office and opened the door. Hiro stood just inside; waiting in the hell only a parent can know when a child's life hangs in the balance.

He came close, sinking to his knees beside the couch, never really seeing me. He gathered Haruka in his arms, crying as her eyes opened and she murmured soothing words to him.

Old Man stood just behind me. He put his hand on top of my head. "You did good, Caine"

"Drink, gold, sword, in that order, Old Man."

He laughed and went into the bar. While he made drinks for a calibration, I made sure Haruka was still okay. Her pulse was strong, her flesh warm, and vibrant with life.

Haruka said, "Didn't I … die?"

"Yeah," I said, "but you're fine now." I went to grab my drink from Old Man. Side by side, we stared into the living room from the bar. *Family, so embarrassing*. I looked at Old Man. "I'm so glad you're not like that. I would have to shoot you."

Sometime later, Hiro placed a call. A car must have been cruising the neighborhood because it was only minutes later that a knock came to the door. I opened it and four black-suited men—replacements for those Salem had killed—walked in carrying briefcases.

I led them in to where Hiro and Haruka waited. If the men wondered why the daughter of their new employer sat on a couch, naked under a blanket, they didn't say so.

Old Man redirected the men into the office and had them lay the cases on the bar, opening them to show the shine of gold bars, a hundred ounces each. The last man had a longer case. He opened and turned it so I could see.

I got hard at once.

It was the new demon sword. I could hear its lust for blood, and feel its murderous aura. I smiled, went over and petted the sheathed blade. *We are going to have so much fun.*

Hiro said to the Old Man, "Thank you for all you have done for us."

"It was nothing, little Hiro."

Yeah, nothing for you—you weren't the one who almost got killed a bunch of times... I felt a deep chill of fear ice up my spine. *...And nearly got married.* I picked up a drink and threw it back. That braced me, chasing the horror away. I returned to the living room to see my clients off.

Haruka bowed deeply. "Caine-sama, I thank you for my life. I cannot express my gratitude."

I waved off her words. "Your gold is reward enough."

Haruka, Hiro, and his men left.

Old Man followed me back to the bar. He watched as I caressed the gold lovingly. He said, "Some of that is mine, you know."

My hands stilled on the gold. "Oh, yeah, that's right."

He continued to stare.

The silence became annoying. "What?" I said.

"Are you going to make me tell him?"

"I'm sure Hiro will notice, once she gets hungry."

"That was not part of the deal."

I shrugged. "The deal was to protect her. Sure, she died, but I brought her back, no harm, no foul."

"She's a succubus now. The ritual in the Mission took effect. Hiro might not consider that *no harm*."

"He can bite me," I said. "She's alive. With a little help learning to control her new nature, no one will ever know. And if they do, her power will ensure their loyalty so they don't go around blabbing."

"She's liable to take over the entire clan. As a succubus, Haruka will not be satisfied with the traditional role of a Japanese maiden."

"You're right, but the deal was for her to be alive and safe." I went behind the bar and started a couple more drinks.

Old Man said, "That's why I'm letting you keep your share of the gold and the sword. However, you need to give the amulet to me."

I cocked an eyebrow at him. "No one should have it. No one should use it." To get my point across, I repeated words he'd taught me as a child, "True power is not given, and never comes without a cost."

He glared at me. Before he could argue, his phone's ring tone went off, playing *Bad Moon Rising*. His face lit up as he answered, "Hey Achill … what? Really, no problem bud. Yeah, I got vintage port chilling for the game. Hmmmm. Oh, no problem, I'll get him on it right away."

I've a bad feeling about this.

The Old Man put his phone away, "Hey, there are a lot of new wolves to deal with, and Angie can't handle them, alone. She called Achill for help, for a new Alpha to be sent here."

I didn't like it, a wolf territory here in L.A., but since the night of the Mission, we've had clanless wolves running wild. That wasn't good either.

Old Man said, "Achill told her he could still feel William out there somewhere, alive, more or less. Long story made short, they can't find him so we've been commissioned to do so."

"William is one of the people I intend to kill. Soon. Let them bring in a new Alpha to subdue the wolves, and take them out of my territory."

"With the slayers setting up their own territory here, we need the strength of the wolves. The council has approved it, so don't kill William … again."

"I know someone who I can call for a line on the Alpha, but if you expect me to swallow this, you're going to have let me keep all the gold."

Old Man looked at me with a mixture of pride and irritation. "Fine, but I want the necklace."

"Only if you destroy it."

"I intend to."

"Okay." By the time he said *fine*, I had my phone out, searching my contact list. I found *her* and pressed the button for the long distance call down to Texas. "Hey Cassie, I need some…"

"Caine! Are you in town?"

"Sorry, no."

"Hey, Grace got that sword you recommended. Now she just has to learn to do something with it besides ninja poses."

"Great, listen, I need some help retrieving a body picked up by the PRT here in L.A. Do you happen to know where they might have…?"

"Yeah, sure. Got a pen?"

"Just a second." I made a writing motion in the air and Old man slid a writing pad and pen across the bar to me. "Okay, go." I wrote down the address she gave me and ended the call.

"You've got a contact in the PRT?" Old Man asked.

"She's not local, or I would have called her for backup against the warlock." I started for the door.

"Where are you going?"

I waved goodbye without looking back. "No rest for the wicked." I got out of the house, and strolled next door to William's place. I knocked on the door and waited for Angie. I heard her moving in the house and a second set of footsteps as well. The door didn't open, but I felt the presence of two people on the other side.

I kicked the door. Hard. "Okay, get out here. I'm going to pick up William and need you to come along to make sure he stays calm. I'm doing this for Achill so I'm not going to kill William. Again."

The second I said *Achill,* the door opened. Angie stood in the doorway, tall and busty, her long red hair sleek and ember-red. Sarah stood behind her, looking completely different from before. More innocent, less driven. I understood, having held the amulet. Those who use it do not stay unchanged. As I looked at Sarah, Angie stepped over to block my view.

Angie said, "Caine, she's not evil anymore. You don't have to hurt her."

I put on my serious-as-death face. “But what if I want to?”

She growled at me. “Get over it.”

I laughed at her. “Yeah, I get it, don’t worry. Look, I know where William is, but I need to make sure he doesn’t make me kill him. Again. So, you coming?”

Sarah slid out past Angie. She looked like a lost teenager, scared and hopeful, “Gramps is really alive?”

“Yeah, whatever you and the amulet did, keeps bringing him back, and not as a zombie. What kind of spell did you use?” I asked.

“I don’t really remember. It’s like I’ve just surfaced from a dream and all the details are fading.”

“Fine. Are you both coming?”

They both said, “Yes.”

“Okay, but if I hear any complaints, I’m blowing shit up,” I said.

They didn’t say anything, shutting the door, following me to my mustang at the curb. We piled in and headed for the highway. There was a covert government installation waiting for my personal attention.

FORTY

"A demon by any other name
... still smells like trouble."

—Caine Deathwalker

We reached the address Cassie had given me, and parked outside the gate of a Hollywood FX Studio. People knew of Area 51. They knew of the Illuminati. They knew about the magic bullet and the grassy knoll. They knew of a Kenyan-born president's photoshopped birth certificate.

But they don't know about this place.

We climbed out and headed for an unassuming gray brick building.

Smart, if any one sees unnatural bodies they'll just think they're props.

A small shed stood near the gate, a uniformed security guard on duty.

"Are you going to kill him?" Sarah had a troubled look on her face.

Walking between the girls, I draped my arms over their shoulders. I activated the *Demon Wings* tattoo on my back, and endured a grinding pain, as if all my bones were being crushed to powder. Had I still been on the Red Moon, real wings would have speared from my back, fanning out in a shocking display, but I was on Earth again. The pain eased and my presence was erased, along with that of the girls. Shielding us all had hurt more than normal, and wouldn't last that long. *We needed to hurry.*

Once past the guard shack, and inside the warehouse, I whispered to

Angie, "Use your nose, and don't worry about the tingly feeling on your skin; it's just my magic."

She guided us past a receptionist that frowned at the door which seemed to have opened and closed itself. We moved on past oblivious security cameras, as the receptionist went to the front door, stared out, and shrugged. While she had her back turned, we went through another door, closing it softly behind us.

I whispered, "Keep your hands on me. Break contact and they'll see you." We went along a wide hallway, past numerous doors of frosted glass, until Angie stopped us.

"Here," she said.

I pulled out my lock pick mini-gun, stuck the prongs in the lock, and a few squeezes of the trigger later, the door was open. We walked in, careful to stay clustered together. Angie pulled us past a number of stainless steel slabs. We saw savaged bodies from the bloody battle, legs and arms lying in piles. We stopped in front of a frosted door and listened to the people inside.

"Damnedest thing I've ever seen."

A cool, feminine voice said, "Don't worry about it. These things happen. Just clear everyone out of this area, and I'll see what I can do about stopping the next zombie apocalypse."

I knew that voice. *Cassie? She got here fast.*

I pulled the girls out of the way as the door opened and numerous workers in white coats left in a hurry. Cassie was the last to go. She looked like a supermodel with dazzling smile, blond hair, and a knock out figure. I'd met her, and her daughter, on a recent trip to east Texas where I'd left a few bodies lying around.

While a respected PRT member, Cassie was laid back enough not to count every unnatural creature of the night as a threat to mankind. This generosity of spirit came from the fact that she herself was only passing for human. Not something commonly known.

Angie growled low in her throat as Cassie went by.

Cassie's gaze flicked over us. I saw recognition in her face as she easily pierced our protective shroud. She winked at me and kept going.

Angie whispered, "Kitsune bitch thinks she's all that!"

"There's a reason for that," I said.

"What?" Sarah whispered.

I smiled. "She *is* all that, *and more*." I only wished I knew it from personal experience.

We went in, separating as the cloaking magic failed at last. The room looked like a film set version of an autopsy room. Tiles lined the floor and walls. Circular lights were suspended over stainless steel slabs that had drains for blood and other bodily fluids. There were water hoses for clean up and cabinet doors in the walls where bodies were stored, waiting their turn at examination.

William was the star attraction, occupying the central slab. His naked body looked freshly dead. His severed head balanced on a supportive yoke, eyes closed. The body was intact except for the hands. They lay near the damaged stubs of his wrists.

One of the hands began tapping two fingers.

They other hand picked up the rhythm, tapping along.

The corpse's eyes snapped open, scanning the ceiling, shifting to us. He frowned. Tendrils of white flesh were rising like worms at the end of the wrists. The strands wiggled in the air, searching. Similar strands from the amputated hands reared as well. As the strings met, they fused. They contracted. The wrists were pulled back into place. I shifted my gaze to the neck and head. A similar process was in effect. Ropes of tissue filled the gap between head and neck. The ropes pulled. The head returned to its proper place. All signs of the previous amputations faded.

Angie turned away, holding her stomach like someone trying not to be sick.

William Cooper blinked. He drew a deep breath. He kept breathing. Slowly, He sat up.

Uncle William!" Sarah had stood in a state of shock, as if she'd not seem him in pieces before. Now, she ran and threw her arms around him, crying against his naked chest.

He patted her a little clumsily, as if this was new to him. I understood. William was an Alpha wolf. Showing a soft side of his nature could be interpreted as weakness. That led to challenges in the pack. And to gruesome, bloody deaths. Alphas therefore didn't often go in for public displays of affection—except toward their mates.

I walked over to William, gun in hand. He looked up at me over Sarah's head. His eyes snapped over to my gun. His eyebrows bridged, arching in a silent question.

"Shut up," I said, "it's over, I won, you lost, Angie and Sarah get to live. Because you were stupid enough to oppose me however, the rest of your little pack paid the price. They're dead."

His muscles bunched, like he wanted to shove Sarah aside, jump me, and rip my still-beating heart out of my chest. My gun was pointed at the back of Sarah's head.

He controlled himself.

I continued. "Your Fenris wants you to control the new wolves made that night—before they go nuts on the townspeople and have to be put down. In other words, clean up the mess you made."

I stepped to the side so Sarah wasn't between us anymore, made a show of almost putting my gun back in the holster, only to lash out with the hilt, pistol whipping William across the face. His head rocked. His eyes blazed a deeper yellow. He bared white fangs.

I did put my gun away then, trusting my protective shield. "That's for making my job harder. Now, I'm going home. You take things from here with these two."

* * *

The sound of hammering and power tools, and the metallic smell of dwarf magic, made it hard for me to enjoy my Blue Lagoon. Old Man had imported some Iron-Clan dwarfs to fix up all the damage in the office that William's wolves had done. He was billing William for this of course. Leona was still getting comfortable with Osamu hanging around, having moved into an empty bed room. She *did* like him; I was just hoping she didn't eat him. He was handy to have around, especially since he made his own sake—by the barrel. This had instantly endeared him to Old Man.

Izumi had returned from Under-the-Hill with her mom. They were now out terrorizing Rodeo Drive in Beverley Hills. *Women—fey, human, and otherwise—do love their shopping.*

Leona was parked on a bar stool next to me. She was convinced the dwarf workmen would steal everything not nailed down if not watched closely. She'd been listening to my story of Vivian and the Slayers. "So, how did you get past them without handing over the necklace?"

They weren't happy to lose the amulet. It went all the way back to the original founder of their group, Mordred Pendragon."

"Club-footed bastard," Leona opined.

I slid off the stool and went around the bar to make a pitcher of *Cachaca*, distilled sugar cane, fresh lime juice, water, and sugar. Diabetic suicide.

"I suggested the necklace was demonic and red moon an omen of doom. Then I offered to get the necklace back for them. They refused my generosity, smelling a trap."

The leopard nodded. "Humans always think the worst of demons. Hey, I'm surprised you didn't want to keep the relic. With all that power, you could have done *anything*."

"Free power isn't real. That thing should never have been made."

Magical clouds swirled by the fireplace.

Osamu put a hand over his gun, but I put my hand up to stop him. He obeyed, but seemed uneasy with restraint.

The clouds thinned and Old Man was revealed. I didn't wait for him to ask; I just started pouring him a drink.

"I got a new job for you," Old Man said.

I looked at him and went for my gun.

He put up his hands. "Wait, don't worry. This is *your* kind of job, so, are you in?"

"Do I get to kill, and only kill?"

"To your heart's content."

"I'm in."

"By the way, have you heard what everyone's calling you now?"

"Don't really care."

"You have a new name, Red Moon Demon."

I looked at the Old Man and smiled. "Red Moon Demon. I like it."

Made in the USA
San Bernardino, CA
08 March 2015